Rhyannon Byrd is the national bestselling author of forty contemporary and paranormal romantic thrillers *London Affair* a books have been translated into enjoying the California sunshine beautiful Malvern Hills in Englar ever-growing collection of concer... shirts and coffee mugs.

For more information on Rhyannon's books and the latest news, you can visit her website at www.rhyannonbyrd.com or find her on Facebook at www.facebook.com/RhyannonByrd or on Instagram @RhyannonByrd.

Praise for Rhyannon Byrd:

'*London Affair* is signature Rhyannon Byrd – exciting, sexy, and romantic. Byrd brilliantly crafts a steamy love story with a couple that dazzles, and I couldn't put it down!'
Virna DePaul, *New York Times* bestselling author

'From London to the English countryside, Jase and Emmy burn up the sheets'
P.T. Michelle, *New York Times* bestselling author

'Raw, addictive, and blisteringly hot . . . a sizzling success'
Romantic Times (Top Pick)

'No one writes lip-biting sexual tension and sizzling romance like Rhyannon Byrd'
Shayla Black, *New York Times* bestselling author

'Rhyannon Byrd has a gift for beautiful, sensual storytelling'
Cheyenne McCray, *New York Times* bestselling author

'Filled with love, lust, loyalty, betrayal, sensuality, and heady romance. Readers will find themselves reaching for a Kleenex and fanning themselves all at the same time as they devour this page-turner'
Night Owl Reviews

'Combines passion and suspense with a touch of deadly danger guaranteed to keep you reading until the very last page'
Joyfully Reviewed

'Hold on to your iceboxes, girls! This one is a scorcher!'
A Romance Review

By Rhyannon Byrd

London Affair
New York Scandal

Dangerous Tides Series
Take Me Under
Make Me Yours (e-novella)
Keep Me Closer

NEW YORK SCANDAL

RHYANNON BYRD

HEADLINE
ETERNAL

First published in 2022
by HEADLINE ETERNAL
An imprint of HEADLINE PUBLISHING GROUP

1

Cataloguing in Publication Data is available from the British Library

ISBN 978 1 4722 8132 6

Typeset in 11/14 pt Minion Pro by Jouve (UK), Milton Keynes

Printed and bound in Great Britain by Clays Ltd, Elcograf S.p.A.

HEADLINE PUBLISHING GROUP
An Hachette UK Company
Carmelite House
50 Victoria Embankment
London EC4Y 0DZ

www.headlineeternal.com
www.headline.co.uk
www.hachette.co.uk

*This one is for the awesome
Kate Byrne.*

~

Endless gratitude and thanks for your wonderful insight,
guidance and support, Kate. You're an absolutely brilliant
editor, a truly lovely person, and it's always such a joy
and pleasure to work with you. Thank you a thousand
times over for all that you do!

NEW YORK
SCANDAL

Prologue

Early August

THE WATCHER

As I listen to the newlyweds arguing in their stateroom, I place one wet, gloved hand against the wall of the rich boy's luxury yacht to steady myself, my clothes drenched from the short swim I took to reach them. The 40-foot *Olly's Girl* is docked in a quiet cove off the Amalfi Coast in Italy, the sea so calm it's easy to find my balance. But inside I'm a storm. It's my racing pulse that's made me light-headed, the exhilaration of finally having Lottie Fleming right where I want her playing complete hell with my system. I've waited so long for this night, planning it down to the tiniest detail from the moment it'd been decided that things could no longer go on the way they were.

From the moment it'd been decided that she had to die. That death would be the price of thinking her pathetic jackass of a husband's money could actually protect her.

I'd known it had to be perfect. *Had* to be, or I'd . . . No, I don't even want to think about what will happen if I fail. But there's no need to worry about repercussions, because *this* is perfection at its finest. It's . . . sublime. Like manna from heaven.

Out here on the water, she can't evade me . . . like she has before. There's no escape, and the spoiled pretty boy won't do anything to stop me. Not this time, when I'm armed.

Theirs is hardly a love match, and I knew, from the second I started watching him and learned what he's really made of, that the only things Oliver Beckett truly cares about in this world are himself and his money. Plus, I'm bigger and stronger than he is, so the guy poses no real threat now that he's on his own with her.

Lottie's usually soft voice sounds shrill as she shouts at him. I can only just make out her words, and I would laugh at the surprising subject of their argument, but I'm too busy hoping that she spits fire at me this same way when I have her beneath me. Unlike the last time I had my hands on her, there'll be no need to gag her beautiful mouth tonight. She can scream as loud as she wants, but there'll be no one to hear her.

Unable to wait any longer, I surge forward and throw the door open, the smile on my face impossible to contain when I take in his stunned expression . . . and her horrified one. She starts to cry out, but I'm already moving, the gleaming six-inch blade in my hand lifted high as I close in, the rush of excitement so intense it nearly stops my heart.

I've waited for this moment for so long.

Waited for this girl.

And now she's *mine*.

Chapter One

Thirteen months later . . .

CALLAN

'Clara,' I mutter into my phone, dodging some asshole who's decided to jog down the center of the sidewalk on a busy Friday afternoon in Brooklyn, 'you know I love you, but this shit has got to stop. I'm not your campaign's gigolo service. Let Marissa Abernathy find her own damn date to the fundraiser tonight.'

'Did you seriously just say that out on the street? Can people hear you?' my younger sister groans, the sound of exasperation in her voice one that's grown painfully familiar over the past few weeks. She's currently embroiled in a bitter, brutal battle for the office of New York City mayor, and the campaign has taken its toll not only on her, but on our entire family. And given that we still have two months to go, I'm genuinely starting to wonder if I should think about leaving the country for a while.

Since I'm not a prick, I want to be supportive. I really do. But the fact that I'm both single *and* have good name recognition in the city, thanks to my personal protection company taking on more than a few high-profile celebrity clients in the past few years, has made me Clara's first choice when it comes to escorting her rich society friends – the ones she's made through her charity work – around town. The circles they move in aren't really my down-to-earth, work-your-fingers-to-the-bone sister's scene, but in the cutthroat world of political elections, it's always better to have more friends than enemies. Or at least that's the line that Carl Deevers, her campaign manager, keeps throwing at us, whenever anyone in the family voices an opinion that the douchebag doesn't like.

'I'm sorry, Clara, but I'm done,' I tell her, knowing I can't stomach another endless night of hell with a woman whose favorite subject is herself. Fifteen months ago, I might have been able to see it through. Hell, I probably would have slept with a few of them as well, so long as they understood that it was nothing more than a fun hook-up between acquaintances, and would never be anything more.

But I'm not the same man I was back then. Not even close. And even though I'd take a bullet for my sister, I'm drawing a line in the sand about this that I don't intend to step over.

'Fine,' she says with a resigned sigh, too sharp to have missed the conviction in my voice. 'Can I at least put you down for phone calls on Saturday?'

'Of course, honey. I'll make as many as you need. I'll talk the city's ear off about how awesome you are and how much good you're going to do once elected.'

Her soft laugh brings a brief smile to my face, which is rare for me these days, and I squint as I turn a corner, facing right into the late-afternoon sunlight. It's a gorgeous September day, and I wedge the phone between my ear and shoulder so that I can roll up the sleeves of my casual button-up, since I'm roasting in the thing, when the sound of another laugh catches my attention, stopping me dead in my tracks. Low and husky, that

bone-melting sound is the same exact one I've actually fanta-
sized about hearing again. Especially when I make the mistake
of thinking about what I refer to as the 'weekend from hell' –
which is far more than I should.

Someone runs into my back, their gruff curse reminding
me that now *I'm* the asshole disrupting the flow of movement
on the sidewalk. I tell myself to keep walking, seeing as how the
owner of that sexy-as-sin laugh is a woman I have no business
getting involved with, much less even talking to. She's wanted
for the murder of the same jackass I had to watch her marry on
a sunny summer day in England last year, and has been on the
run ever since their extended honeymoon in Italy took an ugly
turn. The husband was found brutally stabbed to death on his
yacht . . . and his beautiful wife, Lottie Fleming, fled the country and was never seen again.

Until now.

Well, maybe. I still haven't turned around to verify the
laughing woman's identity, and the curses being thrown my
way by my fellow New Yorkers who have places to be and don't
appreciate my huge frame blocking their path are only getting
louder.

Since when did you become such a chickenshit? I ask myself,
gripping my phone so tightly I'm surprised it hasn't shattered.

I'd only ever heard Lottie laugh once, the one time we were
alone together, but it . . . Yeah, it obviously made a hell of an
impression, because I'm still thinking about it over a year later.
Pathetically imagining I'm hearing it in the middle of one of
the most crowded cities in the world.

Christ. Stop stalling, dickhead, and just get on with it.

I suck in a quick breath, force my body around and then
immediately scowl with disappointment at what I find. Instead
of the slender, big-eyed blonde I was hoping for, some redhead

is standing there, delivering food to a table at a busy café, laughing Lottie's laugh. But then the young twenty-something turns her head, giving me a view of her complete profile . . . and, son of a bitch, it's actually *her*.

Either she's dyed her hair or she's wearing a wig. A long, curly wig that looks all wrong on her. I mean, she's still gorgeous, but this look is too brash and bold for the blushing postgrad who damn near knocked my feet out from under me the first time I ever laid eyes on her.

'Holy hell,' I hear myself mutter, 'I've gotta go.' I hang up on Clara without so much as a goodbye and finally move out of the center of the sidewalk. I take a few steps forward, drawn to this woman with a pull that I've spent over a year second-guessing, trying to convince myself it was only in my imagination. That I hadn't really been that insanely attracted to her. My ploy was just bullshit, though, because right now, woman-on-the-run or not, all I want is to take Lottie Fleming – I refuse to call her by her married name, even in my head – into my arms and fuck the ever-loving hell out of her. It's such a primitive reaction that I'm almost embarrassed by it. But there's no denying that it's exactly how I feel, as if laying claim to her body will somehow keep her from slipping away from me again, when I know that's nothing but a pipe dream.

Done at the table, she smiles at the older couple she was serving and walks back inside the café, her plain black leggings and long white T-shirt with *Lenore's*, the café's name, written flamboyantly across the back looking incredible on her. I lose track of how long I stand off to the side of the sidewalk, my brain working overtime as I try to come up with some kind of plan for approaching her. But it's nearly impossible to concentrate because the sense of relief pouring through my system at the fact that she's alive and well is nothing short of staggering.

Yeah, I logically knew that she hadn't been killed when Oliver was murdered – by who I've always believed was either a woman he'd screwed over or a jealous, jilted husband – because she'd boarded a flight from Italy to California the next morning, twelve hours after what the coroner had established as the time of death. But the trail had gone cold in Los Angeles, and despite the team of investigators that my friend Jase Beckett, who is Oliver's cousin, has had looking for her, not a scrap of proof that she was still alive was ever found.

And that had damn near destroyed me. In ways I'd spent a hell of a lot of energy over the past year trying hard not to think about.

Before I can decide on a plan of action, Lottie comes walking out of the café with a black backpack slung over her shoulder, apparently done with her shift, and I have no choice but to move my ass if I don't want to lose her on the crowded street. She's wearing a pair of gray Converse that don't give her any extra height, but at just under six-five I'm easily able to keep my eye on her lithe five-seven frame.

It's evident from the way she moves through the crowd of pedestrians that she's been living here in New York for a while now. She doesn't have that nervous flinch that makes it so easy to spot a newcomer. But even though I can tell that she's at ease with the city, she's definitely on the lookout for something. Or someone. We haven't walked for more than a block, but she's already glanced over her shoulder three times, luckily not clocking me, since I'm trained to go unnoticed when I need to.

Then again, maybe I'm not as good at it as I thought, since she suddenly ducks down an alleyway on our right. I reach the shadowed entrance just in time to see her take a left at the end and I run like hell to catch up with her. She dodges a couple of skateboarders, then turns again, and I nearly wipe out on a spilled bag of French fries, but thankfully stay on my feet. She breaks right, and I know I'm screwed when I watch her run headlong into a crowded neighborhood street party.

'Goddamn Fridays,' I mutter, stopping and spinning in a circle as I search the noisy street. Dozens of laughing kids are running barefoot through a series of sprinklers that have been set up in the middle of the road, while their families congregate around portable barbecues and music pours from the windows that have been left open in the long, parallel rows of brownstones. The sunny day, after nearly two weeks of constant rain, has brought out what looks like the entire neighborhood, and I want to roar with irritation because I have no idea where Lottie has gone. But in an unlucky twist for her, since I know she's wearing it to disguise her appearance, it's the brash red wig that enables me to spot her again after I jump onto the base of a streetlight like someone out of a movie. She's already nearly half a block away, so I jump down and take off running, throwing out apologies left and right as I jostle my way through the throng of people.

I chase after her for nearly another block and a half, the crowd slowing me down until I'm all but choking on my frustration. Then I catch a glimpse of her slipping into another slim alleyway between a Cuban bakery that smells amazing and a hair salon. The street party is thinning out at this end of the road, as it blends into a retail zone, and I finally catch up with Lottie just as she takes a right and starts to run up a set of wide stone steps that belong to a tall, thin apartment building that looks like it's from the 1930s. I reach out with one hand before she can climb the second step, bracing for the impact of her slamming into my chest as I spin her around. But she surprises the hell out of me by bending her leg, using her momentum to drive her lifted knee straight toward my crotch. I shift my weight at the last second, taking the blow on my hip, and grab her other wrist before she can start wailing on me.

'Jesus Christ, Lottie, stop fighting!' I snarl, giving her a little shake. 'It's me!'

Her body freezes as her head shoots back, the vivid blue eyes that I constantly see in my sleep wide with shock as she gapes up at me. 'Callan?' she gasps, and I can tell from her reaction that she'd had no idea it was me she was running from.

'Yeah,' I grunt, expecting her to relax now that she knows she's not in any danger. But I feel the tiny hairs start to rise on the back of my neck when the opposite happens . . . and her distress turns into something truly chilling.

'Let me go,' she wheezes, going unnaturally pale beneath the vivid splotches of color burning in her cheeks.

And her eyes . . . *Christ.*

I've never really been all that into art museums, probably because I grew up getting dragged to numerous ones all over the world on every family vacation we ever took, and right now, staring into Lottie Fleming's scared eyes, I feel that same uneasy sensation I'd get when looking at a work by Edvard Munch. Anxiety is all but seeping from her pores, her skin too pale, those dark blue eyes so huge they pretty much swallow her face. It makes me feel like a dick, as if I'm responsible for her distress, and even though I know that none of this shit is my fault, there's no doubt that *I'm* the one scaring the hell out of her at the moment.

'You don't need to be afraid,' I tell her, working hard to keep my voice gentle. 'I just want to help.'

'Fuck you!' she snaps, tugging hard at her wrists.

Before I can think better of it, I hear myself say, 'Whenever you want, sweetheart. I'm all yours. But right now we need to get you somewhere safe.' I jerk my chin at the building behind her, judging it with a swift glance. 'This neighborhood is too rough for you.'

A bitter, almost hysterical-sounding laugh slips past her trembling lips. 'Wow, sound like a snob much? I'll have you know this is an awesome neighborhood.'

'And I happen to know that last week there was a brutal murder just a few blocks over.' My company provides personal security for the family who owns the restaurant where the homicide took place, and while it was a shock that one of their employees was tortured and killed while locking up for the night, it turned out that the guy had owed a serious amount of money to some dangerous people. Ones who are apparently making a move to take over this part of the city.

But Lottie doesn't even flinch at the news. She just shakes her head and laughs again. 'Is that meant to scare me, Hathaway? Have you forgotten that *I'm* a murderer?'

My mouth flattens into a hard, tight line. 'The hell you are.'

'Nice try,' she scoffs, curling her upper lip, 'but I'm not going to fall for it.'

'Fall for what?'

'Whatever stunt you're trying to pull.' Suspicion coats her words, her sexy British accent harsher than I remember it, her anger hardening the edges of each consonant. 'Did you call the cops the second you spotted me? Is that why you're trying to keep me here? Are they already on their way?'

I'm furious that she thinks I would betray her that way, even though I know my fury is completely illogical. She has no reason to trust me. Hell, she doesn't even know me. Not really. But I plan on changing that.

Sweat dots her upper lip, her skin dewy from her frantic run to get away from me. She looks earthy and real and wild, a far cry from the perfectly polished poetry scholar I met last year who bore an uncanny resemblance to Michelle Williams – but I've never wanted a woman as badly as I want her in this moment. It's probably a thousand kinds of wrong, given the grim circumstances, but I want inside her so badly I can taste it, the warm, feminine scent of her body making my damn mouth water.

I swallow hard against the untimely lust that's pounding through my system, and fervently tell her, 'I didn't call the cops, Lottie. I would never do that to you. And in case you were wondering, I happen to believe you're innocent.'

'Then you're the only one,' she shoots back, shaking so hard I'm surprised her teeth aren't chattering. She sucks in a sharp breath, clearly struggling to calm down as she looks me hard in the eye. 'But even if you're not going to turn me in, you still need to go. Just let go of me and . . . run.'

'I'm not going anywhere.'

'God, don't do this. *Please*,' she pleads, casting nervous looks around us, while her pulse pounds at the base of her throat. 'You need to leave me alone. Just leave, right now, and don't come back.'

I shake my head when she looks back up at me, hating the panic that's all but coating her skin. 'I'm sorry, Lot, but that's not gonna happen.'

'I'm bad news!' she suddenly shouts, struggling again to free her arms, the lingering sounds of the street party probably the only reason her cries haven't brought someone to her rescue. 'God, Callan! Just stay away from me! If you don't want to die, just stay away!'

I narrow my eyes as I carefully tighten my grip on her, determined not to let her go, knowing damn well that if I lose her now, I might never get her back. 'What the hell are you talking about?'

'I . . . I can't,' she chokes out. 'I can't do this. I can't go through it again. Not with you. Please, just walk away.'

I want to demand to know what she means by the 'Not with you' part, but I sense this isn't the time. So I tell her, 'Again, Lottie, that's not gonna happen.'

She opens her mouth, probably on the verge of telling me to go to hell for my high-handed tactics, when someone calls down, 'Lana, are you okay?'

We both freeze, my brows raised with curiosity as I look up to find a cute Hispanic kid who must be about seven or eight standing on a rickety balcony about fifteen feet above our heads, his brown eyes huge as he stares down at us.

'I'm fine,' she calls up, but her voice is shaky, and the child's worried frown stays in place. 'Really, Nico,' she adds, forcing a smile onto her face for the boy. 'I just . . . ran into an old friend who surprised me. But we're all good. Now go back inside and do your homework before your *abuela* gets upset.'

I'm by no means fluent in Spanish, but I know enough to recognize that *abuela* means grandmother.

'Now, Nico,' she tells him, kindly but firmly, and I can see from the exchange that these two know each other well. I can also tell that she's angled her body so that the kid can't tell that I'm restraining her.

'Okay,' he mutters. 'But you'd better still come over later like you promised and play Mario Kart with me.'

Before he heads inside, Nico gives me a dark look of warning that makes me want to smile at his bravery, but I fight it back, not wanting to insult him. As much as I hate that Lottie is obviously living in this rundown building, it eases something inside my chest to know that she's had this little guy to spend time with . . . and to look out for her.

'Why don't we finish this argument up in your apartment,'

I suggest, knowing I've assumed right about this being where she lives when her shoulders sag with defeat. She gives me a tight nod, and I release her wrists, frowning when she immediately rubs at the red marks on her right one, and then the left. 'Shit. I didn't mean to hurt you, Lot.'

'You didn't.' She hikes her backpack higher onto her shoulder as she turns and heads up the steps, leaving me to follow her. 'I just bruise easily.'

'I'll remember that,' I say under my breath, doing my best to keep my eyes off her perfect ass as she opens the huge front door that was left unlocked and walks inside, not even looking back to see if I'm still here. But then, I've made it clear I'm not going anywhere.

As we climb the stairs, I can hear the TV blaring in Nico's family's apartment, but the others are quiet, the residents most likely still out for the day. As unkind as I was in my assessment of the building, it's clear that the people who live here look after it. The stairwell and landings are spotless, with the fresh scent of lemons in the air and colorful artwork hanging on the walls. When Lottie notices me taking in one of the surrealist paintings that reminds me of the Chagall that Jase had bought for his fiancée, Emmy, at Christmas, she murmurs, 'Nico's mum, Eva, is an amazing artist. I keep telling her that she should try to sell them, but between working as a bike courier and taking care of Nico, she claims she doesn't have the time.'

'I'll tell my sister Chloe that she needs to take a look at these.'

'Why?' she asks, shooting me a surprised look over her shoulder.

'She's an interior designer, and these would go great with her signature style,' I explain, knowing that Chloe would be impressed that I even know what her 'signature style' is. 'Plus, I hate to see talent go unrecognized.'

She reaches the next small landing and stops, an odd expression on her face as she turns to look at me. 'What?' I ask, pushing my hands into my front pockets so that I'm not tempted to reach out and touch her. 'You thought I was just muscles and a pretty face?'

'You're not *that* pretty,' she deadpans, and I can't help but let out a loud, genuine laugh.

'Ouch, Lottie. Knock a guy when he's down, why don't cha?'

'You're hardly down, Callan,' she murmurs, eyeing up my tall frame with a flash of heat that's so quick I almost miss it.

'Maybe not on the outside,' I say, my low voice soft but serious, while my gaze moves greedily between her pink lips and those storm-dark eyes. 'But on the inside, honey, I'm still licking my wounds over your less than joyous reaction to me finding you.'

She rolls her eyes and turns away, but I think that might be so that I don't see the way her mouth seems to tremble with emotion. And, hell, I know it's not the time or place, but I'm not above using some humor to ease things up between us, because she's still strung tighter than a bow string. 'I'm just real thankful that my balls are still in one piece,' I drawl, 'your best intentions to squash them aside.'

She doesn't say anything in response, but I didn't really expect her to. Instead, she just gives a delicate snort as she pulls a set of keys from the front pocket on her backpack and walks over to the brightly painted door that sits at the end of the landing, then unlocks it. I follow her through the doorway, having to duck so that I don't smack my head on the six-foot door frame, and work hard to conceal my shock at how small the place is as I watch Lottie drop her backpack onto a yellow loveseat.

'So, now that you've seen me safely home, you can go,' she says, her arms wrapped around her middle as she stands with her back to the room's only window, her chin set at a belligerent angle that perfectly matches the anger that's still smoldering in her eyes. Anger . . . and a touch of fear, since I still haven't convinced her that I'm not here to cause her any trouble. That I only want to help.

But her anger and fear, as well as my simmering irritation, aren't the only things here in this tiny apartment with us. There's a visceral tension that's so thick I feel like I could reach out and grab it, the heaviness of it making it difficult to breathe. It's made up of heat and need and physical hunger, even more potent than it'd been the last time I'd seen her, when she'd been walking out of Jase's family home, leaving for her honeymoon with another man. But her eyes had been on *me* as she'd climbed into Olly's sleek sports car, and I'd had no doubt that she wanted me as badly as I wanted her.

I'd silently begged her not to do it. Not to leave with him.

And it'd cut like a knife when she'd looked away and slammed the passenger-side door shut, making her decision clear.

The asshole hadn't even helped her into the low-slung Porsche, but that hadn't been surprising. After having helped Jase deal with the distraught, pregnant nineteen year old who had shown up out of the blue to confront Olly two nights before, I'd understood exactly how much of a self-centered prick he was. Christ, he'd spent the entire weekend screwing his way through the wedding party, and even though I knew damn well that Lottie was aware of it all, she'd still married the prick. Still driven off with him while I'd just stood there on the steps with the rest of the wedding guests, feeling like a fool.

'Callan,' she says, pulling me back to the moment, and my frown deepens as I recall that she's still desperate to get rid of me.

'How many times do I have to tell you that I'm not going anywhere?'

She takes a quick breath, looking as if she's fighting for patience, and crosses her arms so tightly I'm surprised she has any circulation left in them. 'You know, this kind of behavior could easily be construed as harassment.'

'Bullshit, Lot. I completely support a woman's right to do whatever the hell she wants, but this isn't a normal situation and you know it. You need help, but are being too pig-headed to take it.'

'So you're going to *make* me? Talk about a freaking hero complex.'

'I'm going to make sure you're okay,' I grind out, shoving my hands back through my hair in a burst of frustration. 'And while I'm doing that, I'm going to find a way to help you get your damn life back.'

'Why?' she cries, sounding completely baffled as she throws her hands up in the air.

'Why what?'

'Why would you do that? Any of it? It's insane!'

There are a thousand different reasons I could give her that would probably just send her running again, so I go for the one that hopefully sounds the most reasonable. 'Because it's the way my mom raised me.'

She gives another snort, only this one is sharp with derision. 'To take on charity cases?'

I slowly exhale, striving for patience of my own. 'No. To help those in need, when we have the means. Those means being my background and my business. And you, honey, are definitely in need of help from someone like me.'

'You're a bodyguard, Callan. Or . . . you were. What exactly do you think I need protecting from? The police? Wouldn't that make you a criminal?'

'Not the police,' I say, feeling like I might finally be starting to make some sense of the bizarre situation. And why she's so desperate to get rid of me. 'Yeah, I know you must be scared shitless of getting caught, and given how things have gone, I don't blame you. But what I think is really scaring the hell out of you is the idea of whoever killed Oliver tracking you down.'

She sucks in another sharp breath, her face so white she looks like a goddamn cadaver.

'Christ, Lot. What the hell is going on?' I demand, my thoughts racing as I try to wrap my head around this new revelation.

'I can't . . . I don't . . .' She turns her face to the side, obviously struggling for composure. I know she's found it when she smooths her hands down the front of her T-shirt and looks over at me with an expression that's so eerily composed it's unsettling, as if she's taken every bit of emotion inside her and buried it down so deep, she can no longer even feel it. 'I don't have much to offer you to drink,' she eventually murmurs, as if I've just dropped by for a casual visit, 'but I bought some sodas last night. Want one?'

'Sure, thanks,' I reply, playing along even though I'm dying to press her for an explanation. But my gut tells me it's not the time to keep pushing, so I bite my tongue as I watch her head into the cramped kitchenette that I can just see through the beaded curtain that hangs over a small archway.

Since I'm on my own, I take a moment to give my surroundings a closer look. I'm standing in the center of a studio apartment that's actually smaller than the living room at my place here in the city. The floors appear to be the old original hardwood planks, but they're spotlessly clean and gleaming. There's no TV, but a dated laptop sits on top of an end table that's been painted in a beautiful cherry-blossom motif that looks as if her neighbor Eva probably did it for her. And through a small archway on my left, I can see what looks like an air mattress that's been neatly covered in purple sheets lying on the floor, the sight of it making me want to get my hands on whoever's responsible for putting her in this situation and make them pay.

'Go ahead, say it,' she murmurs, catching me studying the place as she walks back through the beaded curtain and hands me a cold soda can. 'My place is a piece of crap.'

'It's cute,' I tell her, meaning it as I pop the top and take a drink. While it pisses me off that she's living in a damn shoebox, the quirky style of the studio fits her perfectly, and I can tell that even though she's clearly struggling for money, she's worked hard to make it as comfortable as possible. Chloe would probably call it Boho Chic, if I've understood anything from her design lectures over the years. But to me it's just feminine and inviting, with lots of white and soft splashes of color. And yet, as cozy as Lottie has made the place, it's making me uneasy, and I know that's my gut trying to warn me that she's not safe here. That there's a hell of a lot more wrong with this woman's life than the fact that she's wanted for murder.

Bringing my hard gaze back to hers, I say, 'It's your security that's shit, Lot. The building is completely unprotected against break-ins, and the lock on your front door is pathetic. I could probably bust through it with a single kick.'

She lifts one golden eyebrow in a perfect arch. 'Yeah? Then I guess I'll just take all my loads of cash that I have lying around and go buy myself a brand-new door that's Callan-approved.'

Ignoring her sarcasm, I give her a sharp smile. 'There's no need, honey, because you're not staying here.'

Her blue eyes narrow at my words, the look on her face saying she thinks I've completely lost my mind. 'Excuse me?'

'You're coming home with me. I have a place here in the city, in Manhattan, in a secured building, with an alarm system that's the best on the market.' Plus, she'll have *me*, but I know better than to point that out.

'Well, huzzah for you, Hathaway. But I don't really give a damn where you live.'

'We can waste hours arguing,' I tell her as I walk over to the small table that's set against the wall with a single chair – she probably uses it to eat her meals at or as a desk – and set the soda can down. 'Or you can accept the inevitable and do what's right.'

'What's right is kicking you out the door.'

'Why? So you can pack up and do another runner?' I slowly shake my head as I turn to face her again. 'I don't think so.'

'Why? Because it's not what *you* want?'

'Damn straight,' I reply, pushing my hands back into my pockets. 'But more than that, it's not smart, Lottie. And I know you're sure as hell not stupid.'

A harsh, bitter laugh slips past her lips. 'Look around you. The current circumstances of my life don't exactly speak to my intelligence.'

'And you know better than to blame the victim. I *know* you do.'

Her gaze is uncomfortably piercing and direct, making me feel as if she can see right inside me. As if she can analyze my mind like one of the poems she used to study and write papers about, and I try not to flinch, too aware of how much I have in my head that I don't want her getting anywhere near. Not when she so desperately wants rid of me.

'You could get in trouble for helping me,' she finally says, tossing the soft words out like a challenge.

'I could,' I agree. 'But I won't.'

'You don't know that,' she argues with exasperation.

'I'm a grown man, Lot. I know what I'm doing.'

'God, you're not going to take freaking no for an answer, are you?'

'No, I'm not. So all you need to decide is if you want to deal with just me, or if I should call Jase and Emmy and get them here to help me talk some sense into you.' They were both at Lottie's wedding, and I know she spent quite a bit of time talking to Emmy Reed, who had been Jase's date that weekend. She'd seemed to get along better with Emmy than with anyone else at the wedding, including her own family.

'You wouldn't dare.'

'The hell I wouldn't.'

'Are you . . . Are you saying that they think I'm innocent, too?' she quietly asks, the faint strain of hope in her voice making my insides twist.

'Of course they do,' I lie, since only half of that statement is true. Emmy has been my biggest ally in arguing for Lottie's innocence – though I think that has more to do with the fact that she *wants* it to be true, rather than actually believing it – but neither of us have managed to sway Jase to our way of thinking. He honestly believes Lottie stabbed his cousin over thirty times, then left him to bleed out on the deck of his yacht, the backbone of his theory being that Olly was a big enough asshole to drive *anyone*, even an amazing person like Lottie, to do something that violent and horrible.

We've argued about it more than once, and will most likely argue about it again, given the path I've chosen today. But I have no doubt that I'll pull my friend around to my way of thinking. I won't accept anything less, because I know, deep down in my bones, that despite the fingerprints found all over the knife that cut Oliver Beckett to shreds, there's no way in hell the woman standing before me is responsible.

'Just trust me, Lottie. Please,' I plead, the uneasy feeling in my gut that she's not safe here only growing stronger. And when I sense that she might actually be wavering, I go in for the kill. 'Look at it this way – if you're in danger, do you really want to bring that danger here, into the same building where families live?'

She flinches, making me feel like a complete shit for saying it. 'That was low.'

'But true, and you know it.'

Silence stretches out between us, heavy enough to feel like a physical force, and then she finally looks away, her eyes closing as she gives a quiet, defeated sigh. 'Fine. It's a stupid, asinine idea, but I'll do it.'

Relief sweeps through me, stunning and sharp, but I'm smart enough to keep my mouth shut as I watch her walk into the tiny bedroom and open her small shoebox of a closet, where she's got a duffel bag on the top shelf. She sets the bag on the air mattress, and starts packing in another wave of heavy, angry silence, while I take my phone out.

But as I pull up the number for my car service, I hear her mutter a dozen or so sharp, grim words that tell me what really lies at the root of her fear.

I just hope you're not the one who ends up regretting it.

Chapter Two

CALLAN

I lock my front door, then turn and watch as Lottie makes her way across the hardwood floors and thick rugs that my sister Chloe had found for me when I bought the sprawling apartment last year. We took a car from Lottie's neighborhood, but didn't talk on the ride over, which was probably for the best. Nothing I wanted to say to her could be said in front of a nosy driver, and she'd still looked furious, so I think the silence suited her just fine.

It's grown dark in the past half hour, and we're high enough up that the impressive view of Manhattan is all glittering lights and soaring skyscrapers. I prefer the woods to the city, but if I have to be in town for work or my family, then this is the way to do it, high above all the noise and commotion, with nothing but the clouds for company.

Setting her duffel on the floor and my keys on the waist-high chest that sits in the entryway, I notice that Lottie's carefully edging a bit closer to the far wall that's made entirely of glass, her movements careful and tinged with fear. The glass is fortified,' I murmur, trying to put her at ease, while enjoying the way her work leggings hug her long legs, though it concerns me that she looks even slimmer than she had at her wedding. 'You don't have to worry about getting too close.'

Her shoulders stiffen, but she doesn't turn around as she quietly says, 'I wasn't.'

'If you're afraid of heights, honey, it's nothing to be ashamed about. Everybody's afraid of something.' I don't add that my greatest fear for the past year has been that I would never see her again, knowing damn well it would be the wrong thing to say. But it's the truth. And no matter how irritated she insists on acting, the overwhelming sense of relief that I experienced when I found her today just keeps growing, making me feel lighter than I have in months. Hell, if I can convince her to share a bed with me – for safety purposes at this point, of course – I might even be able to sleep peacefully tonight.

'My fears are none of your business,' she mutters, pulling me from my thoughts, and I bite back a sigh, figuring she'd probably rather sleep in a pit of rattlesnakes right now than beside me.

'Well, in case there's any curiosity mixed in with all that anger you're feeling, I bought the place specifically for that view. Thought it was pretty spectacular.'

A soft, bitter laugh shakes her shoulders, and she grabs her backpack as it starts to slip, setting it on the floor by her feet. 'Is that the standard line you use with the women you bring up here?'

'Not standard, no.' I scratch at the evening bristles on my jawline, trying to decide if she sounds jealous or just annoyed. 'I've lived here since just before your wedding. And I don't have any lines, Lottie. Not anymore,' I tell her. And then some of the bitterness that I've carried for so long, from having to watch her marry another man, leaks into my tone as I say, 'It's not really any of *your* business, but you're the only woman, other than ones who work for me or that I'm related to, who's ever seen this place.'

She shoots me a skeptical look over her shoulder. 'You expect me to believe that you haven't brought a woman home with you in over a year?'

'Believe what you want. But it's the truth.'

'Sure it is,' she scoffs under her breath, looking back at the view. She hasn't paid much attention to the big, high-ceilinged room around her, and I can't help but wonder what she thinks of the style. I've always felt that Chloe did a perfect job with the place, but there's no getting away from the fact that it's vastly different from Lottie's own apartment – and I don't just mean cost-wise. The lush houseplants and the richness of the deep teal and dark chocolate color scheme are cut by the harshness of wood and metal, making it a purely masculine setting. One that only accentuates the soft vibrancy and strength of her femininity.

She's like a beautiful gazelle trapped in the tiger's jungle, and I choke back a laugh when my stomach suddenly gives a bestial growl, reminding me that I haven't eaten since my lunchtime meeting with Deanna Brannon, a great, badass lady and my newly appointed Head of Operations at Hathaway Security.

'Are you hungry?' I ask Lottie, opening the top drawer in the chest that holds all my takeaway menus, since it's the easiest place to stash them when I come in with my mail.

She shrugs her shoulders in a noncommittal response.

'Well, I'm starving. Thai food okay with you? There's a great place not far from here that delivers.'

Another shrug, and I bite back a surge of frustration, knowing I need to be patient. She's obviously on edge and doesn't want to be here, so I need to be happy with my big victory in just getting her through the door, and not worry about gaining any smaller ones at the moment.

'Okay, then,' I mutter, taking out my phone as I head toward my bedroom so that I can finally get out of this shirt. 'Make yourself comfortable while I change and order us some food.'

LOTTIE

I take a deep breath and work to calm my racing pulse, still desperately trying to wrap my head around what is happening. Still trying to come to terms with the fact that Callan Hathaway, the gorgeous, bronze-haired stranger who's haunted me for the past fifteen months, has guilted me into going home with him . . . because he claims he wants to help me. As if such a thing is even possible.

God, what the hell have I gotten myself into?

We've been here for about thirty minutes, but he spent most of that time having to deal with an emergency call that came in from someone at Hathaway Security, the personal protection company that he owns. From what I could make out from his side of the conversation, it sounds as if he'd been walking by the café today because of a meeting he'd had with a potential client in that particular part of town. A part that's actually much more awesome than Callan was giving it credit for, its numerous families and authentic feel so much more comforting to me than the parts of Brooklyn that have been taken over by trendy, overpriced shops and housing.

After his call, the food he'd ordered was delivered, and now he's sitting on the huge leather sofa that faces the one I'm sitting on, his mouthwatering body dressed in jeans and a faded Metallica T-shirt that looks ridiculously good on him. Enough incredible-smelling food to feed an army is laid out on the rustic, square-shaped coffee table that sits between us, and I blink as Callan extends one of his long, muscular arms to hand me a huge plate that's a beautiful swirl of copper and black, the crooked half-smile on his wide mouth doing something strange to my already racing pulse.

The entire situation is surreal, and far too intimate, like something plucked right out of my fevered midnight fantasies. The embarrassing ones where I wake up thrashing in my cheap sheets, my body burning with need for a man I barely know – who was only at my wedding because his mum had been too ill to make the flight – but had made such an impact on me, I'm still struggling for a way to put him out of my mind.

And, God, he's somehow even more stunning than I remembered, with all that shaggy hair and the bronze stubble on his jaw. More rugged and male and devastatingly sexy. More . . . *everything*.

'Come on, Lot,' he murmurs in his deep voice, jerking his chin at the food. 'Eat up.'

I've always been one of those slender girls who could eat anything they wanted without putting on weight, while longing for the kind of lush curves that most men find far sexier than my tomboy look. And it hasn't helped that I've barely been able to eat during the past year, my nerves shot and worry constantly roiling in my stomach. But this spread looks too delicious to refuse, and I find myself reaching for the closest open box and start spooning a fragrant chicken dish onto my plate. Then I reach for the next one . . . and the next.

'Shit. I forgot the beers.' He looks at me with that sexy tilt of his head that seems almost primal. Almost animal-like, as if he's so much more than just a man, but that's probably just my longtime love of paranormal romance coming through. My tired brain is getting tangled up trying to decide if he would be a wolf or a grizzly shifter, when he asks me, 'You a beer drinker, Lottie?'

'As long as it's not Guinness. That stuff makes me shudder.'

His laugh is low and deep, and I squirm a bit on the comfortable leather cushion as I watch him rise to his feet, my gaze glued to his muscular arse as he heads toward what I assume is the kitchen. From what I've seen, this entire apartment is like something out of *Architectural Digest*, and while I knew that Callan owned a successful business, I'd had no idea that he was this well off.

And though the money might have been a turn-on for some women, I've been around enough snobby rich boys to know that they're definitely not my type.

Only . . . there's not a single snobbish thing about Callan Hathaway, and you know it, an annoyed voice murmurs in my head. It's the same one that's been screaming at me for acting like such a bitch to him, but I keep ignoring it, too afraid of what might happen if I stop.

When he sits back down with two icy bottles of the best-selling IPA that we serve at the café in his hands, I notice the way that his jeans pull tight across his thighs, allowing me to see the sexy cut of muscle in his long, powerful legs. He somehow manages to look like he belongs on the glossy pages of a magazine even when dressed in well-worn jeans and an old T-shirt, his big feet bare and tanned, and I hate that I'm self-conscious of my grubby work uniform, since looking good for this man is the absolute *last* thing in the world I should be caring about.

He pops the top off one of the bottles, then reaches over the table again to hand it to me just as his phone starts vibrating for what must be the sixth time since he found me. 'Thanks,' I murmur, watching as he pulls the phone from his pocket and hits ignore, after only briefly glancing at the screen, which he's done for every call except the one from his company. 'You should go ahead and take it,' I say casually, worried I'm doing a crap job of hiding my true feelings on the subject. 'Your girlfriend must be worried if she keeps calling.'

'I don't have a girlfriend, Lot.' The corner of his mouth twitches, like he's trying not to laugh at my embarrassing flare of jealousy. 'The calls I'm ignoring have all been from one of my sisters.'

I latch on to the topic of his family like an overboard sailor grasping for a lifeline, since it will safely steer us away from the uncomfortable subject of his love life. 'You have three of them, right? And three brothers?'

'That's right,' he says, looking down at his plate, but I swear I see the corner of his freaking mouth twitch again, as if he can see right through me. And for some inexplicable reason, the idea is as arousing as it is worrying.

'Well, don't you want to make sure it's not an emergency?' I ask, turning my focus to my own plate, since the tasty Thai food is a hell of a lot safer than Callan Hathaway.

'It's not,' he replies with a sigh. 'She's just being nosy.'

'Oh.' I take a bite of the coconut shrimp and try not to moan, but the taste is blissful. I swallow, take a sip of my beer, and ask him, 'So which sister is it?'

He still isn't looking at me, but a kind of tightness suddenly settles over his huge body, as if something troubling has just occurred to him. Something he obviously doesn't want to share, since he changes the subject completely. 'Your accent sounds different than it used to. Why is that?'

'Habit, I guess. I've tried not to make it too easy for people to place where I'm from,' I murmur, leaving him to his secrets, since God knows I want to be left to mine. 'You know how it is. My current life of glamour is all part of this on-the-run thing I've had going.'

A low laugh slips past his soft-looking lips, and I mentally give myself a hard shake when I realize that I've just been sitting here, staring at the guy's mouth while he eats. Nervous energy buzzes beneath my skin, my scalp prickling, and I finally can't take wearing the wig a second more. Setting my plate on the coffee table, I wipe my hands on the linen napkin he'd given me earlier and reach up, pulling the pins out that hold the nightmare in place. I almost moan again as I pull it off, using my fingers to massage my scalp after I toss the godawful wig onto the arm of the sofa, then finger comb my hair into what's hopefully some semblance of order before reaching for my plate again.

'This food is amaz—' I start to say as I glance over at Callan, but the words die on my tongue when I realize that his warm brown eyes have gone dark, his gaze unmistakably hot as he takes in the way my wavy blonde hair is falling over my shoulders now, the ends just curling above my breasts. Fighting the self-conscious urge to fiddle with it, I cough to clear my throat, and murmur, 'It's, um, grown out a lot since you last saw me.'

That dark gaze slowly lifts back to my eyes, and there's a distinct edge to his voice as he tells me, 'It looks gorgeous, Lot.'

I shift a bit nervously, having no idea what to make of him . . . or the compliment. 'Um, thanks,' I mumble, before focusing back on my food. And even though he starts eating again too, I can feel the blistering force of his gaze every breathtaking time he looks over at me, the heat that starts climbing into my cheeks making it painfully clear that I'm blushing like an idiot.

'Okay, you got me here,' I blurt, sounding belligerent, even as I take another bite of the sumptuous food that he's bought for us. Talk about ungrateful. 'So what happens now?'

'That's easy. Now you talk.'

'Yeah? About what?'

'Everything.' He takes a long swig of his beer, then locks his sharp gaze with mine as he says, 'Starting with why you married that son of a bitch.'

My anger flares so quickly it's like being dunked in icy water, and I hear myself snap, 'You shouldn't talk about him that way!'

His head cocks a bit to the side again, the look in his eyes one of surprise and confusion. 'Lottie, you're not stupid. In fact, you're probably one of the smartest people I've ever known. So believe me when I say that I *know* you know that Oliver Beckett was a piece of shit.'

I want to ask why he thinks he knows a damn thing about me, but I'm too emotional to focus on anything but what he's said about Olly. 'He might not have been a great guy, sure. But he was a brave one. He . . . He . . .'

Callan's brown eyes turn piercing. 'He what, Lottie?'

Setting my plate back on the coffee table, I somehow manage to push my response past the lump of gratitude and regret that's nearly choking me. 'Olly saved my life.'

He stares, looking at me as if I've just told him that I'm really the Queen of England.

'It's true,' I whisper, my throat so tight I can barely swallow. 'And trust me, I was as shocked as you are when it happened.'

Something even darker, and infinitely more dangerous, filters into his gaze, and I know he's gone into some kind of protective-alpha mode when he quietly asks, 'Saved it from who?'

Instead of answering the question, I take a page out of his

own book and deliberately change the subject again. 'How did you even recognize me today? When I'm wearing the wig, I don't look anything like the woman you met last year. I barely even look like her now.'

He lowers his face again, but not before I see the tinge of pink in his bristled cheek, the recessed lighting that runs about a foot under the ceiling's perimeter catching softly on his bronze stubble. 'What?' I press, wanting to know what this rugged, confident, damn near god-like man could possibly find embarrassing.

'It was your laugh,' he mutters, before stuffing his ridiculously sexy mouth full of noodles.

I blink, wondering if I actually heard him right. 'My . . . laugh?'

'Yeah.'

'That's . . .' My voice trails off, and I swallow so hard that it hurts, swimming in confusion as I run my damp palms over the tops of my thighs. 'I honestly don't even know *what* that is.'

He rolls one of those hard, muscular shoulders and grunts something unintelligible under his breath, reminding me of a surly bear. Then he looks up at me and says, 'If you don't want to talk about what happened in Italy yet, fine. We'll get to it later. But at least tell me what you've been doing this past year.'

Despite the unbearable tension of the entire situation, I actually laugh. 'What do you think I've been doing, Callan?'

'I know you've been hiding. But how? Where? Why?'

I pull in a deep breath, then slowly let it go. 'I . . . Let's just say that before he died, Olly provided me with a very special gift. One that gave me the means to live under a different identity if I ever needed to.'

'Jesus Christ,' he says, his voice whisper-soft, and there are about a-million-and-one questions burning in his beautiful eyes. But he doesn't press me for details, and I'm so grateful that I go ahead and briefly answer his other two questions.

'So that's the how. Ever since I landed in Los Angeles, I've been Lana Hill, a waitress who's half-American, half-British. And as for the where and why, I rented a car the day I got to LA and just kept driving until I'd reached New York. I've lived here ever since. And the reason,' I explain, forcing myself to keep holding his piercing gaze as I scrape out this last part, 'is that I had no doubt the police would believe I'd killed Olly, and no way to prove that I hadn't. So like a coward, I've been hiding ever since.'

'From them and the real killer,' he murmurs, not even voicing it as a question. But he doesn't need to. He's studying me so carefully, reading my expressions so easily, he knows damn well that he's right.

'So what about you?' I ask, before taking another sip of my beer.

'Work,' he tells me, setting his own near-empty plate on the table. 'A vacation with my brothers over the winter at a ski resort. A few road trips on my new Harley with my friend Seb. More work.' He picks his beer back up, giving me another wry half-smile as he adds, 'And I've spent a hell of a lot of time looking for you.'

My spine shoots so straight, I probably look like I've just been zapped with a jolt of electricity. 'What does *that* mean?'

'It means exactly how it sounds, Lot.'

I shake my head in confusion, while my pulse pounds in my ears. 'But . . . why? You don't even know me.'

'That's not entirely true,' he disagrees, then finishes off his beer. 'And just because I had to watch you marry another man doesn't mean your disappearance didn't completely wreck me.'

I look away from him, unable to cope with the things he's

saying when he's looking at me like I'm somehow . . . I don't know. Important to him, which makes absolutely zero sense.

'And I do know you,' he tells me with a bitter laugh. 'Trust me, after talking to pretty much anyone who's ever been a part of your life, I've learned a hell of a lot.'

No matter how freaking awkward the situation is, my gaze is pulled back to his as if it has a will of its own. 'You . . . investigated me?' I ask, sounding more than a little outraged. But I'm not really angry. I'm just . . . shocked. 'How?'

'When Jase called to tell me what had happened in Italy, I hopped on a flight the next morning for England.' He sets his empty beer bottle beside his plate, then leans back, his muscular arms, with their cut lines of muscle and sinew, stretched out along the back of the sofa in a pose that's as masculine as it is mouthwatering. 'Usually, in cases like these, if a person's in trouble, they turn to someone they know for help. So I started by talking to your aunt and uncle.'

I lift my brows in surprise. 'Aunt April and Uncle Liam?'

Callan nods. 'But they were almost in too much shock still to be of much help. All they could really tell me is that you'd come to live with them at the age of fourteen, after your parents died in a car accident, and that you'd always been a gifted, hard-working student. The only odd thing your aunt mentioned was that you'd been quite social, with lots of friends, until you turned sixteen. After that, you stopped going out and just spent all your time studying.'

'I wanted to get into a good school,' I murmur, staring at the backs of my hands as I press them against my thighs, determined not to let his words jar me into revealing too much.

He waits, as if hoping I'll just start pouring out my life story. When he finally realizes it'll be a cold day in hell before I open that depressing vein, he leans forward, bracing his elbows on his spread knees, and my gaze is instantly drawn to the impressive, denim-covered bulge between his legs. When it occurs to me where I'm staring, I rip my gaze away, completely mortified that I'd been ogling him like a piece of meat – but he plays the part of a gentleman and doesn't even call me out for it.

'So after talking to your family, I tracked down your ... friends from university,' he tells me, and I swear his voice is a bit rougher than it was before. 'The ones you lived with until just before your marriage.'

I notice the way he paused before the word 'friends', and I understand why. Despite the fact that most of them were good people, I wasn't ever close to any of them. Hell, I lived with Sasha, my maid of honor, for nearly three years, but didn't ever really know much about her – other than the fact that she was smart, liked to party ... and had shagged Olly on my wedding night.

Flopping against the back of the sofa, I stare up at the off-white ceiling and laugh softly. 'I bet they were all pretty shocked, huh? I can't imagine they ever thought that dull, mousy Lottie would be wanted for murder.'

'First of all, there's not a single dull or mousy thing about you. And secondly, you should give them more credit. They're genuinely worried about you.'

I lift my head, trying to judge if he's telling the truth from his expression, but there are times when the guy's got an unbeatable poker face – a trait that I can't help but envy. 'Maybe some of them are,' I say quietly ... grudgingly, 'but you don't have to sugar-coat things for me, Callan. I know damn well that Olly was in Sasha's bed on our wedding night.'

Something flashes in his eyes that I sincerely hope is anger and not pity. But I'm grateful that he doesn't keep forging down this awkward path, and instead shocks me when he says, 'I also talked to your supervisor, Dr Hoffman.'

That bit of news has me sitting upright again. 'You didn't!'

'I did.' There's a gleam in his dark eyes that I don't quite understand, but it has my pulse quickening. 'She's worried sick about you, Lot. And proud as hell of your master's thesis. She even showed me some of your work.'

'You're kidding,' I say with surprise.

He flashes me a crooked smile. 'Nope.'

'Oh God,' I groan, covering my warm face with my hands. 'I'm sorry,' I mumble, feeling ridiculously embarrassed for a woman who's been on the run for the past year. 'That must have been so boring for you.'

'Are you kidding me? It took some significant flattery on my part, but I finally persuaded Hoffman to send me a copy of your poetry compilation.'

I peek at him from between my fingers. 'The one about the Greek gods?'

'Yeah.'

'That's . . .' I exhale sharply as I push my hair back from my face, then press my palms back against the tops of my thighs to keep from fidgeting. 'Yeah, I honestly don't know what to make of that either.'

He laughs, low and rough again, the sexy sound sliding down my spine like a physical touch that makes me shiver with awareness. 'I can't claim to be smart enough to understand all of it, but I love the way I can get almost lost in it. The way your words make me . . . feel. You're incredibly talented, Miss Fleming.'

I know I should say thank you – and probably correct him on my last name – but my throat is suddenly too tight for speech, and I take a deep breath as I look around the insanely awesome room, trying to make sense of what's happening here. But the entire evening, from the moment I looked up into his gorgeous eyes when he'd caught me on the steps of my building to this precise second, has been surreal. I'm like Alice, falling head-over-feet down the rabbit hole, and I'm still tumbling, with no idea what's going to happen when I finally hit the bottom. The only thing I know with any certainty is that it's going to hurt, because as much as I love to have my head in the clouds when it comes to literature, life has made me into a stone-cold realist.

And Callan Hathaway is too goddamn perfect to be real.

Quietly, and with some kind of wild, visceral emotion rising up inside me, I look over at him again and ask, 'What's really going on here, Callan?'

'Nothing,' he says, his broad shoulders lifting in an easy-going shrug, 'except one friend helping out another friend.'

'I'm not buying it,' I argue, surging to my feet. 'Because no one is *this* freaking righteous. No one is this freaking nice!'

'Bullshit,' he says, tilting his head back. 'There are good people all over the place. You just apparently haven't known many of them, Lot.'

'Like hell there are!'

'Emmy was sweet to you.'

I pause, shoving my hands back through my hair again, feeling trapped. 'That . . . That was a long time ago.'

'It was a year,' he replies drily. 'We're not talking decades here.'

He's right, but I'm too confused to keep arguing. So I take the coward's way out and do a hard retreat. 'Look, I worked a ten-hour shift today and I'm exhausted, not to mention filthy and I still smell like the café's tuna melt special. Do you mind if we hold off on the rest of the inquisition until tomorrow? I'd love to just use your shower and go to bed.'

'Not at all.' He moves to his feet with an athletic prowess that should be impossible for a guy his size, the way his muscles move beneath the golden sheen of his skin making my pulse jump. 'I want you to feel at home here, Lot, so use whatever you want. It's all available.'

I give him a sharp look, trying to decipher if there was a sexual offer hidden in those innocent words, but it's too difficult to tell. Everything the man says in that bone-melting, slightly gruff voice comes off sounding sexual. Either that, or I'm so attracted to him, lust is affecting how my ears work.

'I'll grab you a towel and show you where the guestroom is,' he says, already heading around the sofa.

'Wait,' I blurt, remembering my manners. 'Let me help you clean up first.'

'Don't worry about it,' he tosses over his shoulder as he walks into the entryway and grabs my duffel. I quickly pick my backpack up from where I'd left it on the floor, and hurry after him, since he's already on the other side of the room, heading through a high arch that leads into a wide hallway.

Without looking back at me, which is a good thing since I can't seem to stop watching the way his backside looks in his jeans, he asks, 'Do you need to call and let them know you won't be at work tomorrow?'

I frown at his back. 'I'm not quitting my job,' I tell him, while his wide shoulders seem to stiffen with tension. 'But we don't have to argue about it right now. I actually have the weekend off.'

He grunts something under his breath as he opens a tall, modern-looking chest that sits against the hallway wall, then pulls out a thick, fluffy white towel. Closing the chest, he turns and offers me the towel, but I just stand there, staring at the way the veins in his arm are pressing up beneath his tanned skin. It's so outrageously rugged and sexy, it's unreal, and I feel like an idiot when he clears his throat to get my attention.

Shaking myself out of my lust-induced trance, I grab the towel and quickly lower my gaze, staring down at the toes of my faded pink socks.

'Yeah, so, the guestroom is right over here,' he says, and I look up to see him walking over to a dark, exquisitely carved wooden door. 'It has its own bathroom and a mini fridge stocked with bottled water and juice,' he adds, opening the door and then propping his shoulder against the pale gray wall, 'so you should be set for necessities. But my room is just at the end of the hallway, so I'll be close by if you need me.'

'Thanks,' I say softly, careful not to touch him as I slip past his tall body, my eyes widening as I enter the room. It's beyond lovely, the back wall covered in a tropical-style wallpaper in peacock blue, gold and orange that goes perfectly with the high bed that's made of polished bamboo. It's obvious that the entire apartment has been professionally decorated, the work of his older sister, I'm guessing, and I can see what he means about Eva's paintings, because they really would look perfect in a room like this.

I hear Callan enter the room behind me, and I glance over my shoulder to see him set my duffel bag on the floor beside a beautifully painted chest of drawers. Looking away, I walk over to the bed, set the towel and my backpack down on the silk bedspread that's in a slightly lighter shade of blue than the wallpaper, and can't resist running my hand over the sumptuous fabric.

'Okay, then,' he says. 'Just give me a shout if you need me.'

I look over and manage a brief smile that hopefully conveys my appreciation for the way he's trying to make sure that I'm comfortable in his home, while the look in my eyes no doubt still shows my frustration at the fact that I'm even here in the first place. 'I'm sure I'll be fine.'

I can tell that there's more he wants to say, but he simply responds with a masculine nod and turns to walk out of the room, while I follow behind him.

'Hey, Lottie,' he murmurs, turning to face me again a second before I start to shut the door, his warm gaze locked in hard and tight on mine. 'I just have one more question.'

'What is it?' I ask, gripping the doorknob so tightly I'm surprised it hasn't snapped off.

He pushes his hands into his front pockets and does that sexy head-tilt thing again. 'Why New York? I mean, you knew I lived here, right? So why come *here*?'

'Don't be so full of yourself, Hathaway. It had nothing to do with you. I just thought it would be the easiest place to get lost in.'

'You could've gotten lost in LA,' he points out in an easy-going tone that's at complete odds with the intensity of the way he's searching my expression, hunting for even the slightest crack in my emotional mask.

'I could have,' I agree. 'But I don't happen to like LA.'

'Everybody likes LA,' he argues with a soft laugh. 'Hell, it's all sunshine and beaches, Lottie. What's not to like?'

Since I don't have a single freaking answer for him – at least not one that won't reveal far more than I can handle – I simply say, 'Goodnight, Callan.'

Then I shut the door in his face.

Chapter Three

CALLAN

It no doubt makes me a total shit, but I wait until I hear the shower running, then use the key I keep in my bedside drawer and unlock the door to the guest bedroom, grabbing Lottie's backpack off the bed. Taking it into my office, I work fast, slicing open a portion of the seam on the bottom edge and inserting one of the small tracking dots that my company uses for our clients. The only difference is that they always know we're tagging their possessions, whereas if Lottie knew what I was doing, she'd probably try to smash my balls in again.

With the tracker in place, I glue the seam shut – it's faster than sewing it – and slip back into her room, leaving the backpack where I found it, then quickly get the hell out of there, relocking the door behind me.

Seeing as how I still need to clean up the takeaway, I head back out to the living room, but stop just as I'm about to pick up the first plate and walk over to the entryway instead. I know it's probably overkill, but I grab one of the Converse that Lottie had slipped off after coming inside, then take it back to my office. Peeling up the insole, I insert another tracking dot, push the insole back into place, and take the shoe back out to the entryway, placing it in exactly the same spot where I found it.

With that done, it takes me only ten minutes to deal with the takeaway cartons and stash the plates and silverware in the dishwasher, then set the alarm. As I head back to my bedroom, I can no longer hear the shower running, and there's no light coming from under the guestroom door, so I figure Lottie's already crawled into bed. It takes all my mental willpower not to picture her in there on the queen-sized bed, since I know that will only string my sex-starved body even tighter, and I'm already strung tight enough as it is just from having her here, in my home.

When I reach my bedroom, I shut the door, suck in a deep breath as I take my phone from my pocket, and finally make the one call I've known, from the moment I found her, that I was going to have to make.

'Hey, man,' Jase says after only two rings, sounding genuinely happy to hear from me, and I realize it's been a few weeks since we've spoken. And since he also doesn't sound like I've just woke him up, I'm guessing he and Emmy are in California, rather than their place in London. 'What's up?'

'I, um, have some news.'

He must hear something in my voice, because his tone is more careful as he says, 'Okay.'

I start pacing across the black hardwood floor, a gritty laugh on my lips as I tell him, 'And I need you to not freak the hell out.'

Jase snickers like a jackass. 'What am I, a teenaged girl?'

'Hey, don't be a sexist twat,' I growl.

'Christ, I'm not sexist. It's just a say—Ow, damn it! Shit, Em, stop giving me a noogie!' he yells, just before she squeals like she's being tickled and they both dissolve into muffled laughter.

'Jesus,' he mutters into the phone nearly a half-minute later. 'Now you've got Emmy ganging up on me and that woman's vicious.'

'Your stupid mouth did that all on its own. But this is important, so I need you to focus.' I take a breath, then just blurt it out. 'I found Lottie today and she's staying with me.'

I hear something clatter, as if Jase has dropped the phone. Then his deep voice is back, thick with shock as he says, 'What the fuck?'

'I found Lottie, Jase. Here in New York. She's in my guestroom as we speak.'

'Holy shit. How? How did you find her?'

I give another low, gritty laugh and reach up with my free hand to rub at the knotted muscles in the back of my neck. 'Pure random friggin' chance, if you can believe it.'

'I don't,' he grunts, clearly as skeptical as ever when it comes to this girl.

'Well, it's true, man. I was just walking down the street today, and found her working at a café in Brooklyn.'

'Where the hell has she been?'

'Right here in the city,' I tell him, which still blows my mind. 'She drove here after landing in LA and has been working as a server ever since.'

'For Christ's sake, how?' he demands, his British accent crisp and sharp. 'She's a wanted woman, Callan. It's not like she could just apply for a bloody work permit!'

'Yeah, well, Olly gave her a gift on their honeymoon.'

'What kind of gift?' he asks, sounding completely baffled.

'From what little I know, it was a new identity package, in case she ever needed to run.' And I still can't quite believe the guy had done it. God knows I hadn't thought he had it in him to be that generous, and it's driving me crazy, wondering what finally got through to him. What finally opened his eyes, enabling him to see what was right in front of him, to the point that he would actually do something to help her. Something that had no benefit to his own sorry ass.

But even more than that, I need to know why he thought she would need that damn package in the first place. And Jase is apparently thinking the same thing.

'Why would Olly buy her a new identity?' he asks. 'That doesn't make any sense.'

'I have a feeling that it does,' I rumble, still pacing. 'I just don't have all the details yet.'

'Jesus. This is so messed up.' My longtime friend exhales a heavy breath, and I can hear what sounds like waves crashing in the background, telling me that he's probably standing out on his and Emmy's sprawling deck that overlooks one of the most beautiful beaches in the States. 'What are you going to do?'

'What do you think? I'm going to help her.'

'Callan, have you really thought about what you're saying? You could end up in a shitload of trouble if this goes south.' He pauses for a moment, probably trying to figure out how he can word this next part without pissing me off. And sure enough, his next question is 'What about Clara?'

I feel a twinge of guilt – similar to the one that had hit me after I'd ignored Clara's call out on the sofa during dinner – over the fact that I hadn't once thought about how any of this would affect my sister when I was arguing so hard for Lottie to come home with me. Because Jase is right. If this thing goes sideways on me, and the fact that I'm helping a wanted woman, whether she's innocent or not, gets leaked to the press, Clara's mayoral campaign will be nothing but a smoldering pile of ashes. Then I'll have not only screwed over my sister, who I love dearly, but the entire city of New York, since they'll be stuck with goddamn Rick Wainwright as mayor – a lifelong politician who is as useless and crooked as they come.

But in the end, there's only one thing I can say to the guy who I love like one of my own brothers. 'I can't turn my back on an innocent woman.'

'But that's just it, mate. You don't *know* that she's innocent.'

'I do,' I clip, my normally easy-going voice sharp with frustration. 'And you and your private detective have your heads up your asses if you still believe she's guilty.'

'You're not thinking clearly,' he argues. 'She could be a killer.'

'She's not. She's just someone who's been seriously screwed over. She's a woman in need, Jase.'

'A woman you're obsessed with,' he points out, proving just how well he knows me.

'A woman who needs my *help*,' I growl, keeping the fact that she doesn't actually want that help to myself. 'And if you've listened to me at all, then you'll understand that this is happening.'

'Shit,' he mutters, and I can tell from his tone that he's finally accepting the inevitable. 'So what have you learned?'

'Not a lot,' I mutter back, the tension in my neck knotting tighter than ever. 'I've asked a lot of questions, but she's being careful with her answers.'

'I would be too if I was—'

I cut him off, snarling, 'She's not a criminal or a murderer, you prick!'

'—her,' he finishes wryly. 'If I was *her*. So there's no need to fly to La Jolla right now to kick my arse.'

I grunt in response, and the bastard actually laughs at me. Then he sobers, and quietly says, 'You know, if she's still holding her cards close to her chest, then she obviously doesn't trust you.'

'Not yet. But she will.'

'You better hope so,' he drawls, 'if you want her to stick around long enough for you to solve all her problems.'

'She won't run,' I say in a low voice, hoping to God that it's true. 'But no matter what happens, I'm not walking away from this. I'm not walking away from her.'

He sighs with resigned acceptance, before reminding me exactly why we've been friends for so long . . . and why I'd trust him with my life. 'Okay, mate. What do you need me to do?'

Chapter Four

LOTTIE

With all the crap going on in my life, why can't I stop thinking about the sexy New Yorker?

This is the question I keep asking myself as I lie on the beach lounger beneath a sweltering Mediterranean sun beside my new husband. Unfortunately, the man on my mind isn't Oliver Beckett, the one I spoke vows to back in June. We're on an extended honeymoon as Olly takes us around Italy's Amalfi coast on his ridiculously extravagant yacht, and I swear it's been the longest weeks of my life.

I'd hoped that getting away from England for a while might make it easier to breathe . . . to relax, but so far that hasn't been the case. Instead, I feel like there's a constant itch at the back of my neck. A familiar prickle of unease that forms the entire reason I'm lying on this beach in the first place, wearing Olly's embarrassingly huge diamond ring on my finger.

I'd tried talking to him about it – about my feelings of growing apprehension – but in typical Olly fashion, he'd just told me to chill out and enjoy myself. Now that we're no longer in England,

I know he's not taking the danger as seriously as he needs to. But then, Oliver Beckett has never really taken anything seriously but his playboy lifestyle. And yet, as annoying as it is, I can't even be irritated by his attitude. Not after the surprisingly thoughtful gift that he gave me last night.

That gift will be a lifeline if the situation ever . . . No, I don't even want to think about how bad things would have to get for me to actually contemplate starting a new life somewhere. Because as amazing as it would feel to just be free of it all – the fear and loneliness and constant worry – it kills a part of me to think of never seeing my shy, sweet uncle again . . . and leaving behind everything I've worked so hard for.

After waiting tables to pay my way through school, I finally uploaded my master's thesis last week, and in the winter, I'm meant to start my PhD program. Something that I've wanted ever since I was a girl and would listen to my mum talk about her love of poetry and how it could tap into the very essence of what it means to be human. At the time, I was too young to fully comprehend what she meant, but her passion was spellbinding and magical, and it'd sparked a fire inside me that's never gone out.

I turn my head on the beach lounger to tell Olly thank you yet again, but for some illogical reason my entire body turns with the movement, and now I'm just rolling and plunging into a shockingly cold, inky darkness that has me crying out in fear. The breeze and sand and blazing sunshine are gone. There's just this constant tumbling into nothingness, until I'm suddenly standing in the middle of our stateroom on the yacht, my head spinning with confusion, and I can hear Olly shouting at me.

'Christ, Lottie! Did it never occur to you that maybe I act like a dick because I know that's what you're thinking every single time you look at me? That it's the same damn thing everyone's thinking!'

'Don't you dare throw that in my face!' I shout back, the words tearing out of me like the rehearsed lines of a play. Or . . . like something I've already said before. 'People treat you the way you've asked for them to treat you with your shitty behavior! If you want that to change, then you have to stop treating everyone like dirt!'

He starts to take a step toward me, his expression showing more emotion than I've ever seen from him as he pulls in a shaky breath. But before he can make his next argument, the door to our room is thrown open and we both look over at the same time, our gasps of horror drowned out by the roaring in my ears.

My greatest nightmare is standing in the doorway, dripping with seawater, the salty scent tickling my nose. He looks different from the last time I saw him, as if the madness he's carried inside for so long has finally found its way to the surface. His usually styled blond hair has been cropped brutally close to his scalp, his blue eyes, once so similar to my own, now red and lined with exhaustion.

And in his right hand is a gleaming, familiar-looking, red-handled butcher's knife.

I take this all in within the blink of an eye, because he starts running toward me only seconds after throwing the door open, the knife held high in his hand, his intent written across his obsession-ravaged face like bold, black ink on a page. I want to flee, but I'm frozen by shock, my feet nailed to the floor like a helpless sacrifice. I close my eyes, waiting for the visceral pain of that first strike . . . but it never comes. Instead, I hear a noise so disturbing it nearly makes me vomit, and I open my eyes to a true nightmare.

Then I scream . . . and scream . . . and just keep screaming, until Olly's blood-spattered face turns toward me, and he croaks one hoarse, commanding word . . .

'Run!'

CALLAN

I jerk awake with a gasp, unsure of what has woken me. And then I hear it again. The most bloodcurdling scream imaginable.

'Lottie,' I whisper, already rushing to my feet. I run like I have the devil on my ass and try to open the guestroom door, but it's still locked, and I'm cursing my stupidity the entire way back to my bedroom, almost wiping out on my recently polished hardwood floor. I grab the key from my bedside table and hurry back, opening the door and nearly dying when I see that the bed is empty. But then I hear a small, frightened sound, like a child's whimper, and I turn my head toward the far corner of the room. I have to squint, but I can just make out Lottie's huddled form in the rays of early morning sunlight that are streaming in through the gauzy curtains that cover the room's glass wall.

'Lottie,' I whisper again, my heart pounding so hard I feel like it's echoing all around us. I slip the key into my pocket and take a cautious step in her direction, but stop when she flinches. Sinking down to my knees, because I'm not above crawling for this woman if that's what it takes, I work to make my voice as gentle as possible as I say, 'Baby, you must have been having a nightmare, but it's over now. You're safe, okay? You're here with me, in New York, and you're safe.'

Her breathing is still hard and fast, but she's no longer making that soft, terrified sound that felt like a fist reaching into my chest and pulverizing my heart. Then she blinks a few times, looks up at me, and croaks, 'C-Callan?'

'Yeah, it's me.'

'Oh God,' she groans, wetting her lower lip with a nervous flick of her tongue, her long lashes glistening with tears. 'I'm . . . I'm sorry. This is so embarrassing.'

'The hell it is. Everyone has nightmares, Lot. And after what you've been through, it would be weird if you didn't.'

She pulls in a deep breath, then slowly lets it out. 'I just . . . I can't believe I was screaming loud enough to wake you up.'

'Hey, it was time for my lazy ass to get up anyway,' I drawl, hoping to make her smile. But she doesn't. I don't know if it's residual fear from her nightmare, or the fact that she's alone with me in a bedroom, but I can sense her uneasiness, so I say, 'Come on. We can sit out in the living room and watch the sunrise while we talk. It's bloody gorgeous, as you Brits say.'

She doesn't move, just stares back at me, still taking those deep breaths, her blue eyes storm-wrecked with emotion.

'Come on,' I say again, determined to find a way to help her relax as I move back to my feet. 'I'll even make you a cup of my world-famous coffee.'

I almost sag with relief when I finally get the briefest twitch of a smile from her. 'World famous, huh? That's a pretty big brag.'

'But completely true, I promise.'

'Okay. All right.' She looks down at her thin tank top, then self-consciously crosses her arms over her chest, since her tight nipples are poking against the fabric. 'Just let me grab something warmer to put on.'

'Hold that thought,' I grunt, having to cough to clear the untimely knot of lust from my throat. 'I'll be right back.'

I quickly walk back to my room, make a fast stop in my bathroom to brush my teeth, then grab my favorite hoodie – an ancient, super-soft Oxford sweatshirt from my days at university with Jase – and head back into the guestroom to find her standing at the foot of the bed in a pair of pajama shorts that are so short, they nearly stop my heart. 'You can wear this,' I tell her, offering it over, and she takes the sweatshirt with an expression on her beautiful face that seems equal parts self-conscious and touched. And, hell, maybe even still a bit pissed off, since I haven't forgotten what it took to get her here.

'Thanks,' she says so quietly it's almost a whisper, before slipping the hoodie over her head. It nearly falls to her knees, and she has to roll up both sleeves several times to keep them from swallowing her hands, but she looks gorgeous. She isn't wearing a stitch of make-up, her hair completely tousled from what was undoubtedly a restless sleep, and yet I swear I've never seen a more breathtaking sight than Lottie Fleming dressed in my clothes.

But despite how badly I want this woman, I'm in control of my body's reactions, not even sporting an ill-timed chub. That is, until Lottie turns the tables on me. I'm only wearing a pair of loose black pajama pants, so this is the first time she's ever seen me shirtless, and the instant she seems to realize it, I know I'm screwed.

Her gaze focuses in first on the intricate design of the Celtic tattoo that covers my left shoulder, then slowly moves over my collarbone, before dipping down to my pecs. Heat filters through her lingering upset over her nightmare, and I don't have a single goddamn clue what to do. I never thought I'd be lucky enough to even see this woman again, much less have her look at my scarred body the way she's looking at me right now, and my dick starts to go rock hard without a single conscious directive from my brain. Thankfully, my common sense kicks back in just a second later, and I realize the only thing to do here is to get the hell out of the guestroom, before Lottie accuses me of being a total prick.

'I'll go put on the coffee,' I rumble, quickly turning to go. 'Take your time and come out when you're ready.'

'Okay,' I hear her say, but I'm already hightailing it down the hallway. When I reach the kitchen, I stop, jam the heels of my palms against my eyes, and suck in a couple of my own deep breaths until my body finally starts to behave.

'Work with me here, you bastard,' I mutter down at my crotch, then have to laugh at myself for trying to have a conversation with my brainless dick. Christ, if I hadn't already accepted that Lottie Fleming makes me completely crazy, I'd be hard-pushed to argue it now.

Getting my ass in gear, I set about making the coffee, plate up a couple of pastries that my housekeeper, Rita, must have bought yesterday during her morning shift, then do a precarious job of grabbing everything when I hear Lottie coming down the hall.

As I walk into the living room carrying two steaming mugs in one hand, the plate in the other, Lottie quickly grabs two coasters from their holder and places them on the coffee table. Since she put them both on the same side, I do exactly what I wanted to do the second I walked in and saw her sitting there in the early morning sunshine, and sit down next to her as I place the mugs on the granite coasters.

'Again, I'm sorry I woke you up.' She tucks her legs up underneath her, but doesn't try to scoot away from me, which I count as a win. 'You were right about me having a nightmare.'

'About that night?'

She nods, her slender throat working as she gives a hard swallow. Then she reaches toward the table, grabs her coffee, and says, 'Do you mind if we talk about something . . . easy? At least for a little while?'

'Not at all.' I grab my own coffee, along with one of the maple twists. 'Whatever you're up for, Lot.'

'Then tell me about your company.'

'Yeah?' I ask, pleasantly surprised that she's taking an interest in my life.

'Yeah,' she says with another brief half-smile, each one making me want to pump my fist in the air like a damn idiot. But I know this woman hasn't had much, if anything, to smile about in a hell of a long time, and I can't help but want to change that for her.

And since I'm all about giving Lottie what she wants – so long as it's not me leaving her to deal with all of this shit on her own – I tell her about how I decided to start Hathaway Security six years ago and explain that there are now seven headquarter hubs along the Eastern seaboard, while she sips her coffee and nibbles on a maple pecan swirl. We talk about some of the company's clients, as well as its employees, who I'm all damn proud of, and then I tell her about Deanna. As I answer her questions about Hathaway's new Head of Operations, I can tell that Lottie's impressed not only by Deanna's credentials – the woman served two tours in Afghanistan, before retiring from the military and joining the private sector – but also by the fact that I'm not too egotistical to admit that Deanna could easily kick my ass in a fight.

I'm so caught up in enjoying her company and the ease with which we can talk to each other – as long as the topic isn't her messed-up life – that I'm not even thinking about our insane physical attraction. I'm just enjoying having her here, in my home, eating up every moment that I get to spend with her like it might very well be our last – the all-too-real prospect that she might suddenly decide to say *Piss off* and bail keeping a small knot of dread churning quietly in my gut. One that will no doubt eventually give me one hell of an ulcer.

But then she flicks the tip of her tongue across her bottom lip, swiping at a bit of maple glaze, and that's all it takes for my goddamn dick to decide that it's behaved long enough. And as luck would have it, she chooses that exact moment to reach over to take my empty mug from my hand, her beautiful blue eyes shooting wide when she notices the unmistakably long, thick ridge in my pants.

'Lottie . . .' I murmur, knowing I need to apologize as she sets both of our mugs on the coffee table. But I never get the chance.

'You're hard again,' she whispers, a pink flush covering her cheeks even as she suddenly reaches over and boldly grips my cock, shocking the ever-loving hell out of me.

'Shit! I'm . . . *Shit!*' I gasp, not even sure what I'm saying, my heart pounding so hard I'm surprised it isn't bursting out of my chest like in that gory scene in *Alien*. The simple touch of her hand, even over my pajama pants, is so good it nearly has my eyes rolling back in my head.

'Don't be sorry,' she tells me, sounding more in control – more *determined* – than I've ever heard her sound before. 'I want this.'

I blink at her, wondering where in the hell this complete one-eighty has come from, half-terrified that it's all a dream. 'Jesus Christ, Lot. Are you sure?'

A soft, breathless rush of laughter bursts from her lips, and then she gives me another crooked smile that's so incredibly sexy, I nearly lose it then and there. 'Callan, I'm the one who just reached over and grabbed your package. Maybe I should be asking *you* that question.'

My brows draw together in what I know must be a look that's caught somewhere between extreme confusion and visceral, primitive lust. 'I just have a bad feeling that doing this right now is going to put me in some serious dickhead territory.'

'Again, I'm the one grabbing *your* junk. If anyone's a dick here, it's me.'

'Bullshit. You're perfect.' And since it's far past time for me to become an active participant in whatever the hell it is that's happening, I reach over and grasp the bottom of the hoodie, then tug it over her head, which unfortunately means she has to let go of me, but also means I get to see her in that sexy tank again. But then, as if to prove that she's out to destroy me, Lottie grabs the hem of the top and pulls it off as well, the sight of her bare, pale breasts so mouthwatering my hard-on literally jerks in my pants. 'Every single damn inch of you, Lot. Perfect.'

'Hardly,' she murmurs, and I want to argue, to tell her how wrong she is, but my ability for speech dies the second she grips the waistband of my pants and tugs them down over my crotch, my dick springing up so fast it thumps against my abdomen.

'Oh! Oh wow,' she whispers, curling her hand around the base, the warm sound of appreciation in her voice hardening my cock until the bastard looks obscene. The broad head is so slick it's gleaming, and I can't take my eyes off the way her feminine hand doesn't even reach all the way around the ridged shaft as she pulls it upright.

'Lottie,' I growl, struggling for control – which proves pointless when the woman leans over and breathes against my heavy, bruise-colored tip, my fingers digging into the sofa cushions so deeply, I'm surprised the leather hasn't ripped. 'Holy shit, Lot!'

She wets her lips with a nervous flick of her tongue, then just goes for it, and the instant those pink lips close around me, I make a sound unlike any I've ever made before. It's all raw, guttural aggression – just like an animal – and I don't even know who I am anymore as I suddenly grasp the sides of her head and carefully pull her down another inch, pushing myself deeper into her warm, wet mouth.

'Jesus,' I hiss, shaking, my entire being focused on the sight of her taking me in. 'I should probably warn you that I haven't been with anyone since before we met,' I groan, panting, sounding like I gargled with a mouthful of gravel. 'So this is going to be over a hell of a lot faster than I want.'

Her eyes shoot up to mine as she slowly pulls back, releasing me with a wet pop that's so damn sexy it makes me wince. 'Are you serious?' She must read the answer on my face, because she immediately follows that first question up with a second one. 'Why?'

Why? Why the hell does she think? I haven't been with anyone because the only woman I wanted was not only hiding from the world, she was also hiding from *me*. But instead of trying to explain something that I know sounds completely crazy, I choose action over words, rearing up and bending her back over my arm. Her fingers dig into my biceps as I lower my head and greedily take one of the pink tips of her pert breasts into my mouth, the soft cry of pleasure that she gives by far the sweetest sound I've ever heard. I work her with my lips and tongue and teeth, then flick my tongue against her other sweet peak, before sucking on it so hard she instinctively grinds herself against my thigh.

Needing to see just how ready she is for me, I lay her down on the sofa, rip her pajama shorts over her hips, and have just grabbed the sides of her tiny black panties when she cries, 'Wait! Not . . . Not yet. It's still my turn.'

I suck in a deep breath, but it does nothing to calm me down. 'To hell with your turn.'

'No fair,' she huffs, proving that despite her kind of shy demeanor at times, she's actually every bit as gutsy as I've always suspected. 'I was having fun.'

I stare down at her as we both breathe deep and fast, our bodies so hot we're practically steaming in the chilly morning air. And we both already know *exactly* how this is going to play out, since the woman has me completely wrapped around her little finger. 'Christ,' I grunt, sitting back, my hands clenched into fists against the sofa so that I don't grab hold of her, toss her over my shoulder, and carry her to my bed, where she belongs.

Her face is flushed, those blue eyes bright with physical hunger – and more than a bit of triumph – as she stands up. Then she turns and walks a few feet away, and my starved gaze doesn't know where to land, her heart-shaped ass and long legs even more beautiful than I'd imagined. And God only knows that from the moment I met this woman, I've spent a hell of a lot of time doing just that.

'Get over here on the floor and stretch out,' she says, turning to face me, while the sunlight streams in behind her through the wall of glass, making her creamy skin and golden hair shimmer as if she's some otherworldly creature. One who's apparently been sent here to drive me out of my goddamn mind. 'I want to be able to touch and see every single inch of you.'

A stunned laugh jerks up from my chest, gritty and deep. 'Jesus, Lot. I had no idea you could be so evil.'

'A woman dying to go down on you is evil?' she drawls, perfectly arching one of those sweeping blonde eyebrows at me.

'She is when I want to get my hands and mouth on her so badly it's damn near killing me,' I tell her.

'Well, you're a big, tough guy,' she murmurs with a teasing twitch of her lips. 'I think you can handle a little torture.'

I give another low laugh that's edged with frustration as I drop my head back, wondering if she has any clue how difficult it's going to be to give her what she's asked for. Hell, what she's *demanded*. Not that it matters. She's had such limited control over her life this past year, I can't help but secretly love that she feels confident – as well as safe – enough with me to take some here.

When I stand up, my pajama pants slide down my legs,

pooling on the floor at my feet, and she looks my naked body over like she wants to taste it from head to toe and then eat me alive, making every grueling minute I've ever spent on my fitness more than worth the pain. My pulse continues to roar in my ears like an engine at full throttle as I do as I've been told, stretching out on the sun-warmed floor at her feet, and she wastes no time kneeling beside me. I shove my hands behind my head, locking my fingers together to keep from reaching for her, because I can tell from the hungry, determined look in her eyes that she's about to drive me mad.

'You're so bloody gorgeous,' she whispers, her tone almost reverent as she moves into a kneeling position between my spread legs. Then she places her hands on my chest and strokes them down my scarred torso, my abs twitching as she glides over them, going lower and lower, until she's finally holding my rigid cock again.

'Hell,' I grate, my entire body shaking, muscles bulging with strain as I struggle for control. 'Lot—' I start to say, but her name ends on a guttural shout as she leans over and takes me in again, soaking me in the hot, slick heaven of her mouth. I tremble and curse, the muscles in my neck aching as I keep my head lifted so that I can watch her with narrowed, burning eyes, determined not to miss a single second of the way she looks kneeling over me with one hand braced against the floor at my side, while her other hand holds my shaft up, keeping it right where she wants it. I bend my right leg, the roar in my ears getting louder, and I have a fleeting thought that I should let her know I'm already close. But then it's too late, and I bellow like a madman as it crashes over me.

'Lottie!' I growl, expecting her to lift up and work me through the orgasm with her hand. But she doesn't, staying with me instead, and I come harder than I ever have before, with all of the hunger and despair that have been my constant companions this past year.

'That's so goddamn good,' I force through my clenched teeth, my chest heaving. I'm sweating and swearing, the pleasure only made more intense by the way her dark eyes are locked tight with mine, burning at me, telling me she's getting off on this blisteringly raw, possessive act every bit as much as I am, which doesn't seem possible. But it sends me to a place that's so far beyond mere physical need and desire, it's not even in the same ballpark, and I drop back on the floor with a thud, chin tucked in, eyes still glued to the sight of her. 'Lottie,' I groan, my voice so guttural it doesn't even sound human. 'Jesus, that's so hot.'

And the second I'm spent, I try to warn her with my sharp, heavy-lidded gaze to get ready.

To be prepared for payback.

Because now it's *my* turn.

Chapter Five

CALLAN

Lottie gasps my name in shock when I suddenly take hold of her and reverse our positions, pulling the tiny black panties down her long legs so quickly I hear a seam rip.

'Sorry,' I bite out, even as I'm already pushing her slender thighs wide, my greedy gaze locked in hard and tight on the mouthwatering sight of her pink, glistening flesh. 'Sorry,' I say again, my voice sounding muffled in my ears as my pulse keeps roaring like some kind of starved, primal beast. 'I just needed to see this.'

'Oh God,' she moans as I slide my hands down the soft inner surfaces of her thighs, until they're framing that gorgeous, most intimate part of her, and my mouth literally waters.

'Unbelievable,' I husk, stroking two fingers down her plush, slick cleft, thinking she's the most exquisite thing I've ever seen. 'You really are perfect, Lot.'

She gasps as I flick the callused tips of my fingers across her sensitive clit, and since I'm far too gone to remember that I'm meant to be reining myself in, I move those two big, long fingers back down to her very pink, very delicate opening, and push them inside, watching as her body stretches to take me in. She's snug and deliciously drenched, soaking my fingers as I slowly pull them out to the knuckle, then work them back in, unable to wrap my head around how *tight* she is. Or how quickly she's started to breathe, her cushiony inner muscles already giving little pulses that tell me she's getting close.

'That's it, sweetheart. You gonna come for me already?' I rumble, unable to get enough of the way she smells and feels and looks. And when she suddenly starts to crash, it's with the softest, sexiest cry I've ever heard, and I groan at the feel of her tender sex convulsing around my fingers as her entire body shivers with release.

'I hope to God you're comfortable on this floor, because I'm about to go down on you for hours on end,' I mutter, already lowering my head. 'I'm keeping my mouth on you all goddamn day, Lottie.'

'But I want another—'

'Callan? Honey? Are you okay?' a painfully familiar voice suddenly calls out from the entryway, cutting her off, and I realize with horror that I've been so focused on Lottie's perfect body, I completely missed the sound of my mother unlocking my front door! 'Callan? Clara says you haven't been answering your phone! Are you here?' she asks loudly, the beeping sounds telling me that she's trying to turn off my alarm.

'Shit,' I quietly growl, unable to believe this is happening. It's like some kind of twisted Freudian nightmare come to life, and I glance up at Lottie's bewildered expression as I shake my head in apology and carefully pull my fingers out of her.

'What's happening?' she squeaks, blinking up at me.

'My mom is here,' I whisper, then quickly turn my head and yell, 'Mom, stop!' before the woman walks so far into the living room she can see around the sofa, and ends up witnessing something neither one of us is going to be able to stomach.

'What? Why?' she asks, though her heels are thankfully no longer clicking against the floor. 'What's going on? Where on earth are you?'

'I'm on the floor and I'm not alone. So if you don't want to get an eyeful of my bare ass, then you'll stop and give me a friggin' minute to get decent!'

'Decent?' she gasps with enough dramatic flair it could earn her an Oscar. 'Callan Robert Hathaway, are you having hanky-panky right now? And in your living room of all places?'

'Oh Christ,' I huff under my breath, before a brief smile kicks up the corner of my mouth at the muffled sound of Lottie's laughter. One look at her pink face tells me that she's completely mortified to have been caught in the act by my *mom* – but this girl has an awesome sense of humor, and it's obvious that she's also seeing the awkward hilarity of the situation. She bites her lip, clearly trying not to laugh out loud, and it's one of the most painful things I've ever had to watch as she scrambles out from under me, grabs her clothes and starts pulling them back on.

'How do I get to the guestroom without her seeing me?' she whispers, yanking her shorts up over her legs.

'You can't,' I tell her, shoving a hand through my hair as I sit back on my ass. 'We're just going to have to tough this one out.'

Her eyes go so wide I can see white all around that deep, beautiful blue. 'No way. I can't meet your mum, Callan.'

'We're both adults,' I say casually, trying to put her at ease. 'We've done nothing wrong.'

'It's not that. Or . . . it's not *just* that,' she hisses. 'Are you forgetting that I'm on the run?'

'Don't panic,' I murmur, taking her hand as she kneels

beside me so that I can give it a reassuring squeeze. 'It's going to be okay.'

She looks at me as if I've suddenly sprouted a third eye. 'How could this possibly be okay?'

'No one in my family has ever even seen your photo,' I point out, choosing to address the part of her worry that I can at least alleviate. 'She won't even know who you are.'

Since she looks slightly less panicked, I let go of her hand and finally reach over for my pants, rolling onto my back as I pull them on. We're both depressingly decent now, so I go ahead and move to my feet, a quick glance at the entryway showing my mom standing just inside the living room with her back to us. Shaking my head over how much shit Jase is going to give me when I tell him about this – there's no point in try-ing to keep it a secret, since he's close enough to my mom that she'd definitely rat me out the next time she sees him – I reach down for Lottie's hand again and tug her up beside me.

Just as I'm about ready to tell my mom that it's safe to turn around, I spot Lottie's bright red wig beside the coffee table. She'd left it lying over the arm of the sofa last night, and we must have knocked it to the floor while we were getting started with what was easily the hottest make-out session of my entire life, though I'm hating that I wasn't able to get my mouth on her. And seeing as how I don't want to have to explain the wig's existence, I stop and quickly kick it under the sofa, then pull a reluctant Lottie along beside me as we make our way around the seating area.

There's no missing the tension that's all but rolling off the girl in waves, and I feel like shit about it, wishing I could put her at ease. But I don't know how without ripping off the meta-phorical Band-Aid and just getting through this next rough part, so I clear my throat and finally say, 'Okay, you can turn around now, Mom.'

She spins on her red heels, looking like someone on their way to New York Fashion Week, her still-bronze-colored hair styled in an intricate French twist, and the diamond earrings my dad had given her before he died glittering in her ears. She shoots Lottie a bright, friendly smile, proving that there's not a judgmental bone in her body, then glances beyond us and nearly stumbles back in shock as she shouts, 'Good God, Callan! Were you mauling the poor girl right in front of the windows? Anyone could have seen you!'

'I was hardly mauling her,' I drawl, then scratch the edge of my jaw in confusion. 'And we're fifty floors up, Mom. Who exactly is gonna be looking through my windows?'

She stares at me as if I'm daft. 'Drones, Callan. Some pervert could be spying on you with a drone. I saw a whole special about it on the news.'

I pinch the bridge of my nose with my free hand, striving for patience, and don't even waste my time explaining to her again that it's one-way glass, when I've already told her numerous times before.

'And then there's *me*,' she adds, sounding even more dramatic than usual. 'I mean, this isn't really what I want to see on a Saturday morning.' She gives a delicate chuckle as she pats her hair, even though not a single strand is out of place. 'Or on *any* morning, for that matter.'

'Then maybe you shouldn't just let yourself into my place,' I point out, my tone so dry it has her arching one elegantly shaped eyebrow at me.

'In my defense, sweetheart, I thought you might be dead or dying.'

I arch an eyebrow right back at her, taking in her perfect appearance. 'But you took the time to do your make-up and hair before rushing right over to save me?'

'Well,' she murmurs, smoothing her hands over her sleek black dress, 'I never know when I might run into that adorable Cassel fellow when I'm here.'

'Oh God,' I laugh, thinking she's probably one of the only people in the world who's not the least bit intimidated by the enigmatic, undoubtedly dangerous Frenchman. 'I would pay money to see you call him "adorable" to his face.'

'I'm sorry, but who is Cassel?' Lottie asks, still trying to surreptitiously pull her hand from mine, no doubt so she can flee at the first opportunity.

'Seb Cassel, the gorgeous French Interpol agent who lives next door,' my mom explains, answering Lottie's question with another bright smile, having no idea how much shit she's just landed me in. 'He and Callan are best friends.'

'First of all, I'm a thirty-four-year-old man,' I sigh, 'so I don't have a best friend. But if I did, it would be Jase. And second—'

Before I can finish my argument, Clara bursts in through the front door dressed in another one of the ugly neutral-colored pants suits that Carl is always insisting she wear these days, already complaining. 'Thanks for leaving me to deal with the taxi, Mom. I barely had enough ca—' She breaks off the instant she sets eyes on me and Lottie, her entire body freezing in the entryway, and I can see the exact moment that her infamous temper gets the better of her. 'What the hell? Is *this* why you couldn't escort Marissa last night?' she snarls, pointing at Lottie as she barges into the room, and I literally see red.

'If you're going to act like a rude brat,' I force through my clenched teeth, 'then you can get the fuck out!'

'Callan!' my mom gasps, but I'm too damn furious to worry about shocking her with my language. Not to mention embarrassed that this is going to be Lottie's first impression of my family.

'Sorry, Mom. But she doesn't get to come in here and pull this shit,' I growl, jerking my chin at Clara. 'And she also doesn't get to comment on a situation that she knows absolutely fuck all about!'

I rarely raise my voice, and the fact that I've done so now has clearly startled my sister, her green eyes, which she got from my dad, clouding with confusion.

'Who's Marissa?' Lottie quietly asks at my side, sounding completely mortified.

I shake my head at her, hating that her face has gotten even pinker, and give her a look that hopefully lets her know I'll be happy to explain everything later, when it's just the two of us.

Unfortunately, Clara mistakenly decides that her best course of action is to just keep going on the offensive, obviously having no idea when to shut up. 'Well, thanks to you, Marissa decided not to go last night, and now your dick has blown—'

'That's enough!' I roar, pulling Lottie with me as I take a furious step forward. 'I don't even know who you are right now, Clara, because you sure as hell don't sound like my sister. I thought you went into politics to make the world a better place for people. Not to become just another self-inflated jackass who treats everyone like shit.' I pause to pull in a deep breath, but anger is still burning through my veins, and I can't stop myself from quietly adding, 'I never thought I'd be ashamed to call you family, but right now you're making it damn difficult not to feel that way.'

For a moment, my sister simply appears dumbstruck, her eyes huge in her slightly round, freckled face, lips parted in shock. But then she flinches, and it's almost painful to watch the realization of what she's done spread over her like a chill. 'Oh God. You're right,' she croaks, sounding truly chastened. 'I'm so sorry.'

'I know you're stressed about the campaign. But this isn't you,' I mutter, still stunned that she's pulled this crap. 'And as for Marissa, you know damn well that she only sits on the literacy committee because she thinks it makes her look good. She doesn't give a damn about helping anyone better their lives, and she cares even less about helping you get elected.'

'Oh . . . wow. You're Clara Hathaway,' Lottie suddenly murmurs, before looking at me with profound confusion, as if she can't understand how this has happened. 'Clara Hathaway is one of your sisters. The same Clara Hathaway who's running for mayor. She's the one who was calling you last night?'

'Yeah.' I give her hand a gentle squeeze, then realize that's not nearly good enough and let go of her hand so that I can wrap my arm around her waist, tugging her up against my side, where she belongs. 'I'm just sorry she's made such a shitty first impression.'

Clara groans as she covers her face with her hands, her petite frame, nearly three inches shorter than Lottie's, looking as if it's going to crumple under the weight of her guilt.

'I'll go and put on a fresh pot of coffee,' my mom quickly announces with a loud clap of her hands, her cheery tone setting my back teeth on edge, since I'm still pissed at the way Clara has acted. And I haven't missed the fact that my mom hasn't even asked for an introduction to Lottie. No, she's just barreling straight ahead, acting as if we've all known each other for years, which has always been her go-to when things might steer even the slightest bit toward awkward.

'I really am sorry, Cal,' Clara says, while my mom clicks away on her heels. 'I . . . It's early, but it's already been a shitty morning. I'm down in the polls again, and Wainwright's latest ad plays me up as some spoiled rich girl who's never had to work a day in her life.'

'That's bullshit,' I growl, same as any protective big brother would do, though in Clara's case it's completely true. She was born with a passion for public service that saw her voted in as the youngest-ever city councilor in our home district when she was only twenty-three. And she didn't just sit around enjoying the perks of political office, but instigated real change, championing women and minorities, as well as starting local literacy groups and a therapy center for young people suffering from eating disorders. 'I honestly don't think I've ever known anyone who works as hard as you do.'

'Yeah, well, the voters unfortunately seem to be eating his lies up like a bear with honey.' She twists her long, wavy hair, just a shade darker than my own, over her shoulder, the same way she's always done whenever she's stressing out. 'But it's still no excuse for me to act like such a bitch. Forgive me?'

I glance at Lottie, who finally stops trying to pull away from me long enough to give me a quick nod, then look back over at Clara. 'Yeah, I forgive you, you little shit.'

Her lips twitch with a brief, wry smile. 'As eloquent as always, big bro. But thanks.'

'Ah, good. So everything's all sorted then,' my mom says, coming back into the room with perfect timing, which tells me she'd been listening to every word we said from the kitchen.

'Okay, so let's start this nightmare over. Mom, Clara, this is . . .' I catch the look of pure panic on Lottie's face from the corner of my eye, and find myself saying, 'Lana. Lana Hill.' It's currently the name she's going by, so at least I'm not completely lying to my own mother, even though I know that's a flimsy excuse. 'Lana, this is my sister Clara and my mother, Margot.'

'Hi,' Lottie murmurs, giving them both a small, strained smile.

'It's so nice to meet you, Lana. And I really am sorry I came in acting like such a raging psychopath,' Clara says sheepishly, just as her phone starts letting out a shrill ring in the purse she has slung over one shoulder. She takes the phone out and glances at the screen, then immediately frowns. 'Shoot, I've got to take this.'

She walks to the far side of the living room as she answers the call, and even though she's speaking so low that we can't hear what she's saying, we can all tell from her body language that something's wrong. 'Oh dear,' my mom frets when Clara slips the phone back into her purse and turns toward us, looking like she definitely just got some bad news.

'What was that about?' I ask as she walks back over to where we're all still standing.

'Someone claiming to be close to me is going to give an interview to one of the local news channels this morning,' she says as she starts to rub her forehead, appearing to have one hell of a headache coming on. 'They're apparently backing up Wainwright's entire story about me being nothing more than a spoiled princess.'

'Who on earth is it?' my mother gasps with outrage, reminding me of how she would always champion us when we were younger. Hell, she still champions us today, and we all love her for it.

'Clara,' I prompt, when a few seconds go by and she still hasn't answered the question. Then I understand why, because she kind of grimaces as she looks my way, telling me the answer isn't one I'm going to like.

'It's Jessica,' she mutters.

At first, I'm sure that I didn't hear her right. 'Say that again.' She gives a heavy sigh. 'It's Jess, Cal.'

Rage, blistering and raw, rises up inside me like some vicious force of nature. 'Motherfucker!'

'Callan!' my mom huffs, though if you ask me, she looks angry enough to drop a couple of F-bombs herself right about now.

'That lying, psychotic bitch,' I snarl, still working to wrap my head around the fact that my ex is obviously trying to screw with my sister's campaign.

'I've got to go and try to . . . I don't even know,' Clara says, looking completely at a loss for how she's going to handle the situation. 'Carl says there's time to talk to her before she goes on the air in two hours, since the studio is close by. But I've never managed to have a sensible conversation with Jessica in my life. I have no idea how—'

'I'll go with you,' I cut in, knowing – without any doubt – that it's the right thing to do, even though I hate the idea of leaving Lottie's side.

Clara looks at me with surprise. 'Are you sure?'

'Hell yeah.' Taking hold of Lottie's hand again, I add, 'I just need to talk to Lana for a moment, so grab some coffee with Mom while I get dressed. And there are pastries if you guys are hungry.'

I don't give anyone time to say anything, already pulling Lottie, who still hasn't uttered a word about any of this craziness, with me down the hallway. The last thing I want to do is leave her – especially given what just happened between us out in the living room – but I know a busy TV station isn't someplace she'd be willing to go with me right now. And it's not like she won't be safe here in the apartment. The building's security is top notch, and she'll be with my mom, who I taught how to use the gun that I keep in my office years ago.

And the unarguable fact of the matter is that this is the right thing to do. Clara doesn't know it, but I owe her for the risk that I've put her campaign in by bringing Lottie here, instead of taking her straight to the police. Not to mention the fact that the only reason Jessica is trying to mess with my family in the first place is because of me. Because I've refused to have anything to do with the lying viper for years now. So I'll be the one who deals with her.

'I hate to leave you,' I say to Lottie, as soon as I've shut my bedroom door behind us, 'but you'll be safe here. No one can get into this building without security clearance.'

She doesn't say anything in response, and I reluctantly let go of her hand as she pulls away from me. Scrubbing my fingertips over my jaw, I watch as she crosses her arms over her middle and turns in a circle in the center of the room, her curious gaze taking in my private space, with its stark black-and-white landscapes on the pale gray walls, dark wood furnishings and massive king-sized bed.

And since being in here reminds me of how our morning started, I tell her, 'And we might have gotten a bit sidetracked, but the second I'm back, we're going to have that talk about who and what you're terrified of, Lottie.'

'Is that right?' she asks with a soft, humorless laugh, her blue eyes shadowed with a dark torrent of emotion when she brings her gaze back to mine.

'I can keep you safe here, but I won't be able to help you get your life back until you come completely clean with me.'

She shakes her head, and says, 'You make it all sound so simple, Callan, but it's not. It's a nasty, sticky spider's web, and once you're caught in it, it's impossible to get out. Just look at what happened to Olly.'

'I'm not going to trash-talk him. Not after what he did for you. But I'm not him, Lot. I've spent my entire adult life training to handle every kind of asshole there is. Whoever it is that you're hiding from, I can deal with them. I promise you.'

She looks away, staring at my unmade bed as she pulls in a

deep breath, then slowly lets it out. 'So who's Jessica?' she asks, pushing her hands into the hoodie's front pocket.

'She's an ex, and one of the biggest bitches you'll ever meet.' I pause, rubbing at the back of my neck this time, since talking about Jessica never fails to make me tense. 'I normally don't like to use that particular word, but I swear, Lot, it's the only one that really works for someone like her.'

She glances over at me with one of those wry half-smiles. 'That sucks.'

'You have no idea,' I murmur, since getting involved with Jessica Marten remains, to this day, one of my most costly mistakes. A mistake that not only made me question my own judgment, but completely killed any desire I had to offer another woman anything beyond some hot, sweaty time between the sheets – until that fateful weekend when I met Lottie. I still don't know how to explain the strange connection that I instantly felt with her that had damn near knocked me on my ass. A connection that had reawakened those parts of me I'd thought I'd lost forever. That had enabled me to not only trust again, but to actually hope for something more than what I had.

If I ever tried to explain it out loud to someone – like I had with Jase, and to a lesser degree with Seb – I just came off sounding crazy. But now that I've found her, I know better than to question its existence, because it's as real as the building standing around us. As real as the danger that hangs over her life like a cloaked shadow, the weight of it so heavy I can see how she's constantly struggling not to be crushed beneath it, even when she's just standing here in my bedroom with me, talking about my psycho ex.

'Do you think you'll be able to get her to change her mind?' she asks.

I scowl as I tell her, 'I think the whole thing is just a childish ploy for attention, since there's no way she'll really go through with it. Not when I have dirt on her that could destroy her if it ever gets out.'

Her golden eyebrows lift with surprise. 'Oh wow. So then this is all just because she wants to see you?'

I snort with derision. 'The woman just wants attention, plain and simple. It's what feeds her toxic ego.'

'She sounds lovely,' she comments in a dry tone.

'Trust me, she's a mistake that I seriously wish I could go back and change.'

'Yeah, I'm pretty familiar with those,' she murmurs, that invisible shadow seeming to get even heavier. Then she draws her shoulders back as she pulls in another deep breath, and there's a definite edge to her soft voice as she says, 'And the more I think about it, the more I think I should really just grab a taxi and head back home while you're gone.'

'What? No goddamn way,' I argue, closing the distance between us, though I stop short of touching her. 'I don't want you going back to that place until we've got all this shit handled.'

She stares up at me like what I'm saying is crazy. 'Callan, I can't just stay here while you try to sort out all my problems for me. That's ridiculous!'

'It's not and you know it, Lottie. So please stay,' I mutter, knowing in my gut that it's not safe for her to go home. 'If not for yourself, then for me. I can't go and help Clara if I'm scared shitless you're going to leave the second I'm gone.'

At first, she doesn't respond. She just stares back at me with those dark eyes that are carrying more secrets than any one person should ever have to carry on their own, no matter how strong they are.

'Fine, I'll stay,' she eventually huffs, and my ego takes a hit from her obvious lack of enthusiasm. Not to mention the tiny scowl that's settled between her brows. 'But what am I meant to do? Just hang out with your mum? Because that's going to be pretty awkward, considering how crappy I feel for lying to her.'

'Don't. You have nothing to feel guilty about, because none of this is your fault,' I tell her, believing it with the same conviction that I believe in my family's love and the immutable fact that after the sun sets tonight, it will rise again in the morning.

'You know, you don't *really* know that, Callan.'

LOTTIE

'What? That you're innocent?' he murmurs, and the next thing I know I'm in his arms, which feels strangely like it's *exactly* where I'm meant to be, and he brushes the corner of my mouth with his warm lips, making me shiver. I shake with a desire that's unlike anything I've ever experienced, this poignant moment somehow even more intimate than anything we just did to each other out on his living-room floor, and I break a bit inside, no longer capable of dealing with tenderness. God, I don't know if I've *ever* been able to deal with it. But certainly not *now*, when this incredible man simply holds me tighter as I start to shake even harder, his strong arms pulling me so close that when I turn my head, I can press my cheek against his broad chest, his heart beating loud and steady beneath my ear.

And then, as if he knows I'm too on edge to keep talking about anything serious at this point, I can hear the smile in his voice as he simply says, 'Thank you.'

'For what?' I mutter, sounding like a sulking child.

His chest shakes beneath my cheek with a low, rumbling laugh. 'For not running scared when my crazy but lovable mother barged in on what was hands down the best moment of my entire life.'

I start to smile too, my body shivering with the memory of having him under my mouth and hands, until I remember one of the surprising exchanges between him and his mum, and I shove so hard against his chest, I almost succeed in knocking him back a step. Which is impressive, given that he's a bloody mountain of a man. 'What the hell, Callan?' I snarl, glaring up at him as I angrily brace my hands on my hips. 'I can't believe you live next door to a cop and actually thought it was a good idea to bring me here. I thought you wanted to help me, not get me arrested!'

'Don't worry about Seb,' he says with another bone-melting smile, my outburst not even fazing him in the slightest. 'He's a cool guy.'

I know it's childish, but I find myself rolling my eyes at him. 'He could be the freaking Fonzie Fonzarelli, but it doesn't mean I want to run into him.'

'Fonzie Fonzarelli?' he snickers, still grinning like a jackass. 'God, you crack me up. You're so young, I can't believe you even know who he is.'

I blink at him, wondering what planet he thinks I've been living on. 'Are you kidding me with that crap? Henry Winkler is a legend. We're talking twenty-four-freaking-carat gold.'

He laughs like I've said something funny as he suddenly moves around me, heading toward what appears to be an immense walk-in closet on the other side of the room, and my eyes nearly pop out of my head when I follow him inside it. Jesus, his entire apartment is unreal, but this closet . . . Yeah, I could seriously fall in love with this thing.

I'm so focused on taking in the built-in, glass-fronted wall of drawers and sumptuous, leather-covered settee, that I completely stop paying attention to what Callan's doing, which proves to be a massive error when I turn around and get hit with an overload of the gorgeous male beast wrapped up in a custom-made navy suit, crisp white dress shirt and yellow-and-navy-striped tie. He looks like he's just stepped off the cover of *GQ*, and I wipe at the corner of my mouth with my fingertips, just in case there's an embarrassing drop of drool collecting there.

Completely oblivious to my ogling, he straightens the tie, shoots his cuffs, then walks over to the wall of drawers, opens one, and takes out a hefty metal wristwatch that looks like it probably cost more than my entire university education. Next, he grabs a pair of aviator sunglasses from another drawer, tucking them into the jacket's inside pocket, then picks up the brush that's sitting on top of a wooden chest and runs it through his hair a few times, the thick strands gleaming beneath the golden glow of the modern light fixture that hangs from the center of the high ceiling.

By the time he looks back over at me, I'm actually fanning my face with my right hand, and he arches one of those slashing eyebrows at me in silent enquiry.

'Don't mind me,' I murmur. 'You just, um, clean up really well, Hathaway.'

He laughs, but I love the tell-tale flush of pink on his cheekbones. He still hasn't shaved, the almost-auburn stubble on his jaw only accentuating the rugged angles of his handsome face, his lips so freaking kissable, I have no idea why I didn't do exactly that when I decided to act like a wild woman and jumped his gorgeous bones out on his sofa. The guy is too bloody stunning for his own good – but unlike so many other ridiculously attractive people, he isn't cocky about his looks. If anything, his arrogance comes from his impressive abilities, but not in a way that's off-putting. He's simply a man who knows what he's good at, which from what I've seen, appears to be just about everything.

'Will you really be okay while I'm gone?' he asks, the way his dark gaze goes warm with concern putting another chink in the emotional armor I'm trying so hard to keep in place.

'I've been a fugitive on the run for over a year now,' I tell him, lifting my shoulders in a casual shrug, as if I'm not secretly terrified by the idea of him leaving me here with his mum. 'It might be awkward, but I think I can handle your mother.'

'I admire your courage,' he says with a low laugh.

'Come on,' I murmur. 'She can't be *that* bad.'

'Oh, she's great. Just ask her about the grandkids my oldest brother and sister have given her. That'll keep her busy for at least an hour, and I promise to be back before then.'

'You'd better be.'

'You gonna be worried about me?' he asks, his gaze searching, as well as undeniably hot, and the next thing I know, he's done letting me have my space and is pulling me back into his strong, powerful arms.

For a moment, my very real fear for his safety almost has me lashing out at him, telling him to back the hell off so that I can retreat and regroup behind the thick, spike-covered walls I've spent so many years building around me, their existence the only reason I'm still able to get up every day and go through the motions of living. But I manage to fight back that all-too-natural-to-me-now reaction, and completely surprise myself when I'm able to quietly admit, 'Of course I'm going to worry about you.'

'Good.' He stares down at me with so much intensity, I find it kind of difficult to breathe. 'Because God knows I'm going to be worried about you, honey.'

I swallow so hard that it hurts, my heart pounding hard and fast, and without any conscious direction from my brain, I find myself lifting onto the tips of my toes as I curl my hands around the back of his warm, strong neck, and it feels like the world is moving in slow motion as I pull him down to me . . . and finally, for the first time ever, touch my lips to his. He stiffens for only a second in shock, then gives a low, masculine growl and bursts into action, his big hands gripping my waist so that he can lift me off the floor as he slants his head a bit to the side, and suddenly our lips are parted, our tongues rubbing and tangling in a sensual battle for control. I kiss him as if I want nothing more than to crawl up inside him – as if it's vital that I taste every part of his hot, deliciously maple-flavored mouth that I can – painfully aware that I might never get a chance like this again. Not with this life I've been dealt, every minute I manage to survive on this earth a bonus that I know I'm lucky to have. And so I kiss Callan Hathaway like I've wanted to kiss him from that very first time I ever laid eyes on him.

I kiss him like it's the last kiss I might ever have, and completely lose all sense of time – all sense of anything but the way his addictive mouth tastes and feels against mine – until a persistent noise comes from what seems like miles away, and through the fog of hunger and lust that's overwhelming me, I realize that someone is knocking on Callan's bedroom door. He makes a low, guttural sound when I reluctantly tear my mouth from his, both of us panting as we stare eye to eye, my dazed brain trying to figure out at what point I'd wrapped my legs around his waist and he'd pushed me up against one of the sturdy closet doors, his massive erection pressed up hard and tight against my abdomen.

I lick my lips, tasting him there, and breathlessly say, 'I . . . I think that must be Clara.'

'Shit,' he breathes, resting his forehead against mine for a moment, before finally lowering me back to the hardwood floor and stepping away. 'I'll be right there!' he calls out, and I can just make out the faint sound of footsteps heading back down the hallway.

Callan runs both hands through his hair as he exhales a rough breath, gives me a scorching look that tells me *exactly* what we would be doing right now if not for the fact that he needs to leave, then turns and walks back into his bedroom.

'Lottie,' he says, when he reaches the door and glances back at me.

'Yeah?' I reply from where I'm leaning against the closet doorjamb, my legs still not quite steady enough for me to stand on my own.

'No matter how much of a handful my mom might be,' he murmurs, his brown eyes promising me he means every word, 'you'd better be here when I get back.'

Chapter Six

THE WATCHER

I count backward slowly from a hundred as I watch Callan Hathaway leave his building with a petite woman who I can only assume is his sister, seeing as how she'd arrived not long ago with an older female who was undoubtedly his mother, the three of them all having the same striking shade of bronze hair. But despite my attempts to stay calm, it isn't helping to soothe the fury scraping through my system like a nail-covered spike.

No matter how I look at it, I simply can't comprehend why Lottie went home with this jackass.

I mean, he's a good-looking guy, I'll give him that, if Viking warriors are your thing. But I can't imagine that would be my refined little bunny's taste. The American is basically just a walking, talking primate, showing up and beating his chest like bloody He-Man. And the lust that had carved his features last night – as he'd stared down at her on the front steps of her apartment building – had been so disgusting, I'd actually lost the contents of my stomach while I'd watched them.

When they'd left, it'd been so easy to follow his car service in my rental, the New York City traffic making it impossible for him to race away with her. Not that it would have mattered, given the precautions I've taken. But as it turned out, I hadn't even needed to use them.

I wonder if he even knows it's me that she's running from like a frightened rabbit. Has she shared our juicy secrets? If so, then I hope he felt like a fool when she told him. Hope he accepted that I'm more exceptional than him in every way that counts, since he was too cocky to see the truth when he was staring it right in the face over a shitty cup of coffee.

As I watch him standing there with his sibling on the busy Manhattan 'sidewalk', as they say here in America, the morning sunlight glinting against the stubble that now covers his jaw, instead of the heavy beard he'd had last year, I reluctantly accept the fact that I was also too cocky to see him clearly. If I had, I would have recognized the danger he posed and killed him the moment I'd learned he had a thing for *my* girl. It'd been so obvious when we'd met in London, his dark eyes filled with frustration when I couldn't give him the answers he'd wanted about where she might be, who she might be with . . . and why she was running in the first place.

Thinking about that meeting with Hathaway takes me back to the blood-drenched event that had prompted his tracking me down, and it's all I can do not to get hard in my jeans as I huddle behind the wheel of my rental that's parked across the street from the bastard's building. When I'd burst in on Lottie and her husband that night, I'd gone for her first, just as I'd planned. But my intention hadn't been to kill. No, that would have ended my fun too quickly.

Instead, I'd only planned to hurt her a bit, just enough to keep her from running while I took my time with ol' Oliver. But the pretty boy had surprised me. Hell, he'd surprised

Lottie too, when he threw himself in front of her, taking the blade to his chest like a champ.

As a black Mercedes SUV pulls up in front of Hathaway and his sister and they climb inside, I want to follow them so badly I can taste it, my need to deal with the prick once and for all nearly too much to resist. But I fight back the dangerous impulse, digging my nails into my palms so deeply they draw blood, knowing it's not the time. Not when he's made such a cardinal mistake and left Lottie alone with his mother. I focus my attention on his sibling instead, holding her image in my mind's eye, thinking that she looks vaguely familiar, though I can't recall where I might know her from. But regardless of who she is, the important thing is that she's more than pretty enough to keep my interest, if I come to need a distraction to tide me over until I decide it's time to bring my fun with Lottie to an end.

Until I decide that our game of cat and mouse is finally due a spectacular finale.

I'm far more intelligent than most, so I haven't indulged my darker fantasies often. But over the years, there have been times when I . . . Well, when I *required* an outlet. And I know how to cover my tracks, so discovery has never been an issue.

And there's something almost sweetly poetic about the idea of taking something of importance away from Hathaway. Of giving him a taste of pain that's so bitter to swallow, he bloody well chokes on it.

But I won't rush this and risk making a mistake.

I can bide my time and play this smart.

Because I'm by far the better man . . . and soon they're both going to know it.

Chapter Seven

LOTTIE

Ten minutes after Callan has left, I'm still standing in the door-way to his walk-in closet with my lips tingling and my arms wrapped around my middle, the loss of his delicious heat leaving me cold, even though the luxurious bedroom is warm and inviting. But as much as I would prefer to simply hide out in here forever, which sounds like a hell of a plan – and a far saner idea than going out there and continuing this charade with his poor mum, who seems like a riot and a genuinely nice person – I know that I can't.

And yet, if the woman had any idea who her son had actually left her alone with, the sad truth of the matter is that she would probably run screaming from the building. Because God knows that just because Callan believes in my innocence, it's no guarantee that his family will.

Taking a deep breath, I walk across his beautiful bedroom and carefully open his door. Peeking my head into the hallway, I make sure the coast is clear, then hurry over to the guest bed-room and quietly shut the door behind me, since it would definitely be awkward if she heard me in here. After what she walked in on this morning, his mum clearly thinks that we're involved, and I'm too tired to come up with a clever reason that would explain why I'm staying in Callan's guestroom, instead of in the master bedroom with him.

Walking over to the gold-framed, full-length mirror that sits in one corner of the room, I can't help but wince, since I look like someone who's just been completely turned inside out. But I guess it's not all that surprising, considering I basically had been, in a purely breathtaking, sexual way. No, the surprising part is that *I'm* the one who'd initiated it, and standing here now, I honestly don't know where I'd found the courage. Or *what the hell* I'd been thinking.

I could rationalize my actions by blaming them on a need to experience something that was wildly blissful and sweet, after so many months of nothing but constant fear and remembered tragedy. A primal, undeniable need to experience something that made me feel alive . . . and wanted. But the honest to God truth was that I simply couldn't fight it anymore. I've wanted Callan Hathaway for so long – have thought about him nearly every minute of every day for the past year – and when given the opportunity, I'd been helpless to do anything but take it.

And I'm not regretful of it . . . or the crazy, so-good-I'd-wanted-to-scream way that he'd made me feel.

No, what I regret is that I now know he's every bit as addictive as I'd suspected. And seeing as how I have nothing but a questionable future ahead of me, there isn't the slightest chance I'll have the time to get my fill of him before this thing undoubtedly blows up in our faces. If such a thing as 'getting one's fill of Callan Hathaway' is even possible, which now that I've had a taste, I seriously doubt.

There's a sudden clatter from what sounds like the kitchen

that makes me jump, and I exhale a shaky breath, fully aware that I need to stop stalling and start making myself presentable. I didn't bring a lot of clothes options with me, but that's mainly because I don't have many ... and I certainly hadn't planned on meeting any of Callan's family members. After digging through my duffel bag, I choose a pair of gray jeans that will go well with my Converse, and an oversized white top that slopes off one shoulder and has a cute asymmetrical hemline, figuring they'll have to do. I also don't have much in the way of make-up other than some blush, mascara and a nude lip gloss, so there's no help for the dark smudges under my eyes. But a good brushing at least has my hair looking decent, so I pull in another deep breath for courage and finally brave leaving the room.

I find his mum in the massive, jaw-droppingly gorgeous kitchen, and when she beams a smile at me that's warm and friendly, it makes me feel like an even bigger tool than I was already feeling. And that's before she so kindly says, 'Lana, please let me apologize for barging in on you two this morning. And for Clara's unfortunate outburst. I swear she's normally my most laid-back child, but this campaign is really taking its toll on her.'

'I can't even imagine how stressful it must be,' I murmur as I slide up onto one of the leather stools at the granite-topped breakfast bar, feeling like absolute crap over the fact that this sweet woman doesn't even know my real name. The bar sits opposite from where she's leaning against one of the gleaming countertops with a cup of coffee in her hands, her chocolate-brown eyes, so like Callan's, filled with a mother's worry for the happiness of her child.

'I don't know how much of the campaign you've been following,' she says, her elegantly shaped eyebrows drawing together in a small frown, 'but Clara's opponent – Rick Wainwright – is horrifically brutal, for lack of a better word.'

'Brutal how?' I ask, while she sets her mug on the counter and pulls a clean one down from one of the cupboards.

'In every way you can imagine,' she tells me, pouring me a cup of coffee from the expensive-looking coffee-maker that's still making percolating sounds, the rich aroma of freshly ground coffee beans filling the air. 'He's a talented political manipulator, only telling people what they want to hear, without any plans for implementing his growing list of promises. And he's the dirtiest politician I've ever seen. He'd rather sling mud than have an honest debate – and his history with women is . . .' She shudders as if thinking of something truly repulsive. 'God, it baffles the mind to understand why anyone would support him. But they do.'

'Unfortunately,' I murmur, 'there are some people who will always gravitate toward the voice that's telling them what's wrong and who to blame for it, rather than the one offering them real solutions.'

'Isn't that the truth,' she says, giving me an approving smile as she sets the steaming mug in front of me, along with the sugar pot. 'You know, it probably sounds horrible, but I can honestly say that I haven't always been a fan of the women my Callan has chosen to date,' she adds in a softer voice, leaning forward a bit like she's telling me a secret. 'But after meeting you this morning, I'm thrilled to be able to say that his taste has clearly improved.'

'Oh, uh, thank you,' I just manage to push past my lips, and as I watch her turn and walk over to the huge stainless-steel refrigerator and pull out a carton of coffee creamer, it takes everything I have not to slink to the floor and crawl under one of the stools, the entire situation like something out of a dark, it's-actually-painful-to-watch comedy. Coughing to clear the lump of guilt and dread in my throat, I thank her again as I take the creamer from her when she offers it to me, and make a desperate bid to change the subject as I say, 'I just hope Clara wins in November. I've read all about her platform and I believe she could truly bring about change if she's given the opportunity.'

'That's so sweet of you, Lana. Thank you.'

'Well, I really mean it,' I murmur, stirring a teaspoonful of sugar into my coffee before taking a sip.

'I'm surprised that you hadn't made the connection between her and Callan before this morning,' she says with a slight look of concern as she picks her coffee back up, 'but then I know how frustratingly private he can be.' Giving me an apologetic smile, she adds, 'Would it be beyond rude of me to ask how long you two have known each other?'

'Oh. We, um, met last year.' I don't say in England, because Callan had mentioned, the night before my wedding, that he was there representing his family. His mum would have made the trip, but her rheumatoid arthritis had been acting up and she hadn't been able to fly at the time. And given how horrific my marriage had turned out, the last thing I need is her bringing up anything to do with that entire weekend. 'He . . . He's a regular at the café where I work in Brooklyn. But we've only just recently started to, um, casually date.'

'Oh phooey on that "casual" nonsense,' she says with another warm smile, my response thankfully seeming to alleviate any worries she'd had over the fact that I hadn't known about Clara. 'He's obviously crazy about you. A mother just knows these things.'

'Mrs Hath—'

'Please, call me Margot,' she cuts in, giving me a mischievous wink. 'And I promise I won't be a meddler. It's just . . . I was really worried he wouldn't ever get serious about anyone again. That he would be alone forever, after the whole Jessica debacle left him so jaded.'

I inwardly cringe again, thinking she couldn't be further from the truth. Callan might want to nail me, and help me out of some inherent sense of honor, but I'm not a woman he could ever be 'serious' about. And he sure as hell wouldn't want his mum spilling any details to me about his nightmare relationship with this Jessica woman, but she just keeps forging ahead like a beautiful, exquisitely dressed wrecking ball. 'I mean, after Jessica, who was such a destructive, manipulative user . . . Well, I'm sure it isn't hard for you to imagine how angry and distrustful he was when it all came crashing down. It absolutely broke my heart to see him that way.'

'Um, that's . . . awful,' I murmur before I take another sip of my coffee, painfully aware that I need to steer this conversation in a new direction. One that's as far away from Callan's personal life as I can get it, since I know this is a thousand kinds of wrong. But instead, I'm horrified when I hear myself ask, 'Were they married?'

The sour expression on her still smooth face makes it even clearer that Margot isn't a Jessica fan. 'No, but she was his fiancée. For a brief time, at any rate.' She leans in a bit closer, like she's about to impart another particularly sensitive secret, and her voice is noticeably softer as she says, 'You see, not long after their engagement, Callan discovered that the horrid she-witch had been—'

I'm on the edge of my seat, but the sudden ringing coming from the stylish purse that's sitting on the counter not far from us has caught Margot's attention, and she reaches over to pull out her phone. 'Oh, shoot,' she says when she looks at the screen, then gives me another apologetic smile. 'I just need to take this quickly. It's my youngest son, Connor. But I promise I won't be long.'

'Please, take all the time you need,' I tell her, and she flashes me another lovely smile before she answers the phone, her heels clacking against the rustic stone tiles as she gives her son a cheery hello and walks across the kitchen. I can hear her chatting away as she continues down a back hallway, then turns into another room for privacy, the emotion in her voice as she relays what's happened with his sister's campaign making it clear how invested the family is in Clara succeeding. A success that I'm putting in jeopardy just by being here.

I suck in an unsteady breath, my hand shaking as I carefully set my mug down, the already hefty load of guilt I'd been feeling for discussing Callan's private life with his mother suddenly morphing into something monstrous and sickening. Something that's now twisting through my insides like a serpent, because of the indisputable fact that it's not Jessica who's the real threat to Clara's campaign – *I* am. Hell, I could completely destroy it, and I know, without any doubt, that the best thing for everyone, Callan included, would be for me to get the hell out of here as quickly as possible. And then out of their lives for good.

God, talk about being a destructive user! It kills a part of me inside to admit it, but his manipulative ex doesn't have anything on my own behavior. I might not have sought Callan out, but I came here with him, into his home, and accepted his generous hospitality.

Then all but gobbled him up like a freaking succubus.

And yet, even though I know it's wrong for me to be here, I still can't regret what happened between us before his family showed up. Those intense, pleasure-drenched moments had been some of the most insanely sweet minutes of my entire life, and as long as I can slink away before causing any real damage to these people, they're ones that I'm always going to keep safely locked away with the very best of my memories. And if a miracle occurs and I somehow manage to live beyond my youth, I'll probably still be taking this particular memory out in the quiet of night and reliving it, second by second, amazed that my messed-up self ever managed to capture the attention of an incredible man like Callan Hathaway in the first place.

'So that's that,' I murmur under my breath, knowing damn well what I have to do, regardless of what I'd told Callan. And as I look around the empty kitchen, it occurs to me that this will probably be my best and easiest opportunity, so long as he didn't reset the security alarm when he left.

Sliding off the stool as quietly as possible, I hurry out into the living room, then over to the entryway, my heart in my throat as I catch sight of the green light on the control panel. And I already know, from when his sister walked in this morning after his mum had disabled the alarm, that the door doesn't beep when opened.

Rushing over to the nearest sofa, I kneel down to fish my godawful wig out, then quickly head back to the guestroom, where I'd left my duffel bag and backpack. Unfortunately, I can't exactly be stealthy with both, so I throw the absolute essentials into my backpack – toiletries bag, some clothes and my laptop. It's already full, but just as I'm about ready to zip it up, I realize I'm a sentimental sap, because I grab Callan's hoodie and shove it into the pack as well, before quietly making my way back out to the living room. I can hear his mum's voice still coming from that back room, but it's difficult to make out what she's saying over the heavy thudding of my heart. And my stupid lashes are wet again, which doesn't make any sense, until I realize that I'm crying. It's a dangerous sign of weakness that I absolutely can't afford, given the state of my life, and I harden my jaw, more confident than ever that I'm doing the right thing here.

And while Callan is probably going to be furious when he first realizes I'm gone, I honestly don't think it will take long before he understands just how massive of a bullet he's dodged. He might even end up thanking me. Though I doubt I'll ever know, since I'm most likely never going to see him again.

'I'm sorry,' I whisper to the empty room, trying to commit every detail, from the beautiful furniture to the stunning view, to memory. 'But I promise you're going to see this is for the best.'

Then I quickly put my shoes on, swipe angrily at my damp cheeks, and silently walk out the door.

Chapter Eight

CALLAN

Sitting in the backseat of the SUV beside Clara, who's on the phone again with Carl, I try to shake off the uneasy feeling in my gut. Miraculously, the confrontation with Jessica had been a non-event, so I know that's not the source. As soon as she set eyes on me *and* Clara walking into the TV studio, she'd looked ready to make a run for it. I have no doubt that she'd planned all of this knowing we'd find out about it, and that *I'd* be the one who came to deal with her. But she definitely hadn't antic-ipated Clara showing too, probably assuming she would be too busy with the campaign, and I'd had to bite back a laugh at the look on her face. Because if there's one person in this world guaranteed to put the fear of God into Jessica Marten, it's my younger sister.

When Jessica had pulled the shit that ended our two-year relationship, it'd been Clara who had been the hardest on her, telling her exactly what she thought of her every time they ran into each other. An occurrence that had happened quite often, given that Jessica had moved into the same building as Clara after I kicked her out. I have no idea what Jess had been think-ing at the time – whether she'd thought she would be able to get Clara on her side or if she simply wanted to make a nuisance of herself – but whatever her plan, it had massively backfired, seeing as how I've never met anyone who can hold a grudge the way Clara does. And this was all without her even knowing the real story, since I hadn't wanted my siblings to find out just how much of a pathetic shlump I'd been. Instead, they'd all assumed that Jess had cheated on me, and while I'd never confirmed their assumptions, I'd also never told them the truth.

But whatever Jessica had hoped to achieve with today's stunt, it'd been a wake-up call for me, and I'd pulled her aside before we left to make it clear what would happen if she ever tried something like it again. And while I think she's been walking around since our break-up confident in the fact that I would never do anything that would permanently damage her career, I'm relieved to see that I finally got through to her today. I might have let her get away with annoying shit for the past few years, but she went too fucking far when she involved my family, and now she knows the gloves are off.

Now she understands that I no longer give a damn if telling the truth makes me look like an idiot. If she pisses me off again, I'm going to finally let the world know what really happened between us . . . and afterward, she'll be forced to kiss her pre-cious career goodbye. Hell, she'll be lucky to get a two-bit part at some shitty dinner theatre.

So given that I'm feeling satisfied with how the Jess situation turned out, I'm guessing that this growing sense of tension right now is stemming from the fact that I left Lottie behind. But then, it could just as easily be that I still have more ques-tions than answers when it comes to the beautiful Brit, the list of things that I know with any certainty about her situation entirely too short for comfort.

Firstly, whoever it was that had murdered Olly had been ready to kill Lottie as well, though I'm still not sure if he was the target . . . or if she was.

And secondly, after some of the things she's said to me, I'm certain that at least part of her reticence in coming home with me was her fear that something might happen to me, too. Which means that she believes there's a strong chance some asshole out there is still looking for her, with the intent of hurting her, and the rage that moves through me with that thought has a low growl surging up from my chest that draws a startled look from Clara.

I wave off her worried frown and scrub my hands down my face, feeling hobbled by all the unknowns. But my gut . . . Yeah, I might not have a shred of proof to back it up, but my gut is telling me that Lottie is the real reason some psychopath attacked her and Oliver, and not the other way around, as I've always assumed. And if that's true, then maybe it can explain the bizarre shift in Lottie's social life when she was only sixteen and had gone from being a popular, outgoing teenager, to a complete loner, because no one changed *that* drastically without a reason. And it wasn't going to be because of the tragedy with her parents, seeing as how this shift in her behavior had happened two years after their deaths. She'd grieved for them, her aunt and uncle had told me, but her close network of friends had gathered around her at the time, offering all the support that they could.

Until she'd cut each and every one of them out of her life, just a couple of years later.

My gut twists even tighter as I consider all the horrific shit that could have been the impetus for her withdrawal, and it kills me to think of her suffering from some kind of abuse, though I'd be remiss to discount it. I'm turning my brain inside out, trying to figure out what it will take to finally earn her trust so that she'll open up and let me help her, when my phone starts buzzing loudly in my pocket, ripping me from my troubled thoughts with the even more troubling warning that Lottie has left my building.

'Oh shit,' I mutter to myself as I pull my phone out, and sure enough, the tracking dots that I hid in her things last night have activated, just like I'd programmed them to do before going to bed. And given how fast she begins moving, I figure she must have just jumped into a taxi.

'Son of a bitch,' I snarl, then lean forward and start barking orders at our driver, since I have no doubt that she's headed back to her apartment. 'I'll give you a five-hundred dollar tip if you can get me to the corner of Hammond and Second in Brooklyn in the next twenty minutes.'

'Callan!' Clara gasps, quickly grasping for the back of the seat to steady herself as the driver hits the gas and we speed forward, the guy already weaving through the late-morning traffic like a Nascar champion. 'What the hell?'

'I'll explain later,' I tell her, too on edge to even try it now, since it would mean divulging things that I still have no idea how to explain to my family. Or if I even should.

Thankfully, Clara decides not to push, and we spend the trip just holding on for dear life while the driver earns every cent that I promised him. We've made remarkable time, and are only two blocks from Lottie's apartment, when the tracking app on my phone tells me that she's out of the taxi and is now moving on foot.

'Stop!' I shout, and the driver brakes so hard that Clara and I are both jerked back by our seatbelts. Cursing under my breath, I struggle to unhook the damn thing, then open my door and climb out onto the SUV's running board, scanning the area for any sign of Lottie, since the app is only accurate within a fifty-yard radius. We're still far enough away from her place that I figure she must be scared if she's taking these kinds of precautions, possibly thinking someone might be watching the front of her building. But, Christ, it's not like she has any training in spotting surveillance. Even if she's being careful, she's still likely to walk into a trap, and the thought makes me want to throw my head back and roar with frustration. But there isn't any time for me to act like a jackass, so I keep scanning the crowds of people on the sidewalk, and finally spot that godawful red wig about twenty yards behind us.

Sticking my head back inside the SUV, I catch my sister's confused gaze and quickly say, 'Get back to my apartment and tell Mom that everything's okay. Then set the alarm for me when you guys leave. I'll be in contact as soon as I can. And make sure this guy's tip gets put on my account.'

'Callan, wh—?'

'Sorry, Clara, but there's no time for explanations right now. I've gotta go.'

I jump down onto the sidewalk and slam the door shut, then take off after Lottie, who's moving quickly in the opposite direction from her building, making me think she must be planning to loop around the block, possibly using some of the narrow alleyways that can't be accessed by car, and go in a back way. 'Lottie, wait!' I shout, when she's only ten feet in front of me, and while I half-expected her to take off running at the sound of my voice, she stops and reels toward me instead, her blue eyes wide with shock as I close the distance between us.

'Callan? How did—? What are you—?' She sucks in a sharp breath as I grab her upper arm and pull her with me into the recessed entrance of an out-of-business pet shop, so that we're no longer standing in the busy flow of pedestrians. 'Wait a minute,' she snaps, glaring up at me as I step closer. 'Did you put some kind of tracking device in my things?'

'Damn straight I did,' I seethe, my terror receding now that I can see for myself that she's okay, while fury that she's not only put herself in danger, but felt she had to sneak away from me like I was some kind of goddamn jailor, swiftly takes its place. 'And a good thing too, since you apparently have a death wish!'

She rears back from me, her face pale but for the twin bright splotches of color on her cheeks that tell me she's angry, too. 'I don't know why it's such a shock to you that I ran!' she yells, shivering so hard that she's shaking, despite it being hot as hell out. 'I told you I thought I should go back to my apartment, so you had to know it was a possibility. God, Callan, I hadn't even wanted to go home with you in the first place!'

I open my mouth to argue, but as some asshole tries to shove past a slow-moving group of elderly couples on the sidewalk, he veers close to where she's standing, and though he doesn't touch her, she flinches like the guy had just brandished a knife in her face.

'Christ,' I mutter, knowing damn well that she reacted like that because she's terrified of being out on the street. 'I know there's shit you're not telling me, Lottie. I just want to keep you safe. Is that really so fucking awful?'

'It's not your job, Callan. I'm not your responsibility. So just leave me alone!' she snarls, shoving against my chest so hard that it nearly knocks me back a step. 'I don't need another bloody stalker!'

This time, *I'm* the one who flinches, feeling like she's just punched me in the stomach. Or reached into my chest and squeezed my heart between her delicate hands, until it's nothing more than a pulpy mess of muscle and tissue. 'Just so we're clear here,' I scrape out, 'are you seriously comparing me to the sick shit who killed your husband?'

She sucks in another sharp breath, but doesn't tell me I'm wrong. That I misunderstood or she didn't mean it. She just lifts her chin at that belligerent angle I'm becoming all too familiar with, and I find myself taking an instinctive step back from her. Then a second. And a third.

'All right.' A bitter, hollow laugh jerks up from the deepest point of my chest, scratching my throat, and it's a heavy-hitting dose of reality that has me saying, 'You wanna go, go then. I honestly don't care anymore. I'm done with this shit.'

I'm turning before the last gritty syllable has even left my lips, not even allowing myself the chance to take in her expression. I might have been stubbornly slow on the uptake, but I've finally gotten the message, and now I just want to get the hell out of here so that I can try to figure out where exactly I went wrong with this woman.

And why I ever gave a damn in the first place.

LOTTIE

Every part of me wants to run after Callan as he walks away and throw myself at him, clinging to his huge body like a vine, but I fight the purely selfish impulse. Instead, I hike my backpack higher onto my shoulder and force myself to start walking in the opposite direction, but it's impossible to see where I'm going, and at first I don't understand what's happening. Then I feel dampness at the corner of my mouth, my tongue flicking out to taste the saltiness of tears, and I realize they're running down my face again. I'm quietly crying as I try to weave my way through the crowd of people on the sidewalk, every step I take only making me cry harder.

Callan was *wrong* to put whatever he did on my things to track me, but I know why he did it. The crazy man truly just wants to help me – and he must have known, deep down in his gut, that I was going to do exactly what I've done today: thumb my nose at his insanely generous offer and head back out on my own, putting myself in danger.

But whether he was right or wrong to do what he did, I had no right to say those horrible words to him, and it's killing me inside to know that I had the power to hurt him like that. I hadn't understood it back then, and I still don't understand the stunning connection that had formed between us the weekend when we first met – but there's no denying that it existed. That it was *still* there, vibrant and breathtakingly real, every time we so much as looked at each other . . . until just a few seconds ago, when I took a bloody mallet to it and smashed it into a million tiny, unrecognizable pieces.

Nice going, Lot, I silently mutter, so disgusted with myself I feel ill. *You told off the one person in the entire world who believed you were innocent, and for what?*

Well, for him. For Callan. Because despite what the rest of the world might think of me, I'm not a cruel bitch bent on wreaking pain and destruction. I'm a freaking poet, for crying out loud! So really, what other choice did I have? Was I really just meant to accept help from the only person who genuinely wants to be there for me, when it would mean taking a wrecking ball to his entire life, as well as his sister's career? Yeah, I don't think so.

I hear a strange, almost high-pitched laughter buzzing in my ears, but don't realize that it's actually coming from me until I catch the way people are staring at me, as if they're frightened for my sanity. And, hell, maybe they should be. I honestly don't know anymore, because life . . . All this cruel, twisted irony that *life* keeps throwing at me is taking its toll, so if I don't start laughing my arse off about it, I'll just end up sinking down onto the grimy sidewalk and sobbing like a baby.

'Isn't it time, then, to finally toughen up and get the hell on with it?' I ask myself, drawing more concerned looks from those around me. I plaster a sharp, don't-screw-with-me smile onto my face and swipe at the tears on my cheeks, using every ounce of strength I have left to force myself to stop thinking about what I've lost, and focus instead on what comes next. Sure, it's a short-term solution that really doesn't have a chance in hell of working, but if it gets me back to my apartment without someone calling the cops on the crazy woman crying hysterically as she walks down the street talking to herself, then I figure I really ought to give it a shot.

I can smell the mouthwatering scent of Rosita's Bakery up ahead, and I rub at my eyes again, then straighten the wig I'd put on while taking the elevator down from Callan's apartment, trying to pull myself together in case I run into Eva. I have no doubt that she would take one look at me today and go into her motherly protective mode, wanting to make sure I'm okay, when all I need is to be left alone so that I can finally do what I *should* have done weeks ago.

I realized, while getting bitch-slapped by guilt in Callan's kitchen this morning, that there's really only one course of action for me now – and it's one I should have taken as soon as I'd first started to feel that uncomfortable prickle at the back of my neck again. I should have run the second that happened, before someone else ended up getting hurt because of me, the same way that Olly had. But like a selfish bitch, I'd stayed here in Brooklyn. I'd told myself that I was just being paranoid, since I couldn't face leaving the small, but relatively safe-feeling life I'd started to build for myself here. Told myself that the smartest move was to just keep laying low, when my instincts had kept screaming at me that something wasn't right.

That something was, in fact, very, very wrong.

'At least I'm ready to do something about it now,' I grumble, so focused on planning what I'll be able to take with me from my apartment, once I've rented a car, that I completely forget to pay attention to where I'm walking.

'Oh, I'm sorry!' I gasp, reaching out to steady the tall body that I've just barreled straight into, nearly knocking the poor guy off his feet. But as I tilt my head back, I find myself looking up into a familiar pair of deep-blue eyes, and my heart lurches so badly, I swear I can feel it lodged in my throat.

'Hey there, Lottie,' the man drawls with a wide, terrifying smile. 'I've missed you, little bunny.'

Chapter Nine

LOTTIE

For one heart-stopping moment, I just freeze, exactly like I did when this asshole first busted into mine and Olly's stateroom, brandishing that gleaming knife. But then I see the flare of triumph in his eyes – that spark that says he's won because I'm weak and pathetic and no match for him – and a fury unlike anything I've ever known grabs hold of the terror that's locking me in place and starts shaking the ever-loving hell out of it. And yet, the anger doesn't transform me into some badass heroine from an action movie, no matter how desperately I might wish that it would. Instead, I just start trembling like someone with a high fever, while a low, keening sound crawls up from my throat, like a wordless cry for help. But by some bizarre stroke of luck, it actually works.

'Hey, is this guy bothering you?' someone asks from my side, the stranger's deep voice gruff and filled with concern. I have no idea what this Good Samaritan looks like, because I can't tear my horrified gaze away from the now scowling bastard standing in front of me, but I've never been so happy to hear another person's voice in my life.

'Yes! Yes, he is!' I manage to scream, stumbling back a step, my legs like jelly. The psychotic killer who's haunted me for so long lurches forward to grab at me, but the helpful stranger shoves him back, and I don't wait around to see what happens next. As if a shot of adrenaline has just been injected directly into my bloodstream, I turn and take off running, while the sound of a fight breaks out behind me. I send up a fervent prayer to whoever might be listening that the guy who stepped in to help me will be okay, and risk a quick look over my shoulder, relief piercing my chest when I see that others have joined him, and I catch someone shouting, 'Hey, shithead! Get the hell out of our neighborhood!'

I would laugh with glee over the fact that the 'shithead' probably has no idea how to deal with an angry crowd of fierce, protective New Yorkers, but I'm still too filled with terror and fury and a wild, desperate desire to survive to do anything but flee. I don't even know where I'm running to, just that I need to put as much distance between us as I can, until a shaft of sunlight breaks through the pillowy clouds and I spot the most beautiful sight I've ever seen up ahead, walking down the sidewalk on the opposite side of the street.

'Callan!' I scream, his thick hair gleaming like bronze in the warm September sunshine, and I'm so desperate to reach him that I don't even look before running into the busy road that stretches between us. I hear the godawful sound of screeching brakes, followed by a strange gust of wind at my back, and quickly glance over my shoulder again to see that I've just nearly been hit by a bus.

'Watch where you're fucking going!' the grizzled driver

shouts at me through his open window, shaking his fist, but I can't even tell him I'm sorry. No, I'm stuck on some kind of autopilot, Callan's name the only sound that will come out of my mouth, so I just keep shouting it, over and over, as I try to weave my way through the braking cars, while horns honk and drivers keep yelling harsh obscenities at me.

I'm panting by the time I nearly reach the curb, covered in sweat, and I trip over someone's discarded work boot that's just been left in the road, pitching forward, my backpack only adding to my momentum. I brace for impact with the hard ground, knowing it's going to hurt, but it never comes, two strong hands suddenly catching me by my upper arms and yanking me up onto the sidewalk as if I weigh no more than a feather.

'Callan!' I gasp, knowing instantly that it's him before I've even tipped my head back to take in his outrageously gorgeous, fury-darkened face, the look in his eyes telling me that I just scared ten years off his life.

'What the hell, Lottie?' he roars, giving me a little shake. 'You nearly just got yourself killed!'

'I had . . . Had to reach you,' I ramble, still breathing too fast, the tickle at the back of my throat telling me that I'm only seconds away from bursting into tears again. 'I'm so s-sorry!' I sob, fisting my hands in the front of his crisp white dress shirt. 'What I said before, I didn't mean it. You're n-nothing like him. Nothing! But the last thing I want is to ruin your l-life. I . . . I couldn't stand it if something happened to you because of me!'

'Yeah, you keep trying to save me,' he mutters in that deep, delicious voice that never fails to make me shiver with awareness, even when he's clearly still furious with me . . . and I'm in the middle of a monumental breakdown. 'Keep trying to protect me from getting hurt. But do you know what would completely destroy me, Lot? Making you deal with this shit on your own. That's not something I can live with.'

'But what about Clara's campaign?' I ask, and as he places his big, warm hands on the sides of my face and gently brushes my tears away with his thumbs, I can see that he's starting to get a clearer picture of what sent me running.

'It's going to be okay,' he murmurs in a low rumble, the brutal, jagged edges of his anger softening with his understanding. 'I'm not going to bullshit you and tell you that I've got all the answers, because I don't. But I promise that we can figure this out together. If you'll just trust me, I'll work myself to the bone to find a way to get you out of this nightmare, Lot, without you, me *or* my family getting hurt.'

'I won't run again. I promise,' I gasp, and while they're not the words of trust that he was hoping for, he accepts them with a rugged jerk of his chin, and I nearly sag with relief.

'What happened after I left?' he asks, his dark gaze moving over my tear-drenched face, reading me like a book.

'I, um . . .' I start to say, but have no idea how to even begin, and Callan thankfully takes mercy on me, choosing not to force an explanation. At least for the moment. Instead, he throws up his hand in that way that only born-and-bred New Yorkers can do, and a taxi screeches to a halt at the curb within seconds.

'Where to?' the driver asks, after we've both climbed into the backseat.

'Take us to the Fairfax,' Callan tells him, and with a brief nod from the driver, we're on our way.

'Why are we going to a hotel?' I quietly ask, aware that the Fairfax is one of the newest hotels that's been built here in Brooklyn, the project one that had gotten a lot of media attention because of its dedication to sustainability, without skimping on luxury.

'Because my mother's no doubt still at my apartment,' he murmurs, reaching over and grabbing my hand, 'and we need privacy for the conversation we're about to have.'

'Oh. Okay.' I take a deep breath, trying to mentally prepare, but my thoughts are nothing but a blur of chaos, so I keep talking instead. 'What were you doing, just walking down the street?'

He gives my hand a gentle squeeze, his voice rough and his dark eyes locking with mine as he says, 'I just needed to get some fresh air before calling for a car.'

'I'm sorry,' I say again, guessing that he was walking off the hurt and anger that I'd caused with my callous words.

'I know something scared you,' he mutters, a frown knitting its way between his masculine brows as he gently rubs his thumb across the sharp points of my knuckles. 'You nearly got run over trying to get to me, Lot. And while I'm fully aware that there's this . . . kind of pull between us, my ego's not so huge that I can believe you were willing to risk death to catch up to me. Not when you know where I live and could have easily found me there.' He tilts his head toward me, his piercing, worried gaze searching mine. 'You were running after me because something scared the shit out of you. What was it?'

'In the room,' I whisper, my heart thudding painfully in my chest as I cast an uneasy look toward the back of the driver's head. 'I promise I'll tell you everything when we get to the hotel.'

Though it's clear that he's frustrated, he accepts my response with another gentle hand squeeze, and we're quiet the rest of the drive, which only takes a few minutes. I stand nervously by Callan's side while he talks to the friendly employee at the front desk, the fact that neither of us has so much as a single piece of luggage, apart from my backpack that he's carrying for me, not even earning a flicker of her lashes, which I find impressive. The whole transaction takes less than a minute, and then we're riding the elevator up to the twentieth floor. I use the time to ask him about what had happened at the TV station with his ex, but all he tells me is that it's been handled. And once we reach our floor, there's only a brief walk down a wide hallway, and then Callan is using the key card he's been given to unlock our room's door, holding it open for me as I walk inside.

Everything seems strangely surreal for a moment as I stand in the center of the room and watch Callan close the door behind him. I'm only vaguely aware of the modern, expensive decor that surrounds us, the true center of my focus none other than the tall, outrageously gorgeous man who's now walking toward me. There's a small table and two chairs situated over by one of the windows, so I go and sit down, still feeling unsteady, while Callan places my backpack on the bed, then slips out of his suit jacket and lays it across the back of the other chair. His tailored shirt fits his broad shoulders to perfection, and I simply sit there in silence, watching as he rolls up his shirtsleeves, revealing his sexy, corded forearms. Then he looks over at me with those beautiful, worried brown eyes, shoves his hands into his front pockets, and says, 'I don't want to sound like a pushy prick, sweetheart, but start talking.'

I'm not sure if I'm desperate for more time to put my thoughts together, or if it's that I'm simply dying of curiosity, but my tone is steady as I hold his gaze and quietly say, 'Tell me what happened with your ex – I mean, why the two of you broke up – and I'll tell you why I had to marry Olly, as well as what happened in Italy.'

Surprise flickers across his handsome face, just before he gives a sharp, gritty laugh. 'Nothing happened with her, other than her being a total bitch.'

'Your mum said she made you jaded.'

His eyebrows lift with another jolt of astonishment. 'Jesus, you couldn't have spent more than thirty minutes with my mom, Lot, and she managed to gossip about Jessica?'

'Well, she's, you know, worried,' I explain with a shrug. 'Especially about how emotionally destroyed you were after she broke your heart.'

'Christ,' he mutters, scrubbing a hand down his face. 'First of all, now is not the time to get into this. But Jessica did *not* break my heart. And for the record, *I* left *her*. Not the other way around.'

Now I'm the one feeling surprised. 'Oh.'

'And just so you know, my mom's going to be gutted that you ran out on her,' he tells me, obviously deciding to give me some payback for bringing up the whole Jessica thing. And it works, because I feel like crap about it.

I bite my lip for a moment, then say, 'Should you call her and . . . God, I don't know. Try to explain?'

A bronze lock of hair falls over his brow as he shakes his head. 'Not now. I told Clara to tell her that I'd be in touch later.'

'Oh,' I say again. Then I pull in another deep breath, because I know I've stalled long enough. Grabbing one of the glass bottles of water that are carefully arranged on the table in the shape of the hotel's logo, I twist off the top, take a sip, then force myself to start. 'So I, um, married Olly because we could both offer something that the other one needed,' I say in a soft voice, my gaze focused on the bottle as I hold it in one hand and pick at the stylish paper label with the other. 'He needed to finally get serious about a woman and marry her, or his bitch of a mum was going to cut him off financially, and he knew she wouldn't buy him marrying one of his usual hook-ups. Plus, he doubted any of them would actually sign a prenup. And I . . . I had – *have* – a stalker. An insane one, as crazy as that sounds. He's extremely dangerous, and someone I've known for years.'

I expect him to demand a name, but he doesn't. He just

starts pacing back and forth at the foot of the king-sized bed, and asks, 'Olly knew about the stalker?'

'Only by accident. I wouldn't have deliberately told him, because I've never told anyone. But Olly was a customer at the restaurant where I worked in London while I was going to university, so we knew each other in a purely professional capacity. Then he started sleeping with Sasha, who, as you know, was one of my roommates. One night, when I was home alone, this . . . stalker broke in. But Olly and a few of his friends showed up out of the blue, and they scared him off,' I explain, surprised that this condensed version of the story is coming far more easily than I had thought it would. I'm actually a bit lightheaded, as if finally sharing the load with someone is lifting some of the weight that I've been carrying on my own for so long. 'A week later, Olly came into the restaurant and asked me to have coffee with him. I agreed, and he told me that he'd come up with a plan that just might work in both our favors.'

'What exactly was the plan?'

'Like I said, his mother was threatening to cut him off if he didn't settle down and get a wife. So he told me that if I would sign a prenup and agree to stay married to him for a minimum of five years, which was part of her conditions, then he would use his money and influence to help me with *my* problem.'

'Did you start dating him?'

I stop picking at the label and look up at him in surprise. 'God, no. I mean, not really. We just went out for show, so that people would believe us when we announced the engagement. But it was never sexual between us.' The corner of my mouth twitches for just a moment with a wry smile. 'Trust me, we really weren't each other's types. And Olly had enough girls to keep him busy without trying anything with me.'

'Not even on your wedding night?' he presses, and there's a

raw edge to his deep voice that makes it more than clear how he feels about the subject.

I shake my head, looking away from him. 'No. You already know he was with Sasha that night,' I reply, thinking about how I'd felt when I'd realized what was happening . . . and then later, when I'd been alone with Callan in the Becketts' music room. Clearing my throat, I can feel the frown settling between my brows as I go on. 'He, um, was willing to give me time before we had to "seal the deal", as he called it. But he'd started . . . talking about it more often, in those last weeks of our honeymoon.'

'Yeah, I bet he had,' he mutters under his breath.

'I don't know why,' I admit with a quiet laugh, shaking my head again. 'But our agreement had been that we would eventually consummate the marriage, so that his mum couldn't screw him over if she ever tried to claim it was all a sham. So maybe that was it.'

'You said that the identity package was a gift,' he murmurs, thankfully moving on from that awkward aspect of mine and Olly's fake relationship. 'Why?'

'It was weird, the way it happened. Olly had gotten seriously ill before he gave it to me – I think it must have been from some dodgy oysters he ate at this street vendor one day when we went to a local village fair – and I . . . I took care of him.' I focus on picking at the label again, a rougher tone to my voice as I say, 'I'm not sure anyone had ever done something like that for him before, and I think he genuinely appreciated it. So much so that he gave me the package a week later, and I know it must have cost him a fortune. Not only because of its quality, but also the short notice.'

'Had you talked about one before then?'

'Not really,' I admit with another quiet, sad-sounding laugh.

'I think I'd said something, one night at dinner, about how much I would have loved to have an alternate identity that I could use to run away one day and start my life over, if I ever needed to. But I didn't think he'd taken me seriously, until he gave me exactly what I'd wished for.' I look up at him again, wondering if he can see just how awful I feel as I tell him, 'The attack happened just two days later.'

His deep voice is gruff with understanding and compassion as he says, 'I hate to ask, Lot, but can you talk me through what happened?'

I give a hard swallow, but nod, understanding that it's not some prurient interest driving him to ask this of me. Things like this are a part of his profession, and he's determined to help me, which means he needs to know every detail that I can stand to give him. So after pulling in a shaky breath to compose myself, I take another sip of the water, then keep picking at the label as I try to figure out where to begin. 'I, um, guess the first thing you need to know is that despite the threat my stalker posed, Olly hadn't thought we would need any protection while we were in Italy. So it was just the two of us. We'd, um, spent the day in this quaint, beautiful seaside town, and Olly had had a few drinks, so I'd driven us back to the yacht for dinner. I cooked some chicken risotto, and then we sat in the TV room and watched some ridiculous movie that Olly had picked out.'

My lips twitch with a brief smile as I recall how we'd both laughed afterward, unable to believe how such a terrible script had ever been funded by a major studio. As I set the water bottle down on the table, I turn my head to stare out the nearby window, then start rubbing my damp palms over the tops of my thighs, my stomach churning as the memories of what happened next rise up inside me.

'After the movie,' I murmur hoarsely, focusing on the sun-dappled clouds that dot the sky like puffs of cotton candy, 'we went to our stateroom. Olly was exhausted, so I thought I'd read for a while. But then . . . we started talking, and that's when *he* burst into the room, soaking wet and holding a huge knife in his hand.'

I glance over at Callan, and though he looks as if there are about a hundred different questions he wants to ask me, he sits down on the foot of the bed, exhales a rough breath, and simply says, 'Had he swum out to the boat?'

I nod as I say, 'I think so.'

He must sense that I'm not ready to go into greater detail, because he doesn't interrupt and ask me to elaborate when I go on. 'After . . . After Olly saved me, I was hysterical, but I thankfully managed to grab my purse, because it not only had the keys to our rental car in it, which we'd parked near the cove where we were anchored, but also the identity documents that Olly had given me. I held the purse above the water while I swam toward the shore, then ran like hell for the car and managed to get away.'

It'd all been so terrifying and unreal, I hadn't even shivered from my wet clothes when I'd climbed up onto the beach, despite the night being colder than usual, and looking back, I can't help but wonder if I'd been close to going into shock. I'd certainly been functioning on some kind of autopilot setting, my brain locked down by the sheer horror of what I'd seen and been through.

'I would have died a horrible death that night, if Olly hadn't protected me,' I quietly add, clenching my hands into fists and pressing them against my thighs. 'I have no idea why he did it, Callan, but it was the most selfless thing I've ever seen. It . . . defied logic.'

CALLAN

Lottie might not know why Oliver Beckett had done what he did, but I'm fairly certain that I do. That Olly had known, deep down, that he didn't deserve her. And maybe there'd also been a shred of decency in him that felt like shit for the way he'd treated her during the weekend of their wedding, even if their marriage had been more of a pact than a relationship. There must have been, or he wouldn't have done what he could to make sure she had a way to disappear if she ever needed to. And he sure as hell wouldn't have put himself between her and the murderous psycho screwing with her life.

And while I know she's left Everest-sized gaps in the story, I have faith that she's eventually going to tell me everything. After keeping it all bottled up inside for so long, it can't be easy for her to spill her guts to me now, and so I shove back my impatience and remind myself to be grateful that she's finally opening up and talking about what had happened at all.

'So that's my pathetic story,' she says, pulling me from my thoughts. 'I'd hoped that I would be able to come up with a plan to take the bastard down. Hoped that I could somehow beat him at his own twisted game –' another soft, bitter laugh falls from her lips, and she shakes her head with disgust – 'but it's been over a year now, and I'm still just this jittery, frightened loser who's accomplished nothing.'

'Bullshit,' I grunt, hating to hear her talk about herself that way. 'Christ, Lottie. Most people would have been completely destroyed by what happened to you. But here you are, working your ass off in this massive city, still fighting for survival. You're a goddamn miracle.'

'But I haven't achieved anything,' she argues. 'Not a single freaking thing.'

'You've kept going. You might not see how amazing that is, but I do.'

She laughs again, though this one is full of quiet embarrassment, while she stares at me with those stunning blue eyes, looking as if she can't quite figure out if I'm for real or not. Then her lips twitch with the briefest, saddest of smiles, and she throws my entire world off kilter when she says, 'You know, I had thought fate was being so cruel, bringing you to the wedding instead of your mum. Putting you in my path the way that it did, but only when it was too late. When I couldn't have you, even if you'd wanted me. And now . . .' She pulls in another deep breath, then slowly lets it out. 'Now you're somehow back in my life, but there are still so many bloody obstacles stacked between us, destroying everything.'

'You're no longer a married woman,' I point out, my low voice gritty with emotion, unable to believe she's just said those mind-blowing things to me.

'True,' she murmurs, and my chest gets tight when I see the fresh tears glistening on her long eyelashes. 'But I still have this nightmare hanging over my life, Callan. And I'd honestly rather have to deal with it alone, than risk you getting hurt because of me.'

'I won't,' I vow, wishing there was a way to make her believe it. To make her believe in *me*.

'You don't know that,' she counters with a heartbreaking hitch in her voice.

'Hey, have some faith, okay?' I walk over and crouch down in front of her, placing my hands over her small fists as I give her what I've often been told is my most charming, slightly crooked smile. 'Believe it or not, Miss Fleming, I can be every bit as badass as you are.'

For a moment, she just stares back at me with those

gut-wrenching, tear-drenched eyes that have a thousand different thoughts flickering through them. Then she actually smiles, just a little, but it's enough to make me feel as if I had *finally*, for the first time since I heard her laughing yesterday, found the right damn thing to say. 'Do you really believe that?' she asks me, the small note of hope in her voice impossible to miss. 'That I'm not weak?'

I give her hands a gentle squeeze, hoping she can see in my expression just how honest I'm being when I say, 'Why wouldn't I, when it's the truth?'

'It doesn't feel true. Not at all,' she whispers, and as she blinks away her tears, those beautiful blue eyes turn smoky with need. 'But it's one of the sweetest, hottest things anyone has ever said to me.'

From one breath to the next, lust fires through my body like an inferno, and I jerk away from her as I straighten back to my full height. 'Jesus Christ, Lot,' I croak, quickly loosening my tie and undoing the top button on my shirt, feeling like I'm burning with fever. 'Don't even think of looking at me like that right now.'

She tilts her head a bit to the side, and I swear there's another tiny twitch of her lips as she asks, 'Like what?'

'Like you want me inside you,' I growl, shoving both hands through my hair so hard that it hurts. 'Because it's what I want too, more than I thought was even possible. But I'm not fucking you in some unsecured hotel room when I still don't have any idea what scared you today.'

And just like that, the heat in her eyes is gone, and I watch the way her slender throat works as she swallows a few times, then quietly says, 'He was here. In Brooklyn.'

I freeze, not even breathing. 'Your stalker?'

'Yeah,' she chokes out, wetting her lips with a nervous flick of her tongue. 'I literally ran right into him after I was such an arse to you.'

I curse under my breath, so furious I could put my fist straight through the nearest wall. 'It can't be a coincidence that he was in your neighborhood. He knows where you live.'

'I know.' She licks her lips again, then pulls the bottom one through her teeth, looking more anxious than I've ever seen her. 'And I, um, think it's all my fault.'

'What? Why?'

'Because I did something stupid,' she tells me, and I can see her pulse speeding up at the delicate base of her throat, her breath quickening.

'I seriously doubt that,' I say as gently as I can, which isn't easy, given the anger that's simmering beneath my surface. But my rage is the last thing in the world that she needs right now, so I bury it down deep as I tell her, 'You're a lot of things, Lottie – some of them frustrating, most of them completely awesome – but stupid isn't one of them.'

'What I did was . . .' She looks so miserable, it's taking everything I've got not to walk to her and pull her into my arms. But I'm terrified that if I do, she'll stop talking, and I know this is something I need to hear if I'm going to be able to protect her. 'I . . . contacted my uncle.'

Since that was one of the last things I expected her to say, I frown with confusion. 'Why would that—?'

She cuts me off before I can even finish the question. 'Because my stalker . . . His name is Andrew, Callan. Andrew Christopher Fleming.'

Chapter Ten

CALLAN

'Your stalker is your goddamn cousin?' I bite out, slaughtering the words, unable to wrap my head around what I've just heard. 'The one you grew up with? Tall, blond guy who works as a profiler for Scotland Yard?'

Her brow creases with confusion, pink lips parted in shock, before she pulls herself together and asks, 'How do you even know that? Did you see him today?'

'No. But I interviewed him last summer, after you disappeared.'

She grips the arms of the chair, her spine so straight it looks like she's grown another inch in height. 'You didn't tell me that!'

'I told you that I talked to the people closest to you.' I turn and start pacing at the foot of the bed again, my thoughts spinning so quickly I'm surprised my damn head is still on straight. 'Christ, I had coffee with the son of a bitch, and he played me like a fool. When I asked him why he hadn't been at the wedding, he told me he'd been working a case and couldn't get away. Then the jackass actually got teary-eyed talking about the murder.'

'He's . . . sick. But most people find him incredibly charming. It's why he's managed to do so well at work. He's only twenty-nine, but everyone at Scotland Yard thinks he's a bloody genius and a saint.'

'I'm not pissed because I found him charming,' I mutter, shoving my hands through my hair again, 'and I sure as hell didn't think he was a genius. I'm pissed because I wrote the bastard off as kinda creepy, but harmless.'

'He's far from harmless, Callan. There was an article in *The Times* last year, after he helped solve a murder case, that claimed he has "an uncanny insight into the mind of a criminal". But that's only because he is one.'

As a trained professional, I know that losing my shit isn't going to help anyone, or make either one of us feel any better, so I force myself to stop pacing and pull in a deep breath. Then another. It takes a couple more, but eventually I'm able to sit back down on the foot of the bed, my elbows braced on my spread knees as I lean forward and lock my gaze with Lottie's. And while I'm desperate to know how this shit with Andrew began, I'm not about to put her through that *and* a retelling of what happened in Italy, so I'm forced to choose the story that's resulted in her being on the run not only from the law, but for her life, and shelve the other for when I've finally gotten her someplace where she can hopefully start to relax. 'I know it sucks, baby, but I need to know exactly what happened on that yacht.'

She gives me a small nod, and though I hate putting her through this, I can't help but admire her strength as she quietly says, 'Like I told you before, I had mentioned to Olly that I was feeling uneasy, but he . . . He hadn't thought we would need protection when we were so far away from England. So far away from Andrew.'

'So it was just the two of you the entire time you were on your honeymoon?'

'Yes.' She exhales a shaky breath, and it's only then that I realize how tense she's gotten, her knuckles white from how tightly she's gripping the arms of the chair. 'And to be honest, until he saw Andrew with the knife in his hand that night, I'm not sure Olly had truly understood just how crazy my cousin is. I mean, he definitely knew he was dangerous. But . . .'

'But he underestimated what he was capable of.'

'Yeah,' she agrees with a nod. 'When Andrew burst into the stateroom, he had the most terrifying smile on his face as he ran toward me with the knife. It was as if all the evil and madness that he'd hidden from others for so long had finally broken free. And Olly . . . Olly just threw himself between us, taking that first strike straight to his chest.'

'Jesus Christ,' I mutter, sickened not only by what had happened to Oliver, but also by the fact that she'd had to go through something so terrifying.

'But it . . . it didn't kill him,' she explains, a hollowness to her words that's as eerie as it is heartbreaking, as if living through something so horrible had somehow scraped out a part of her that she still hasn't managed to regain. That still hasn't managed to heal. 'He fought back, punching at Andrew, until Andrew cut him again. And I was . . . At first I was just frozen, unable to even move, but I came out of it and started looking around for something that I could fight back with. But then Andrew tackled Olly to the ground, and Olly looked over at me as Andrew stabbed the knife into his stomach, and he shouted at me to run.' She swipes at the tears that have started spilling over her pale cheeks again, her voice shaking as she says, 'And like a c-coward, I did. Even as Andrew was stabbing him to death, Olly kept shouting for me to r-run.'

I scrub my hands down my face, not sure how to process what I'm hearing. Emotions are crashing into me from all sides, and I take a moment to try to process it all. The rage. The gratitude. The shock. The reluctant admiration. I've spent so long pouring my dislike onto Oliver Beckett that I don't quite know how to accept the fact that he went out a goddamn hero. One who saved Lottie's life, even though he would have likely made it a living hell if they'd stayed married.

Eventually, I say, 'You did the right thing, Lot, because the bastard would have killed you, too. It's why you're still here today.'

'But I didn't even run away right,' she counters with a bitter laugh, that godawful wig she's still wearing moving over her shoulders as she shakes her head. 'I was too slow and had only just made it up onto the foredeck when he caught up with me. So I grabbed a wine bottle that Olly had left out and smashed it, holding the jagged top half in my hand like a weapon to keep Andrew from charging at me. But he wouldn't shut up. He just kept bragging about how brilliant he was at covering his tracks. Told me that I could run, but that my life was over. That everyone was going to believe I'd killed Olly, because the bloody knife in his gloved hand was from the galley on the yacht. The same one he knew I'd used to make us dinner that night. He'd found it in the dishwasher, which we'd forgotten to turn on.'

'That's why your fingerprints were all over the murder weapon,' I murmur, hating that the bastard had been so clever.

'And he said no one would ever even believe that he'd been there, because he'd hired some conman who looked like him to stay at his house and drive his car around the village he lives in in Oxfordshire, making sure the locals had seen him. He hadn't even traveled on his own passport, but had used a fake one.'

'That son of a bitch. That's why no one in England suspected a damn thing.'

'And given how everyone knew about Olly's sleeping around the weekend of our wedding, I could see exactly what Andrew threatened playing out. Could see how the police would view me as the scorned newlywed who lost it and finally took her anger out on the man who'd hurt her.'

'Which is exactly what they did,' I mutter with disgust.

'Even though I had the broken wine bottle in my hand, I knew it was only a matter of time before Andrew came at me, and that there was a good chance I was going to die. But Olly . . . God, I don't even know how he was still breathing, much less able to move, but he somehow made it up onto the deck. He looked like someone out of a horror movie, completely covered in blood, but he was carrying a hammer that he must have grabbed from the toolbox he kept in his closet. He aimed for the back of Andrew's head, but I could see that the blow wasn't delivered with enough force to kill him. Andrew staggered, though, and that's when I jumped overboard. I thought for sure he would be right behind me, but I managed to make it all the way to the rental car without any sign of him, so maybe Olly actually managed to knock him out for a while.'

'So Olly played the hero twice.'

'He did.' She licks her lips and exhales a trembling breath. 'But it was for nothing.'

'Not nothing. You're here now, Lottie. That's not fucking nothing.'

'But Andrew was right. He's had me trapped all this time.' She places her hands on her thighs again, rubbing them there in a nervous gesture that makes me want to pick her up and hold her on my lap. But I fight the impulse, not wanting to interrupt her as she keeps going. 'After I called emergency services and told them that Oliver was in desperate need of medical assistance and where to find the yacht – which ended up taking them forever, because Andrew had turned off the yacht's tracking signal and pulled in the anchor, so it'd just floated out to sea – I thought about the things he'd said the entire drive to the airport, and I couldn't see a way through that didn't end with him walking free and me going to jail. I mean, they freaking love him at his work. No one was going to believe that he could be capable of something so evil and psychotic.'

'Why would they?' I mutter, my jaw so tight I can feel a muscle pulsing under my skin. 'I'm guessing that jackass has been getting away with evil shit for a long time now.'

She gives another nod as she looks out the window again, catching her lower lip in her teeth, and while I'd planned to wait before asking her how the shit with Andrew had started, I find myself rubbing my jaw and saying, 'I need to ask you something, sweetheart. But I don't want you to think that I'm judging you . . . or blaming you.'

'You want to know why, if he'd been stalking and harassing me, I'd never turned him in to the police,' she says dully, still not looking at me, that weight seeming to crush her down again, until she looks painfully small sitting there in the chair, as if a strong gust of wind could just blow her away.

'Yeah.'

She takes a few deep breaths, then wraps her arms around her middle, her gaze still focused on the bright blue sky, the sunny day seeming shockingly incongruous to our grim conversation. 'As you probably learned last year, my parents were killed in a car accident just after I'd turned fourteen. So I went to live with my aunt and uncle, April and Liam Fleming, who are Andrew's parents. Liam and my dad were brothers.'

Since she pauses, I go ahead and tell her, 'I was introduced to them both at the wedding, and then later, I met them for coffee, like I mentioned last night. That was the day before I met with Andrew.'

'Right. So, um, the first couple of years, he . . . kept his distance. He was older and away at school, so he was never around that much anyway. It wasn't until I'd turned sixteen, and had suddenly started to look . . . more mature, that he tried to touch me. But I was lucky that day, because my aunt came home early, and he stopped as soon as he heard her car in the driveway. But when I . . . When I told him I was going to tell her what he'd done, he said that if I ever told anyone or went to the police, he would kill me.' She finally looks away from the window, bringing her tortured gaze back to mine, her voice barely more than a jagged shard of sound as she says, 'But before he "cut my throat from ear to ear", he said that my best friends would die first, in the same way. That he would go after anyone who was close to me. Anyone I cared about . . . and make them pay. And I believed him.'

As the horror of what she's told me sinks in, and understanding dawns, I work my jaw a few times, then have to swallow the knot of raw, blistering rage that's lodged in my throat before I can quietly say, 'That's why you pulled away from everyone.'

'I had to.'

'And you haven't allowed anyone to get close to you since.' I say it as a statement, not a question, but she answers anyway.

'How could I? I know he's watched me every step of the way. He's been an evil shadow hanging over my entire life, and it's only been by some kind of blind, stupid luck that I've always managed to get away. That he's never been able to follow through on his sick, twisted plans for me.'

'So what made you finally take a step toward . . . freedom?'

'That night that Olly and his friends just let themselves into the flat I shared with Sasha and the others, I have no doubt that Andrew would have raped me if they hadn't shown up. He'd surprised me when I came home from work, and even though I tried to fight him off, it only took him a few minutes to get me tied to my bed and gagged. I could see in his eyes exactly what he had planned, and I was trying to scream around the scarf he'd shoved in my mouth, and that's when Olly and the others got there. But they were out in the living room and couldn't hear me.'

'Shit, baby. I can't even imagine how terrifying that must have been.'

'It . . . It was like a nightmare,' she murmurs, looking as if she's trapped back on that horrific night, rather than here in the room with me, her blue gaze dark and unfocused as she stares at some distant spot on the gray carpet that covers the floor. 'Andrew hadn't shut my bedroom door fully, thinking everyone would be gone for hours, and by chance, Olly saw us when he walked down the hallway to use the bathroom. I didn't know him very well, but he'd always been an arse whenever he'd come around, and for a split second I was so scared he was going to just keep on walking and not give a shit. But he took one look at the terror on my face and started shouting at Andrew as he charged into the room, scaring him off.'

'So he saved you that night, too,' I rasp, trying to reconcile this version of Oliver Beckett with the one that Jase and I had known.

'He did. And after he untied me, he kicked his friends out and demanded to know what had been going on. When I refused to tell him, he threatened to call the police and report what had happened, so for the first time ever, I found myself opening up to another person about Andrew.' She blinks a few times, then brings her troubled gaze back to mine. 'Olly stayed until one of my roommates came home, then left, and I didn't see him again for five days. That's when he showed up at the restaurant after one of my shifts and asked if I would have a coffee with him to talk about something important, which turned out to be his crazy offer.'

'Crazy, yeah. But for the first time, you could see a way out,' I murmur, finally understanding why I'd had to watch her climb into Olly's Porsche and drive away from me at the end of that godawful weekend. Finally, for the first time since we'd met, able to wrap my head around why it'd been possible for her to look at me the way that she had, and still just leave me standing there on those steps, while she went off with another man.

'I could see what I'd *hoped* was a way out,' she says, suddenly reaching up and taking off the wig. 'And I realized that if I didn't take that step right then, then I probably never would. I would just live my life in constant fear, until the day Andrew eventually won.' For a moment, I think she's going to start ripping the wig into pieces, no doubt seeing it as a symbol of everything she's gone through this past year. But then she pulls in an unsteady breath and lays it on the table instead, her jaw tight as she looks back over at me. 'I was determined not to let that happen. So I did the most selfish thing a person could do, and I accepted Olly's offer, even though I knew it was wrong. That I was putting him in danger. But no matter what I said to him, he would always just tell me not to worry. And I tried to fool myself into thinking that maybe he was right, and it would all be okay, since he'd held up his end of the bargain while we were in England, hiring a personal security company to shadow both of us throughout the day. Plus, he'd had a high-tech alarm system installed at the flat we moved into just after we announced our engagement.'

'Which company did he use?' I ask, surprised that I hadn't uncovered any of this last year, when I'd gone back to England to investigate her disappearance.

'Masterson's.'

'They're good. Expensive, too.' And then, just because it's the truth, I add, 'But not as good as mine.'

As if she's found what I've said funny, she gives a soft chuckle that makes me smile. 'Wow. Ego much, Hathaway?'

'It's not ego, baby. It's fact. But I know Ian Masterson personally and he's a good guy. I think Olly must have paid extra to have everything kept completely confidential, but if I call Ian directly, I should be able to get him to send over any information they have. Do you know if Olly gave them Andrew's name?'

'I think so,' she replies with a nod. 'I'm pretty sure Olly had given them as much information as he could, though I never talked to them myself.'

'When I tailed you after you left the café yesterday, you kept looking over your shoulder, like you were worried someone was following you.'

'I've been feeling like . . . like I have this constant itch on the back of my neck,' she says with a rougher edge to her voice, her blue eyes shadowed as she reaches up and places her hand on her nape, under the fall of her hair. 'It's the same feeling that I would sometimes get back at home, which usually meant that Andrew was watching me. I had a similar feeling in Italy. And now here.' She lowers her hand, then nervously rubs her palms back over her thighs. 'It's, um, actually been going on for a couple of weeks now.'

'If you've managed to stay away from him for so long, how do you think he found you?'

She frowns, curling her hands back into fists. 'I told you, I messed up.'

'You said you contacted your uncle. Did you tell him where you were?' I ask, though I know damn well that she wouldn't have done anything that risky.

'Of course not,' she replies, her frown deepening.

'Then why do you think that led Andrew here?'

'Because it did.' She sighs, then starts to explain. 'I've been too paranoid to get another phone, even a burner one. And my laptop is just for my writing – it doesn't have internet access. But just over three weeks ago, on my birthday, I was feeling . . . low, and so I borrowed Eva's phone to check on how some of the people I'd known were doing back home. That's how I saw a post from one of my second cousins about my uncle. He'd . . . He'd had a heart attack.'

'Shit.'

'Naturally, I was worried and freaked out that I wasn't there, though I saw a second post that said he'd come home from the hospital.' She pulls in another deep breath, then slowly lets it out, her expression miserable as she says, 'But I still wrote to him.'

'You emailed him? From Eva's phone?'

'I did,' she groans, reaching up to tuck her hair behind her ear on the left side. 'I know it's stupid, but I logged into my old email account and sent him a brief message, just to tell him that I was sorry to hear he'd been so poorly and hoped he was feeling better. Then I immediately logged back out. I didn't even check my account again to see if he'd written me back. But Andrew is like a genius with technology, so he must be monitoring their accounts and somehow managed to trace my location.'

'Was that the first time that you'd contacted your uncle since Oliver was killed?'

'No. I sent him and my aunt a message from my phone in Italy, before I ditched it and got on the plane to LA.' She bites her lip again for a moment, her face seeming even paler as she says, 'I told them that something horrible had happened and that they probably wouldn't hear from me for a while. And then I . . . I actually warned them to be careful around Andrew.'

I frown at this bit of news, seeing as how her aunt and uncle never mentioned a single word about Lottie's communication to me. 'Did you tell them what he'd done?'

She shakes her head, looking sick with guilt. 'I know I should have, but I honestly didn't know how. I just . . . I couldn't find the words.'

'Christ, Lottie, don't feel bad about it. You were probably still in shock.'

'Maybe. All I know is that I got on that plane, cuddled up under a blanket, and didn't wake up until we'd landed at LAX.'

I rub my hand against the scruff on my jaw, my thoughts racing as I try to make sense of what I've learned. 'Why do you think your aunt and uncle didn't tell me any of this when I spoke with them? They knew I was trying to help you.'

With a soft, but unmistakable edge of bitterness in her voice, she says, 'My aunt has never liked me. I'm worried that she convinced my uncle I ran because I was guilty. And they dote on Andrew like he's the freaking messiah. To be honest, they probably didn't give my warning any credence at all.'

I'm too restless to keep sitting on my ass, so I stand up and start pacing again. It's a bad habit that I've had since I was a kid – one that's always driven my mom crazy – but that I've never been able to break.

'What are you thinking?' she asks, giving me a deep, searching look.

Maybe I should sugar-coat my response, but I've asked her for complete honesty and know she deserves the same. 'I'm thinking that I intend to find this asshole, get a confession out of him before ripping him to fucking pieces, and end this nightmare for you once and for all.'

Instead of cheering my plan on, she looks instantly terrified. 'You have no idea how dangerous that would be.'

'I do,' I reply with a grim smile. 'I just don't give a shit. I want this over and your name cleared, no matter the cost.'

'But we don't even know where he is,' she points out, sounding like she might be taking a small comfort from that fact. But I know it's only because she's petrified of the son of a bitch hurting someone else who's close to her.

'Not yet, but we will. I need to make a quick call to Deanna. You okay with me having her put a team on this, so that we can start compiling a full background check on him? I promise it won't go beyond Deanna and my employees.'

'All right,' she agrees, gifting me with a bit more of her trust, even though her fear is clearly still keeping her in a tight stranglehold.

She stays in the chair, listening while I make the call. Deanna must be able to pick up on the tension in my voice, because she doesn't waste time pressing me for details, even after I tell her to take Thompson and Robbins, two of our best employees, off their current assignments so that they can be sent up to the company safehouse in Hayford. She just assures me that everything will be taken care of and that she'll be in touch the second they have anything that might be of interest. I thank her and end the call, but keep the phone in my hand while I try to decide what mine and Lottie's next move should be. Or, more to the point, how we're going to get there.

'So now what?' she asks, obviously thinking about the same thing that I am.

'Now we get somewhere safe and hope Deanna comes back to us with a way to find this asshole.'

'And when we do find him?' she presses. 'What happens then?'

'Then I deal with him.' And even though it's neither the time nor the place – but because I'm completely crazy about this woman and desperately want to put a smile back on her gorgeous face – I tell her, 'And once it's over, I'm taking you back home with me, putting you in my bed and fucking your beautiful brains out, all night long.'

'Is that right?' she asks with a sudden burst of laughter, her blue eyes just a tad brighter as she covers her smiling lips with her hand. 'I have to say, that sounds like quite the celebration.'

'I plan on making an impact, you can count on that,' I drawl, having no doubt that the lust I feel for her – this ever-present, visceral, gut-clenching need – is written all over my face as clearly as a neon sign.

'Well, I'd be lying if I said I wasn't looking forward to it, so long as I get a chance to wreak havoc on your brains as well,' she murmurs, giving me a provocative look that damn near stops my heart. 'But are you really going to make me wait till then?'

'Lottie, I'm going to be lucky if I can control myself long enough for us to get out of this room. So no, baby, we're not waiting till I can get you in my own bed,' I reply with a low laugh, loving that she's not at all shy when it comes to our physical attraction. The emotional stuff might still scare the hell out of her, because I know she's afraid of being hurt. Afraid of reaching out for something, and then losing it. Having it ripped away from her in a way that's violent and raw and world-changing.

But when it comes to her body, she's made it clear that she's more than willing to entrust it to me – a fact that has me dangerously close to letting my cock start making the important decisions, which is never a good idea, seeing as how the bastard has a one-track mind.

'What's wrong with this room?' she asks, her blue eyes innocent and wide, but I just snort as I shake my head, aware that the little Brit is only teasing me.

'We know he's close and that he's been watching you, which means it's stupid for us to stay in the city,' I say, finally going with my gut and pulling up the number I need to call – even though it's going to land me in a ton of shit – as she moves to her feet. 'So use the bathroom if you need to, honey, because we've got one hell of a long drive ahead of us.'

Chapter Eleven

LOTTIE

It's cold as we step off the hotel elevator and onto the lower parking level – which, according to the sign on the wall, is meant to be for employees and hotel vehicles only. But this is where Callan has arranged for us to be picked up, since he didn't want me standing out on the sidewalk in front of the hotel in broad daylight. The smell of oil and exhaust fumes is strong, but I've smelled worse places in the city. It's the cold that has me frowning, my white shirt and jeans not doing much to keep me warm in this cavernous concrete box.

'You chilly?' Callan asks, when he notices me shiver.

'Freezing.'

'Here.' He sets my backpack on the ground between his expensive dress shoes, then slips out of the jacket he'd put back on before we'd left the room and offers it to me like a true gentleman. 'Wear this.'

'Are you sure?' I ask, as he picks the backpack up again and hooks it over one of his broad shoulders. 'I don't want you to be cold, too.'

He gives me one of those sexy, bone-melting smiles that has undoubtedly put some color back in my cheeks, my pale face a shocking sight when I'd looked in the hotel room's bathroom mirror while washing my hands. 'Honey, I'm roasting in this suit. So trust me, I'm sure.'

'Then thanks,' I tell him, gratefully taking the jacket, which smells nearly as good as Callan does as I slip it on. It's about ten sizes too big for me, but I'm afraid of ruining it if I roll up the sleeves, like I did with the hoodie. So I just carefully push the sleeves up until I can finally see my hands, then ask him if I can borrow his phone.

'Of course.' He pulls his black, top-of-the-line smartphone from his pocket and unlocks the screen for me, then hands it over.

'Thanks,' I say again, as I start punching in the number I need to call. 'I just realized I need to let the café know that I probably won't be in on Monday.'

He reaches over and touches my arm, his sexy smile replaced by a grim look of concern. 'Don't give them a return date.'

'As awesome as that sounds, I can't just quit work, Callan. I need the money.'

'No, you don't. And we're not going to argue about it.'

'We aren't?' I ask with a harsh laugh, my thumbs momentarily paused over the touch screen. 'Do you have any idea how—?'

'Think about it,' he cuts in, his deep voice rough with impatience. 'He probably knows that you work there, Lot. We don't have a fucking clue how long he's been watching you.'

I shudder in response, and he immediately frowns. 'Shit, I'm sorry,' he mutters. 'I hate making you feel uneasy. Hell, I hate that you even have to think about that sick shit at all. But there's no way I'm letting you step foot in that café again.'

'I understand what you're saying, Callan, and that it's coming from a good place. But . . . for now, I'm just going to tell them that I've had a family emergency and need a few days off. Whatever happens after that, I'm honestly too tired and too much of a mess right now to figure it out.'

He accepts my decision with a masculine jerk of his chin, though I can tell he isn't happy about it. But since he isn't a know-it-all, misogynistic jerk, he keeps his irritation to himself, and stays quiet while I call the café. One of my co-workers who I've gotten pretty friendly with since she started working at Lenore's a few months ago – a cool thirty-something named Ruby who's studying to be an actress, like so many others in this infamous city – answers the phone. She tells me that our manager, David, has gone to the bank, but promises to give my message to him as soon as he's back, along with an apology for the fact that I'm giving them such short notice.

After Ruby says that she hopes everything's okay, we say goodbye and I end the call. Just as I'm handing the phone back to Callan, it rings, and even though I'm standing right next to him as he answers it, I can't make out much of the conversation from his clipped remarks. All I know is that he's just learned something that has seriously pissed him off.

'What is it?' I ask, as soon as he thanks whoever he's been talking to, ends the call and slips the phone back into his pocket.

'That was Deanna. She's already made a few calls and just learned that Fleming took a leave of absence from Scotland Yard three weeks ago.'

'Right after I sent that email,' I groan, feeling like such an idiot.

'Don't do that. Don't let him make you feel bad for having a heart and worrying about people.'

'But if I'd—'

'If you'd what, Lottie? Just not given a shit about your family?'

'No. But—'

'Our ride is here,' he cuts in, his tone an unusual mix of frustration and relief. The frustration is probably because of me – the relief no doubt coming from the fact that we're finally getting out of here. I'm feeling a wave of relief as well, until I look over to the far side of the parking level and see a sleek, expensive-looking Mercedes in an amazing shade of gunmetal gray coming down the wide row that's two over from the one we're currently standing in, behind a long line of shiny SUV hybrids that are plugged into a bank of charging stations.

I'd thought Callan had called his car service again while I was freshening up in the bathroom, but now I'm not so sure. As nice as the SUV was that had driven us to his building last night, this car looks like it's someone's pride and joy, and there's an unmistakable note of wariness in my voice as I ask, 'Who's that?'

He reaches over and takes my hand in a firm hold, then sighs before he says, 'It's Seb.'

'The Interpol cop?' I reply with a wry laugh. 'Is that some kind of joke?' Because surely it is. But when I look away from the Mercedes, which is still too far away for me to make out the driver, to glance up at Callan, I immediately get a sick feeling in the pit of my stomach. 'Ohmygod. You didn't!'

'Trust me, it's going to be okay.'

'Are you freaking serious?' I growl, tugging my hand from his. 'I can't believe you thought the perfect person to call for help was your bloody cop friend and neighbor! Have you lost your mind?'

'We can argue about my sanity once we're on the road,' he mutters, curling one of his big hands around my upper arm and urging me forward.

'Or we can – *oomph!*'

One second I'm giving Callan hell, and in the next, I'm lying on the hard concrete, my knees and elbows scraped, completely winded. It takes me a moment to figure out what's happened, but then I hear what sounds like the thick, meaty sound of a fist connecting with flesh, and I roll over to see Callan and my cousin exchanging vicious blows like a couple of boxers.

'Callan!' I scream, scrambling back to my feet, but he's too focused on the arsehole in front of him to answer me.

'Stay down where I put you, Lottie,' Andrew sneers, and I realize he must be the reason I'd ended up on the ground. But unlike the last time this bastard went after someone in front of me, I'm not going to run and play the pathetic role of the coward. Instead, after pouring my grisly story out to Callan up in that hotel room, reliving all those remembered horrors, I'm filled with an explosive, volcanic rage over the fact that this psychopath has dared to attack us, my vision nothing but a pulsing sheen of red as I scream and practically launch myself onto Andrew's back, clawing at his neck and head like a wild woman. He curses and quickly throws me off, backhanding me across the face so hard that I'm sent spinning into one of the SUVs, and through the ringing in my ears, I hear Callan let out a bloodcurdling roar of fury. Then there's a nauseating crunch, and as I shove my hair out of my face with shaking hands, I see the wash of blood pouring from Andrew's nose.

'You don't fucking touch her. *Ever*,' Callan snarls, the molten burn of rage in his dark eyes telling me that he has every intention of ending Andrew's life, here and now.

'I'll do whatever the hell I want,' Andrew mutters, wiping the back of his wrist over his bloodied mouth. He's wearing a pair of sneakers, jeans and a white T-shirt, his blond hair longer than I've ever seen it, looking every bit like the consummate

American just out to enjoy the sunny day – but it's his eyes that give him away. Unlike Callan's angry gaze, Andrew's stare is strangely blank, as if he can no longer even compute emotion. He's just this human-looking shell for the disgusting evil that lives inside him, and as he charges Callan again, I'm torn between running to get Seb, so that he can help, and trying to do something myself. But I'm hopelessly untrained in this kind of thing, and as I look around, I can no longer even see the Mercedes. Seb must have parked somewhere on the other side of this stupid row of SUVs, and I can't believe he's so close, but has no idea about the danger his friend is in.

The only good news is that Callan is clearly the better fighter. And while I'd known, on some level, that he must have combat training, I'd never really thought about what that meant. But he *is* a highly trained bodyguard – one of the best in the world, I'd heard Jase say at the wedding – so I have no excuse for being surprised that he's kicking Andrew's arse. My cousin is a giant of a man, but Callan has at least an inch on him in height and is broader, too. And yet, his muscular body moves with a sleek, predatory power and grace, his movements naturally fluid, making Andrew look sluggishly clumsy each time he tries to land a punch. And like the heroic figure he is, I realize Callan is keeping his body placed between the two of us, ensuring that the psychotic killer doesn't get close to me again.

Unfortunately, Andrew must realize that he's outmatched, because he decides to resort to his weapon of choice, pulling a switchblade from his back pocket. As he flicks the knife open, he grins like the maniac he is, then lunges toward Callan with the blade held tight in his hand, slashing toward his chest, but thankfully misses.

'Taking her to your home was one thing, Hathaway. But did you really think I was just going to stand by and let you shag her like some cheap whore in a hotel room?' he sneers, spittle and blood spraying from his lips as he swipes at Callan again, nearly losing the knife when Callan delivers a punishing blow to his arm that makes Andrew cry out.

'The days where you have so much as an ounce of control over Lottie's life are over,' Callan tells him, his deep voice soft, but guttural. 'You're done, Fleming.'

My cousin smiles so wide I can see his blood-covered teeth, the animalistic look fitting him to perfection, since any humanity he ever had has been crushed beneath the vile, sadistic urges that have overtaken him. Or maybe he was always like this, and as the years have gone by, the thin veneer of civilization he'd managed to wrap around himself has simply been worn down, becoming thinner and thinner, until the cracks have started to show.

'I'm going to enjoy cutting you to pieces,' he pants, sounding winded, 'just like I did with the last one.'

Callan doesn't even bother to respond, the deadly look in his eyes when he gives me a swift glance making it clear that he has no interest in conversing with this bastard. He just wants to rid the world of him, once and for all.

He stays light on his feet, dipping and swaying to avoid the blade each time Andrew tries to cut him. But he isn't just a passive player in this nightmare. He's still making his own moves against my cousin, and landing nearly every punch, the sight of the blood that keeps gushing from Andrew's nose, running down over his chin, giving me a feral hit of joy.

'Lottie, get your ass to the car!' Callan shouts as they move closer to where I'm standing, but I shake my head. No way in hell am I scurrying off and leaving him, even though it's probably the most logical thing to do. I mean, it's not as if I'm offering any help here, and I hate how useless I feel, my hands clenching at my sides as the need to beat Andrew as badly as Callan is beating on him fires through my body like a fever.

'Lot—' Callan starts to growl, but his gruff voice is suddenly drowned out by the ear-piercing roar of an engine, and I look over to see Seb's Mercedes speeding straight for us. The guy clearly has some kind of insane specialized driver's training, because he puts the car into a controlled spin that nearly takes Andrew out with the back end.

'Get in!' Seb shouts through the lowered passenger-side window, and Callan rips one of the doors open, practically tossing me into the backseat. I expect him to climb in after me, but he doesn't, and I realize that he's looking around, trying to find Andrew, who has obviously decided he's outnumbered and made a run for it. Finally, Callan curses under his breath, grabs my backpack from the place on the ground where he'd dropped it after Andrew had launched his attack, and climbs into the back seat with me. The second he slams the door shut, Seb hits the gas, tearing down the row and up the parking structure's spiral ramp like he's Vin Diesel himself.

Glancing up at us in the rear-view mirror, he speaks in a smooth French accent as he says, 'I'd wondered what was taking so long for the two of you to reach the car, then got worried enough to drive around for a look.'

'I appreciate it,' Callan grunts, and we both have to reach up to hold on to the roll handles when Seb steers the Mercedes out of the building and onto the road. 'Even though you scared the asshole off.'

'If you don't like the way this turned out,' Seb drawls dryly, 'then next time, my friend, kill him faster.'

'I plan on it. In fact, the next time I get my hands on him, I'm ripping his fucking head off.' His low voice is cut with a deadly rage, and I have no doubt that he means every word.

'How d-did he even know we were there?' I stammer, then clench my jaw to keep my teeth from chattering, my pulse still hammering in my ears like a frantic drumbeat that's giving me one hell of a headache. Though after I reach up to touch my pounding temple and my fingertips come away bloody, I realize the source could also be from the fact that I'd smacked my head against the SUV after Andrew had hit me.

'He could have been following us,' Callan mutters in response to my question, his own brow creased with a scowl. 'I didn't know you'd seen him, so I wasn't exactly trying to blend in when I flagged down that taxi. He could have grabbed one right behind us.'

'I guess, but it seems unlikely. When I literally ran into him on the street, someone noticed how terrified I was and confronted him. As I ran away, I think a fight actually broke out. So I'm not sure he could have caught up with me in time to follow us.'

'Shit,' he grunts. 'You said he's some kind of tech genius, right?'

I give a shaky nod.

'Then there's also a chance that he could have hacked into the tracking . . .' His voice trails off, and instead of finishing his sentence, he suddenly grabs for my backpack, which he'd placed on the seat between us, feeling along the seams. When he gets to the top of the pack, where the hanging loop is, he curses and grips either side of the seam, yanking until it rips apart, and I gasp as a small silver disc falls out onto the seat.

'Is that one of yours?' I ask, even though I have a horrible feeling that it's not.

'No,' he grates. 'I put mine in the bottom, under the padding.'

'Ohmygod. How did he . . .? How in the hell did he get that thing in my backpack?' I half-gasp, half-cry, my breaths jerking in my chest as the reality of what this means starts racing through my head.

'Give me your shoes.'

I don't even ask him why, too nauseous to open my mouth as I reach down and quickly undo my laces. When I hand the shoes over to him, he begins inspecting them, and finds another silver disc hidden between the rubber sole and heel of my left shoe, then turns to me and tells me to take off his jacket. As soon as I'm done, he places his hands on either side of my throat. I'm about to ask him what he's doing, when he starts running his hands down over my torso, and I realize he's checking to make sure my clothes weren't tagged as well. When he's done with my shirt and jeans, he makes me turn so that my back is to him and he lifts my top, checking where my strapless bra clasps together. Then he lowers the shirt for me, and as I turn to face him again, I see that he's already unzipped the top of my backpack and is carefully inspecting everything inside, as well.

'Okay, I think we're clear,' he mutters, zipping the pack back up.

'He . . . h-how?' By this point, I'm shaking so hard that I can barely speak, so that's all I can get out as I watch Callan lower the back passenger-side window and toss the two tracking dots out. But when he looks back over at me, I can tell from the grim expression on his face that he knows exactly what I'm asking.

'If it was just your backpack, I'd say he probably snuck into the café one busy afternoon and tagged it then, without anyone noticing. But your shoes . . . That's a different story, honey.'

'Oh God,' I whisper, realizing the most likely answer is that Andrew had broken into my apartment at some point and tagged them then. And since they're basically the only pair of shoes I ever wear these days, it was probably while I was at home, either sleeping or taking a shower!

I shudder with revulsion and rub my arms, since my skin is crawling. As if he knows just how badly I need to feel safe right now, Callan pulls me onto his lap, tucks my head under his chin, and holds me as if he means to never let me go. 'I'm so sorry, baby,' he murmurs, pressing his lips against the top of my head in a kiss that's pure, sweet comfort. 'But we're going to fix this. I swear to you, that bastard's not getting anywhere near you again.'

'I second this vow,' Seb says from the driver's seat, still expertly maneuvering the beautiful car through the ever-present New York traffic. 'And while I have about a million questions, my friend, for the moment, they can wait. Just tell me if the plan is still the same.'

'You don't mind driving us?' Callan asks, catching Seb's gaze in the rear-view mirror.

The Frenchman lifts his broad shoulders in a laid-back shrug. 'You're in need, so I am here.'

'Then the plan's the same. We're taking her up to the safe-house in Hayford.'

'Good choice, given that you seem to have a psychotic ass-hole after you.'

'Man, you have no idea,' Callan mutters. 'But I'll fill you in once we're out of the city.'

'In the meantime, perhaps an introduction, no?'

'Lottie, this is Sebastian Cassel, a pain-in-the-ass-at-times but good friend of mine, who I seriously owe for helping us out today. Seb, this is Lottie Fleming.'

I watch in the rear-view mirror as Seb's dark brows lift with surprise. 'The Lottie Fleming?'

'One and the same,' Callan replies, the arm that's wrapped around my waist tugging me just that little bit closer to him, as if he's afraid I'm going to bolt now that Seb has made it clear he's heard of me. Which means there's also a chance that he knows I'm wanted for murder, and he's a freaking *cop*. But seeing as how he isn't arguing that I should be taken straight to the local police station, I decide not to panic, my poor system having already been through enough stress for one day.

'I have heard of you, *ma chérie*,' Seb drawls, catching my gaze for a moment in the mirror, before safely focusing back on the road. 'And let me just say, while I'd thought he was surely exaggerating, you're even more beautiful than Callan claimed.'

'Um, thank you,' I murmur, taking a moment, now that my heart is no longer beating like it's trying to burst its way out of my chest, to take in the striking attractiveness that is Seb Cassel. His dark hair is cut stylishly short, his cinnamon-brown eyes a riveting contrast to his mocha-colored skin, and while it's difficult to gauge when he's sitting down, I have a feeling he's just as tall and muscular as Callan, though his facial features are a bit more classically handsome compared to Callan's rugged good looks.

'You know,' I say, turning my head to look Callan in the eye, 'your mum definitely wasn't lying about him being hot.'

Seb gives a low laugh up in the front seat, while Callan just shakes his head and mutters, 'He isn't *that* good-looking.' Then he arches an eyebrow at me. 'And I thought you were pissed that I'd called him.'

I arch an eyebrow right back. 'Just because I don't particularly want your cop friend anywhere close to me doesn't mean I can't appreciate the view.'

For a moment, he just studies my face, his dark-chocolate gaze moving from feature to feature, until he finally looks into my eyes again. 'Where did my shy Lottie go?' he quietly asks, reaching up to gently brush away the blood on my brow with the pad of his thumb.

'She died on a boat back in Italy,' I deadpan, making him flinch, which immediately makes me feel like a jerk.

'The hell she did,' he argues in a tone that's soft, but gruff. 'And before you start spinning this around in your head, I don't give a shit if you're shy or outspoken. I like you just the way you are, tender and rough edges alike.'

I pull in an unsteady breath, stunned by how easily this magnificent man can get to me, and am trying to figure out what the hell to say back to him, when he takes mercy on me and tells me he needs to make another call. Though he complains about losing me on his lap, I'm calm enough that I can sit on my own now without breaking down, and as I tell him to put his seatbelt on while I clip my own belt into place, he gives me one of his sexy, lopsided smiles and does as he's been told. Then he lifts his hips so that he can pull his phone from his pocket, and makes his call, which is to Deanna, and I'm relieved as I listen to him tell her that he wants security details put on everyone in his family. It's a cautious but smart move, given that Andrew made a vicious assault on his life today . . . and could probably track down the members of Callan's family with relative ease. He also asks her to have someone check the CCTV footage from the Fairfax, which is another smart move, since it would be visual proof that Andrew had violently attacked us.

Eventually, we hit so much traffic that not even Seb can weave his way through, and it feels like hours have passed before we're finally surrounded by trees and no longer driving through the streets of a concrete jungle.

As if he's read my thoughts, Seb speaks up again from the front seat. 'Okay, my friend. We are no longer in the city.'

Callan has been staring out his side window for the past half hour, seeming lost in his thoughts, but at Seb's words, he turns his head and looks at me. 'You can trust him, Lot. I promise.'

'You *promise*?' I echo with a sarcastic laugh, feeling too many raw emotions again now that I've been put on the spot. Because while I might be comfortable getting a ride in Seb Cassel's luxurious car to wherever it is we're headed, that doesn't mean I'm ready to open a vein for the guy and spill my deepest, darkest secrets. 'To be honest, Callan, I'm not even sure that I trust *you* right now,' I mutter, giving him my best glare. 'Not after this stunt.'

Seb whistles under his breath, clearly enjoying the hard time that I'm giving his friend, which endears him to me a bit. But I'm still wary of everything he represents, given that I've been living in fear of an unjust arrest for more than a year now. Call me touchy, but that kind of thing can really wear a girl down.

'Look, baby, I know you're scared,' Callan murmurs, reaching over and taking my hand in his bigger, stronger and slightly battered one, the calluses that roughen his palm making me shiver with sensual awareness despite my pissy mood. 'But you don't need to be. Not about this. Seb is a good guy.'

'He's a freaking cop!' I snap, sounding embarrassingly belligerent. 'A hot one, yeah. But still a cop.'

'He's my *friend*.'

'That doesn't mean anything, and you know it,' I argue, thinking that Andrew is my cousin, related to me by blood, and he *still* wants to do horrific things to me . . . and then watch me die.

'It means something to *me*,' he counters, his deep voice firm with conviction. 'And to him, too. Right, Seb?'

'Let me put it this way, *ma chérie*. If you two kill someone and need help burying the body,' Seb drawls in his provocative accent, 'I trust Callan enough not to ask what happened. I will only assure him that I am exceptionally good with a shovel.'

'Yeah, well, I didn't get to kill anyone today,' Callan complains, sliding Seb a disgruntled look, 'because *you* scared the bastard off.'

'And helped save the beautiful Lottie,' Seb murmurs, tilting his head in a regal nod, 'so you're welcome.'

Callan's lips twitch with a smile. 'Yeah, all right,' he concedes. 'I owe you for that one.'

'You owe me *many*, but who's counting?' Seb quips.

'You, apparently,' I remark dryly, which makes him laugh.

'I just like giving him a hard time,' Seb explains. 'But the truth is that I trust Callan implicitly, which means that you can trust *me* to be respectful of his judgment.'

Figuring I might as well cut right to the heart of the matter, I say, 'Even if that means helping someone who's wanted for murder?'

'You're *innocent*,' Callan growls before Seb can even respond, giving my hand a gentle, but firm squeeze.

'He doesn't know that!'

'*He* doesn't really know much of anything at the moment,' Seb points out, 'except that Callan has been worried sick about you for the past year, and that the deranged bastard back there was trying to kill you. So why don't the two of you finally bring me up to speed?' He catches my gaze in the rear-view mirror once again, and in a low voice that sounds like he's making me a vow, he tells me, 'On my mother's grave, Lottie, I give you my word that I'm not going to do anything to hurt you, or to threaten your freedom.'

After that, there's really nothing else for me to do but give in with a sigh. 'Okay. All right. I'll trust you.'

'See, Lot?' Callan murmurs, giving me a smug look that

kind of makes me want to kick him in the shin like a bratty schoolgirl. 'I told you everything was going to be okay.'

'I have a psychotic stalker after me, Callan. What the hell about my life seems okay?'

Lacing his fingers with mine, he lifts my hand to his mouth and presses a soft kiss to my knuckles. 'The fact that you're not alone anymore,' he replies. 'That you've got people in your corner now.'

'People he can hurt to hurt *me* even more than he already has,' I say shakily. 'How is that a good thing?'

The edge of his mouth kicks up with a crooked, ridiculously sexy smile, the look in his eyes so warm I actually feel a bit flushed. 'Have a little faith, sweetheart. And I'll keep saying it as many times as I need to, because it really is going to be okay.'

'Listen to him, Lottie. He knows what he's talking about.'

Sounding far more tired now than I do angry, I ask, 'And how exactly would you know, Cassel?'

He flashes me a sharp smile in the mirror, and there's something behind the determined expression on his handsome face that makes me damn happy he's on *our* side, and not against us. 'Because like Callan just said, Lottie, you have people in your corner now. And whoever that shithead was back there at the Fairfax, his days of endangering you are over.'

Chapter Twelve

CALLAN

The sprawling modern safehouse in upstate New York is eerily quiet as I lock the front door behind us. Lottie had barely said anything when I'd introduced her just now to Trey Robbins and Danny Thompson – the two security experts I'd had placed here when I'd first spoken to Deanna today, who've worked for my company since the beginning and who I trust implicitly. She's still silent now that we've come inside and it's just the two of us, and doesn't even look around with her normally curious gaze, her slender body frozen in place in the slate-tiled entryway, her clothes filthy from where Andrew had tackled her to the ground. She just stands there and watches me with those tired blue eyes, her pale face smeared with blood from the small cut near her brow that's reopened since I last cleaned it for her, when we'd stopped for food. The sight of her injury makes me want to tear something apart with my bare hands, but I choke back the impulse, knowing that the last thing she needs right now is my anger.

What she needs is comfort. And while that's not been my

strongpoint for a long time, I'm determined to find a way to take care of her, giving her everything she deserves.

'Come on, baby,' I murmur, taking her cold, delicate hand in mine. 'Let's get you into a hot shower, fill your belly with some food if you're up for it, and put you to bed.'

She follows silently behind me as I navigate my way through the shadowed house by memory, our footsteps echoing through its empty rooms. We're high enough up in the hills that we're surrounded by woodland, and an early evening storm is raging outside, darkening the sky, so it feels later than it is. But the long-ass drive has worn us out, and I wish that Seb had been able to take me up on my offer of a hot meal and a cup of coffee, as well as a room to stay in for the night. He has an early meeting in the morning, though, so he left immediately after dropping us off, since he still has a long drive back to the city ahead of him.

I lead Lottie directly back to the master bathroom, set her backpack on the counter, and start the shower for her, wanting it to be hot by the time she climbs in. And even though I want to fall all over her now that it's finally just the two of us again, and we're someplace safe, I give her space, telling her where to find clean clothes when she's finished with her shower, then close the bathroom door behind me.

There's another full-sized bathroom off the hallway, so I grab a towel and head there. As I strip out of my blood-spattered shirt and trousers and set my phone on the counter, I think back to the worried call that Lottie had made to her friend Eva, after she'd shared her horrific story with Seb. When he'd posed the question of how easy we thought it would have been for Andrew to gain access to her building, Lottie had panicked and asked if she could borrow my phone so that she could call Eva and warn her to contact the police if she saw anyone hanging around who matched Andrew's description. When her friend had pressed her for details about what was going on, asking if she was in any trouble, Lottie had said she was sorry but that she had to go and disconnected the call, the guilt on her face as she'd handed the phone back to me something that I hope she never has to feel again.

We'd stopped for lunch around twenty minutes later, and though she'd claimed she wasn't hungry, Seb and I were able to convince her to eat a cheeseburger and some fries, explaining that it would help with the adrenaline crash. The weather had still been good at that point, so we'd set our bags of food on the hood of the Mercedes and stretched our legs while we ate. When we were ready to get back on the road, Lottie had argued that I should sit up front, so that my long legs wouldn't be cramped in the backseat. And while I'd wanted to climb into the back with her again anyway, just so that I could stay close to her, I'd figured that maybe she wanted some time to herself, so I'd done as she suggested and sat up front with Seb.

Lottie had dozed off not long after, and I'd taken a moment to send a text off to my mom, letting her know that we were okay. I'd also asked her to make sure that the family didn't blow my phone up with messages once their new security details showed up, seeing as how there was nothing that I could tell them at this point, and promised to be in touch again soon. Then I'd messaged Jase to give him an update, since he'd texted me while we were eating, and after that, Seb and I spent the next hour discussing his latest case. It's a grim one, involving tracking down a doctor who Interpol believes is performing illegal organ transplants with hearts and livers purchased on the black market, and I could tell by the sound of Seb's voice that the case has been taking its toll on him. Then Deanna had called again, and it had only been more bad news.

I'd hoped we might be able to get our hands on the CCTV footage from the Fairfax, thinking it could be used to argue Andrew's guilt and Lottie's innocence, since he'd perpetrated a violent attack on us. But their security staff had contacted Deanna with the message that the cameras had been disabled on that level of the parking structure, which was undoubtedly Andrew's doing. And the traces our team of tech experts had run on his electronic devices had each led back to Oxfordshire, meaning the prick had left them all at home. If he has a phone now, it's a burner one. There also haven't been any financial transactions linked to his name here in the States, so he's either traveling around on a fake identity again or using cash. Either way, we're no closer to having a way to find him, which means Lottie and I definitely made the right move in getting out of the city.

And I'd be lying if I said I didn't believe the fact that Andrew had taken a leave of absence this time, rather than pulling the body-double stunt like he had when he tracked Lottie and Oliver down in Italy, means he's in no rush to bring this shit to an end. No, I think the sick bastard has been getting off on taking his time, watching her squirm whenever she's been out in public, and God only knows how many times he might have broken into her place while she was at home – a thought that will no doubt give me more than a few sleepless nights in the days to come.

Starting my own shower, I wait until it's steaming hot and then climb in, the strong water pressure feeling great on the sore muscles across my neck and shoulders. Since I don't know how long Lottie will be, I hurry with the shampoo and body wash, then climb out and head into one of the other bedrooms to grab some clean clothes.

Given that we never know what circumstances we'll have to use the safehouse for, we keep it stocked with both male and female clothing, in an assortment of sizes, in all the rooms.

When I run into Lottie in the hallway, I see that she's chosen a slouchy gray shirt and a comfortable-looking pair of black leggings, while I'm in another pair of black pajama pants and a white T-shirt. Then again, the clothes might be her own, since I know she had a few clean things in her backpack, and either way, she looks beautiful. Her damp hair is brushed back from her face, her peaches-and-cream skin scrubbed clean of makeup, and there's a slight bruise coming up above her right eye, but I swear I've never seen her look more lovely.

She also appears rejuvenated enough to eat before heading to bed, so we talk about the house as we make our way into the spacious, high-ceilinged kitchen, with its charcoal-colored cupboards, cream marble countertops and stainless-steel appliances. Either Robbins or Thompson have thankfully made a run to the store, the fridge and pantry already stocked with a variety of foods, and I find some hearty chicken soup that I heat up for us, along with some fresh-baked rolls.

We sit at the breakfast bar in the kitchen while we eat, and I put a local news channel on the TV that hangs on one of the kitchen walls. Despite the dramatic events of the day, our conversation is natural and easy, each of us asking the other's opinion on a particular news story or engaging in good-natured debate if we happen to disagree on a political issue. I'm loving getting a sharper insight into the way her keen mind works, but it doesn't take long for us to finish the meal, and Lottie cleans the counters while I load up the dishwasher. Then we finally head back to the master bedroom, without even having to discuss the sleeping arrangements, and crawl into bed together.

And while I'd doubted I would be able to sleep, given how I've wanted to get this woman into bed with me since first setting eyes on her over a year ago, once we're lying under the covers and she cuddles up against my chest with a soft sigh, sounding as if she feels safe for the first time in forever, I find myself simply wrapping her up in my arms and crashing right along with her.

The next time I open my eyes, it's still dark out, and I'm confused by the sound of someone playing the piano, seeing as how I'd just been dreaming about the night of Lottie and Oliver's wedding, when I'd found her down in the Becketts' music room, playing their priceless Steinway. I'm no music scholar, but I'd recognized her talent, the melancholy piece she'd been playing one that had moved through me like an emotion.

It's the same piece that she's playing now, out on the baby grand that sits before the massive bay window in the living room.

As I throw my legs over the side of the bed and shove my hair back from my face, I recall how Lottie had nearly bolted when I'd come into the music room that night in the Becketts' mansion, mortified that she'd woken someone up with her playing. But I'd assured her that I simply hadn't been able to sleep, so had decided to come downstairs for a whiskey, and at my urging, she'd finished the piece.

The cavernous room had been filled with shadows, the only light coming from an antique lamp in a far corner, the golden hue painting Lottie in an ethereal glow. She'd looked so beautiful she hadn't seemed real, and I'd felt like I'd stumbled upon a magical creature that wasn't meant for this world . . . or for me.

But I hadn't cared if it was right or wrong.

I'd simply wanted her to be mine.

LOTTIE

As my fingers move over the ivory keys, my mind keeps drifting back to my wedding day. But not the jaw-clenching hours that I'd had to spend by Olly's side. No, I keep remembering that night, when I'd been playing in the Becketts' music room . . . and Callan had stumbled across me on his way to find a drink.

I'd been introduced to him two days before, and had blushed like a freaking schoolgirl when he'd shaken my hand and given me one of his deliciously wicked, crooked smiles, thinking he was the most gorgeous thing I'd ever set eyes on. We'd spent the next two days at a variety of wedding events, never really speaking much – but whenever I'd glanced in his direction, I'd found him watching me with those dark, beautiful eyes.

Each time.

Every time.

Surprisingly, though – given my past – his attention had never made me feel uneasy, probably because I'd been watching him just as intently. Just as hungrily . . . and with more greed than I'd ever thought I was capable of.

No, the only thing that had bothered me about Callan's gaze that weekend was that behind the smoldering need, there'd been a constant question: *Why are you doing this, when you so obviously know it's a mistake?*

That night, when I'd finished the piece I'd been playing, we'd started to talk, and I can't even recall exactly what we'd said to each other. But the words hadn't been important. What mattered was the way it had *felt* to be alone with him, as if every inch of my skin had been charged, my body more alive than it'd ever been before.

It was like he'd flipped a switch with his presence, and I'd suddenly been turned on. Awakened. Somehow even . . . *connected*. To him. To this beautiful stranger who I barely knew.

And since I didn't have any idea how to handle it, considering the state of my life, I'd simply run. Just like the frightened bunny Andrew had always accused me of being.

As I finish the last notes of the piece, I pour every ounce of the anguish I'd felt that night into my playing, finally letting it go, since there's no sense in carrying it around with me anymore. I'm a different person, in a different world, and whatever it takes, I'm determined to stand my ground.

No more running.

And no more being too scared to take what I want . . . or to admit what that even is in the first place. Because if I don't do it now, when the hell will I? The answer is *never* – and I refuse to just roll over and let that happen. I bloody refuse to give Andrew that kind of power over my life, when he's already controlled so much of it, for far too long.

'Callan!' I gasp, startled to find him leaning against the archway into the living room as I swivel to the side on the piano stool, getting ready to stand. I have no idea how long he's just been standing there with his muscular arms crossed over his bare chest, the soft glow of light from the single lamp I'd turned on glinting against his tousled bronze hair and the stubble that will soon be a short beard on his rugged jaw.

'Nice hoodie,' he murmurs as his heavy-lidded gaze moves over me, and I can feel the heat that crawls into my face over the fact that he's caught me wearing the Oxford sweatshirt I'd taken with me when I'd snuck out of his apartment this morning, my cheeks burning like they do when I've sat for too long out in the sun.

'Oh, um . . . I—'

'It's okay, little thief,' he drawls with a quiet laugh, looking happier than I've ever seen him, an unmistakable flicker of satisfaction in his eyes. 'I'm glad you took it with you.'

'God,' I groan, covering my face with my hands as I lower my head. I know he must have seen the hoodie when he was check-ing my backpack for more of Andrew's tracking devices, though he hadn't called me out on it. But then, that had hardly been the time for teasing – unlike now. 'This is so embarrassing.'

Taking mercy on me, he changes the subject. 'I know I told you this before, the last time I found you sitting at a piano in the middle of the night, but you play beautifully, Lottie.'

'Thank you.' I lower my hands as I lift my head and look at him, smiling as I say, 'I actually can't remember a time when I didn't know how. My mum started teaching me when I was only four.'

'Yeah?' He moves away from the archway, pushing his hands into his pockets as he walks over to me, and I can feel his excitement – *and relief* – over the fact that I'm finally sharing something with him about my life. Something that's important to me, and that has nothing to do with Andrew and the pain he's caused. 'She must have been a talented musician.'

'She was amazing. At music, and pretty much everything else,' I say thickly, tilting my head back so that I can hold his gaze as he comes to a stop only a few feet away from where I'm still sitting. 'But I'm sorry that I woke you with my playing. I guess I wasn't thinking about how loud it would be.'

A bronze lock of hair falls over his brow as he gives a brief shake of his head, murmuring, 'Don't be. I'd much rather be out here with you, than in that bed alone.' He comes even closer, until he's standing right in front of me. So close that the warm, masculine scent of him fills my head with each breath that I take, so delicious it makes my mouth water, while my pulse kicks up like a storm, whooshing in my ears.

'That bastard got you good,' he mutters, gently touching the skin around the small cut by my right eyebrow, which thank-fully hadn't needed stitches, but had accounted for most of the blood that had been on my face before I'd showered. And I was already starting to develop one hell of a bruise. 'He's a good fighter. Good enough that I still can't quite understand how you were able to get away from him on that yacht.'

'I had Olly's help, obviously,' I say so softly, it's almost a whisper. 'And . . . I had good motivation. To, um . . . survive.'

'Yeah?' His dark eyes burn with curiosity as he locks his heavy gaze with mine, his thick, curling eyelashes no doubt the envy of every woman he meets. 'What was it?'

'I . . .' My voice trails off, and I can feel the heat pulsing in my cheeks as I try to find the courage to give him the truth.

'Come on, Lot,' he urges, searching my eyes for the answer, as if he knows it's going to be a changing point for us. One that I won't be able to come back from, after I've taken the leap. 'Tell me.'

'I think it was because I wanted *this*,' I somehow force out, as I wrap my arms around my middle, needing them to hold me together in this critical moment of vulnerability. 'I wanted the chance to see you again one day.'

His brown eyes flash with a torrent of raw emotion as he sucks in a sharp breath, and I feel myself sinking into the confession – into the need and the want and the blistering hunger that burns between us. The visceral, poignant, beautiful hunger that I no longer feel driven to fight against. I'm so tired of battling against everything that could make me happy, for the fear that it will all be ripped away from me. But now that Callan Hathaway is standing so close I could reach out and touch him, staring down at me like he wants to eat me alive, it's as if I've somehow been granted a freedom that I've never had, and I just want to dive right into him. I want to drown in what he makes me feel, and enjoy every exquisite second of it, without a single moment of doubt or hesitation.

Wetting my lips, I pull in a deep breath, then slowly let it out as I say, 'I wanted the chance to be with you, Callan. I just wanted to be with you.'

He makes this guttural, primitive sound that reminds me of the way he sounded when I first touched my tongue to him this morning, the things we'd done to each other on his living-room floor feeling like they happened a thousand years ago. Then I'm suddenly in his arms, cradled against that mouthwatering chest, and he carries me over to the sofa that's placed against the wall, sitting down in the middle of it as he settles me on his lap.

'I wish you'd come to me, instead of hiding all this time,' he scrapes out, his dark eyes molten with desire as he places a warm hand against the side of my throat, the callused pad of his thumb stroking so softly against the corner of my mouth, I can't help but remember what it had felt like between my legs. 'You should have come to me, Lottie. You should have flown straight to New York and fucking come to me.'

A startled laugh jerks from my chest, catching us both by surprise, and I reach up to clasp his shoulder, terrified he's going to pull away from me as I quietly say, 'I might have had a huge crush on you, Callan, but I didn't know you well enough to just show up on your doorstep, begging for help. I mean . . . I barely even know you now.'

His eyebrows knit with a frown, and there's a guttural edge to his deep voice as he argues, 'That's bullshit, Lot. You know you can trust me, and that's the most important thing.'

'You're right, I do trust you,' I tell him, smiling again. 'But doesn't it bother you that there's still so much we don't know about each other?'

'Then let's fix that,' he murmurs, the sudden gentleness of his voice at complete odds with the fierce determination in his narrowed gaze. 'What do you want to know, baby?'

'Anything,' I say with another laugh. '*Everything.*'

'Everything, huh?' The edge of his mouth kicks up with another one of those sexy, crooked half-smiles that I'm already becoming addicted to, and he places his big hand over the top of my thigh, his palm so hot I can feel its heat through my leggings. 'Okay, let's start with the basics. You've met my crazy mom and Clara, but I have an older brother named Colin and an older sister named Chloe, who's the designer. Then there's Cade, who gave me the tattoo on my shoulder and is just a year older than Clara. And the youngest are the twins, Coco and Connor, who are both in their last year at university. I also love a good action movie and the Foo Fighters, but have been known to listen to a country song or two. And I never missed an episode of *The Sopranos* or *Breaking Bad.*'

'What about *Game of Thrones*?' I ask, and since my arms are now looped around his powerful shoulders, I reach up and play with the ends of his hair that are curling at his nape.

'What about it?' he replies, cocking his head a bit to the side as he holds my stare.

'Did you watch it? Because having an extensive knowledge of *GoT* is kind of a dealbreaker for me,' I inform him with a teasing smirk.

'Not yet, but I'll get right on it,' he claims with a low, rumbling laugh, his dark eyes shining with humor. 'What about you?'

'Hmm. Well, you already know my family situation, so we won't go down that road. But as for the rest, I'm a huge fan of a good thriller or romcom, and I never let a Christmas go by without watching *Die Hard* at least a dozen times. I also love Florence and the Machine and Tori Amos, and Fleetwood Mac and Elton John are always on my playlists. And when it comes to TV, in addition to *Game of Thrones*, I'll pick *Parks and Rec* or *Stranger Things* every time.'

'All solid choices, honey.'

'Yours, too,' I murmur, hyperaware of the way his big hand is stroking its way up to my hip. And there's no missing the massive ridge that my other hip is pressed up tight against, the proof of just how badly this magnificent male wants me, making me want to rub all over him like a cat in heat. But I pull in a deep breath and do a good job of controlling myself, since I'm curious about a thousand different other things, from what books he likes to read to his favorite foods – until he completely shatters my self-restraint with the touch of his big hand sliding into the top of my leggings.

'You really do know me, Lottie. You know how hard you make me. What I taste like. How I reacted the first time I ever set eyes on you.' His hand pushes into my panties, his long fingers sliding across my already slick flesh, and I give a shocked, breathless cry when he suddenly strokes my entrance, then pushes two of those big, hot fingers inside me. 'You know what it feels like to have my fingers buried deep inside your tight little body,' he groans, leaning over and gently nipping the trembling edge of my jaw, 'while you squeeze them, drenching them, and come all over my hand.'

As if he's some kind of Pied Piper, I lean back against the arm that's wrapped around me, spreading my legs as far as I can with the damn leggings on, desperate for his touch. My sex is already clenching around his fingers, my orgasm so close I can almost taste it. Then he presses the callused pad of his thumb against my swollen, sensitive clit, working it even better than I can, and I come with a broken moan that almost sounds like I'm in pain, the pleasure so intense it consumes me, taking me completely under as I ride out the mind-shattering waves.

When I can finally breathe again, I blink my eyes open to find Callan's scorching gaze moving over my flushed face, and

I gasp as he pulls his hand from between my legs, lifts it to his lips, and slips the two slick fingers that had been inside me into his mouth, sucking on them like they're the sweetest thing he's ever tasted. Like *I'm* the sweetest thing he's ever tasted, and I make a sound that I didn't even know I was capable of. One that's all carnal hunger and insatiable desire, like I'm some wild thing that knows only craving. Only lust and heat and the seething need to be taken by this gorgeous, insanely sexy male until I no longer even know my own name.

'Where are we going?' I gasp, when he suddenly takes his fingers from his mouth, curls his arm under my legs and picks me up again, carrying me from the room like he's a man with a mission.

'Bedroom,' he grunts, every ripped muscle in his tall body rigid with urgency, the vein at the side of his strong, corded throat pulsing hard and fast as he carries me down the shadowed hallway. 'One of the guys will be doing regular checks on the house throughout the night, and I don't want them walking in on us.'

It takes less than a minute for him to reach the master bedroom, and after he lays me down on the bed, he flicks the floor lamp that stands in one corner onto its lowest setting, then goes back to the door to shut and lock it. By the time he's walked back over to me, I've eagerly stripped out of my clothes, the way his hot, heavy-lidded gaze moves over my naked body making me warm all over, despite the chill in the air. And as I watch him grip the waistband of his pajama pants and shove them over his hips, his veined, breathtaking shaft huge and hard as it jerks upright, I feel tears start to burn at the backs of my eyes, but I'm not sad. I'm just . . . overwhelmed . . . unable to believe that after thinking I would never see him again, he's here. Right *here*, standing in front of me with the hungriest, most incredible look of need on his gorgeous face, his jagged breaths lifting his broad chest like a bellows, and I know, with every part of my being, that this is *fate*.

This, right here, is how our first time was *always* meant to be. It's just fifteen months late – but that time we were forced to wait has only solidified the stunning connection that's binding us together, like some kind of cosmic pull. Despite being a poet at heart, I don't normally buy into these whimsical sorts of ideas, but I'm not sure how else to explain it.

'Callan,' I whisper, staring up at him as he just keeps running that ravenous, greedy gaze over my blushing body. 'Please, stop torturing me and just touch me already.'

'Sorry,' he rumbles, finally climbing over me. 'You're just so goddamn beautiful to look at, Lottie. I can hardly believe you're real.'

I place my hands against his warm, solid chest, with its scattering of scars, then run them up over his golden skin, ready to curl them around the back of his neck and pull him down to me, so that I can kiss the hell out of him. But he slips out of my grasp as he shifts lower on the bed, his big hands shoving my thighs wide, and then his mouth is *there*, between my legs, a sharp gasp on my lips as he thrusts his tongue inside me, tasting my body like he owns it.

'Ohmygod,' I pant, unable to believe how freaking good it feels as he spreads me with his thumbs, licking at my slick flesh in a way that leaves no doubt about how much he's loving what he's doing. And the sounds that he's making . . . God, they're the most provocative things I've ever heard, guttural and greedy and raw, my eyes nearly rolling back in my head when he latches on to my clit and starts working it with his lips and tongue like he won't be happy until he's driven me completely out of my mind.

This moment – it's so perfect that it frightens me. But not nearly as much as the idea of never experiencing it. Never experiencing *him*.

'Callan!' I cry out, when he pushes his tongue back inside me, and as I lift my head to look at him, his hungry gaze locks with mine, and he growls as he grips my hips and jerks me even tighter against his mouth, like he's terrified I might be ripped away from him before he gets what he wants.

Which is me, falling apart for him. And that's exactly what I do, a throaty cry on my lips as my head falls back to the bed and I fist my hands in the snowy white sheets, holding on for dear life as I crash over that blinding, devastating edge of pleasure, coming for him so hard I literally scream his name.

Chapter Thirteen

CALLAN

As Lottie's voice echoes through the room, I'm unable to get enough of her, the taste of her warm release so sweet, I'm already addicted. I stay with her until the very end, and then just keep nuzzling her, her mouthwatering sex as wet as a lake. Then I hear her start begging for my cock, and my pulse roars in my ears, my body so hot I'm surprised I'm not steaming. But as desperate as I am to get inside her, I'm having too much fun where I'm at, and so I just keep licking her until she reaches down, fists her hands in my hair and wrenches my head up.

'What the hell, Callan? Stop making me wait!'

'Easy, sweetheart,' I murmur, giving her a playful wink as I tease her precious clit with the tip of my tongue, loving the way it makes her gasp. Her body is so responsive, it's like she was made for me. 'You've just gotta have a little patience.'

She looks so beautifully outraged, I can't hold back the graveled laugh that surges up from my chest as I start kissing my way up her trembling body, eagerly tasting her silky flesh with my tongue, until I finally reach her breasts and can take one of those plump, candy-pink nipples into my mouth, sucking on her like I want to swallow her whole.

'I swear to God,' she pants, the feel of her short nails digging into my biceps so good, I want to feel her grip me like that all over my body, 'if you don't get inside me in the next five seconds, I'm going to scream!'

'I hate to point out the obvious, baby, but you're already screaming,' I rumble, flicking her other plump, pink nipple with my tongue as I reach down and grip my shaft. I give it a brutal squeeze, like a non-verbal warning to behave. And then, since I'm every bit as desperate as she is, if not more, I notch myself against her. But just as I start to push forward and get that first mind-blowing glimpse of how it's going to feel when I'm buried to the hilt inside her snug, cushiony body, I realize why this feels so unbelievably good.

'Shit,' I hiss, forcing my hips back as I lock my frustrated gaze with hers.

'What? What's wrong?' she gasps, blinking up at me.

I groan like someone who's in agony. 'I'm not wearing a condom, Lot.' Shoving the guttural words through my clenched teeth, I add, 'And I'm pretty sure that Thompson and Robbins wouldn't have thought to grab us any when they went to the store earlier.'

'Oh. Of course,' she whispers, her gleaming gaze shifting to some unknown spot over my shoulder as she catches her lower lip in her teeth, the notch between her brows telling me that she's as devastated by this news as I am. Then she pulls in a deep breath, looks me right in the eye, and shocks the hell out of me as she says, 'I'm not on the pill or anything, which probably doesn't surprise you, considering the state of my life at the moment. But I, um . . . Well, I know it sounds crazy, but I don't care if you don't, so long as you . . . you know, pull out. I just want you.'

I know there's undoubtedly a serious, extremely in-depth discussion that we should probably have at this point, but the woman who's been at the center of my entire existence since the moment I first met her – even when I didn't have a single clue where she was – has just told me that she wants me, condom or no condom, and any chance at control I might have had is completely obliterated. I immediately shove myself inside her, so much harder and deeper than I meant to, but her slick, plush sex is like a dream, and I'm nothing now but raw, animal instinct.

I haven't had sex without a condom since I was old enough to know better – and I know, without any doubt, that it had never felt like *this*. I'm not even all the way in, but my body is in heaven, and as I press my forehead against hers, I suck in a sharp breath, hoping to God I can hold back long enough to make it good for her. Because there's no way I'm going to leave my woman hanging, *ever*, but sure as hell not the first time I finally get inside her.

'Keep going! I want . . . I want all of you,' she moans, rolling her hips against me, trying to take me deeper, and the sound that jerks up from my chest is some kind of graveled cross between a sob and her name.

'I'm never going to stop,' I snarl, gripping her behind her left knee and lifting it toward her chest as I work against her body's tight resistance, determined to give her every part of me, exactly like she's asked for – like she's *demanded*. And when she finally takes that last broad, veined inch, where I'm the thickest, I collapse over her as I brace myself on my forearms, pretty sure I can see the inner workings of the goddamn universe burning against the backs of my eyelids. I gasp and growl and curse, my open mouth pressed against the vulnerable side of her throat as I tell myself that I just need to *Get. My. Shit. Together.*

I repeat the guttural words like a mantra in my head. But, Christ, it isn't easy to do when she keeps rolling her hips against me, driving me mad with the breathtaking feel of her. I groan like I'm in a world of pain, and it nearly kills me when she runs her hands down the sweat-slick length of my back.

'Callan,' she sighs, rubbing her heels against my calves as she strokes her hands lower, over my taut ass. 'Why aren't you moving?'

'Trying . . . to give . . . you . . . time,' I bite out, then kiss my way up the sensitive side of her throat until my lips are at her ear. 'You're tighter than a fist, Lot, and I don't want to hurt you.'

'You won't. Not when I want you this badly,' she argues, the catch in her voice reaching straight into my chest and squeezing my thundering heart. 'I've . . . Because of Andrew, I've only done this a couple of times, and they were just . . . just meaningless hook-ups.' The embarrassment in her tone matches the pink I can see in her cheeks as I lift my head. 'I know that sounds pathetic, that I've never been with anyone I was in a relationship with, but—'

'It doesn't,' I cut in, pushing her hair back from her face, hating that she feels that way. And while I might be possessive as hell where this girl is concerned, I fucking despise the fact that she had to hold herself back from the things that other people so often take for granted, like companionship and pleasure and simple closeness with another human being. Despise the thought of her being deprived of them because of that sick, twisted bastard.

'But,' she goes on, her blue eyes hungry and bright as she stares up at me, 'I want this with you so badly, Callan. Every part of it. I just want to lose myself in it, so *please*,' she pleads, placing one of her soft hands against the side of my hot face, 'don't you dare hold back on me.'

I swallow so hard that it hurts, and accept that there's really only one thing to do now, which is to give my girl *exactly* what she wants.

'Do you know what you are, Lottie? Because it's sure as hell not pathetic. And you're not alone anymore. Not ever again. You're just amazing and awesome and *mine*,' I growl as I draw my hips back. Then I lower my head, nipping at her plump lower lip as I start feeding the hard, brutal length of my shaft back inside her, determined to take her with more meaning than I've ever given to anything in my entire life. 'Every beautiful little inch of you is *mine*. And I'm yours, baby. I'm all yours.'

'Yes. God, yes,' she moans, wrapping her arms around my shoulders as she presses her lips to mine, and as the kiss turns wild and voracious, I start moving inside her harder . . . faster . . . deeper, until I'm hitting the end of her with each powerful thrust. Until I'm fucking the ever-loving hell out of her and her breathless cries are filling my mouth, while my own guttural sounds spill into hers.

I take her so hard that the headboard starts banging against the wall, but there's no controlling this primal, greedy desperation that we have for each other, my starved body ready to gorge on her for as long as it can. And then suddenly there's this blistering moment where she tears her mouth from mine as her voluptuous inner muscles somehow tighten around me even more, squeezing me to the point that it's almost a sweet, savage pain, and it's like that silent eternity in the eye of a storm. We're caught there, suspended on the tip of a needle, breathless with the devastating need that's binding us tighter and tighter together, until we finally snap from the build-up of pressure. I snarl like a damn animal as I slam my hips against her, making sure she has every rigid inch of me, and she gives a keening, breathless cry as she starts coming so hard it nearly destroys me, the feel of her pulsing around my shaft the most stunning thing I've ever experienced.

I roll my hips, grinding against her clit, determined to wring out every last ounce of pleasure for her that I can, and though I want this to last forever, my own orgasm bears down on me like a freight train, and there's only time for a few more deep thrusts before I have to rip myself from her tight hold. Bracing myself on one shaking arm, I fist my soaked shaft and aim for her belly as my scalding release erupts from me with so much force it steals my breath. The intensity of sensation goes on and on, until I'm finally, mercifully spent, and I collapse onto my side like a used, wrecked thing, my chest heaving as I struggle to catch my breath, my mind completely blown by what we've just experienced.

When I can eventually move again, I force myself to my unsteady feet and head into the bathroom to grab something I can clean her up with. I find a washcloth beneath the sink and run it under some warm water, then walk back to the bed and sit down by Lottie's hip, acutely aware of her watching me from under her heavy lashes as I wipe her clean, and I swear I can feel her gaze like a physical touch. It's as if the searing act of intimacy we've just shared has somehow super-charged our connection, my senses sharper as I listen to the still jagged sound of her breathing, while the warm, delicious scent of her body fills my head.

Tossing the washcloth on top of the hamper that sits in a corner of the room, I walk over and turn off the floor lamp, the nightlight that someone's left in an outlet by the bed providing enough of a golden glow for me to easily make my way back to Lottie. I lift the covers from the foot of the bed and pull them over us as I lie back down on my side, feeling fucking lucky as hell when she immediately turns and snuggles up against me.

'Callan?' she whispers, tilting her head back so that she can press a gentle kiss to the underside of my chin.

'Hmm?' I murmur, sifting my fingers through her thick, golden hair, then stroking my hand down the silky length of her back, thinking her skin is the smoothest, softest thing I've ever touched.

'Is it wrong that I want to thank your mum for being too ill to attend my wedding last year?' she asks, and even though I can't see her face, I can hear the smile in her voice, and my chest shakes with a low rumble of laughter.

'Not wrong at all, baby. I feel the same way.'

She presses those smiling lips to my shoulder, then starts tracing her delicate fingertips over the swirling design of my tattoo, until I reach up and cover her hand with mine. 'Sorry,' she says, as if I'd found her touch annoying.

'Don't be sorry.' I pull her tighter against me, the incredible feel of her breasts smashed against my chest making it damn difficult to rein in the beast. 'I love your touch, sweetheart. A bit *too* much, which is the problem, seeing as how I'm trying to show you that I can be a gentleman and give you some recovery time, instead of acting like the sex-crazed animal you turn me into.'

She wriggles in my arms until she's lifted herself up high enough that she's sharing my pillow, the flush that's still on her cheeks seeming to deepen as she strokes a single fingertip along the edge of my jaw. 'You know, when I was sitting across from you last night while we ate, I kept thinking that you were too rugged and wild to be just a man.'

'Oh yeah?' I drawl, lowering my head and nipping at her throat.

She laughs and moans all at once, arching her head back for me, so I just keep kissing her soft skin as she says, 'It's true. I was actually trying to decide, if you were a shapeshifter, whether you would be a grizzly or a wolf.'

I brace myself on an elbow and grin down at her, loving this playful side of her personality. 'Do you have a preference?'

'You,' she whispers, looking at me as if she honestly means it – and knows *exactly* what her response is going to do to me. 'If I could have anything, it would just be you.'

'Christ,' I groan. 'You're killing me, Lottie.' And even though I'd promised myself that I'd let her rest, there's not a chance in hell I can stop myself from kissing her after she says something like *that*, so I don't even try. I just take her sweet, beautiful mouth with mine, kissing her for long, exquisite minutes, until I finally force myself to stop so that she can get some more rest, loving the way she curls up against me again, as if it's where she belongs. Our breaths have only just started to even out, the steady rain that's falling against the roof lulling us to sleep, when my phone suddenly vibrates on the bedside table with a message alert. We both instantly stiffen, knowing that at this time of night, whatever the news is, it can't be good.

'Shit,' I curse, jerking myself up into a sitting position as I reach over and turn on the bedside lamp, then grab the phone, a scowl knitting between my brows as I read the text from Charles Dillon, Deanna's personal assistant.

'What's wrong?' Lottie asks, clutching the sheet against her chest as she sits up beside me.

'Someone's launched a massive cyber-attack against our main server at the New York office. Deanna's got our tech department shutting it down, but whoever it is, they're trying to hack into the company's personnel files.'

'It's Andrew! It has to be.' She pushes one hand into her hair, shoving it back from her stricken face, her words tripping over themselves as she starts to panic. 'He's trying to find out if you have any other properties that we might have gone to. God, Callan, I told you—'

'Don't,' I clip, cutting her off. 'Whatever happens, this isn't your fault, Lot.'

She lowers both hands to her lap, looking at me as if I've lost my mind. 'Are you serious? Whose fault is it if not mine?'

'It's that asshole's fault,' I mutter, my jaw so tight I can feel a muscle pulsing there beneath my skin. 'His and his alone.'

'But the only reason he's screwing with your life is because of *me*! And he'll come here, and you'll—'

'Lottie, listen! He's not going to be able to find this place, even if he makes it through our firewalls, which there's not a chance in hell of happening, because it's not even listed in the company's files.'

'It's not?' she whispers, looking slightly less panicked as she pulls in a shaky breath.

'No, baby,' I assure her, taking one of her cold hands in my free one and giving it a gentle squeeze.

Her shoulders sag with relief. 'That's . . . That's good, then.'

'We've kept this safehouse completely off the books, in case we have a situation where we need to help someone disappear. Completely,' I repeat, wanting her to be reassured. 'So even if we lowered our firewalls and invited him in, there's nothing he could uncover about this place. And the whole point of having Seb drive us here, instead of taking the car service, was to keep the trip off the records. So he's got no way to trace us to this location.' Then I smile a little, my tone wry as I tell her, 'I mean, we could have taken my Harley, but we haven't really talked about whether or not you like bikes, so I figured Seb's Mercedes was the safest bet.'

For a brief moment, she looks like she might smile back at me. But then she grimaces, saying, 'I bet Deanna must be seriously pissed off that someone's trying to mess with your server.'

I shake my head, wishing she wouldn't keep taking all this shit on as her own. Guilt is like this girl's closest, constant companion, and I hate that for her. Wish I could change it for her as badly as I want to get my hands around Andrew Fleming's throat and squeeze the goddamn life out of him.

'I . . . I should go,' she says in a tight voice that sounds like it's been crushed down into something small and painfully hard, and she pulls her hand from my grip. She's no longer even looking at me, her gaze now focused on some distant point on the far side of the room. 'Rent a car and just head out on my own, before anything else happens.'

'Fuck. That.' I don't shout the words, but I'm angry enough that they still make an impact, her troubled gaze flying back to mine.

'I'm serious, Callan. Because you know it won't be long before he connects you to Clara. If he hasn't already.'

I work my jaw, aware that of all the arguments she can throw in my face, this is going to be the hardest one to convince her to let go. 'If that happens, then we'll deal with it. But there's nothing—'

'Can you imagine how much damage he could do?' she cries, working herself up into another panic.

Keeping a calm, easy tone, I say, 'And we can damage him right back, Lottie.'

'How?' she demands. 'We have no proof! Not of anything he's done.'

'It's not just your word against his anymore,' I remind her. 'He came at me with a knife today.'

She scoffs with derision. 'And any lawyer worth their salt would simply say that you were lying to protect me.'

I sigh, accepting that we're just going to keep going round and round right now. And, hell, the last thing I want is to go to the cops, but not for the reason she's assuming.

No, I don't want Fleming falling into the system, doing his time, and then walking the streets a free man one day, putting Lottie's life in danger once more.

I want this finished *now*.

I want the chance to take the bastard out for good.

Because that's the only way to ensure that this amazing woman – who's taken so many hits it's a miracle that she's even still standing – won't ever have to worry about him again.

Chapter Fourteen

CALLAN

In the bright light of day, the problems that Lottie and I are facing don't look any better. And despite having had the most mind-blowing, God-I-can't-wait-to-have-it-again, incredible sex of my life, neither of us slept well, our bodies too restless for the remainder of the night.

After Charles's bombshell of a text, and mine and Lottie's argument about how to react to the attempted hacking, she'd thrown the slouchy gray top she'd been wearing earlier back on and had sat up against the headboard with her knees drawn to her chest, listening while I slipped into my pajama pants and called Charles, then finally got a call from Deanna and talked things over with her.

With nothing left to be done last night, Deanna and I had agreed to talk again this morning, and then I'd crawled back into bed with Lottie. As we'd lain on our sides, facing each other, she'd asked me if I thought we should warn Clara about the possibility of Andrew trying to mess with her campaign. I'd told her no, not yet, since there was no sense worrying my sister over something that hopefully wouldn't be an issue. But I knew she'd been right to be concerned, so after Lottie fell asleep, I got back out of bed and headed into the living room to call Jase, even though it was the middle of the night, to ask for his help.

If there were a physical threat against Clara's life, then I would know how to help her. But the brutal, manipulative world of PR is one I have no idea how to navigate, and I trust Jase to be able to come up with a better plan than I could, in the event this all blows up in our faces.

After finally grabbing a bit more sleep, I woke up at dawn, took a long, satisfying moment to appreciate how beautiful Lottie looked lying beside me, then carefully climbed out of bed so that I didn't wake her. I changed into some workout shorts, then did a long run on the treadmill, and grabbed a shower before heading into the kitchen to put on the coffee. As I wait for it to brew, I have a long call with Deanna, then pour two cups and carry them back to the master bedroom. I find Lottie awake and sitting up against the headboard with her knees drawn up to her chest again, just staring through the huge window that looks out over the lake that runs along the back of the property.

'It's a gorgeous view,' I say, but my gaze is focused on *her* as I set her coffee mug on the bedside table, because she's infinitely more beautiful than any picturesque scenery.

'Thanks for the coffee,' she murmurs, bringing her tired gaze to mine. 'Have you been up long?'

I shake my head as I pull the comfortable chair in the nearby corner closer to the bed, then take a seat. 'Not really. Got in a run on the treadmill, then spoke to Deanna.'

She sits up a bit straighter, and there's a noticeable tension around her eyes and mouth as she asks, 'Did something else happen?'

I shake my head again. 'No. But they were able to track the hacking signal to the general area of Brooklyn before shutting it down.'

'God,' she whispers, wrapping her arms around her knees as she shudders. 'He's been staying close to me, hasn't he?'

'But he's not close to you now, honey. And that's how it's staying.'

'Anything else?' she asks, and I know she's enquiring about Clara's campaign.

'Nope.' I take a sip of my coffee, then jerk my chin at her as I move back to my feet. 'Now come on. It's time I made my woman some breakfast.'

I'm happy to cook for her but she insists on helping, so we make eggs, bacon and toast, eating at the breakfast bar with the news on again, and while we both seem to be doing our best to keep the conversation flowing, the heaviness in the air isn't something that can be ignored. We're both tense, knowing that Andrew's hacking move won't be the last thing he tries, and I feel a powerful, consuming wave of protectiveness for Lottie move through me every time I think about what the bastard might be planning. One that only intensifies when I catch her delicately probing the tender skin around the cut on her brow, and so after we wash up, I decide that there's a hell of a good way we can spend the next few hours that doesn't involve worrying ourselves sick or pacing with frustration.

'Where are we going?' she asks, after I take hold of her hand and start pulling her along with me down the long back hallway.

'We converted one of the bedrooms back here into a gym a few years ago.'

'Are you going to work out again?' she asks when we walk through the open double doors that lead into the sunny, spacious room. It's filled with a wide range of workout equipment, as well as a twelve-by-twelve padded mat that sits in front of another huge window. But instead of looking out at the lake, this view is of the surrounding woods.

'Naw,' I drawl in response to her question, leaving her standing in the center of the room as I let go of her hand and walk back over to the doors, closing them and flipping the lock. 'I'm going to teach you how to fight back.'

She gives me a look of confusion as I come back to her. 'I don't understand.'

'Self-defense, Lot.'

Her eyebrows lift with surprise, which instantly makes her wince because of the cut. 'Callan, you've met Andrew. He's nearly as tall as you are.'

'Doesn't matter,' I tell her, shaking my head. 'You can still learn how to hurt him, and I'm going to make sure that you know how.'

I read the fear that moves over her face, and instantly feel like a jackass for not handling this better. 'Hey, I don't plan on letting that son of a bitch get anywhere near you, okay? But if there's one thing I've learned in my line of work, it's that shit happens, and it's better to be prepared than to hope it's all just going to work out the way you've planned.'

'You're right,' she agrees with a nod, looking nervous, but willing to give it a go.

'Good. Now strip down to your panties,' I tell her, jerking my chin at the leggings she'd slipped back on.

She arches one of her golden eyebrows in a look that's as wry as it is sexy. 'I thought this was meant to be serious.'

'It is,' I assure her, giving her a wicked smile. 'But that doesn't mean I can't enjoy the view.'

'Perv,' she laughs, rolling those beautiful eyes at me.

'You know you love it,' I toss back, getting a kick out of teasing her.

'Hmm,' she murmurs, before nodding her head toward the huge, curtainless window. 'You don't care that Thompson and Robbins will be able to see us if they walk by?'

'It's one-way glass, just like at my apartment. And you just watched me lock the doors, so no one can walk in on us.'

She gives a dry laugh. 'Seems you've thought of everything.'

This time, I'm the one who arches a brow. 'You really think I'd let one of those guys get a look at you in your undies?'

She smirks as she shakes her head. 'You know, I'm starting to think you have a one-track mind.'

I can't help but smile again as I say, 'If that track is Lottie Fleming, then hell yeah, guilty as charged.'

She pulls in a deep breath, then lets it out with a soft puff as she rubs her hands together. 'Okay, enough teasing me, you big flirt, because I'm ready to learn how to kick ass. *But* I'm keeping my clothes on.'

'Spoilsport.'

With another laugh, she asks, 'So how do we do this?'

And just like that, my smile fades, because I know this next part is going to completely shred me. 'I don't want to make you uncomfortable, Lot, but the best way for us to start is for you to, um . . .'

'Tell you the ways that he's attacked me?' she finishes, when I'm unable to get the words out.

'Yeah,' I rasp, trying to mentally prepare myself for what I'm about to hear. But it's a useless exercise, because there *is* no way to brace yourself for this kind of twisted shit.

She sits down cross-legged on the center of the mat, and I'm in awe all over again of her inner strength as she begins to relay the different situations that she's found herself in with the bastard over the years, as well as how he managed to get her tied up and gagged the night that Olly had scared him off. As I listen to the telling, I can't stay still, the fury searing through my veins sending me pacing back and forth in front of the window, my hands clenching and unclenching at my sides as I imagine wrapping them around Fleming's throat.

When she's done, she looks up at me, her lashes glistening with tears as she says, 'You must think I'm so stupid for putting myself in situations where he could get to me.'

'The hell I do. What were you meant to do? Hide away in a locked room every day for the rest of your life? You had to get out and live, Lot, and sometimes things went wrong for you. But that's got nothing to do with your strength or intelligence. It doesn't even have anything to do with your training, because things can go bad for everyone. You think I've never been shit on or gotten kicked in the teeth?'

'Look at you, Callan. You're like a god of a man. You're larger than life. Super smart and gorgeous and funny, with family and friends who not only love you, but clearly think the world of you. I doubt you even know what it feels like to be broken or made to look like a fool.'

'You're wrong.' I pull in a deep breath, then let it go with a rough, bitter laugh. 'Shit, I didn't want to get into this,' I mutter, rubbing my jaw, 'because this woman has no hold on my life at all anymore, other than to play the part of the occasional nuisance, like she did yesterday.'

'You're talking about Jessica?' she murmurs with a note of surprise, pulling her knees into her chest and wrapping her arms around them.

'Yeah.'

There's a tiny crease between her brows as she stares up at me, her tone soft as she says, 'Damn it, now I feel bad for what

I just said. Because I definitely got the sense from your mum that it was an ugly break-up.'

'Ugly is putting it lightly, Lot.' I grab the end of one of the lifting benches, pulling it closer to the mat, and as I sit down, I say, 'Jessica is a famous actress. She—'

'Wait a freaking minute,' she gasps, and her eyes have gone huge with shock. 'Is your ex bloody Jessica *Marten*?'

'Yeah,' I answer with a scowl, leaning over so that I can brace my elbows on my spread knees.

Still looking completely dumbstruck, Lottie whispers, 'I had no idea, Callan.'

'I met her at a fundraising gala just over five years ago, and we started dating not long after,' I explain, wanting to get the story over with as quickly as possible. 'Things weren't great, but we were . . . steady, I guess you could say. Only Jessica decided that she wanted to get married, and I wasn't really feeling it. But her publicist went ahead and announced the engagement, thinking it would be good for Jess's publicity, and the next thing I knew, I was going along with it, just so I wouldn't have to deal with the tantrum I knew Jess would throw if I didn't.'

'Wow,' she murmurs, running her palms along her shins. 'That's—'

'It was fucked, honey. Seriously *fucked*. But that's not even what drove the final nail in the coffin.' I move my head from side to side a few times, trying to work out the tension that's knotting in my neck, the bitterness in my voice only getting harsher as I say, 'Jessica's last movie hadn't done as well as the one before it, and the reviews were horrible, but she was enjoying the boost our engagement was giving her while getting ready to film her next project, which was this thriller about a famous singer who's being stalked by an obsessed fan. So she and her publicist got together and hatched up another plot to keep her popularity on the rise. Only this time they went too far.'

'Announcing an engagement that hadn't really happened was already going pretty far,' she comments, sounding as disgusted as I'd felt at the time.

'Yeah, well, this time they . . .' My voice trails off as my chest rumbles with another gritty laugh, and I rub at the back of my neck, still finding it difficult to wrap my head around what they'd done. 'Christ, Lot. They started encouraging one of her stalkers for the news coverage it could give her.'

She blinks a few times, looking as if she can't quite believe those words have just come out of my mouth. 'That's . . . It's . . . That's *insane*.'

'Trust me, I know,' I sigh. 'She would receive some extreme fan attention, like so many in the industry unfortunately do, but luckily never anything that went too far. Then this one guy who would send her written letters, instead of email, along with drawings that he'd done of her, got flagged by the team who monitored her communications. It seems the letters had not only taken a graphic turn, but they'd also started showing up with more frequency, and the drawings had gone from ones of her face to full-body nudes. I got worried and put a team at Hathaway on tracking the guy down, in addition to increasing her security detail, and suggested she keep a low profile until we'd found the asshole. But someone on her PR team leaked the story to the press, and the entertainment blogs and TV shows went crazy over it. Ryan, her publicist, was all but drooling over the exposure, and Jessica strangely didn't seem to be all that bothered by it. But then the guy started writing that he'd found a way to give her what she'd told him *she wanted*, and things changed. She began acting paranoid, as if the situation was really getting to her. Then she demanded that if I cared about her at all, I'd find him and deal with him.'

'Deal with him how?' she asks, lifting her brows.

'I still don't know exactly what she was hoping for, and at the time I didn't ask. I just wanted to find this asshole so that I would know she'd be okay after I was out of the picture, since I'd decided to end the engagement and move on from what was clearly a huge-ass mistake. So I put every other part of my life on hold and went after him with everything I had. And the entire time, she never even had the goddamn decency to come clean with me and tell me the truth about what she and Ryan had done.'

'How did you find out?' she quietly asks.

'The really fucking hard way,' I say with a harsh laugh, rubbing at my chest as if I can still feel the pain of the wounds Robbie Deacon had inflicted there, even though they're nothing more than scars now. Ones that are a constant reminder of my stupidity. 'I eventually tracked him down, and when I confronted him, he came at me with a knife. He'd obviously had some combat training and got me in the chest a few times, but they were shallow cuts, and I was able to draw my gun and hobble him with a shot to the leg.'

'Bloody hell, Callan.' Her soft voice is rough with concern, the look on her beautiful face one of absolute horror at what I'd gone through. And it's something she can unfortunately picture far too easily, given what she'd seen happen to Olly in Italy.

'And that's when it all came out,' I mutter. 'I got him into a chair and had him use a belt to tourniquet his leg, while I called the emergency services, telling them we needed an ambulance and the police. Then he starts going on about how he'd only been doing what Jessica had wanted, and he had proof. At first

I just thought it was bullshit from someone who'd lost their grip on reality, but he told me to look in the top drawer of his desk, and that's where I found them. The notes and photographs that *Jessica* had been sending *him*. Intimate ones, sprayed with her perfume, with messages about how she knew they were meant to be together one day. And I knew it was all real, not only because it was her damn handwriting, but some of the photographs were ones she'd actually sent to me from her phone, when she'd been away on location for a shoot.'

'Ohmygod,' Lottie whispers, her expression mirroring the disbelief I'd felt that day.

'Yeah, it was messed up. I told him he'd been played by a sick bitch and her publicist, and the next thing I knew, he made a run for it, jumping out a second-story window. He disappeared into the woods that surrounded his property before I could catch up with him, and though I put a search party together made up of Hathaway employees, it was a week before he resurfaced. That was the night he drove into the city and set himself on fire in the middle of Times Square.'

'I remember seeing something about that on the news,' she says, shocked. 'But I had no idea it was because of Jessica Marten.'

Rubbing my jaw again, I admit, 'That's because I pulled in every favor I was ever owed to keep her name away from it. I knew that she and Ryan would try to put some kind of spin on the whole thing that made her look like the victim, and there was no way in hell I was going to let her capitalize on what she'd done.' I grimace as I think back to the conversation I'd had with Jessica that night, and there's a deeper, gruffer note of disbelief in my voice as I say, 'And after all that, it actually came as a surprise to her when I told her to get the hell out of my place. In her mind, it made perfect sense to use me to clean up her mess, once she realized it'd gone too far and she needed a way out. She didn't even feel guilty about any of it, and couldn't understand why I was so angry. Can you believe that shit?'

'No. It's . . . crazy. All of it.'

Another bitter laugh jerks up from my throat, the entire story leaving a bad taste in my mouth. 'Yeah, it was. And I still fell for it. All of it. I was just the big ol' dumb slab of muscle to them. One they thought they could control like a puppet on a string, just playing some pathetic part they'd written for me, and all so she could get more likes and retweets and whatever else was sucking any humanity she'd ever had right out of her.'

LOTTIE

'She was the dumb one, Callan. *Not you*,' I argue, hating to hear him talk about himself that way. 'You were just the brave, hunky hero trying to save a psycho princess.'

'Well, I felt like an idiot,' he admits, the corner of his beautiful mouth kicking up with a wry grin. 'It's why only my mom knows the truth. I couldn't even stomach telling any of my siblings or Jase about it.'

Softly, I say, 'You can't blame yourself for believing in someone you loved.'

'Can't I? And looking back, I'm not sure if I ever really loved her at all. Because those feelings that I had . . . They don't seem nearly so powerful anymore.' The look in his gorgeous brown eyes gives me chills. 'I mean, I know you better than I ever knew Jessica, and we've only spent a few days together, Lot. And I trust you in a way that I didn't think I would ever be able to trust a woman again.'

At first, I just sit there and hold his dark, intense stare, not a single word falling from my lips as I think about everything he's just said, from beginning to end. As I think about how this man is unlike anyone I've ever known – rough and rugged as hell, but with a sense of loyalty and protectiveness that makes him a bloody hero – and it kills a part of me inside to know that someone had hurt him. Betrayed him. Made him feel even one moment's worth of pain.

Moving to my feet, I walk to him and place my hands on his wide shoulders as he tips his head back, then lean over and touch my lips to his, trying to convey my thoughts and feelings through a simple kiss. But there really isn't anything simple about it at all.

Not in the way I want to make him feel . . . and not in the way he affects me.

He parts his warm lips, and I touch my tongue to his, the taste and feel of him so insanely good that I can hear myself softly moaning through the fog of lust that's clouding my brain. Reason and logic are rapidly fading, replaced by this wild, animal need that he's somehow pulled up from the primal depths of my being and brought to the surface. But it's not that I'm a different person when I'm with him – it's that I'm *more* of a person, my passion for him unlocking emotions and needs that I otherwise might have never even known were inside me.

He's the key. The answer to what I need to feel like this. To feel alive to the point that I'm charged with this wild, terrifying, newfound hope for the future. A future I would give anything to have with him. Literally *anything*.

But I won't make him pay for that possibility by putting himself in danger the way Jessica Marten did. I *can't*. Which means I need to know how to protect myself, and how to help him if it ever comes to that. And if anyone can show me how to do that, after I saw him in action yesterday, I know that it's Callan.

Breaking the kiss, I simply stare down at him, taking him in, while he settles his big hands on my waist and waits for me to say something. He has a slight bruise on his left cheekbone, and his knuckles are battered, but I have no doubt that Andrew is in far worse shape after the beating that he gave him. My cousin is probably sore as hell today, which isn't nearly as bad as he deserves, but makes me feel a bit better anyway.

'I trust you too,' I finally tell him, my voice soft, my touch gentle as I sift my fingers through his thick, beautiful hair. Then I pull in a deep breath, and there's a smile on my lips as I slowly let it out and say, 'So let's do this.'

We spend the next three hours with Callan putting me through my paces, our skin slicked with sweat and my muscles aching, though I'm excited and empowered by everything he's been able to teach me. When we complete another rollover move that ends with him on top of me, his fingers brush against my side, where I'm most ticklish, and as a breathless laugh slips past my lips, his eyes gleam with mischief and the evil man starts tickling the hell out of me, until I'm laughing so hard there are tears streaming from the corners of my eyes.

'That laugh,' he says in a low rumble, finally taking mercy on me as he braces his upper body on his straight arms and stares down into my flushed face, the heat in his heady gaze making me burn. 'I'll never be able to get enough of that laugh, Lot.'

I open my mouth, ready to warn him that payback is going to be a bitch, when he suddenly scowls, gently touching my upper arm with his fingertips as he growls, 'Shit! Are these from me?'

I lift my arm until I can see what he's looking at, and sure enough, there are several faint purplish marks that were made during our self-defense lessons. 'Oh, don't worry about them. It's no big deal.'

'The hell it isn't,' he clips.

'Callan, I bruise easily,' I explain with a soft sigh, looking back up into his worried gaze. 'I always have. But it doesn't mean that I'm made of glass.' Reaching up, I cup the side of his rugged face in my hand, his skin warm to the touch, and harden my tone as I say, 'I don't want to be treated like something fragile and weak. I want to be treated as your equal.'

'My equal?' he grunts, shaking his head. 'Jesus, woman. I'm lucky you let me get anywhere near you. You're perfection that I don't come anywhere close to.'

'And you're crazy,' I laugh.

He doesn't laugh along with me, though. No, he just smiles at me instead, with a crooked tilt of his lips, the smoldering look in his eyes making my chest feel tight, as if I can't draw in enough air. 'I wish you could see yourself the way I do,' he says in a low voice that's soft, but rough. 'I mean, you're incredibly gorgeous. But it's not just the way you look that has me wanting to follow you around like a puppy, begging for attention. It's how brave you are. How smart and funny and kind, along with about a million different other things that make you . . . amazing. I swear to God, Lottie, most of the time I can hardly believe you're not just something that I've dreamed up.'

'Callan.'

CALLAN

She says my name like . . . Like it has this deeper meaning for her that it's never had for anyone else. And, Christ, does that wreck me, even as it builds me up so high I'm surprised I'm not floating up near the wood-beamed ceiling.

I make a low, rough sound of hunger as I bury my face

against the side of her throat, kissing her there, the taste of her body like sun-warmed honey on my tongue, and I nuzzle the velvety-soft skin beneath her ear, whispering how much I want her. How much I need her.

Before I know it, I've stripped her leggings and panties off, spread her long legs, and have my open mouth pressed against her luscious sex, licking my way to paradise. She's still swollen from how hard I'd taken her during the night, and I know she's too sore to go another round right now. But even though my dick is as hard as a spike, I'm happy where I'm at.

Hell, her taste is so addictive, I could be happy staying right here for the rest of my damn life.

'Turn around for me,' she suddenly moans, and there isn't a chance I can tell her no. But why would I even want to? No, I'm stripping and shifting around on top of her like my life depends on how fast I can get myself in her beautiful mouth and my tongue back inside her plush body. Then we go at each other like we're literally starved for the touch and taste of the other, our hungers wild and urgent, bodies so hot we're practically steaming as we somehow end up on our sides, our hands greedily clutching as our hips roll. And when we finally crash over that mind-shattering, bone-melting edge, the pleasure's so ferociously intense, we can't do anything but pant and shake until we find ourselves spent and gasping for breath as we collapse onto our backs, no doubt looking like two survivors from a violent shipwreck.

Eventually, my chest stops working like a bellows, and there's a wide, satisfied smile on my lips as I reach over, giving her thigh an appreciative squeeze. 'Well, *that's* something I've never done on this mat before,' I drawl.

She responds with another one of those sweet, husky laughs that drive me wild, and we're both grinning like idiots as we lift our heads to look at each other, the sunlight streaming in through the window making her creamy skin gleam with a flushed, golden hue. 'I've never done that *anywhere* before,' she says, looking adorably pleased with herself. 'But it was awesome.'

'It was pure heaven,' I tell her. And even though my body is already gearing up for another go, I ignore it, knowing she must be starving after all the training we've done. 'Now come on,' I say with a playful smirk as I move to my feet and offer her my hand. 'It's time for me to feed my girl some lunch, so that she'll be able to keep up with me later.'

She laughs as she takes my hand and I pull her up, and once we're dressed, we make our way back to the kitchen, holding hands and smiling like a couple of blissed-out lovers. Which is exactly what we are in this brief, stolen moment in time – able to pretend, for just a while, that we don't have a giant, dangerous shadow hanging over our heads.

We find Robbins at the fridge, pulling out the makings for sandwiches for him and Thompson, and I feel like a jealous bastard for noticing the way that he and Lottie keep smiling at each other while they chat about how gorgeous it is out. But the guy looks more like a model than a professional bodyguard, with his chiseled features, olive-toned skin and wavy black hair, so I doubt I'm the first guy to feel a bit green around him. He offers to make sandwiches for us too, but I tell him I'd planned on cooking some omelets, and then we spend a few minutes talking about the attempted hacking.

Since this morning was the first opportunity I'd had to talk to Deanna for an extended length of time without Lottie listening in, I'd used it to give my Head of Ops a full debrief of the situation with Andrew Fleming. So when Robbins mentions the hacking, I can tell by the protective way he glances at Lottie that Deanna has already passed the necessary information on to our security detail, which I'd approved.

And yeah, I'm grateful as hell that they all trust my judgment enough not to question helping a woman who's wanted for murder – but if I hadn't believed they would take one look at the facts of the case and realize Lottie was innocent, especially given Andrew's presence here in New York, then I never would have involved them. I would have found a way to deal with the situation on my own, though I'm glad it hasn't come to that, seeing as how I want this woman to have all the protection and people on her side that she can get.

When Robbins leaves, heading back down to the control room that contains the safehouse's security screens for the multitude of cameras that are positioned around the property, Lottie asks where he and Thompson slept last night. I explain to her that the house has a lower level, accessed through a door at the back of the property, that's completely set up for the security teams who work here. And while there's a kitchen down there, it's company protocol to only keep the main fridge stocked when less than six people are on the premises, which is why he'd come upstairs to make their lunch.

'Is there a grocery store close by that we can go to?' she asks, after we've consumed the killer bacon-and-mushroom omelets that I made for us and we're cleaning up together.

'Sure. But we're still stocked up with a ton of food.'

'I just thought it would be fun to cook my mum's lasagna recipe tonight, when I've got access to such a remarkable kitchen. It was always one of my favorites growing up, and there'll be plenty for us, plus Thompson and Robbins. But we'll probably need to pick up a bunch of the fresh herbs that I'll need from the store.'

'Then I'll take you this afternoon,' I tell her, loving that she's feeling relaxed enough to want to do something that she hasn't been able to do in a long time. Something that it's clear will bring her joy, based on the smile she's giving me.

And that smile . . . Christ, it takes everything I've got to let her walk off to go and get ready without me, once we're finished with the dishes, since I know we'll *never* get out of here if I see her naked again.

After my shower, I throw on a pair of jeans, a gray T-shirt and an ancient pair of sturdy black lace-up boots that I left up here a few months ago, then grab Lottie, who looks gorgeous in another pair of leggings, a long black T-shirt that falls off one shoulder and her Converse, a careful application of make-up perfectly covering the bruise above her right eye. We borrow Thompson's Chevy pickup to drive to the store, declining his offer to come along with us, since the main reason I have him and Robbins here is to keep anyone from getting close to the safehouse, our personal security something I can handle on my own. The skies are clear and the sun is shining, while the forest seems even greener for the rain we'd gotten last night, and as we head down the country road that will take us into the nearest town, I say, 'So tell me about Nico and Eva.'

'Eva's one of the most wonderful women I've ever known, and Nico is awesome,' she replies with enthusiasm, and even though my eyes are on the road, I can hear the smile in her voice. 'He's smart and funny and super protective of his mum and his grandma.'

'No dad in the picture?' I ask, reaching over to turn on the AC.

'Sadly, no.' I can tell from the change in her tone that the story isn't a good one, and I brace as she goes on, saying, 'He worked as a delivery driver and was shot by a gang member who stole his truck.'

'Son of a bitch,' I mutter, hating that they'd had to go through that kind of tragedy. 'It's shit like that that Clara intends to work her ass off to make better.'

'I've read about her in the news and think her policies sound like exactly what the city needs. I just can't believe that I never realized she's your sister.'

I slow the truck down and take the next left, then say, 'With everything you've been through this past year, Lot, it's not like you've had a lot of time to just sit back and take in the world around you.'

'I guess,' she murmurs, and we spend the rest of the drive with me answering her questions about Jase and Emmy, and what they've been up to since she last saw them.

When we reach the store, I can tell that she's charmed by its small-town quaintness, and I'm glad that we made the trip, since it's clear that she craves these everyday slices of normal, after going without them for so long. But even though we're in the middle of nowhere and it's unlikely that she'll be recognized, I still hand her the baseball cap I'd grabbed before we left the house and suggest that she put it on. She does that thing I've seen women do where they pull their hair through the opening in the back, and despite the cap being too big for her, she looks as lovely as ever in it.

As we walk inside the store, I grab us a cart, happy to follow her around while she searches for the things she wants on the various aisles.

'What was that for?' she asks, when I suddenly lean down and brush my lips over hers in the middle of the fruit-and-veg section.

'The brunette over there who's feeling up the eggplants was all but undressing me with her eyes. So I had to let her know that I'm taken,' I whisper with a cocky smirk that makes her laugh in that amazing way that, until a few days ago, I'd been terrified I would never hear again.

'You're so freaking arrogant,' she snickers, rolling those beautiful blue eyes at me. 'It boggles the mind that you can even walk around without that enormous head of yours toppling you over.'

'I've actually heard that a time or two,' I drawl, waggling my brows at her, and this time she laughs so hard that she snorts, which only makes her laugh even harder.

I'm still grinning like a jackass, loving that I've been able to crack her up, when she finally gains enough composure to wipe her eyes and say, 'Yeah, that really doesn't surprise me.'

Leaning in close, I lower my head again until my lips are at her ear, and whisper, 'Then I'll have to think of something that will.'

As if she's thinking about what that 'something' might be, there's a beautiful flush on her cheeks as we head over to the toiletries aisle, since she wants to buy some facewash. When I spot the condom display, I reach out to grab the biggest box they've got, but she stops me with the touch of her hand on my arm and shakes her head.

'It's risky,' I murmur, my tone as gritty as sandpaper and my heartbeat picking up pace as I lock my gaze with her wide, bright one.

From her expression, it seems that she's surprised herself as much as she has me. But then the corner of her mouth twitches as she looks me over, her voice soft as she says, 'Risk is pretty much the theme of my life right now.'

'You taking me bare is the risk, Lottie. *Not* me,' I argue with a quiet growl, keeping my voice low enough that we can't be overheard. 'I'm the surest fucking thing you've ever known. But if you're willing to chance me putting a kid in you, then I'm all for it. The sooner, the better.'

She arches one of those golden eyebrows at me beneath the rim of the cap, and there's a provocative purr to her voice as she drawls, 'Or you can just keep pulling out, Hathaway. It's good practice for your self-control.'

Then she turns away with a mysterious, sexy half-smile curling her lips, getting on with her shopping, and I have to bite my tongue to hold back the words I want to just throw out there. The ones where I make it clear about what I want for us, once this nightmare with Andrew Fleming is over. But since the middle of a damn grocery store isn't the place for that kind of discussion, I simply blow out a rough breath and follow behind her, promising myself that we're going to have *that* particular talk a hell of a lot sooner rather than later.

When we pull back up to the safehouse, Thompson – whose tall, leanly ripped body and shaggy blond hair have earned him the nickname Bodhi at the office, since everyone thinks he looks like Patrick Swayze in *Point Break* – is standing off to the side of the circular driveway, smoking a cigarette. Lottie pulls off the cap and smiles at him as we head inside, and it doesn't escape my notice that there's a shot of heat in his gaze as he smiles back at her. I know, from having watched her the weekend of her wedding, as well as during the trip we'd just taken to town, that she has this kind of effect on nearly every man who sets eyes on her, and no doubt a good number of women, too. And yet, I swear she never even realizes it, because while she has an air of confidence that I find impossibly sexy, there's not an ounce of conceit or arrogance in her, which is just another example of how incredible she is.

We've only just started to put away the groceries when my phone starts ringing, the shrill sound disrupting the easy-going mood that had fallen over us for the past few hours, and I find myself bracing again when I pull the phone from my pocket and see that it's Seb, the strange prickle at the back of my neck warning me that he isn't just calling to check in.

I take the call, and there's no controlling the way I flinch when Seb tells me what's happened. All it takes is for Lottie to get one good look at my face, and she reaches out with her right hand to grip the edge of the nearest counter, discerning from my expression that something horrific has taken place.

Coughing to clear my throat, I tell Seb that I'm going to have to call him back, then put the phone back in my pocket and lock my worried gaze with Lottie's, hating how badly this is going to hurt her.

'What is it?' she whispers, quickly wrapping her arms around her middle. 'What's happened?'

I pull in a deep breath, then slowly let it out as I take a step closer to her. 'Do you know a woman named Ruby Carlisle?'

'Oh God,' she breathes, shivering as if I've just thrown a vat of freezing iced water over her. 'She . . . I . . . We work together at the café. Why are you asking? Is she okay?'

'I'm sorry, baby, but no,' I mutter, shaking my head. 'Seb called to tell me that her body was recently found near one of the fire doors at the back of our building.' I don't tell her that Ruby's throat had been sliced open, not wanting her to have that gruesome mental image of her friend in her head. 'The security cameras that cover that area had been disabled. But they think she was killed earlier today, then moved there sometime in the last few hours.'

'Ohmygod,' she groans in a broken voice, her breath hitching as her face goes deathly pale, and as I reach for her, she rears back from me, holding her hands up in front of her in a move that warns me to stay away. She keeps retreating until she comes up against the stove, her voice painfully shrill as she cries, 'I can't believe I spent today laughing and having fun with you, while my friend was getting slaughtered! What the hell is wrong with me?'

'This isn't your fault,' I growl, wishing she would let me hold her, my insides completely shredded by the heartbreaking look of anguish on her face. 'Christ, you're one of the most intelligent people I've ever known, Lottie. You *know* you're not to blame!'

'What I know is that if I had made it clear I was running, and not just hiding out with you, then he wouldn't still be in the city looking for me!' she shouts. 'And an innocent woman wouldn't be dead!'

She shoves her hands into her hair, pulling it back from her face as she leans forward, making the most raw, keening sound of agony that I've ever heard. And then it all just becomes too much for her to contain, and she lets out a furious, bloodcurdling roar as she picks up the heavy cafetière that was sitting on the counter at her right and hurls it against the wall with so much force, it explodes in a shower of broken, jagged shards.

'Lottie,' I rasp, feeling more useless than I ever have before as I watch her collapse onto her knees on the hard kitchen floor.

Then she buries her face in her hands . . . and bursts into tears.

Chapter Fifteen

CALLAN

The crash is so loud, I know there's no way Thompson won't have heard it, if he's still out front finishing his smoke. And sure enough, not ten seconds pass before there's a heavy, urgent knock on the front door.

Lottie's head shoots up at the sound. When there's another loud knock, she gives me a wrecked, but apologetic look, and I can hear her move back to her feet and follow behind me as I make my way out of the kitchen, down the hallway and into the entryway. I open the door and step aside so that Thompson can come in.

'Everything all right in here?' he asks, shooting me a suspicious look, and while it grates that he's giving me the stink eye, I can't help but be pleased that my employees have taken a clear liking to Lottie. Because while they're paid to be protective, the concern on Thompson's face tells me that her well-being means more to him than his paycheck.

Just as I'm getting ready to explain about the noise, she walks over to join us, and he asks, 'Are you okay, Miss Fleming?'

'Yeah, and please call me Lottie,' she tells him, wiping at the tears that are still spilling from the corners of her eyes. 'I'm sorry for making such a racket. We just . . . We just got some really upsetting news.'

Thompson turns his worried look back on me. 'What's happened?'

I explain about Ruby, and there's a silent question in Thompson's eyes about who I think is responsible. I respond with a brief nod, affirming his suspicion that it was Andrew, and he shifts his gaze back over to Lottie, his normally easy-going tone gruff with sympathy as he tells her that he's sorry for her loss. Then he says that he's going to update Robbins on the situation and lets himself out, shutting the front door behind him.

As soon as it's just the two of us again, I walk over to Lottie, relieved when she doesn't pull away from me. But she's still painfully on edge, so I don't pick her up and cradle her against my chest, the way I want to. Instead, I take her hand and pull her along with me into the living room, and as we sit down on the sofa, she draws in a shaky breath. 'I . . . I only met Ruby a few months ago, but she was really funny and sweet, and it was always a blast to work with her. But we never hung out together outside of Lenore's until last week, when she asked me if I wanted to grab a coffee with her after one of our shifts.'

She's been staring down at her hands as she twists them together in her lap, but she glances over at me when she stops talking, and there's the most gut-wrenching look of guilt in her eyes as she croaks, 'One freaking cup of coffee, Callan. And now she's dead. Because that psycho wanted to lash out at someone to hurt me.'

'Don't do that, sweetheart,' I murmur, placing my hand on the small of her back. 'Don't take the blame for this, because that's exactly what the son of a bitch wants. But this isn't on you. All you did was make a friend, and there's no law against that.'

'Oh God!' she gasps, her tear-drenched eyes suddenly going wide with fear. 'Nico and Eva! They could be in—'

'I'm on it,' I cut in, already pulling my phone from my pocket. 'I'll have Seb go over and talk to her right now. He'll make sure that she goes somewhere safe until this shit is over. Somewhere that Fleming won't be able to find them.'

'Just like that, he'll drop everything and help?' she asks, sending a teardrop sliding down her cheek when she blinks at me.

'Of course. Because he knows I'd do the same for him.'

'Wow. You're really lucky, Callan,' she says softly, the saddest damn smile I've ever seen tucked into the corner of her still trembling lips. 'I mean, to have such good friends and such an awesome family.'

I want to tell her that they could be *her* friends and family too, but bite back the words, terrified that after what's happened, they'll just send her running. So I focus on calling Seb, and just as I expected, he doesn't even hesitate to assure me that he'll head over to Eva's immediately. Then I make a quick call to Deanna, updating her on what's happened, and I notice the way that Lottie flinches when I tell Deanna that I want the security details increased on everyone in my family.

When I'm done, I set the phone on the coffee table in front of us, then grab Lottie's hand. 'Seb's heading over to Eva's right now.'

'Thank you. That's . . . That's amazing.' She pulls in another shaky breath and wipes at her wet cheeks with her free hand. 'She doesn't work on Sundays, so they should be at home. But I should call and give her a heads-up, so that she knows Seb is the real deal.'

I grab my phone again, unlock the screen and hand it over.

'Thanks,' she whispers, and I get up and head back into the kitchen, figuring she's going to want some privacy for her call. And while I can't hear much of what she's saying, I catch enough to know that she keeps apologizing, over and over, which kills me. None of this shit is her fault, but I know she won't ever see it that way.

'Everything all right?' I ask a few minutes later, when I turn away from where I've been unloading more of our groceries into the refrigerator and find her standing in the kitchen doorway.

She gives a nod as she sets my phone on the breakfast bar. 'She's rattled, but okay.' Then her lips twitch with a wobbly smile as she says, 'Though I have a feeling Seb's going to get an earful if he starts trying to boss her around.'

A low, brief laugh rumbles up from my chest. 'Hey, it'll do him good to spend some time with a woman who doesn't fall all over him.'

She smiles again, this one a bit steadier, though the pain in her eyes is still devastating to see. Then her gaze slides over to the broken pieces of the cafetière that are still covering the floor and she immediately frowns. 'I'm so sorry for acting like a . . . a maniac,' she whispers, before bringing that tortured gaze back to mine. 'If you tell me where the broom and dustpan are kept, I'll get it cleaned up. And I can pay for a replacement.'

'You're not paying for anything,' I tell her, trying to keep the frustration I'm feeling from my tone, since it isn't going to help anyone. 'And we've got a shop vac here that I can use to easily clean things up, so it's not something you need to worry about.'

She looks as if she's about to argue, so I just forge ahead, asking, 'Can I get you anything? Something to eat? Or a glass of wine?'

She shakes her head, and is already taking a step back as she says, 'No, but thanks for offering. If you don't need my help with anything, I . . . I think I'll go grab a shower.'

'Okay, honey. Just give me a shout if you need me.'

With another brief nod, she quickly turns and heads for the master bedroom, and while every part of me wants to go after her, I don't. It's obvious that she wants some time alone, and while I hate that I won't be in there to hold her while she cries, I'm going to give her space when she needs it.

I spend the next hour putting away the last of the things we'd grabbed at the store and cleaning up the mess on the kitchen floor. There's a hell of a dent on the wall where the cafetière hit, and I make a mental note to have it taken care of once we've left, since I don't want any workmen coming into the house while we're still staying here.

With things finished up in the kitchen, I send a message to Ian Masterson, asking him to send me over anything he has on the Beckett account, and then check in with Deanna, who doesn't have anything new for me.

But mostly I spend the time thinking, searching for a way out of this shit-storm that will keep anyone else from getting hurt. Physically, that is. Because no matter how I wrack my brain – and I've been doing it from the moment this nightmare began – there doesn't seem to be a way to avoid at least some kind of fallout, and I finally make a couple of the most important calls of my life, since there are things I need to have in place before I can put the plan I've started formulating in motion.

Then there are a few more additional calls to make, which turns out to be a long, grueling process that involves a painful amount of evasion, given that the things I need to confess and explain are ones I'd rather discuss in person than over the phone. But I finally wrap things up after another forty-five minutes. Wanting to check on Lottie, since I haven't heard a peep from her for a few hours now, I walk back to the master bedroom and find her curled up in the comfortable chair that sits in the corner of the room, sound asleep. She's still wearing the gray leggings and black T-shirt that she'd put on before we went to the store, so I know that instead of showering, she'd just curled up in the chair and cried herself to sleep.

As I stand there and stare down at her, the intense wave of longing that washes over me is staggering, and I flex my hands at my sides, fighting back the urge to go and fall on my knees before her, begging her to admit that she's feeling even a fraction of the way I am. That her need for me goes *beyond* the physical, into something that's pure, raw emotion. But my bleeding heart is the last damn thing that she needs right now, so I force myself to turn away and go change into a pair of athletic shorts. Then I spend an hour running myself ragged on the treadmill in the gym again, though no matter how hard I push myself, I still can't sweat out this sick feeling in my gut that keeps telling me things are going to get a hell of a lot worse before they get better.

When I'm done, I grab another shower in the bathroom off the hallway, then wrap the towel that I use to dry off with around my waist and slick my wet hair back from my face with my hands. As I stare at my reflection in the foggy mirror, I run a hand over the short beard growth on my jaw, and wonder if I should go ahead and shave it off. But then I recall how much Lottie seems to enjoy it when I tease her sweet little clit with the scruff on my chin, and I decide the beard will definitely live to see another day.

I'm as quiet as I can be as I walk back into the now shadow-filled bedroom – the sun has long since worked its way across the sky, leaving only starlight in its wake – but Lottie still stirs, giving me a sleepy look as she lifts her head, her eyes red from her crying jag.

'Can I get you anything?' I ask, while walking over to the floor lamp and clicking it on to its lowest setting.

'No, I'm good,' she murmurs, and as I turn back around, I catch the flare of heat in her eyes as she runs her appreciative gaze over my bare chest, her tongue taking a quick swipe over her lower lip. But then she shakes herself back to the moment, giving a heavy sigh as she uncurls her body in the chair, setting her sock-covered feet on the floor. 'I, um, should shower too,' she says in a rush, still not looking at me as she moves to her feet. 'I meant to do that earlier, but got . . . sidetracked.'

Hating the hurt that I can still feel pouring out of her, I close the distance between us until I'm standing right in front of her, then just wrap her up in my arms, since if there was ever someone who just needed to be held and comforted, it's my Lottie. My woman. And seeing as how I'm her man, I'm determined to do whatever the hell I can to help her through this. Not just physically, but emotionally too – because there are times when the wounds we carry inside are a thousand times more painful than the ones that can be seen on our surface.

'If you're tired, you don't have to shower, sweetheart.' I lower my head, burying my face in her golden hair, and pull in a deep breath. 'I promise you still smell incredible.'

'Thanks,' she hiccups with a soft laugh. 'But my face is all salty.'

'You get comfortable in the bed then,' I tell her, giving her a gentle squeeze before I let her go and take a step back, 'and I'll grab you a hot washcloth.'

'Okay,' she whispers, sounding exhausted, and I quickly pull a pair of boxers out of the tall mahogany chest that sits against one of the room's pale gray walls, then head into the bathroom. Hanging my towel up on the hook behind the door, I slip the tight black boxers on, then grab a washcloth from under the sink and hold it beneath the hot water. After wringing it out, I head back into the bedroom and sit down on the side of the bed, by her hip, same as I did last night. But this time I hand the washcloth to her as she sits up, waiting while she wipes the dried tears from her face, then rubs the cloth over her throat and the back of her neck.

When she's done, I get up and toss the cloth into the hamper, but leave the muted light on as I make my way back to the bed and climb in beside her, wanting to be able to see her as I take her precious face in my hands and simply kiss her. And while it's a kiss that's meant to offer comfort, it's only seconds before the wild, visceral need that's always simmering between us flares to life, and by the time I lift my mouth from hers, we're both breathing fast, her soft hands are stroking my abs, and my shaft is as hard as granite.

Rubbing my thumb over the plush cushion of her lower lip, I sound like I've just smoked an entire pack of cigarettes as I say, 'Is it wrong that I love the fact you had my taste in your mouth while you were talking to Robbins in the kitchen this afternoon?'

'Caveman,' she quietly snickers, pulling a hiss from my lips as she runs the backs of her fingers down the rigid length of my cock, the boxers the only thing separating my erection from the heady touch of her skin.

'Guilty as charged,' I rumble, forcing myself to keep my hands on her beautiful face, since she needs to be the one who sets the pace here, not me. 'But I happen to be *your* caveman, so hopefully that makes it more tolerable for you.'

'Well, then,' she breathes with a shaky smile. 'I suppose I'll learn to live with it.'

But will you live with me? I want to ask her. As in moving into my home, wherever the hell she wants it to be. Here.

England. Some private island in the tropics. I honestly don't give a shit anymore, so long as she's there with me. But I swallow back the words, determined not to add to her stress, and simply rub the pad of one thumb against the tender edge of her jaw, always blown away by how deliciously soft she is.

She must read the intensity of my thoughts in my eyes, though, because she asks me what I'm thinking, and the words are spilling out of me before I can stop them. 'If we're going to have any shot at a future, Lot, then the running has to stop. We need to deal with him *now*.'

A tiny notch forms between her brows. 'What are you talking about?'

'I'm talking about having a life once this nightmare is over,' I tell her, pushing her hair back from her face as I keep my determined gaze locked tight with hers. 'And while I'm terrified of scaring you off, because I know it's fast, I'm not a coward so I'm just going to say it. I want you to move in with me, Lottie. Permanently. Not just for safety, but because it's where you want to be.'

I can see her working the things I've just said through her brilliant mind, looking at them from every angle. And while I'm braced for an outright refusal – because while she's made it pretty clear that she wanted me when we first met, and that she wants me now, she hasn't said jackshit about wanting me forever – she shocks the hell out of me when she asks, 'You really think I'm going to live through this?'

'You don't?' I grunt, feeling like she's just clipped me on the chin.

'I honestly don't know,' she answers with a shrug, the casual gesture at complete odds with her passionate expression. 'But, God, I hope so. It would suck so bad to finally have you, and then lose it all.'

I can see in her glistening eyes the same damn emotions

that are tearing through me, and I know that there's more I should say. So much more that I should get out in the open. But I don't, simply murmuring, 'You're not going to lose me, baby. I promise. And I'm sure as hell not going to lose you.'

She gives me another little smile and a nod, and all I can think as I run my greedy gaze over her beautiful face is that she's the strongest, most caring, most fascinating woman I've ever known – not to mention the most stubborn and fiercely independent, which only makes her more appealing in my book. And lying here in this bed with her, just taking the time to appreciate her and soak in all the exquisite facets that are Lottie Fleming, inside and out, I have no doubt that Olly eventually saw them, too. That he finally pulled his head out of his ass and opened his eyes to what was right in front of him. And since I'm completely remiss in doing it, I send up a silent thank-you to the jackass, knowing damn well that he'd earned it.

'There *is* something you can do for me,' she suddenly whispers, running the backs of her fingers over my shaft again. 'You can make me forget, for just a while, how horrible this day has been.'

Shaking my head, I say, 'I'm not going to fuck you tonight.'

Her brows lift with surprise. 'You're not?'

'Naw,' I drawl, leaning in close and nipping her lower lip with my teeth. 'Tonight, I'm going to make love to you, sweetheart. So just lie back and enjoy it.'

'At least you didn't say "Think of England",' she laughs, sitting up and pulling her top over her head. Then she takes her bra off, lies back on the bed, and starts working her leggings and panties down her legs.

'If you're able to think at all when I'm inside you,' I growl, bracing myself on my elbows as I settle between her parted thighs, 'then I'm clearly not doing something right.'

'You do *everything* right.'

'Naw, baby, that's you,' I rumble, reaching between her legs and sliding my fingertips up her slick, sweet sex.

Not to be outdone, she shoves the boxers over my hips, then wraps her delicate hand around my hard, heavy erection. 'You know, I think I could probably get addicted to this particular part of you.' She smirks up at me. 'And all the other ones, too. But *this* one's my favorite.'

'Good. Do it. As quickly as possible,' I mutter, lowering my head so that I can lick and suck on one of her tight, candy-pink nipples. Then I eagerly give the same treatment to her other breast, before I lift up and look back down at her. 'Because you're not someone I could watch walk away, Lot. Now that I've finally got you, I'm holding on tight.'

She tilts her head to the side as she stares back at me, still stroking my throbbing shaft with her soft, feminine hand. 'For how long?'

'For however long we have.' Before she can respond, I pull her hand away, notch myself against her tender opening and start feeding my cock into her, slowly, so she can feel every inch. 'I'm not trying to pressure you,' I growl, rubbing my mouth over hers as I roll my hips. 'But you should know that's what I want. For the two of us to be together. As in for-fucking-ever.'

'God, Callan,' she says softly . . . breathlessly, her eyes glistening with a fresh wash of tears. 'That . . . That would be amazing.'

I'm not sure if it's the words she's just said to me or the stunning way that she's looking up at me – or hell, maybe it's both – but from one second to the next, any control I've been clawing on to is completely shredded. Suddenly every muscle in my body is flexing and releasing as I work myself deeper into her snug, drenched hold, and I love the throaty cry that she gives when I'm finally fully seated inside her, not even a sliver of space between our bodies. She's stretched so tight around me, I can feel the frenzied rhythm of her heartbeat, and even though I know she must be sore, she doesn't tell me to stop or to go easy on her. No, she just wraps her long legs around my waist, lifts her head and gives a provocative nip to my shoulder that makes me somehow push in even deeper, and we both gasp from how impossibly good it feels.

And in this poignant, breathtaking moment, we're both reminded that there's *still* good to be found in this world . . . even when we're caught in the middle of a vicious nightmare.

But here, in this bed, it's just me and Lottie. Just our hunger and our need and this insanely powerful connection that keeps binding us tighter together, and I have no idea how I lasted so long today without getting back inside her. And any plans I might have still had about trying to keep this slow and gentle go completely out the goddamn window.

'I fucking love fucking you,' I groan, watching her face as I pull my hips back, while every tight, cushiony inch of her sex clings to me like it never wants to let me go. And as I push myself back in and start riding her with a hammering rhythm that has husky cries jerking from her lips while she clutches at my shoulders, her cheeks flushed and her pink lips curled in the sexiest smile I've ever seen, I marvel at how I ever lived without this. Without *her*. Because it doesn't make any sense, how I went through each day, living and breathing without her in my life, and I'm only seconds away from telling her *everything* – all of it – when she throws her head back and screams with the powerful force of her release.

She comes so hard it nearly destroys me, drawing me closer and closer to that blinding, soul-shaking edge, and I only pull out at the last possible second. '*Lottie!*' I shout, my voice so gut-tural her name comes out as more of a sound than an actual word, my entire body shuddering with pleasure until I'm completely drained.

When I can finally remember how to breathe again, I suck a desperate gulp of air into my lungs and collapse onto the bed beside her, careful not to crush her, and she turns her head to look at me, her passion-dark gaze locking with mine as we slowly drift back to reality.

'What are we going to do?' she asks, after long minutes have passed and our hearts are no longer pumping to a hard, frantic rhythm, and I can't help but shake my head in amazement. I know she's talking about Fleming, and unlike Jessica, who created a nightmare and then just threw it in my lap, expecting me to deal with it, Lottie refuses to sit back and let me handle this shit-show on my own.

'I've got some ideas,' I tell her, leaning over and placing a kiss on the tender corner of her mouth. Then I lift my head and look into her beautiful blue eyes. 'So you don't have to worry, sweetheart. I won't let anything happen to you.'

She places her hand against the side of my face as she gives me a smile. 'I'm not going to let anything happen to you, either.'

And as she lifts her head and touches her lips to mine, she doesn't stop to ask what my ideas are . . . and I don't stop kissing her back long enough to tell her. No, that conversation can wait for the morning, and I'm grateful for this brief reprieve, because I know *exactly* how my girl is going to react when I share my plan.

There'll be anger . . . and shouting . . . as well as a strong chance that something will probably get broken again.

Because she's going to hate every single fucking part of it.

Chapter Sixteen

ANDREW

If there's one thing that I truly despise in this world, it's being wrong. And while it hasn't happened often, as I sit behind the wheel of my rental on this increasingly busy street, waiting for the Manhattan traffic lights to change as the sun rises over the city skyline, I force myself to face the fact that my plans haven't worked out the way that I'd hoped – first with the hacking attempt on the Hathaway server, and then with the wannabe actress/food server.

Not that the second one hadn't been fun. And a hell of a physical workout, given that Ruby was a fighter. But an entire night has gone by since her body was found, and I'm beginning to think that the whole point behind our time together had apparently been for nothing but my enjoyment.

I'd thought for sure that my playtime with Lottie's pretty co-worker would bring my cousin crawling out from whatever bloody hole Hathaway has hidden her in. Surely she got the message. Or perhaps it's simply the Neanderthal himself who won't allow her to do the *right* thing and immediately come back to me, planting her skinny arse back in her cheap apartment before someone else she knows pays the price for her absence from my life with theirs. In which case, it's time to up the ante and really get their attention.

The light changes, and as I take the next right, driving along the front of Clara Hathaway's building, I'm momentarily tempted to put in a quick call to the press, giving them all the salacious details of how her brother's shagging a woman who's wanted for murder. It would kill her mayoral campaign – which I was able to discover with a simple search of the Hathaway name in relation to New York City on the internet – as quickly as I could take her life with a blade. But I forcefully beat back that desire, since, for the moment, there's something oddly satisfying about keeping that particular cat in the bag, simply because I know they must be shitting themselves over it, constantly worrying when I might finally make the call that could send their precious Clara's future into a death spiral she can't ever recover from.

And while I'd obviously love to have some special 'alone time' with the feisty, freckle-faced politician, she has constant security that was no doubt increased the second they learned about Ruby, which won't do. Not when my timeline has been cut short, and my needs are now calling for a more expeditious option. Something that will start a fire under their arses, and bring my beautiful Lottie crawling back to me on her hands and knees, begging me for sweet, sweet mercy.

Not that I have any for the troublesome bitch.

I curse as I'm stopped by another light, my hands gripping the wheel so tightly, I'm surprised it hasn't snapped, and as I glare through the front windscreen, I watch as a bike courier speeds across the road, before disappearing into the traffic. And just like that, I have the perfect solution, so long as the lovely Eva is still working . . . and they haven't closed ranks around her like they did with Clara. I would laugh at the outrageousness of it, but that's how these things happen sometimes. Pure, random chance that can change your life forever.

Like framing Lottie for the murder of her husband.

When I'd swum out to Beckett's obnoxious yacht that night, that had never been my intention. No, I'd simply planned to finally take what was my due, and then happily kill them both, since she'd destroyed my fun by marrying the jackass. But when the cocky arsehole had ruined my plans, I'd improvised. And as it turned out, taking the knife from the galley had been a stroke of absolute genius. As if the gods themselves had been smiling down on me, I'd used that knife to cut him into so many far more interesting, cleverer pieces than he'd been as a whole, and set the destruction of her entire world into motion, like a boulder rolling over an ant hill.

I'd completely destroyed her life, forcing her away from everything that she'd known and loved.

And now I'm ready to do it again.

Bringing the car to a stop at the side of the road, I pull the new phone that I'd bought when I first arrived in New York from my pocket and scroll through my hi-res photographs, until I get to the image I want. The one of the luscious Eva Diaz, Lottie's friend and neighbor. I've been watching Lottie's building religiously, and took this photo over a week ago, one evening when Eva had been coming home from work. As I move my fingertips across the screen, I'm able to enlarge the image until I can read the name of the company that's written boldly across her gorgeous breasts: *Fairbanks Couriers*.

My chest starts to shake with a low, almost giddy laugh, my dick already hard at this new proof of my exceptional brilliance.

Now all that's left is for me to find the perfect spot for my plans . . .

And book a pickup.

Chapter Seventeen

CALLAN

'Lottie, honey, come on,' I murmur, gently shaking her shoulder. 'You've got to get up and come meet everyone, sleepyhead.'

'What?' she croaks, glaring up at me with only one eye through the golden fall of her hair, the other eye still closed.

'You've already met my mom and Clara, but—'

'Your mum and Clara are here?' she gasps, sitting up so quickly she nearly catches me on the chin. 'What's going on?'

'I'll explain everything in a minute. Right now, I'm trying to tell you that they've brought two of my brothers, Colin and Cade, with them, and they're waiting to meet you.'

'Three of your siblings and your mother are here, and you're only just now waking me up?' she cries, shoving her hands into her sleep-tousled hair. 'What the hell, Callan? I look like a wreck.'

'No, you look beautiful,' I quietly protest, pressing a quick kiss to the tip of her nose. 'Now come have some coffee and breakfast with everyone, and then I'll explain what's happening.'

'Oh God,' she mutters, eyeing me with sudden suspicion as

I stand up from the side of the bed so that she can climb out. 'I'm not going to like this, am I?'

'Probably not,' I admit in a nervous rumble, and there's a grim smile kicking up the corner of my mouth as I shove my hands into the front pockets of my jeans. 'But just remember that you trust me. If you can do that, then everything's going to be okay.'

She climbs out of the bed then, keeping her back to me as she quickly makes her way over to the chest of drawers, and I can tell from the set of her shoulders that she's less than thrilled with how this morning is going so far. 'You know, I'm starting to think the problem isn't with me trusting *you*, Callan, but the other way around.'

Now we're both frowning. 'That's bullshit and you know it, Lot.'

'Do I?' She pulls on a pair of black panties, then arches one of those golden eyebrows at me as she looks over her shoulder, and it's a testament to the importance of this conversation that my attention is still focused on her top half, and not on her sweet little ass. 'You've not only made and implemented plans without me, and without talking things over with me, but you already have your family here to back you up.'

'It's not an ambush,' I argue, even though I know damn well that it looks like one.

'And I'm not Jessica!' she shouts, turning toward me in a burst of angry frustration, her blue eyes narrowed and dark as she clutches the clothes she's picked out to wear against her naked chest. 'I'm not looking for someone to handle all of my problems for me. I just want someone who'll be by my side. A partner. I don't need a bloody parent!'

I take a step toward her, hoping my brothers can't overhear this argument, because it's the kind of thing they would never let me live down. 'And I'm sure as hell not treating you like a child,' I bite out.

Her chin goes up at that stubborn angle I was actually start-ing to miss, even though I know it means I'm about to get my ass ripped into. 'Not when it comes to our physical relation-ship,' she says, her low voice seething with resentment. 'But outside of that, you seem to forget that I'm a grown woman with a mind of her own. One who can make her own damn decisions concerning the direction of her life.'

'No, you can't. Because Andrew took that away from you,' I growl, the words so guttural, it's like they're being ripped up from the deepest, most visceral part of me. 'I'm just trying to help you get it back.'

She shakes her head so hard it lifts her blonde hair from her shoulders. 'No, you're trying to get it back all on your own, while wrapping me in cotton wool, and I hate it. I get that I've failed with all of this at every turn, and you must think I'm completely useless, but damn it, I would rather keep running than sit back and watch you take this burden all on yourself. It's bullshit!'

'It's called being in a fucking relationship!' I roar, no longer giving a damn what my family overhears. I'm just raw, blister-ing emotion, my heart thundering in my chest as I bellow, 'It's called being in love!'

She pales instantly, a quiet gasp on her lips as she blinks back at me in shock, and I swipe my hand through the air, as if I can somehow knock the words out of existence. 'You know what? Let's just forget that happened, because this really isn't the time. Okay?'

Her chin jerks up, her voice tellingly soft as she says, 'Yeah. Sure.'

I drop my head forward, rubbing my thumb and forefinger

over my eyes, knowing I've screwed this entire conversation up from beginning to end. 'We can argue about everything else after we've eaten and had some coffee,' I mutter. 'We both missed dinner last night, so I know you must be as starved as I am.'

I lower my hand and look up just in time to see her glancing over her shoulder as she heads into the bathroom. 'Just give me a couple of minutes to get ready and I'll meet you out there.'

A handful of seconds later, I'm silently groaning *Well, that was a damn nightmare*, as I shut the bedroom door behind me and walk into the hallway. But since I don't see the rest of this morning going any better, I pull in a deep breath to fortify myself and head toward the noisy kitchen. When I walk through the doorway, my mom is nowhere in sight, but I find Clara and Cade sitting at the breakfast bar, while Colin has his head stuck in the open refrigerator. 'You call us up here for an important morning meeting and don't even have anything to feed us?' he grumbles, lifting up until he can glare at me over the top of the door. 'What the hell, dude?'

My chest rises and falls with a heavy sigh. 'The fridge is fully stocked, Colin.'

'But none of it's cooked,' he complains, finally straightening and shutting the door. At six-five, he's as tall as I am, but with a bulkier build that comes from the fact he's still on active duty in the Special Forces. 'I'm starving, man.'

'Christ,' Cade mutters, moving his tall but more leanly muscled body to its feet, the incredible ink on both of his long arms gleaming with vibrant color beneath the golden glow of the overhead lights. 'I'll cook you some damn bacon if you'll just promise to shut up.'

Colin gives a hearty sigh of relief, clapping Cade on the shoulder so hard he nearly topples him over. 'Thanks, bro. You're a lifesaver.'

Clara snickers under her breath at them, but there's an unmistakable look of concern in her green eyes as she locks her gaze with mine, and I know she's worried not only about why I've called them all the way up here, but also because of the extra security they've all had following them around. Well, all of them except for Colin, who, according to Deanna, had laughed in the faces of my employees when they'd shown up at his house, before telling them he could take care of his family and himself without their help.

When they'd all arrived a short while ago, their security details had headed downstairs to catch up with Robbins and Thompson, so it's just the family who's gathered here for breakfast. And since I really am desperate for some food and coffee, I ask Cade if he'll cook the entire pack of bacon that's in the fridge, then walk over to the coffee-maker and get a pot started. My mom comes in just as it begins percolating, unusually quiet as she kisses my cheek before going and joining Clara at the breakfast bar, and I know she's worried, too. I'm trying to remember exactly what I'd planned to say to start off the awkward conversation we need to have, when Lottie walks in. She looks as gorgeous as ever in a pair of dark jeans and a slouchy black sweater, her golden hair gleaming and the shiny slick of gloss on her soft, pink lips just making me want to kiss the ever-loving hell out of her. But this is neither the time nor the place, and seeing as how she's just drawn everyone's attention, I start making the introductions.

Because I'm starving and want to eat before diving into the level of intensity it's going to take to explain who she really is, I go ahead and introduce her to Cade and Colin as 'Lana' for the moment. And I'm thankful as hell that when she met my mom and Clara at my apartment on Saturday morning, she hadn't been wearing the godawful red wig I'd convinced her to throw away before we'd left the hotel room at the Fairfax, since it means we can currently avoid any discussion about why she'd been disguising her appearance.

My mom and Clara both say how good it is to see her again, even though their worried looks only intensify when they note the small, healing cut near her brow and the evident strain on her face, and my brothers are both on their best behavior. I can tell they're dying of curiosity about her, but instead of badgering her with a thousand questions, they just shoot her welcoming smiles, tell her to grab a seat by Clara, and then Colin actually starts helping with breakfast by pulling the eggs out of the fridge and whipping them up in a bowl.

Giving Lottie a warm smile, my mom asks her how she's been.

'Um, fine, thanks,' she replies, before shooting me a nervous look, no doubt terrified that my mom is going to put her on the spot about why she'd run out on her at my apartment. But I just give her a quick grin, silently assuring her that everything's going to be okay, since I'd made it clear to my mom and Clara that they were *not* to interrogate her.

And while I'd been worried that this entire breakfast was going to be a painful experience, my family comes to the rescue with their awesome sense of humors and outgoing personalities, putting everyone at ease. There's talk about the crazy things that Colin's youngest has been getting up to, since the kid is determined to turn my brother gray before his time, and then Cade tells us about the Oscar-winning client who's just hired him to tattoo an image of their beloved pet poodles onto their backside, one dog for each cheek. We try like crazy to get him to divulge the name, but he refuses to spill, leading to us all making hilarious guesses about who it might be.

While Clara clears away the empty plates, I pour everyone a second cup of coffee, then finally suck it up and get on with the reason for them all being here. 'If you guys don't mind,' I say, giving Lottie another reassuring glance, 'I'd like to speak to Mom and Clara alone in the office for a bit.'

Lottie frowns, but keeps whatever concerns or frustrations she might have at being left out of the loop to herself.

'No problem, bro,' Colin murmurs, giving me a hard slap on the shoulder that jars my teeth. 'We'll just keep Lana entertained with stories about how much shit you used to get up to when you were younger.'

'Fuck,' I mutter under my breath, which makes both my brothers laugh, while my mom just tsks with disapproval.

I'm painfully aware of Lottie's sharp gaze boring into the back of my head as I exit the kitchen with my mom and Clara, and while I feel like crap for leaving her with my crazy brothers, this is a conversation that's going to be tough enough without her voicing a new argument every two seconds.

And until she plays her part in my plan, it's critical that she remains in the dark.

After I show my mom and Clara into the safehouse's home office, they both take seats in the chairs that are placed in front of the modern-looking desk, wearing similar expressions of worry and expectancy, so I cross my arms over my chest as I lean back against the front of the desk and start talking.

'Okay, there's a lot that we need to cover in a short amount of time, so I'm just going to get right to it. Lana Hill is a false identity. The amazing woman sitting in my kitchen right now is named Lottie Fleming, and—'

'Lottie? Isn't that the name of the woman whose wedding you went to last year in England?' my mom cuts in, her brown eyes, almost the exact same shade as mine, shooting wide with shock. 'Ohmygod, she's the one who murdered her husband!'

'No, she didn't,' I growl. 'And please just be quiet for two seconds so that I can explain everything.'

Clara, acting with a calmness that I can't help but be grateful for right now, sets her hand on my mom's forearm in a silent communication to relax. 'We're listening, Callan,' she murmurs, giving me an encouraging nod as she looks up at me. 'Go on.'

I start at the beginning, figuring they deserve to know all of it, admitting that I felt a connection to Lottie from the moment we'd first met . . . and how gutted I'd been when she still drove off with Beckett at the end of that weekend. When I get to the part about her cousin, and the horrors he'd inflicted on her over the years, they both go pale with concern, but don't interrupt me. Then they both shudder with shock as I tell them about Oliver's murder, and how Lottie only managed to escape with her life because of his sacrifice. But they both nod with approval when I explain how determined I was to help her, after stumbling across her in the city, even though she was adamant that I should stay as far away from her as I could, terrified that something would happen to me. And they look even paler as I relay the events in the parking structure at the Fairfax, followed by the news we'd received yesterday about Ruby Carlisle.

When I'm finally done, my mom is staring at some distant point over my shoulder, still taking it all in, but Clara's sharp gaze locks tight with mine. 'You're risking so much by having her here, Callan. By helping her,' she murmurs, keeping her expression carefully neutral in the way that only a disciplined politician can. 'And while I'm pretty sure I already know the answer, I'm going to ask you anyway: Is she worth it?'

I give a short, tight nod and her eyes go bright with understanding. 'You're in love with her, aren't you?'

My throat works with a hard swallow, but my rough voice is firm with conviction when I say, 'I am.'

Some of the happiness that had briefly flared in Clara's eyes fades, and she gives me a pointed look. 'And you're sure that's not clouding your judgment?'

Quietly, I say, 'She's not Jess, Clara. She's just a wonderful woman who got caught up in a godawful nightmare, and none of it's her fault.'

'Yeah, I think so too,' she agrees with a sigh. 'But I had to ask.'

'I get that. But you can trust her. I'd bet my life on it.' I look back over at my mom, bracing for her reaction, but while there's a light sheen of tears in her eyes, they're shining with understanding and approval.

'Okay,' Clara says in a let's-get-down-to-business tone, drawing my attention back to her. 'Now you need to tell us your plan. Because I'm guessing that's the main reason that you've brought us up here, right?'

I know this next reveal is going to be even more difficult than the first, and the nervous energy coursing through my veins has me moving around to the other side of the desk so that there's room for me to pace while I talk.

When I've reached the final part, Clara's the one I look to, since what I've just proposed will have a lasting effect on our relationship. 'So when you leave here,' I tell her, 'you need to have your publicist put out a statement saying that for both personal and professional reasons, you're cutting all ties with me. That way you'll be covered no matter how my plan to deal with Andrew Fleming works out.'

'Wow,' she breathes, and though I try my best, I'm unable to read her expression.

'What?' I clip, shoving my hands into my pockets as I come to a stop behind the desk.

'I'm just thinking how fortunate it is that you're so pretty,' she mutters with a dry laugh, 'because you sure as hell aren't smart.'

'Clara—'

'Come on, Callan,' she drawls, rolling her eyes at me. 'Did you honestly think I would go along with this bullshit? Do you know me at all?'

With a scowl settling between my brows, I say, 'I know you love me, but this isn't about love. This is about your future. A future I'm about to throw a damn bomb at. So—'

'Shh,' she cuts in, fluttering her fingers at me.

'Excuse me?' I growl, my scowl deepening.

'Just be quiet for a moment. I need to think,' Clara murmurs, moving to her feet. She links her hands behind her back as she copies my pacing, striding back and forth in front of the room's bay window, her brows knitted with concentration, while my mom and I just watch her. 'Okay,' she says after barely more than a minute has gone by, looking back over at us. 'I've got a plan.'

Despite my tension, I can feel the corner of my mouth twitch with wry amusement as I shake my head. 'Of course you do. I've been wracking my brain for a way to deal with this shit for days, and you've already got the answer. So come on, smartypants, let's hear it.'

Looking me right in the eye, she says, 'I'm going to call Jonathan Clark and set up a private interview with him, during which I'm going to share a CliffsNotes version of what you've just told us and make it clear that you have my complete and unwavering support, with the caveat that he can't release it until after you've given me the all-clear.'

'What? The hell you are,' I laugh, as if she's just told us a joke. Jonathan Clark is a journalist who writes for several of the country's biggest papers, and while he's actually a good guy, there's no way I'm letting her do this. 'That's got to be the dumbest thing I've ever heard.'

'Come on, Callan. You know we can trust him. He'll be direct and won't put any sensationalist spin on the story.'

'He won't need to,' I argue, raising my voice. 'It's sensational all on its own, Clara. And political suicide!'

'Just hear me out,' she murmurs, moving away from the window until she's standing behind the chair she'd been sitting in. Gripping the back of it with both hands, she keeps her determined gaze locked with mine as she goes on. 'I get that I've been acting like a she-bitch lately, but that's only because I've had Carl yammering on in my ear nearly every second of every day and I let the pressure get to me. But I've run my campaign from the beginning on a platform that promotes honesty and integrity, so this is the only logical course of action.'

'The hell it is,' I grunt, my jaw so tight it's pulsing with pain.

Her nostrils flare as she sucks in a sharp breath. 'Your idea is completely crazy, Callan. I'm not going to disown you!'

'And there's no goddamn way I'm letting you throw yourself on your fucking sword!' I shout back.

'It won't be like that,' she argues, her expression turning mulish, 'but even if it was, I don't recall asking for your permission, bro.'

I look at my mom, hoping she can talk some sense into her. 'Mom, help,' I plead.

'Don't look at *me*, sweetie,' she murmurs, arching one of her perfectly shaped eyebrows at me. 'I happen to agree with her.'

'Shit!' I seethe, and obviously seeing how upset I am, my mom doesn't even scold me for it.

'Look, I'm not blaming you, Cal,' Clara says in a calmer tone, and as I shift my focus back to her, there's a sharp burst of pain at the center of my chest as I take in the stunning look of pride and determination on her beautiful face. 'You've done what was right, and I'm so incredibly proud of you for it. I mean, I'm thoroughly pissed that you didn't come to me for help from the start, or share any of what you've been going through this past year with us, and I'm terrified for your safety, because this Andrew asshole is clearly psychotic. But I'm proud of you for not turning your back on her – and I would expect nothing less from you, because that's the kind of man you are. And this is who *I* am.'

'Jesus, Clara,' I huff, sounding as tormented as I do amazed.

'What kind of reformer would I be if I didn't stand up for what's right?' she asks, while her lips curl with a small half-smile. 'Not to mention my family? The people I love, including you, you big idiot?'

'But it isn't fair for *my* choices to interfere with *your* life this way.'

'But *you're* not to blame for that,' she states with firm conviction. 'The person to blame is the one who murdered Oliver Beckett and then put the fall for it onto an innocent woman. The same woman he's spent the past eight years terrorizing.'

Given that I sure as hell don't have an argument for any of that, I finally accept her decision, even though it's making me feel sick with guilt. We hash out a few more critical details, since this definitely changes my original plan, and I'm still feeling a bit green around the gills when the three of us head back into the kitchen. So much so that Lottie's eyes flare when she looks at me, making it clear that I'm wearing my frustration and guilt like a scarlet letter on my forehead.

Scrubbing my hands over my face, I blow out a rough breath, and as soon as my mom and Clara are seated at the breakfast bar with Lottie again, I look at my brothers, who are both leaning against one of the kitchen counters with coffee mugs in their hands. 'There's a hell of a lot that I need to bring you both up to speed on,' I tell them, 'and I promise to do that as soon as I can. But first, I need to explain something to Lottie ab—'

'Don't you mean Lana?' Cade cuts in, giving me a quizzical look.

'Her name is *Lottie*, Cade, not Lana. And that's part of what I'll be bringing you up to speed on. But right now, I'm just asking for your patience while I tell her something important.'

He and Colin both jerk their chins at me in silent agreement, and I shove my hands into my pockets as I look up at the clock that hangs over the sink, then slide my gaze back over to Lottie. 'In twenty minutes, Seb—'

'Is he the hot guy who Mom has a huge crush on?' Cade asks, cutting me off again.

'Christ, Cade, focus,' I snap, scowling at him, and he holds his hands up in a silent apology. Looking back at Lottie, who's clearly bracing herself for some bad news, I go on. 'Seb is going to leak Andrew's name to a contact he has at Bishop International News who knows Seb wouldn't ever feed her a bullshit story. He's going to tell her that Andrew Fleming, a profiler with Scotland Yard, is soon to be considered the number one suspect in the murder of Ruby Carlisle, as well as in the murder of Oliver Beckett. We expect a brief article will show up on their news app within the hour.'

'Ohmygod,' Lottie whispers, looking like she might pass out as she holds on tight to the edge of the bar. 'Are you . . .? Have you lost your mind?'

'Naw, honey. I'm just finally thinking straight and putting an end to this shit once and for all.'

She takes a moment to absorb my answer, and then her creamy skin starts to flush with color again, her eyes narrowing to chips of midnight blue. 'And when exactly did you and Seb agree on all of this?'

'I called him yesterday, while you were sleeping.'

'Of course you did,' she says with a harsh, sarcastic laugh. 'Because that's the Callan Hathaway mode of operation, isn't it? Forge straight ahead and who gives a damn who you bulldoze along the way with your heroics. Sound about right?'

'Look, we can argue about my hero complex later,' I say in a gritty voice, pulling my phone from my back pocket. Then I walk over to the bar, unlock the phone's home screen and set it down in front of her. 'Right now, I need for you to write your aunt and uncle and give them a heads-up, since the UK press will probably be tracking them down for comment the second Andrew's name is out there. And it's okay if you sign into your old email account, because the security features on my phone will make your message impossible to trace.'

'Can't I just call them?' she asks, the anger she's feeling over the way that I've planned all of this without her momentarily buried beneath her look of confusion.

Shaking my head, I tell her, 'Later, when we've got more time. Right now, you need to keep this brief and to the point. I'd rather you not have to do it at all, but the news needs to come from someone they trust, and given your uncle's recent health scare, I don't think he should be blindsided by it.'

'Okay, you're right,' she concedes, picking up the phone. 'What exactly do you want me to say?'

'Tell them that you'll be in touch again soon and will explain everything then, but that they need to be prepared to see Andrew's name in the news today, linked to a troubling criminal case. You can fill them in on everything else later, when you call.'

She keeps her attention on the phone as she nods her head, her fingers moving over the touchscreen as she logs into her old email account. It takes her less than a minute to write the message and give it a quick look-over. Then she hits the send button and peers back up at me. 'It's done.'

'Good,' I sigh, knowing this next part is going to be a real bitch.

'You still haven't explained your plan,' she says, handing the phone back to me, and I swear I can feel a wave of uncomfortable tension vibing off my mom and Clara, since they both know what's coming, while my brothers are just watching us with looks of concerned confusion. 'What does leaking Andrew's name do for us, except piss him off and guarantee trouble for Clara's campaign? I mean, it's not like he's going to be stupid enough to try and make a run for it using his real identity. And we still don't even know where he is or have a shred of evidence that proves my innocence.'

Instead of answering her questions in front of everyone, I walk around the bar and take hold of her hand, tugging on it until she hops off the stool and reluctantly follows me out of the room. 'You guys make yourselves at home,' I call over my shoulder to my family. 'But don't destroy anything or you're paying for it!' I add, which earns a snicker from what sounds like Cade, though it could just as easily have been Colin.

'Callan, what the hell's going on?' Lottie demands, ripping her hand from mine the second I've shut the bedroom door behind us.

I push my hands into my pockets again as I lean back against the door, figuring that with my huge body in the way, she won't be able to storm off in a rage once I tell her what I've done. Though there's also a strong chance she just might knee me in the balls after my confession, but I'm willing to take the beating if it means keeping her in here with me until I've convinced her to forgive me. Or at least found a way to make her understand.

'Okay,' I say, hoping she can see in my expression just how

much she means to me. 'I know you're going to be pissed, but I needed a way to draw Andrew here that wasn't so obvious he would see straight through it. So I had our tech department at Hathaway put a crack in my phone's firewall that will allow him to trace where the email you just wrote to your aunt and uncle came from.'

For what seems like forever, she just stands there in the middle of the bedroom, staring back at me, while her chest softly rises and falls with her deep, even breaths. It's like that heavy, expectant moment of calm before a hurricane hits, and even though you know it's coming, you try to convince yourself it won't be nearly as damaging as you feared.

'Lottie,' I husk, when she just keeps standing there, watching me with those guarded eyes, and though she's standing right *there*, with only a yard or so separating us, it feels like she's a million miles away. 'Come on, baby, say something.'

'You want me to say something?' she asks, the quiet laughter that suddenly spills from her lips so caustic, it makes me wince. 'Okay, Callan. I'll say something.' Her hands clench and unclench at her sides, and I swear I can see the fury rising up inside her like a great, towering swell, her dark gaze burning with fear and rage as she shouts, '*What the hell were you thinking?*'

'I'm not going to just sit around and let this prick keep messing with your life, Lot. Not when he's hurting you and the people you care about. And since we can't find him, it finally occurred to me that the fastest solution was to simply bring the bastard to me, so that this shit can end *today*.'

'So you just decided this all on your own, and my feelings on the subject don't matter? Not to mention the way you just completely used me out there!' she snarls, pointing in the direction of the kitchen.

Since I'm only going to dig myself into an even deeper hole

if I touch any of those questions, I suck in a sharp breath and keep forging ahead. 'We needed a valid reason for you to contact your aunt and uncle, which is why Seb and I decided to leak his name to the press. And while we couldn't make it too easy for him to hack into the system, given that he'd see right through that, with any luck he'll be able to trace the email in a few hours, tops, and be here by tonight. Which means you need to get out of here, the sooner the better.'

She shakes her head as a dazed, bitter burst of laughter falls from her lips. 'I do? And just where exactly am I meant to go?'

'I've talked things over with Clara, and you're going to leave with her and her security detail and head back to the city. You'll be staying at her place until this is over.' Which hadn't been my original plan, but was the one we eventually agreed on.

Lottie's eyes widen with surprise, then quickly narrow. 'I don't understand. Isn't that putting Clara in danger?'

I reach behind my neck to rub at the knotted muscles there. 'You're not going to be in any danger,' I mutter, 'so long as I get you out of here, and neither will she. Because once that asshole takes the bait, he's going to come here as fast as he fucking can. Then I'm going to get a confession out of him, recorded and with witnesses, and after that, make sure he can't harm anyone else ever again. Especially *you*.'

'Bullshit,' she argues. 'I *know* you, Callan. You're not a cold-blooded murderer, no matter how much better off this world would be without Andrew Fleming in it.'

'I didn't say anything about killing him in cold blood.'

'So you're going to what?' she scoffs, the expression on her face caught somewhere between dumbfounded and disbelief. 'Have a showdown *Lethal Weapon* style out in the driveway? Fight him to the death?'

I work my jaw, refusing to lie to her, seeing as how the scenario she's just described would suit me to a T.

'Oh wow. That's one doozy of a plan,' she laughs, the hollow sound so painfully cynical it makes me wince again. Then she crosses her arms over her chest, so tightly I'm surprised she can even still breathe, and says, 'Couldn't Thompson or Robbins have just driven me back to the city? Why on earth did you bring your family all the way up here?'

I shove a hand back through my hair, grimacing not only at her questions, but also from the headache that's started throbbing in my temples. 'I wanted to convince Clara to announce that she was severing ties with me to minimize any backlash against her campaign. And since Colin and Cade are the ones who encouraged her to run for mayor in the first place, I figured if I could make Clara see that this was the best option, then I would be able to talk everything over with them, face to face, and convince them to back up Clara's announcement for the press.' A grim smile twitches at the corner of my mouth as I admit, 'But I didn't even make it past the first hurdle.'

She arches an eyebrow. 'Clara refused?'

I give a tired sigh. 'Yeah.'

'Wow, imagine that,' she drawls with another heavy dose of sarcasm, her blue eyes sparking with a brief shot of satisfaction. 'A strong-minded woman didn't like you telling her what to do. Shocker.'

'Be as sarcastic as you want, Lot,' I rumble. 'I'm only trying to do what's right.'

'You mean what you *think* is right.'

A weighted, suffocating silence settles between us, broken only by the quiet soughing of our breaths, until the sound of a vehicle coming up the driveway has her giving me a questioning look, wordlessly asking who else has come to join our little party.

'That's probably going to be Jase,' I mutter, rubbing my jaw.

The shock that moves through her gaze tells me that was the *last* name she'd expected to hear, and she frowns with confusion. 'Why is Jase here?'

'I asked him to come. In the unlikely event that anything goes wrong, he's going to ensure that you get to safety and are set up with a new life someplace of your choosing.' I know it's a hell of a thing to request of him, but he hadn't even hesitated to agree when I'd called. He'd just told me that he would book a private jet and leave California as soon as possible.

'Well, congratulations,' she murmurs. 'You've really thought of everything, haven't you?'

'I just want you protected, Lottie. That's all that matters to me.'

'You know, I would probably think that was sweet,' she says softly, the disappointment in her beautiful eyes hitting me like a physical blow, 'if you hadn't made it so blatantly clear that what *I* want means nothing to you.'

'That's not true and you—'

'Oops,' she cuts in when we hear Jase knock on the front door. Forcing a bright, phony-as-hell smile onto her face, she says, 'Time's up, big guy. Sounds like we had better get out there and greet your buddy.'

Shit, I think. *This is about to go from bad to worse.*

'Yeah, about that,' I mutter, rubbing at the back of my neck again as I straighten away from the door. 'Before we leave this room, there's something I need to tell you, and . . . you're not going to like it.'

'More bad news?' she murmurs with a mocking smile, shaking her head at me. 'Geez, Callan. This just isn't your day, is it?'

Deciding the Band-Aid method is best and that I just need to get it out there, I go ahead and confess. 'I lied when I said that Jase believes you're innocent.'

She flinches, but doesn't say a single word. All she does is blink at me, and then pull in a deep, trembling breath, and I swear I can see the fury building beneath her surface again like a tsunami rolling across the ocean floor, gaining in strength with each second that goes by.

'Yeah, so, Emmy and I have argued with him about it ever since the murder, but—'

'If he believes that I did it, then why is he here?' she cuts in again, though this time her voice is deceptively calm.

'*But*,' I repeat, determined to try to explain, 'even though he thought you were guilty, he was never against you, Lottie. He believed that Olly must have done something truly horrible that simply pushed you past your limit. But I've explained to him about Andrew, and he finally gets it.'

'Well, then that's just wonderful,' she announces with another one of those bright, fake smiles that looks like it's actually hurting her face. 'I think we should go and congratulate him right now.'

And with those strangely ominous words, she walks right past me and out of the room, and I send out a silent apology to my best friend.

Because I have no doubt that the love of my life is about to kick his ass.

Chapter Eighteen

CALLAN

By the time Lottie and I make it out of the bedroom, my family has already let Jase – who's casually dressed in jeans and a white polo shirt, instead of one of his Savile Row suits – inside the house. They're all standing around together in the living room, exchanging hugs and back slaps as they catch up with each other, and I can hear my mom pressuring him to bring Emmy for a visit as we walk in to join them.

'Hey, Lottie. It's good to see you again,' Jase murmurs with a careful smile, reaching out to give her a hug too, as she walks straight over to him – until Lottie's fist suddenly flies up, popping him right in his left eye.

'What the fuck?' he gasps, looking completely stunned as he stumbles back a step, while the rest of the room goes completely silent. 'Why—?'

'How could you have believed it?' she screams, cutting him off, her slender body trembling with hurt and outrage as she fists her hands at her sides. 'How could you believe that I *killed* him? I couldn't harm a fly!'

'Shit, Lottie. You just harmed *me*,' he grumbles, pressing his hand against his injured eye while he glares at her with the good one.

'You deserved it!' she shouts as I step up beside her, letting her know that I'm close by if she needs me – even though I'm probably the *last* person she wants to turn to right now, which completely kills me.

'Yeah, well, so did Olly!' Jase shouts back. 'People wanted to kill him every time he opened his bloody mouth!'

I can hear one of my jackass brothers choking back a bark of laughter, and as I cut a swift, sharp glance over at my family, I find Clara looking like she wants to cheer Lottie on, while my mom appears torn between comforting Jase or comforting Lottie. And Cade and Colin are just relishing Jase's predicament like a couple of douchebags, obviously enjoying not being in the hotseat themselves for once.

But one look at Lottie's face makes it clear that she doesn't find a damn thing funny about what Jase has said. She turns cadaver-pale as she slams both hands over her mouth, looking like she might burst into tears.

'Shit,' Jase mutters, this time with feeling, as he takes in her shattered reaction. 'I didn't mean that.'

She pulls in a deep breath through her nose, clearly fighting for control of her emotions, then slowly lets it out as she drops her hands back down to her sides. 'I . . . I know he was an absolute arse, and that he could treat people horribly. But he was an arse who put himself through hell in order to save my life.'

'And thank God for that,' Jase murmurs, before his lips twitch at one corner with a brief, grief-edged smile. 'You know, he told me, the day before your wedding, that he had no idea why you were marrying him. But that was a lie, wasn't it?'

I can see her delicate throat work as she swallows. 'It was,' she rasps, wrapping her shaking arms around her middle, looking like a strong wind might knock her over. 'We . . . had a mutual agreement.'

'Yeah, Callan explained it to me,' Jase tells her. 'And I have to say, I never thought Olly would be able to do anything that made me proud to be related to him, but he proved me wrong. I'm glad he was there for you when you needed him, Lot.'

'Thanks,' she whispers, shaking a little harder as she lowers her gaze to the hardwood floor, and I get the feeling she's about to bolt from the room, when my phone starts ringing in my pocket.

'It's Seb,' I say, after taking the phone out. I haven't talked to him since late last night, when he'd called to let us know how things had gone with Eva, and Lottie and I had both been relieved to hear the news that Eva and Nico were now staying with a friend of hers from work. But while his visit with Lottie's friend and neighbor had been a success, Eva hadn't made it easy for him, and when I consider everything the guy's doing for me today as well, I know I'm going to owe him for a long time to come.

I press my thumb to the touchscreen to accept the call, but before I can lift the phone to my ear, Lottie touches my arm as she looks up at me, and almost silently says, 'Put him on speaker.'

I know she'll think I'm still hiding something from her if I refuse, and since refusing her anything is the *last* thing I ever want to do, I hit the icon for the phone's speaker and murmur, 'Hey, Seb.'

'How did she take the news?' he immediately asks, cutting right to the chase before I can warn him that Lottie, along with everyone else in the room, is listening to his every word.

'How do you think?' Lottie drawls, her tone painfully dry.

'Ahh. *Bonjour*, Miss Fleming,' Seb replies with a throaty laugh.

'I hope you're not being too hard on my boy, since you know he means well.'

Seeing as how she only scowls at the phone – her anger with Seb because of his involvement with my plan clearly overshadowing the gratitude she'd felt over his checking on Eva and Nico – I ask, 'How did it go with Jeannie?'

'Exactly as planned. She's going to run the story for us, citing an anonymous source. But I promised her that as soon as I could get her confirmation from the NYPD, I'd be in touch.'

'That's good. Thanks, man. I owe you.'

'Like I've said before, you owe me many, my friend.'

'Trust me, I know,' I agree with a heavy sigh. 'So how long till you get here?'

'I pulled into a Starbucks while I spoke with Jeannie, but I'm back on the road now,' he says. 'The traffic has been light, so I should be there within the hour.'

Lottie lifts her gaze back up to mine, her brows knitted with confusion. 'Why is Seb coming here?'

It's Jase who answers her. 'Because when this idiot told me his plan for Fleming, I wanted to make sure he'd have all the backup he could get. And it will cover our asses to have someone here who's from law enforcement.'

'Huh,' she huffs. 'I *guess* he could be useful.'

'Your confidence in my abilities is almost too much to take,' Seb responds wryly, sounding like he's trying not to laugh.

Lottie rolls her eyes at the phone. 'If your ego gets any bigger, Cassel, it won't fit through the bloody doorway. So make sure to duck when you come inside.'

This time, he can't hold back a sharp bark of laughter before he sobers and says, 'You might be irritated with me, *ma chérie*, but Jase is right. With me there, no one will be able to claim it wasn't a justified kill when Callan removes this lowlife from existence.'

Her jaw is so tight it looks painful, and she keeps her gaze focused on the phone as she quietly orders, 'Just don't let him get hurt.'

'Christ, Lottie, I can take care of myself,' I growl, insulted that everyone's so damn worried about this prick getting the upper hand on me.

'Yeah, well, let's hope you're right,' she murmurs with a heavy dose of bitterness and hurt, before turning her back on me and walking straight out of the room.

Ignoring the worried looks coming from my family and Jase, I follow after her, all the way into the master bedroom, and can hear her collecting her toiletries in the bathroom as I mutter a quick 'See you soon' to Seb, then set my phone on the dresser and lean back against it, waiting for her to return.

LOTTIE

'I should be packed in five,' I tell Callan, when I come out of the bathroom with my toiletries bag and find him waiting for me, 'if you want to let Clara know.'

He looks surprised that I'm not going to argue about staying, but now that he's set this dangerous plan in motion, getting the hell out of his hair is probably the most helpful thing I can do. I'm not trained in combat like he is, or tall and packed with muscle like him, Seb and Jase, so I'd probably just end up getting in the way. Or worse, be a distraction that ended up getting someone other than Andrew killed.

And the truth is that I'm so angry and hurt right now, I just want out of here as quickly as possible. I just want to be *gone*.

'As soon as we're done here,' he says, his deep voice low, 'I'll come to get you.'

'Don't bother,' I murmur, picking my backpack up from where I'd set it on the floor by the chest of drawers and carrying it over to the bed.

'Excuse me?' he grunts, sounding pissed, which almost makes me laugh. As if the jerk has anything to be angry about, when *he's* the one calling all the shots.

Ignoring the throbbing pain in my hand from where I'd shocked the hell out of myself when I'd clocked Jase in the eye, I unzip the pack, saying, 'I think some time apart – which we can use to figure things out – will probably do us both some good.'

'What's to figure out?' he growls. 'We fucking belong together.'

I turn my head to the side, glaring at him through the fall of my hair, and am surprised by how in control I sound, given that I'm freaking breaking apart inside. 'And I don't know how many times I have to say it, Callan. I'm not looking to be coddled and treated like a child.'

His dark eyes are hooded beneath a fierce scowl. 'What the hell did you expect me to do? This asshole is screwing with your life! And now someone else has died. You think I'm going to just hang around and wait until the next person he takes out is *you*?'

'I expected you to talk to me!' I snap. 'I get that I'm not trained to handle what's coming, but this would have all been so much easier to swallow if you'd just trusted me enough to have an adult conversation about it. Not plan it all behind my back and then spring it on me, because you're . . .' A bitter laugh surges up from my chest and I shake my head. 'I honestly don't know *what* your reasoning was. Probably that I would tell you you're completely crazy for taking this kind of risk. And then you could have made your arguments, and maybe I would have come around to your way of thinking. But now we'll never know, will we?'

He curses something soft and gritty that I can't quite make out, looking every bit as angry and annoyed as I am. Though I'm getting the feeling that most of it is directed at himself.

'So, like I said,' I murmur, sounding far calmer than I feel, 'please tell Clara that I'll be ready in five.'

He tips his chin down and exhales a ragged breath, shoving both hands back through his shaggy bronze hair as he mutters, 'Lottie, I'm . . . Shit, baby, I'm sorry.'

'You should be,' I whisper.

He lifts his head, his dark gaze burning with emotion. 'But we're not taking any time apart.'

'And I'm afraid that's not your decision to make,' I counter with a heavy sigh as I look away from him, picking my toiletries bag up from where I'd set it on the bed and tucking it into the top of my backpack.

'Are you saying you don't want me?' he asks, his gruff voice suddenly so close I swear I can feel its warmth against my skin, and as I turn my head again, I find him standing right beside me, the way he can move his tall, muscular body without making a single sound catching me by surprise.

'Sex is one thing,' I tell him, tilting my head back so that I can look him in the eye. 'Emotions and trust are another, Callan.'

'Not when it comes to us,' he states with raw confidence, and the next thing I know, his strong hands are gently holding my face and his lips brush over mine once. Twice. They're so close we're sharing the same breaths, and I can tell by the way he just stops and waits, with his addictive mouth hovering above mine, that he's giving me the chance to tell him to back off, if that's what I want. But when I don't, he makes one of those soft, provocative guttural sounds that drive me wild, just before he starts kissing the hell out of me.

'I want you so goddamn bad, Lottie. Today. Tomorrow. *Always*,' he groans, quickly pushing me down on the bed, and it takes only seconds for him to strip my clothes off, while I frantically pull at his T-shirt, ripping it over his head. Then he's kneeling between my spread legs, his hot, greedy gaze glued in tight on my already slick sex as he snarls and fights with the button-fly on his jeans. I swear we both give gasps of relief when it's finally open and he's shoving the jeans over his trim hips, his magnificent cock rising up hard and thick and heavy from the bronze patch of curls on his groin.

He makes another hungry, masculine sound of desperation as he comes down over me, bracing himself on one stiff arm, his biceps bulging as he fists his shaft with his other hand, notching his gleaming head against my tight, slippery entrance. Then he's gripping my thigh and thrusting inside me so hard and fast that I cry out, my hands clutching at the bedding so that I can anchor myself as he gives me every incredible, blood-thick inch of him, deeper and deeper, until I swear he's hitting the end of me.

Because there's nothing between us, I can feel how hot he is inside me. Feel every mouthwatering detail of his ridged, diamond-hard shaft, and there's no denying that I'm still in shock over the way I'd stopped him from buying condoms at the store. But I don't regret it. If things go bad, and this mind-shattering moment ends up being the last one we ever have together, then I don't want to be denied one single breathtaking part of it.

'Never, baby. I'll never be able to get enough of you,' he growls, his dark gaze smoldering with desire as he stares down into my flushed face, his hips working like a piston as he drives himself into me, again and again. But there's nothing mechanical about him. He's all hot, animalistic need, and I've never felt so wanted. So essential. So *vital*. I watch the way his tight abs ripple as he hammers his powerful body into mine, and then I'm digging my nails into his round biceps as the pleasure slams into me so hard it pushes a throaty cry up from my throat, my sex pulsing around him as I shiver and gasp. And from beneath my lowered lashes, I can see the exact moment that his own climax starts to hit him, his savage expression telling me it's going to be every bit as deliciously wild and intense as mine.

He starts to draw his hips back, his nostrils flaring when he sucks in a sharp breath, and as I reach up to place my hand against his bearded cheek, our gazes lock with a sizzling, crackling connection. It suddenly feels as if there's a physical chain binding us even closer together, when we're already as close as two humans can physically be. He freezes, watching . . . waiting . . . and in this blistering second in time, my thoughts are racing as rapidly as my thundering heart, and I find myself thinking about how I've never – not even once – allowed myself to consider the prospect of having a family of my own one day. Not with Andrew's sadistic shadow darkening every corner of my life.

But with the gorgeous, thoroughly captivating, frustratingly heroic Callan Hathaway braced over me, soaking up the outward beauty of him that's only outmatched by what he is on the inside, I can't hide from the truth. That truth being that he would be an absolutely amazing father. I have zero doubt of it. And while I know the odds are small that I'll get pregnant right now, and that it's utterly crazy to even be thinking about it, I take the biggest risk of my life and whisper, 'Stay. Stay inside me.'

He growls like some kind of wild, primal animal as his head goes back, the tendons in his strong, corded throat straining as he shouts to the ceiling and instantly starts coming so hard it fills me with scalding heat, our bodies locked together in a carnal, voluptuous knot of pleasure that feels like it lasts forever. Only . . . nothing ever does.

'That was the hottest fucking moment of my entire life,' he's eventually able to scrape out, bracing himself on his elbows as he collapses over me, his brown eyes gleaming with satisfaction.

'What's hot is you saying that,' I murmur, running my hands over his broad shoulders. Then I give him a little smile, admitting, 'Or just *you* in general.'

He laughs a deep, bone-melting rumble of sound that makes my toes curl, and I find myself tangling my hands in his hair and tugging him down as I lift up, just enough that I can crush my mouth against his smiling one. He kisses me like it's what we were born for, then pulls his head back, his dark gaze locking with mine as he says, 'I've lusted for you, Lot, from the moment I first set eyes on you. Then I found you playing the piano that night in the Becketts' music room, and it was like you laid some kind of claim on me. One that's only grown stronger and a thousand times more intense.'

'Callan,' I whisper, undone not only by what he's saying, but by the stunning way that he's looking at me, as if I'm his *entire* world.

'And now . . .' His voice drops, graveled with emotion. 'Now I *know* that the reason you have this effect on me is because I love you. So much that I will do whatever it takes to be by your side every single day of my life. Every morning. Every night. For fucking always, Lottie.'

I swallow a few times, blinking up at him, my chest so warm it's like I'm melting from the burning, molten wave of feeling that's rolling through me.

Searching my eyes, he gives me one of his devastatingly

sexy, crooked half-smiles. 'You got anything you want to say back to me?'

I bite my lip as I shake my head, but instead of getting upset, he just gives another one of those low, delicious laughs as he mutters, 'God, you're stubborn.'

'And you're a prick,' I shoot back with a heavy dose of affection, swallowing the tears that are burning my throat. 'A bossy, alpha, know-it-all prick.'

'Yeah, but I'm *your* prick.' He rolls his hips, stirring himself in my drenched depths. 'And in case it escaped your notice, I'm still hard.'

'Trust me, I know.' I tighten around him, clenching my inner muscles, and he makes a rough sound like a sob. I've heard him make that sound before, most notably the first time he ever worked himself inside me, and now I'm helplessly addicted to it. Then I smirk up at him, saying, 'I mean, it's not like I could miss having something *that* ridiculously large inside my body.'

'Did you just call my dick ridiculous?' he asks with a snort of amusement.

'Yeah. But only when referring to how bloody huge it is, so you're welcome.'

He lowers his head, rubbing his smiling lips over mine again as he gives another heady roll of his hips, making me gasp. But before we can get carried away, there's a knock on the bedroom door, and with a deep groan of regret, he carefully pulls out of me.

'Whatever you need, I'll deal with it in a minute,' he yells to whoever's standing out in the hallway, while his heavy-lidded gaze locks in with laser-focus between my legs.

'Christ, that's hot,' he growls, his expression tight with lust as he reaches down and rubs the pad of his thumb over my slick, swollen entrance, and I know he's referring to the fact that I'm wet with his seed.

'Wow,' I laugh, pushing up onto my elbows, 'you really *are* a caveman.'

'Can't help it,' he rumbles, running his appreciative gaze over every part of my sex-flushed body. 'I'm gonna need to see you just like this every goddamn day of my life.'

This time, *I'm* the one who snorts. 'Every day of your life, huh?'

'Hell, yeah.' He lifts his fever-hot gaze back to mine and arches one of his eyebrows. 'Given all that we've said . . . and haven't said – as well as what we just *did* – I'm going to go out on a limb here and guess that you're good with that, yeah?'

He waits for my response, but I'm silent, simply blinking back at him, still too irritated over what he's done, despite the awesome sex we've just had, to give him what he wants – not to mention this gut-wrenching fear for his safety that's still twisting inside me like a snake. It's locking me down, as fiercely as if I were trapped in its jaws, and so instead of talking things out with him, like an adult, I swing my legs up and to the side, then move off the bed and back to my feet. 'Please let Clara know that I won't be long,' I say without even looking at him. 'I just need to grab a quick shower.'

'You take as many as you want,' he murmurs, something in his rough voice telling me that he can see right through me, reading me as easily as a book. 'But I'm just going to fill you right back up again the second all this shit is over, sweetheart.'

I give another snort as I shut the bathroom door behind me, wanting to kick the cocky jackass every bit as much as I want to kiss him again, and I know that my rioting emotions are a result of the panic I feel every time I think about the fact that Andrew could very well already be on his way here. And that once he arrives, Callan's going to . . . *God*, I don't even know. Fight him to the death? The idea makes bile rise into my throat, and I quickly shove it out of my mind as I start the shower, determined to find a way to get through this without completely falling apart.

When I'm finished rinsing off and come back into the bedroom wearing a towel, Callan has gone, so I quickly get dressed, throw on some make-up and brush out the tangles in my hair. Then I grab my heavy backpack, slinging it over my shoulder, and head back out to the living room. I seem to walk into the middle of an argument that's going on between Callan and his brothers, who apparently want to stay and help but are being told to head back home. Everyone stops talking, though, the second I walk into the room, and there's an awkward silence, as if no one knows what to say or do, until Margot marches right over to me, enveloping me in a warm mum-hug. 'You try not to worry and just take care of yourself, okay? I know it's all going to turn out just fine, Lottie.'

'Thanks,' I whisper, when she pulls back and gives me a strained smile, clearly sick with worry herself. 'You be careful, too.'

'Of course I will, honey.'

'We'd better go,' Clara announces, grabbing the purse she'd set on the coffee table, before walking over to Callan and giving him a hard, tight hug. 'Watch out for yourself, you big idiot.'

'You too, brat,' he murmurs affectionately, hugging her back.

We all head outside then, and after I speak to Jase for a moment, then say goodbye to Colin and Cade, I turn and start heading for the SUV that Clara and her security detail have already climbed into, the one parked beside it I'm assuming for her brothers and mum. Thankfully the vehicle is a big one, I'm guessing with extra seats in the rear, since I see Thompson climbing in back there, and as I reach out to open the back passenger-side door, I feel Callan come up behind me, his deep voice soft as he says, 'You know, you never did give me an answer about moving in with me.'

I pull in a deep breath and turn around, tilting my head back as I look up at him. And then my breath just kind of catches in my chest, because he is, without any doubt, the most gorgeous thing I've ever seen. He stares down at me with those dark, piercing eyes, the way the sun is shining behind him making his tall, muscular body look as if it belongs to some kind of god, his bronze hair falling over his knitted brow as he waits for my answer. But as I stare back at him, it's different words than the ones about our living arrangements that are jamming into my throat. Words that, from the time Andrew became a grim, deadly sickness corrupting my world, I not only thought I would never feel, but would *never* be able to say to another person. God, I can't even say them *now*, because all that eventually falls from my lips is a hoarse 'Survive this crazy plan of yours, and I'll give you an answer then.'

With a quiet, gritty laugh, he shakes his head at me. 'Christ, Lot. That's harsh, even for you.'

'Maybe,' I mutter, already turning and ripping the door open. My pulse is rushing in my ears as I quickly hoist myself up into the massive vehicle, then turn to reach for the inside door handle. Before I slam it shut, though, I lock my burning gaze with Callan's again, and say, 'But harsh or not, don't you *dare* freaking die on me.'

Chapter Nineteen

LOTTIE

'I promise this will only take a moment,' I say to Clara, climbing out of the backseat of the SUV to join Danny Thompson on the sidewalk. The weather in the city is rapidly turning bad, ominous-looking storm clouds darkening the afternoon sky, but it's early enough in the day that there are still a good number of people about, which is one of the reasons we're here. If it'd already been dark, I know there's no way I would have been able to convince Clara to agree.

The SUV is parked on the side of the road in front of Rosita's Bakery, since the alleyway leading back to my building is too narrow for vehicles to drive through. So Thompson and I will be traveling on foot the rest of the way, while Clara waits here with her security detail, looking like someone just pissed in her Wheaties.

'Just get your ass back as quickly as possible,' she growls, and I give her a tight smile as I shut the door, feeling guilty as hell for putting her through this. But, really, it's Callan who should be feeling like crap, seeing as how this is all his fault.

The giant know-it-all jackass – who's the bravest person I've ever known, but I'm still pretty pissed at him, so I refuse to think about that right now – had had to go and tell me that he loves me. Words I haven't heard since my parents died, and as we'd driven back to the city, I couldn't stop thinking about my mum and dad, and how the only things I have left from them – their wedding rings – are up in my tiny apartment, hidden under a loose floorboard in my bedroom.

It took some intense arguing to get here, but Thompson finally gave in. And once I had him on my side, we were able to convince Clara's detail that it wasn't the 'monumentally bad idea' she kept calling it.

I swear the more time I spend with the woman, the more I realize that I could seriously love her like a sister. But there's no getting around the fact that she's impossibly stubborn. Even more so than her second-eldest brother.

As Thompson and I climb up my building's front steps, I have a jolting moment where I freeze for a second, since it's just occurred to me that I'm about to walk into this place for the first time ever without my wig. And while I know the odds of someone here recognizing me from an old news article are slim, I'm more determined than ever to make this visit a quick in-and-out. Especially when I consider the fact that releasing Andrew's name to the press most likely means that *my* name and photograph are once again in the public eye.

'Everything all right?' Thompson asks at my side, the sound of his voice jerking me back to the moment.

'Yeah, sorry. I, um . . .' My own voice trails off as I focus on what's in front of me, trying to make sense of the fact that there's a new front door on the building. One that has a keypad instead of a handle. 'What the hell?'

'Ah. I saw something about this on a company memo,' Thompson says. 'If you just give me a second, I can pull up the code.'

I look at him with a confused frown. 'Company memo?'

'Yeah,' he replies, his attention on his phone as his long fingers move over the screen. 'Callan had our installation team at Hathaway come over yesterday and put it in. Apparently the door that was here didn't even have a lock on it, which is completely crazy in this city.'

I just blink at him when he glances over at me again, still trying to wrap my head around what he's told me, so he goes back to searching for the code.

'Here we go,' he murmurs a half-minute later, punching in a series of numbers, and as the green light on the keypad shines in my eyes, the door clicks open. 'I'll go up first,' he tells me, his tone making it clear that the topic isn't up for debate.

'Lead the way,' I say, forcing the grateful smile I've been wearing since he agreed to bring me here back onto my lips, and start following him up the stairs. But the smile begins to slip as I think about what Callan has done for the people who live in this building, which must have cost his company a load of cash – and given that he didn't even tell me about it, I know it wasn't some semi-selfish act that he'd hoped would earn him points with me. No, he'd done it because he's a real-life freaking hero, driven to protect, and my slipping smile turns to one of amazement as it occurs to me that for the two nights that I slept in his arms, I hadn't had a single nightmare.

Even in sleep, I'd obviously known he was there, looking over me, and I wish like hell that I could be back at the safehouse right now, looking over him. Protecting *him* for once, since he deserves it more than anyone I know.

'These paintings are incredible,' Thompson comments,

drawing me from my thoughts again, and as I look over at Eva and Nico's door as we walk past it, my smile fades completely.

I'd written a short note for Nico on Friday, explaining that I had to leave town for a few days and was sorry to miss our Mario Kart marathon, and had slid it under Eva's door as Callan and I had left. So hopefully he got it, since I'd been too distracted by other things – like danger and death – to ask Eva about it the few times we'd spoken on the phone over the weekend. And there's no chance I'll be able to run into him now and apologize, because they're not even here. After coming over to speak with Eva, warning her about the possible danger she might be in because of our friendship, Seb had driven her and Nico over to one of her co-worker's houses.

Thinking about that danger, as well as what's already happened to Ruby, the guilt that's always sitting in my gut like a rock swells up so swiftly, I almost choke on it.

I must make a sound, because Thompson looks back at me. 'You okay, Lottie?'

'Fine,' I tell him, forcing a tight smile – while inside I'm breaking into so many raw, jagged pieces, I can't help but wonder if I'll *ever* be whole again.

When we reach my front door, Thompson takes my keys from me, unlocks it, and is focused on taking a look around the small living room, while I follow him in and close the door behind me. But although my tension has increased to the point that I feel like a loud noise could stop my heart, it isn't from fear of being here. Hell, at the moment, it isn't even from Callan's crazy plan for taking Andrew down. No, something came over me as we reached my apartment, my brain buzzing with the knowledge that it was only just a few days ago that I was walking in here with Callan, after he'd found me, and now . . . *God*, it feels like we've lived a lifetime between now and then, and I'm suddenly beyond pissed at myself for how I handled the conversation we'd had after shagging each other's brains out today. Because I *know* that I made a mistake during that talk. Know that I should have been honest with him. Should have told him the truth.

Damn it, I should have told him that I love him when I'd had the bloody chance!

But I hadn't. No, I'd choked on the words, and now I feel like a total coward for not having the courage to just put them out there. To just lay my beating heart at his feet, like a piece of my soul, and simply admit it, the same way that he'd done.

'You sure you're okay?' Thompson asks again, giving me a worried glance as I just stand here in front of the door, no doubt looking like a deer caught in the headlights.

'Um, yeah,' I murmur, forcing a weak smile onto my lips as I start heading for my bedroom. 'I'll just grab the rings and then we can get out of here.'

It takes me only seconds to kneel down on the floor and push my air mattress to the side, revealing the loose floorboard. I find the notch in it that's just big enough for my fingertip to fit into, then lift it up, and a burst of relief sweeps through me when I see that the velvet box I'd hidden under the board is exactly where I'd left it. Picking the box up, I let the floorboard fall back into place. Then I lift the box's lid and find the wedding rings and chain nestled inside the pink tissue paper I'd used to cushion them before packing them away, just after moving in.

I'd been so terrified that Andrew might have found them, once I thought about them on the drive back to the city, but my hiding place had thankfully worked, and there's another grateful smile on my lips as I quickly loop the long chain over my head. This is how I'd always used to wear the rings, ever since my parents' deaths, but had stopped just after coming to New York, too worried I might get mugged on the street one day and lose them. So I'd decided the safest thing to do was to keep them hidden away.

Tucking the rings under my shirt, I take a quick look around the bedroom to make sure there's nothing else that I need, then walk back into the living room.

'Got them,' I say to Thompson, who's standing with his back to the archway that leads into the kitchen, and as my gaze slides over to the small table that's not far from him, I shiver with a strange wave of trepidation. At first, I don't even understand what's creeped me out – but then I remember.

Callan had set his soda can down on that table on Friday afternoon, and I hadn't thrown it into my recycling bin before we left. So it should still be sitting there . . . but it's not. Which means that at some point since we left here on Friday, Andrew's come back. But if he'd already tagged my things, and had known I was with Callan, why would he . . .?

'Ohmygod,' I suddenly whisper, fear sitting in my throat like a boulder as I swiftly jerk my gaze back to Thompson to yell out a warning. But I'm too late. It feels like I'm watching time move in slow motion as I see Andrew coming up behind the tall bodyguard. Before Thompson even realizes he's there, Andrew has lifted the knife that's in his hand and stabbed him in the back with it.

As Thompson's body falls forward, crashing to the floor, Andrew lifts the dripping knife to his mouth and licks the crimson blood from the blade. 'Well, hello there, little bunny,' he purrs, giving me a sharp smile.

'Stay the hell away from me,' I seethe, feeling behind me for the heavy metal candlestick that I found at a thrift shop and has sat on the table beside my loveseat ever since. During the self-defense lesson I'd had with Callan yesterday, he'd repeated, time and again, to use whatever weapons were at hand, and as I curl my hand around the cold metal, I'm ready to do just that. 'How did you even get into this building?'

'You think doors are the only way inside? Haven't you ever heard of a window?' Andrew drawls, looking worse than I've ever seen him, as if he hasn't slept in days, his wrinkled T-shirt and jeans speckled with dark stains that could all too easily be old blood. 'And seeing as how you're here before I was expecting you, I'm going to assume that the blip in Hathaway's security today was actually intentional. What a clever plan that would have been,' he goes on, stepping around Thompson's still body, 'if only I hadn't been in the middle of my own. You see, I was already committed, Lottie, so I had no need to track you down in his annoying hideaway. Not when it was only a matter of time before *you* would come to *me*.'

I have no idea why he thought I would be coming back here, and I don't care. I just want to kill him for what he's done in the past . . . and what he's done just now to Thompson, who's lying so motionless on the floor I'm terrified he's already dead.

'Let me call him an ambulance,' I say unsteadily, terror shaking each word. 'There's no reason for him to die. He's done nothing to you, Andrew.'

'On the contrary. He was helping to keep you away from me.' He sneers down at Thompson for a moment, and I wince at the brutal kick he gives to the bodyguard's ribs. Looking back over at me, he says, 'He should consider himself lucky that I don't have more time to make him pay for his sins.'

'His sins?' I echo with a harsh laugh. 'God, do you even hear yourself? Do you have any idea how fucking crazy you are?'

Color floods his face at my insult, and his voice lashes out like a whip. 'At least I'm not a useless, pathetic coward like you!'

As his sharp words ring through my head, I'm suddenly reminded of all the times I've thought them myself. Hell, I've probably already said them countless times to Callan just since he found me on Friday, and I am so freaking *sick* of feeling this way. Because it's not true. I'm *not* pathetic. I've fought and survived and I'm still standing, and before I even have time to think about what I'm doing, I hear myself screaming, 'You're the pathetic one, you piece of shit!'

Then I'm running right at him as I swing the candlestick in a wide arc, catching him against the side of his head. He cries out in pain, twisting to the side, and the last thing I see is blood pouring over his left ear before I turn and get the hell out of there.

Even though the stairs are steep, I run like I have the devil himself chasing me, knowing that Thompson's best chance of survival is if we're able to get him medical attention as soon as possible. I'm breathing so hard, I can't even tell if Andrew has recovered enough to chase after me, and I'm not going to waste precious seconds looking back over my shoulder to check.

I tear out of the building and run straight into a blast of pouring, freezing rain, the storm finally hitting with a violence that seems appropriately fitting, given that I'm running for my life . . . and for Thompson's. My gaze darts around for someone who might be able to help, but the thunder and rain have sent everyone to seek shelter indoors. Horrified that my luck could be this bloody bad, I open my mouth as I keep running, thinking a scream would definitely help, but I'm breathing too hard for it to come out as anything more than a wheezing gasp.

Come on. Come on, I'm chanting in my head, the ground so slippery I nearly wipe out twice as I run down the alleyway that leads back to the street. Just as I finally get far enough into it that I can see the front of the SUV through the sideways sheets of rain, I force a painfully deep breath into my lungs, preparing to call out for help . . . only to hear Andrew say five chilling words that stop me dead in my tracks.

'I've got Eva, little bunny.'

And just like that, I feel like I've slammed into an invisible wall. I'm completely frozen, with safety right *there*, within my sights – but the SUV might as well be miles away, because they can't help me now. All I can picture is Nico's tear-streaked face when he realizes that something bad has happened to his mum, and I know I won't be able to take another step forward.

With my heart hammering its way into my throat, I turn to face my deranged cousin, my voice no more than a painful scrape of sound as I say what I'm praying is true. 'You're lying.'

But the bastard just smiles at me. 'Your friend sure would appreciate some company right about now. She's pretty scared being all alone in that big ol' building I've been calling home.'

'I'd be an idiot to believe you!' I growl, fisting my hands at my sides, ready to fight this asshole if I have to.

He just looks at me, though, as if he's trying not to laugh. 'Lottie, why do you think I was waiting for you here? I've been one step ahead of you and Hathaway the entire day, starting this morning, when I discovered he had one of his employees tailing Eva while she worked.'

'What did you do?' I snarl, taking an aggressive step toward him.

'I simply found a lovely Hispanic whore who was fit enough to take Eva's place,' he explains with a shrug, 'and made the switch during one of her drops. Eva's been with me ever since. And when her security detail eventually figures out what's happened, the whore's got a note for them to pass along to your lover. One that says you're to come home, alone, or your pretty friend is going to be sent to her mother's house in a variety of different boxes.'

'Ohmygod, you sick fuck.' I have to swallow a few times to keep from leaning over and retching on the cracked, rain-covered concrete beneath my feet, then curl my upper lip with a sneer as I demand, 'How do I know this isn't a lie?'

'Well, a picture speaks a thousand words, yes?' He takes a few steps closer to me, holding up an expensive-looking cell phone, and I feel bile rise into my throat again as I focus on the shadowy image. It's one of Eva, slumped on a dirty mattress in her spandex shorts and Fairbanks T-shirt, looking so pale I'm terrified she might already be dead. But I can't see any blood, and I'm praying that this bastard has only knocked her out.

'You come with me now, Lottie,' he says as he slips the phone back into his pocket, the calm surety of his tone making it clear that he knows he's won, 'or what Ruby went through is going to look like child's play compared to what I do to that mouthy bitch.'

'God, I'm so sorry,' I whisper to Callan, knowing he's going to blame himself. I hate that for him, even more than I hate the twisted psychopath who's standing there gloating in front of me. But I can't just keep running to save my own skin. Not when we don't have a clue where he's keeping Eva.

'Yeah, okay,' I manage, watching through the rain and my tears as he pulls a gun from the back of his waistband and uses it to motion to me to turn around.

Then there's a sharp pain at the back of my head.

And the world goes black.

Chapter Twenty

CALLAN

'What do you mean *gone*?' I roar into my phone, unable to believe what I'm hearing. I knew the trip back to the city would take more time than usual, since I'd insisted that they use one of the longer routes. Part of the fastest way between here and Manhattan means traveling on a two-lane country road for over an hour, and I hadn't wanted to risk them passing Andrew and being spotted. So given the extra time it would take them, plus traffic, I'd been expecting a call saying that they'd made it safely to Clara's anytime now, and instead, my sister has just told me a story that's so completely insane, I can't even wrap my head around it.

'I'm so sorry, Callan,' she says, clearly struggling not to cry. 'I . . . I don't know what the hell happened. We'd thought he would already be at least halfway to you by now, but he must have been hiding out in her place. When she and Thompson didn't make it back to the SUV as quickly as we'd expected, we tried to call Thompson's phone, but there was no answer. One of my security guys went up and found him in her apartment.

He'd been stabbed, so we've just rushed him to the local ER. But there was no sign of Lottie.'

'*Fuck!*'

She pulls in an unsteady breath, and her voice cracks as she goes on. 'And it's . . . It's not going to help if you put a tracking dot on her. We found a pile of her clothes around the back of the building, in one of those narrow alleyways back there. He must have made her strip down to everything but her underwear and socks.'

'Oh God,' I groan, my heart pounding so hard with fear, I don't know how it hasn't already burst.

I can hear what sounds like a crowd of people talking in the background, and then she says, 'Look, I know there's probably a million things you want to say to me right now but something's happening here, so I've got to go. But I'll call you back as soon as I can.'

'Clara!' I growl, but she's already ended the call.

As I lower the phone from my ear, I start pacing back and forth in front of the piano in the living room, my pulse roaring so loudly it takes me a moment to realize that Seb, who was the only one in here with me when I took Clara's call, is asking me what's going on.

After a long argument, I'd finally convinced my brothers to head back home and to take my mom with them, and I'd sent Thompson to beef up Clara's security detail, since they were meant to be looking out for Lottie as well. So aside from me and Seb, Robbins and Jase are the only other people here, and while I know that Robbins is busy keeping an eye on the monitors down in the control room, ready to alert us the instant Fleming shows up on one of our camera feeds, I don't have a clue what Jase has been doing for the past fifteen minutes.

'Callan!' Seb shouts again, and I finally jerk my gaze over to his worried one. 'Tell me what's happened.'

'The plan's gone to shit,' I somehow manage to respond, when all I really want to do is throw my head back and bellow with rage and gut-wrenching fear. 'They stopped by Lottie's apartment for her parents' wedding rings because she got scared that Fleming might have stolen them from her, and now the bastard's got her. And they've just driven Thompson to the local ER with a stab wound.'

'What the hell?' my friend says, his brown eyes wide with disbelief.

I push my hands into my hair so hard it's a miracle I don't pull it out, but I need the sharp sting of pain to ground me, since there's an endless stream of horrific scenarios of what Lottie might be going through with that sick shit running through my head, threatening to shut me down. And seeing as how me having a mental collapse isn't going to do a damn thing to help get her back, I shove that shit down and force myself to focus.

'Do me a favor and call Robbins on the intercom to let him know what's happened. I . . . I need to get a gun,' I mutter, already heading toward the master bedroom, where we keep a gun safe in the closet. While Seb is armed, along with Robbins, everyone had agreed that I shouldn't be, no doubt worried that I'd lose my shit the second Fleming showed his face, killing the bastard before we could get his confession.

The team of tech experts we have at Hathaway had called me a few hours ago to say that Lottie's email to her uncle *had* been traced, so I know Fleming has the location of this place. So why the hell isn't he on his way here? Why was he lying in wait at her apartment, when he had to know that that's the last fucking place I would ever let her go?

Not that I'd apparently had any goddamn say in it!

I keep having to remind myself to breathe as I pull the safe down from the top shelf in the closet and retrieve one of the Glocks, along with ammo, that we keep stored inside it. Just as I'm heading back into the living room, where Seb is now pacing, waiting for my return, my phone buzzes with a text message. I pull the phone from my pocket, having no recollection of shoving it back in there, and the scowl that's already on my face deepens as I read the message from Leo Miller, who oversees the tech department at Hathaway.

According to Leo, he'd been running a comprehensive check on Lottie's aunt and uncle, which is standard procedure when we're handling cases like hers, since they're Andrew's parents, and had just discovered that they landed at JFK late last night – which doesn't make any sense, given that Lottie hadn't even reached out to them with her email until *this morning*. As a cold chill travels across the back of my neck, I'm in the middle of texting Leo back, asking him to run an in-depth check on the couples' phone records and to get back to me if anything unusual stands out, when Robbins comes tearing in through the front door, yelling, 'Turn on the news! You're not going to believe this!'

I can't imagine what the guy could possibly think is more important at a time like this than us getting the hell out of here and back to the city, but when I look over at the TV that Seb has just turned on, switching it to one of the cable news channels, I see my sister beneath an umbrella that someone's holding over her head. She's standing on the front steps of the hospital that Thompson's obviously been taken to, her freckled face pale behind a cluster of microphones, and I feel my stomach sink like a bag of bricks.

'Oh shit,' I croak, knowing that whatever Clara's doing, it's going to have massive repercussions for her. The interview she'd planned to do with Jonathan Clark was going to be risky enough, but at least then she would have had some measure of control. But this . . . This is going to be fucking anarchy.

'City of New York,' she says, speaking loudly enough to be heard over the rain that's pouring down around her, 'I'm coming to you this afternoon not as a candidate for your mayor, but as a fellow citizen in desperate need of your help. I was planning on sharing the following information with you in an interview that would have gone live within the next twenty-four hours, but the situation has taken another dire turn and I needed to reach out to you as soon as possible.'

She pauses to pull in a shaky breath, lifts up a beautiful 8×10 photo of Lottie that was taken on her wedding day, then goes on. 'We're short on time, so I'm going to cut right to the chase. The woman in this photo, Lottie Fleming Beckett, has been taken by her cousin, a man named Andrew Fleming, who has stalked and terrorized her for years. If you recognize his name, it's because it was leaked to the press earlier today in connection with two murders. Last year, he framed Lottie, who is in a relationship with one of my brothers, for the murder of her late husband, and she's been on the run for her life ever since. Yesterday, Fleming brutally killed one of Lottie's friends and co-workers, a woman named Ruby Carlisle, here in our great city. And now, despite my family's efforts to keep her safe, Fleming has kidnapped Lottie, and I fear her time is running out. We believe he's currently based himself in Brooklyn, and it's critical that we find them as quickly as possible, before she comes to any harm.'

The reporters start shouting questions at her all at once, but she quiets them with a lift of her free hand. 'I've seen what can happen when New Yorkers pull together, and I know that there are few places in the world with more power or heart. So please, if you have any information, contact the number that will be showing on your screens shortly, and I promise you that there will be no questions asked about how you came by anything that you share with us. *Please*, I'm begging you, help my family.'

She turns to start making her way up the hospital's front steps, when one reporter shouts out a question that can be heard above all the others, catching her attention. 'Aren't you afraid of what this will mean for you politically, and more specifically, for your campaign?'

One of Clara's aides grabs a microphone from the podium and holds it up for her as my sister stares the reporter down, before calmly saying, 'I realize that my opponents will try to make this out to be the biggest scandal to ever hit politics in our incredible city, but like I said before, I'm coming to you not as a politician today, but as a fellow human being. Because as badly as I want to be mayor, and as good a job as I believe I can do for this city, do you honestly believe it would mean more to me than someone's life? More than the life of an innocent woman who's already been through a living nightmare, through no fault of her own?'

'You don't know that she's innocent,' the jackass shoots back.

'Like hell I don't.' Then she turns and heads back inside the hospital, and the contact number that she'd promised comes up on the screen, beside another beautiful photo of Lottie, this one of her in her university graduation cap and gown. Then a photo of Andrew follows, taken at some kind of police function, and it requires every ounce of my restraint not to walk over to the TV and put my fist through his face.

'Holy shit,' Robbins murmurs, when the channel goes back to its newsroom. 'That was so badass.'

'And it could be our best shot at finding her,' Seb says, sounding impressed.

I want to agree, but I'm locked down with guilt and regret and a deep, wrenching fear that's unlike anything I've ever known. It's digging down into my bones like a jagged saw, nearly doubling me over, my skin slicked with sweat while I keep swallowing against the urge to puke my guts up.

'Where's Jase?' Robbins asks, and I lift my head, wondering the same thing, when my phone starts ringing in my clenched hand, and I'm not surprised to see that it's Deanna.

'I just saw Clara on the news. What do you need from me?'

Her let's-get-this-done manner reminds me why I've always valued this woman's instincts and work ethic so highly. 'I need a team over at Lottie's apartment immediately. The bastard had her change out of all her clothing, so the tracking dot I had in her shoe is no good to us. But he might have made a mistake and left something behind that can help us locate them.'

'We're on it.'

'And . . . I don't know if this will amount to anything, but I got a message from Leo saying that Lottie's aunt and uncle flew into New York last night.'

'I saw that,' she murmurs. 'And if you ask me, it's weird. Especially since we can't track them down at any hotels. It's like they got here and then just disappeared into thin air.'

'I agree that there's something not right about it. So do me a favor and get their photos to the press. The next time they air Clara's hotline number, have them include the aunt and uncle with the photographs.'

'Good idea.'

I catch sight of Jase finally coming back into the living room, and tell Deanna that I've got to go, a sudden suspicion starting to niggle at the edges of my mind as I think about the timing of his disappearance in relation to what we've just watched on the TV.

'You missed it,' I mutter, locking my angry, worried gaze with his determined one.

He jerks his dark head toward the other side of the house. 'I caught it on my phone back in the office.'

We both know the truth, but I ask him anyway. 'Clara's press conference. That was your doing?'

He pushes his hands into his pockets as he jerks his chin up. 'She messaged me, right after they found Thompson, and asked to talk to me in private. But she already knew what she wanted to do. She just needed me to help her with some of the wording.'

My nostrils flare as I suck in a quick breath, the guilt I feel over Clara's selfless act only adding to my rage. 'I asked you to help save her campaign, Jase! Not completely destroy it!'

He narrows his gaze at me, not the least bit fazed by my outburst. 'And we both felt that saving your girlfriend's life is a hell of a lot more important than Clara becoming mayor. Don't even try telling me that you don't agree.'

'Of course I fucking agree!' I roar, my heart thundering as I fist my hands at my sides. 'I'd give my goddamn life to save hers!'

'Well, hopefully it's not going to come to that,' my longtime friend says with a heavy, concerned sigh. 'But we can try to come up with a plan on our way back to the city.'

'He's right,' Seb murmurs. 'You're going to want to be there the second Clara gets a tip.'

'Call Deanna back,' Robbins says, 'and have her book a local chopper. There's an airfield only twenty minutes from here.'

'You're a damn genius,' I tell him, irritated with myself that I hadn't already thought of it. But then, I'm hardly functioning at full capacity at the moment, the fear chugging through my brain turning my thoughts to sludge, slowing me down.

'I just want the chance to help you get her back, man,'

Robbins says, while Seb jerks his head at the door and clips, 'Let's go.'

We quickly grab what we need and pile into Seb's Mercedes, which is parked in the driveway beside the rental car that Jase drove here in. I call Deanna and ask her to book the helicopter as Seb starts the engine, and then we're heading down the winding country road, and Robbins, who's sitting up front, begins telling Seb the quickest way to reach the airfield.

When my phone rings, we all flinch, and I frown when I see that it's Deanna again, hoping she didn't have any problems with the airfield. 'Were you able to book the chopper?' I ask in lieu of a greeting.

'Yeah. They'll be ready to go when you get there. But I'm afraid we've received more bad news. Brandt was assigned to tail Eva Diaz today, since she refused not to go in for her shift at Fairbanks Couriers. But she's missing.'

'What the fuck?' I mutter, feeling like I'm trapped in some kind of gut-wrenching episode of *The Twilight Zone*. One where everything that *can* go wrong *does*.

'I know, Cal. Apparently there was a switch made at one of her pickups, and a woman who closely resembles Eva took her place. That's who Brandt has been following around on Eva's bike all afternoon, while this woman made her drops and pickups for her.'

'Christ,' I groan, furious with myself for not thinking that Fleming might try this shit. Especially after what Lottie told me he had done in order to cover his tracks when he'd flown to Italy and killed Olly. Goddamn body doubles are in the guy's wheelhouse!

'Brandt's going back to talk to every business on Eva's route today, but this woman says they made the switch hours ago, and that Fleming paid her a grand.' Deanna exhales a rough breath, then goes on. 'She had a note with her, Callan, that she was told to hand over the second she was discovered. It says that if Lottie doesn't want to see her friend's body chopped up and mailed to her mom's house in a variety of boxes, then she'll go back to her apartment, *alone*, and wait for him to contact her.'

'Shit. No wonder my plan didn't work,' I bite out, shoving the words through my clenched teeth. 'The asshole was already setting up one of his own, with Eva as the bait.'

I catch the way Seb's narrowed gaze slices up to mine in the rear-view mirror, his jaw so tight there's a muscle pulsing beneath his dark skin. I know he's going to take this latest bit of news hard, given that he was the one who'd tried to convince Eva to take a few days off until the situation with Andrew had been handled, but had failed.

And I can see exactly how Lottie's kidnapping must have played out. If that sick shit threatened Eva's life if she didn't surrender herself, I have no doubt that my girl would have done whatever it took to ensure that her friend was going to get through this okay. Even if that meant handing herself over to the monster who wants to destroy her.

Deanna tells me that she'll have the helipad at the top of the building that houses our New York Hathaway headquarters ready for our arrival, and then I get off the phone and am once again giving the bad news to everyone.

'So our plan was fucked from the beginning,' Seb seethes, his normally smooth voice more guttural than I've ever heard it, before he slams the palm of his hand against his steering wheel so hard I'm surprised the thing manages to stay in one piece.

'We'll get them back,' I growl, willing myself to believe it. 'Whatever it takes, we're getting them *both* back.'

Seb grunts in response, and the Mercedes lurches forward as he slams his foot down on the gas, taking the turns at a dangerous speed for anyone who doesn't have his skill behind the wheel. But none of us are complaining, just wanting to get to the airfield as fast as we can.

Beside me, Jase reaches into his front pocket, pulling out the ring that Lottie had retrieved from her backpack and given to him just before she left, and I'd recognized it as her wedding ring, which had apparently been a Beckett family heirloom. After the SUV she'd been in had driven away, Jase had explained that Olly had traded the original diamond for the larger one that he'd given Lottie, and we're both amazed that she'd held on to it all this time, hoping to return it to the family one day, rather than pawning the thing for cash that she could have seriously used this past year. It's just another mark of the kind of person she is, and I know Jase is going to carry the guilt he feels over not believing in her innocence for a long time to come.

'If he was waiting for her at the apartment, and told her that he had Eva, you think she probably went with him willingly, don't you?' he asks me in a low voice as he rubs the pad of his thumb over the ring's sparkling stone.

'Yeah,' I husk, scrubbing my hands down my face. 'I think that's exactly what happened.'

'Brave girl,' he murmurs, and I have to choke back a harsh bark of humorless laughter, knowing that if I start, I'll probably just end up bawling my eyes out. But, God, he has no idea. Lottie Fleming is the most courageous person I've ever known, and I'm counting on that fact to keep her alive until I can find her.

When my phone vibrates, signaling I have a new email, I'm tempted to just ignore it, since I doubt that's how anyone would contact me with something to do with the kidnappings. But seeing as how I'm just sitting here, worrying myself sick, I pull it up, and my attention sharpens when I see that the email is from Ian Masterson. He says that after receiving my message, he'd pulled up Oliver Beckett's account, and that there's something in the file that I might find interesting. According to the investigators he'd used to suss things out when they'd first been hired, it was noted that there was something odd about the Fleming family dynamic that warranted a deeper look. Something that went *beyond* Andrew's stalking. But as far as Masterson can tell, nothing ever came of it, because the account was terminated after Olly's murder. But he says that he's going to contact the investigators to see if there's anything additional that they can tell him, and will let me know if there is. Then he adds that after Olly's death, his company actually contacted Scotland Yard, informing them that protection had been hired for Lottie Fleming because of the danger that Andrew Fleming posed to her, but instead of taking them seriously, the Yard had just laughed in their faces.

'Son of a bitch,' I bite out, hating that Lottie had been completely right about the way Fleming is viewed by his peers.

'What?' Jase asks, and I tell them all what I've learned from Masterson. But instead of offering any insights, they're just as confused as I am, and I'm about to contact Leo again, asking how he's coming along with the Flemings' phone records, when my phone starts ringing with a call from an unknown number.

'If that's Deanna,' Robbins starts to say, looking over his shoulder at me, 'tell her—'

'It's not,' I cut in, before answering the call. 'This is Hathaway.'

'Mr Hathaway,' a deep, heavily accented voice murmurs, and if I had to guess, I would say that the guy calling me is Eastern European. 'My name is Jack Pravik. I believe you might have heard of me, yes?'

'I'm aware of who you are,' I mutter, which is true. Pravik is

the one believed to be responsible for the death of the murdered restaurant employee I'd told Lottie about while we were
arguing in her apartment on Friday afternoon – or rather, the
men who work directly for him, since they're the ones who
would have been carrying out their boss's orders. 'What I don't
know is why you're calling me.'

'I saw your sister's press conference. It was . . . quite moving, as well as impressive. So if you're willing to keep things
confidential, I believe that I can help you.'

'I'm listening,' I clip, while my heart starts pounding to an
urgent, painful beat.

'And I have your word not to involve the police?' he presses.

'Of course.' I'm gripping the phone so tightly it's a miracle it
doesn't crack, my voice rough with emotion as I add, 'If there's
anything you can tell me about Andrew Fleming and where he
might have taken Lottie, then I'll do any goddamn thing you
want.'

'So it's like that, then?' he responds with a low, gritty slice of
laughter, and I swear I can hear a note of approval in the crime
boss's voice.

'Yeah,' I reply, 'it's definitely like that.'

'I can respect that, Mr Hathaway. A man is never truly a
man until he's willing to risk everything for something or
someone important to him.'

'Do you know where she is?' I growl, praying that this guy's
not just dicking me around.

'I believe that I do. But I'm only willing to work with *you*,' he
explains, and I hear what sounds like a lighter being flicked,
and then Pravik is pulling in a deep drag on a cigarette. 'No
one else.'

I don't even hesitate to tell him that I agree, even though I
know damn well that it's going to piss off every other person in

this car with me. But they're just going to have to deal, because this might be our only shot at getting both women back. 'Where can I find you?' I ask, assuming he's going to want me to come to him.

'Meet me at the corner of Spratt and Evergreen in Brooklyn.'

'I'm upstate right now, but am about to take a chopper back to the city. So I can be there in –' I run a swift calculation in my head – 'an hour and a half, at the latest.'

'I'll be waiting.'

Before he can hang up, I quickly say, 'We have reason to believe that he's taken another woman as well. Lottie's friend and neighbor, Eva Diaz. She has a son who's only seven.'

There's a soft, guttural curse that tells me this dangerous criminal actually finds Andrew Fleming every bit as vile as I do, and then he says, 'He'll have them in the same place.'

'That's exactly what I was thinking.'

'Then it's a good thing that I'll be there with you,' he drawls, and I swear I can hear a feral smile in his voice, as if he's looking forward to taking Fleming down nearly as much as I am.

'If this works out,' I murmur, 'I want you to know that you're going to have my eternal gratitude for reaching out. So thank you.' And while I might be saying this all to a mobster, I mean every word.

I can hear him take another drag on the cigarette, and as he exhales, he says, 'People like this Andrew Fleming are a stain on our world, on that we can both agree. So trust me when I tell you that removing him from it will be my pleasure.'

The call ends then, and I close my eyes for a moment, working the surreal conversation over in my head.

'Callan,' Jase prompts from beside me. 'You gonna tell us what the hell is going on?'

'I don't really know,' I admit, blowing out a rough breath as

I shake my head. 'But I'm pretty sure I just made a deal with the devil.'

LOTTIE

'Come on, Lottie. Open those pretty blue eyes and let me see that you're awake, little bunny.'

At first, the words sound like they're coming to me in a dream. Or, considering whose voice that is, a freaking nightmare, and I pull in a slow, deep breath, fighting back a wave of nausea, my head pounding. Then I force my gritty eyelids to lift, and as I find myself staring up into my cousin's pale, sweat-covered face as he crouches down beside me, it all comes rushing back.

'Wh-what have you done? Where's Eva?' I stammer, scrambling back from him on what I quickly realize is a filthy, linoleum-tiled floor. There's just enough pale light coming from an old, jittery fluorescent bulb for me to see that I'm in a room that's about the size of a classroom, with a high, cavernous ceiling and tall, small-paned windows, the noise from the rain as it pounds against the old, dirty glass making it sound as if this ancient building might come tumbling down at any moment, and I don't have a single clue where we are.

'Don't worry about your friend,' he tells me, straightening to his full height. 'She's just sleeping off her chloroform in another room, since I still haven't decided what to do with her.'

'You have me now, so let her go!' I shout, but he just laughs so hard that his head goes back and all his teeth show, his maniacal appearance finally matching the madness that he's been able to conceal for so long. At least from everyone but me . . . and the people he's hurt.

I'm still scrambling away from him, and as I come up against a wall at my back, I have a brief flare of hope that one of Callan's tracking dots might lead him here to us, wherever *here* is. But then I look down and see with horror that I'm not only shoeless, I'm also no longer wearing my own clothes, a rain-soaked pair of sweatpants and a T-shirt that look like they belong to a man covering me now instead.

'Where the hell are my clothes?' I snarl with outrage, throwing the words up at him as if they carry physical weight. And, God, how I wish that they did. Because I've got so much anger and hatred built up inside of me for this bastard, I could eviscerate him within seconds with my verbal scorn.

'I had to ditch them once I got you into one of those dark alleyways behind your building,' he says in response to my question. 'Couldn't risk them being tagged and leading your new fuckboy here.' His head cocks eerily to the side, and there's a sickening gleam in his bloodshot eyes as he adds, 'I enjoyed the sight of your nude body, little bunny. But, sadly, that would have drawn attention if we'd been seen as I carried you to my car. So I dressed you in some of my things.'

I want to rip the clothes off, because they're making my skin crawl. But given how that would mean being naked in front of him, I swallow back the bile in my throat and try to calm down, since there's no way I'm going to let this sick shit win. And I'm grateful as hell that my parents' wedding rings are still hanging around my neck, the feel of them pressed between my breasts a small, but much-needed comfort.

I'm about to demand that he let me see Eva, when a loud sound suddenly comes from somewhere below us. I can't tell how far away it is – or even what has made it – but it captures Andrew's attention.

'I'm afraid our reunion will have to be postponed,' he

murmurs, taking a step back from me, while his eyes burn with a deadly rage. 'But if we've somehow been found, then the wait will be worth it, because I'm going to enjoy gutting him even more than I did Olly.'

'Oh God,' I whisper, realizing he's talking about Callan. But I can't imagine he would have been able to find this place so quickly, if ever.

Still, whoever it is might be here to help, so I do my best to stall Andrew, buying them as much time as I can.

'Just out of curiosity, have you seen the news lately?' I sneer, forcing a laugh up from my chest that burns my throat. 'Because your name really was leaked to the press. So if I had to guess, I'd say that's probably the police coming to nail your crazy arse!'

'Oh, I saw that,' he says, waving it off as if it was nothing – though there's a tightness around his eyes that betrays his uneasiness. 'Honestly, Lottie. Did you really think anyone would believe such an outlandish story?' he asks, chuckling, but it's a stark, hollow sound that's incredibly eerie.

'Yeah, and I still do,' I snap. 'Especially if you start leaving a trail of dead bodies behind you.'

At first, he doesn't say anything in response. He just walks across the freezing tiled floor until he's standing right in front of me, and stares down into my wide eyes, before he finally rasps, 'Well, right now, I'm about to go and add another one to the list.'

Then he hits me again, this time with his fist, and as pain radiates through my already aching head, I slump back to the dirty, dust-covered floor.

Chapter Twenty-One

LOTTIE

One ... Two ... Three ...

When I get to thirty, I stop counting and push myself up from the floor, shocked that I was actually able to fool the psycho into believing he'd knocked me out again. My head is hurting like crazy, but I'd turned with the hit, the way Callan had taught me to do, and was able to remain conscious.

As I listen to Andrew open another door in the outer hallway that must lie beyond this cold, dank room that I'm in and then close it, I'm amazed my thundering heartbeat doesn't bring him running back. I give it another thirty seconds, and when there's still no sign of him, I move to my feet. It's difficult to know how long I've been here judging by the storm-darkened daylight I can see beyond the filthy windows, but if I had to guess, I would say it's been for no more than a couple of hours or so.

Which is plenty of time for Callan to have been notified of my disappearance and start making his way back to the city. But surely that's not enough time to have driven all the way here, and I'm torn between relief that it *can't* be him who Andrew's gone to confront, while at the same time terrified over how I'm going to manage to get myself and Eva out of this hellhole alive.

Knowing I need to focus, I pull in a deep breath and make my way over to the door, checking that it's actually locked. I try to twist the cold handle, but it won't budge, and so I bite back a sharp curse and start looking around the empty, dimly lit room. There's nothing but a single door in the middle of the far wall, and I can tell by its size that it's probably for a closet or a bathroom. Still, there might be something on the other side that I can use as a weapon, so I make my way over and pull it open. Looking inside, I see that it's some kind of storage cupboard, the shelves that line the walls disappointingly bare, but as I narrow my eyes and peer more sharply into the shadowed space, I can just make out a large shape at the very back. At first, I'm not even sure what I'm looking at. And then it hits me. I'm staring at a body that's slumped against the back wall, its long legs stretched out over the floor. A *dead* body, I have no doubt – after shoving the door open wider to let in more of the pale light – given the angle of the man's head and the amount of blood that covers his torso, spilling into a puddle on the floor around him.

'Oh God, no. No . . . no . . . no . . . no . . . no,' I croak. This poor stranger isn't even someone I know, but I'm completely horrified by what he's suffered because of my deranged cousin. His blood-soaked clothes look dirty and worn, and I realize he was probably a homeless person who'd taken shelter in this derelict building. Just some poor soul who was in the wrong place at the wrong time, and had clearly borne the brunt of Andrew's psychotic rage at some point.

Stepping back and shutting the door again, I exhale a harsh

breath as I struggle to decide if I should try calling out to Eva, or if that's just stupid, since it could very well bring Andrew running right back up here. Then I hear something in the hallway – just a faint rustle of sound – and I freeze, terrified that he's already returned. But the voice that whispers 'Lottie' on the other side of the locked door is Eva's, and I'm so relieved I almost burst into tears.

'Ohmygod, Eva!' I gasp, running over and pressing my cheek against the door. 'Can you hear me? Can you unlock the door from your side?'

'He's locked it with a key, so just give me a second,' she mutters, sounding like she's concentrating on something. Then I hear a click, and as I step back, she turns the handle and opens the door.

'How did you get free?' I ask in a breathless rush, busily running my worried gaze over every part of her, trying to make sure she's okay. We're nearly the same height, but she has a curvier shape that I would die for, and the most beautiful, exotic brown eyes, creamy golden skin and a sprinkling of dark, tiny freckles that sweep across her cheekbones and the bridge of her nose. She's still wearing her work uniform, though it's smeared with dirt, and her lips are pressed thin and white with fear, the greenish cast to her gorgeous face telling me how unwell she feels. But I thankfully don't see any wounds or blood.

'I was in the room across the hall,' she tells me, sounding like she's having trouble getting enough air into her lungs. 'But he must not have thought I was going to come to anytime soon, because he didn't even bother to lock the door after checking on me just now. I think it was probably the sound of the door shutting behind him that woke me up. And I had a couple of bobby pins in my hair, so I used them to pick your lock.'

'You freaking genius! But are you all right? He hasn't hurt you?' I ask, growing more concerned about her coloring, since she looks like someone who's about to lose the contents of their stomach.

'I'm bruised up, and my head is killing me,' she mutters, rolling her right shoulder, 'but I think that's the worst of it.' She leans back against one of the walls, and her beautiful face suddenly tightens with a grimace as she says, 'But I feel like such an idiot for not listening to your friend Seb when he told me I should take a few days off. If I had, then we might not even be here.'

Shaking my head, I say, 'No, Eva. You did *nothing* wrong. Andrew's the psycho jackass, and this is all *his* fault, okay? He's the only one who has any blame.'

'What are we going to do?' she asks, still looking like she might pass out at any moment.

'Are you sure you're okay?' I question her with growing concern. 'Do you think you'll be able to walk?'

'I'm just a bit dizzy. And getting more nauseous the longer I'm on my feet. But if it means getting out of this place, then I'll run like Bolt himself if I have to.'

'I think you might be having a bad reaction to the chloroform he used on you.' I lift my hand, feeling her forehead, and it's warm and clammy. 'Come on. We need to get the hell out of here and get you to a doctor.'

Taking her hand, I pull her with me into the hallway and can see that there's a huge door at the far end that has 'STAIRWELL' stenciled on it. But when we reach it and I try the handle, it's locked.

Eva gives a low, pained laugh. 'What now?'

'I'm thinking,' I mutter, eyeing the glass panel on the door and wondering if I could break it, though the sound might be loud enough to ruin our element of surprise. I almost laugh at myself for even thinking the words 'element of surprise', as if I'm some badass heroine in an action film, preparing to charge in and save the day. But while I'm pathetically ill-equipped to charge in and save anyone, I'm not going to just sit and cower. Screw that! After I get Eva out of here, I'm going to do whatever I can to end Andrew's life, so that the creep can't ever hurt anyone again.

But even if I could smash the glass out, it's also fortified with metal wire, and without anything to cut through it, I know there's no way we'd be able to push past it in order to reach the lock on the other side of the door.

'Do you think we could shout down to someone on the street from that window?' Eva asks, pointing at the one that's on our left. And unlike the windows in the room I'd been locked in, this one is a wide, single pane of glass that opens outward from the bottom. But after I wrench it open and look outside, into the pouring rain, there isn't a single person down on the street below us.

'I think we're on some kind of old industrial estate,' I tell Eva, still leaning out of the window. 'But I can't see any cars or people. It looks like all of the surrounding buildings are abandoned.'

'Shit,' she wheezes, sounding like she's still having trouble getting in enough air, and I know I have to get her out of here as quickly as possible.

I lean out a bit farther, glancing down, and feel my heart lurch into my throat as I recall how Andrew had broken into my building through a window, which means we could break *out* of this one the exact same way. Only, we're about seven or so stories high! There is, however, a wide ledge that runs around the outside of the building, just under the window, and I'm wondering if I've actually gone and lost my damn mind as I ask, 'Um, Eva? How are you with heights?'

'I friggin' hate them, Lan—I mean *Lottie*.' She gives a soft, tired laugh, and says, 'Seb told me that's your real name, and I'm loving all that gorgeous blonde hair. But, when we're out of this nightmare, you and I are going to have a long-ass chat about how you didn't trust me with the truth, because you're one of my closest friends, and I would have definitely been there for you. And as for my hatred of heights, we're talking a level of dislike where I despise them with the passion of a thousand fiery hells.'

'Yeah, me too,' I admit, feeling as nauseous as poor Eva looks. 'But I'm afraid we're going to need to climb out onto this ledge that's out here. I could see through the glass in the door that there's another window like this one in the stairwell, around the corner of the building. So we need to make our way around to it on the ledge, and then climb back inside so that we can get down the stairs.'

'Oh God,' she groans. 'I *knew* you were going to say that, you evil, beautiful bitch.'

Looking at her over my shoulder, I murmur, 'I'd do it alone, babe, but the lock on the door is another one that needs a key. So I won't be able to go by myself and then open it for you, because unlike you, I've never learned how to pick a freaking lock. Which means we need to go together.'

Her chest shakes with another exhausted-sounding laugh. 'Or I could just stay here and die.'

'Don't even joke about that,' I snap, giving her a fierce look. 'I am *not* going to be the arsehole who has to tell Nico that his mama isn't coming home!'

'I know,' she sighs, her dark curls bouncing as she nods her head. 'You're right.'

'I mean it, Eva,' I growl, ready to slap some sense into her if I have to. 'That little boy needs you.'

'And I need him, too.' She pulls in a deep breath as she straightens away from the wall she's been leaning against, then slowly lets it out as she pushes her curls back from her pale face. 'I can do this,' she says with a fresh surge of determination. 'For Nico, I'll do it.'

Opening the window as wide as it will go, I climb out and then brace myself on the ledge and help Eva out as best I can. When we're both on the ledge, I carefully turn so that my back is pressed up tight against the building, and then I make the mistake of looking down, and I swear I can feel the bacon and eggs that I'd eaten at breakfast nearly come back up. 'Oh motherfucking fuck douches,' I gasp, using one of poor Ruby's favorite, more colorful curses. 'Why did he have to pick the tallest bloody building in the neighborhood?'

'Because he's a sadistic prick, that's why!' Eva moans, sounding as terrified as I am.

'Just . . . Just stay close to me, and tell me if you start feeling dizzy.' I'm practically hyperventilating as I begin inching my way along the ledge, thinking that this is every bit as awful as it always looks in the movies. And of course this is when the skies decide to completely open up, and it starts raining even harder, along with some thunder and lightning thrown in to really spice things up. If I wasn't so petrified, I would cry, because any hopes I might have had that a Good Samaritan would suddenly come along on the empty street down below, spot us and bring help, gets utterly washed away by the downpour.

'You doing okay back there?' I shout, gasping again when I take my next step and realize the rain is only making this even trickier, my wet socks nearly slipping right off the ledge.

'I love you, Lottie!' Eva shouts back. 'But if you don't just shut up and keep moving, I'm going to kick your ass!'

'Okay, babe! I'm moving!'

When we finally reach the window that opens onto the stairwell landing, I nearly have a heart attack when it doesn't budge on my first try, terrified that it's locked. But then I grit my teeth and pull even harder, and it starts to creak open, nearly bringing tears to my eyes. 'Hold on!' I shout to Eva. 'I'm going in, and then I'll be able to help you.'

'Be careful!' she shouts back, and I'm repeating those same words in my head as I complete the tricky task of climbing in off the ledge. But I don't breathe easy until I've helped Eva inside as well, and while I know the entire time we spent out there was only a matter of minutes, it felt like an excruciating lifetime.

We look like a couple of drowned rats, our wet hair plastered to our cold faces, but we share wobbly smiles as we glance at each other, just grateful to be one step closer to getting out of here. But we haven't even been on the landing for more than thirty seconds, both of us still trying to stop panting, when I hear someone coming up the stairs.

'Damn it,' I mutter under my breath, frantically looking around, but the old, dirty bricks stacked in the corner are the only things here on the landing that I might be able to use as a weapon. I pick one up, praying I'll have enough strength to bash Andrew's face in with it, when the person comes around the bend in the stairs and I catch sight of a tall, gray-eyed, incredibly handsome stranger. He's dressed in a pair of designer jeans and a tight black sweater, his glossy, ink-black hair brushed back from a striking, angular face.

But even though he's gorgeous, there's an unmistakable air of danger that surrounds him that has me gripping the brick in my hand even tighter as I snarl, 'Who are you?'

'Someone who is here to offer my assistance,' he replies in a deep voice, his accent sounding either Russian or Eastern European. 'I've come with your Mr Hathaway.'

'Callan!' I gasp, filled with equal parts relief and dismay as I let the brick drop from my hand, which is stupid, since it almost lands on my foot. 'Is he here? Is he okay? How in God's name did he find us so quickly?'

'He's furious, but unharmed. And yes, he's here. I believe he took a helicopter flight back to the city. He's searching floors one through five, while I took six through ten.'

'Why would Jack Pravik be interested in helping us?' Eva asks with a thick note of suspicion, making it clear that she knows the identity of this handsome, mysterious stranger.

His piercing gray eyes do a quick sweep of her trembling form, before he quietly says, 'Because he has no tolerance for assholes who hurt women. And I don't want scum like Andrew Fleming walking my streets.'

'*Your* streets?' I murmur, wondering exactly *who* this man is.

Answering my unspoken question, Eva wheezes, 'He's one of the top captains of a local crime syndicate.'

I frown as I slip my arm around her waist, worried she's going to fall over, her erratic breathing, which is rapidly getting worse, scaring the hell out of me as I mutter, 'Is that meant to be some kind of joke?'

Before Eva can respond, he says, 'I assure you that I don't mean either of you any harm, Miss Fleming. I am the one who reached out to Mr Hathaway and helped him find this place.'

'Yeah, sure you . . .'

'Eva!' I cry, when her voice trails off and she starts to slide away from me, slumping against the wall that's just behind us, her eyes so unfocused I'm not even sure if she can still hear me.

'What's wrong with her?' Pravik bites out, hurrying over to

us and pushing her wet hair back from her face while he studies her eyes.

'Please help her. She's . . .' I shiver as my own voice suddenly trails off, wondering if I'm crazy for trusting this complete stranger with my friend's well-being.

He must be able to read my indecision and skepticism on my face when he glances over at me, because he quickly says, 'There's no cell reception up here, so I can't call him. But in the event that I was the one to find you and had trouble convincing you that I'm here to help, there's something Hathaway told me that he said only the two of you would know.'

Surprise widens my eyes. 'What is it?'

'He said that he's happy to let you keep the hoodie you stole from him, so long as he gets *you*.'

I would smile if I wasn't so terrified for Eva. But since I am, I get straight to the point. 'I think she might be having some kind of reaction to the chloroform that Andrew used on her.'

Pravik's dark, straight brows knit together with concern as he checks her pulse at the side of her throat. 'She needs a hospital.'

'I think so, too. So can I trust you to get her to one while I go to find Callan?'

He blinks as he slowly looks over at me again, his expression making it clear that he thinks I've gone slightly mad. 'You want me to just leave you here?'

I narrow my eyes as I return his intimidating stare. 'Well, I'm sure as hell not going anywhere without him.'

'Christ,' he mutters, shaking his head with irritation. 'I should have known this wouldn't be simple.'

'Since when are rescue operations ever simple?' I ask with a short, dry laugh.

He grumbles something under his breath in a Slavic language, then reaches behind his back. 'At least take this for your protection,' he says, offering me a dark, heavy-looking handgun.

'Um . . .' is about all I can manage as I gingerly take the gun with my free hand, surprised by its weight, while my other hand is still gripping on to Eva, helping her to stay upright.

'Wait. Do you even know how to use a gun?' he demands warily, looking like he might decide to take it back.

'No, but it can't be *that* difficult to figure out,' I state with false confidence as I tighten my grip on the weapon, making it clear that I have no intention of handing it back over to him.

'Just don't shoot me by accident,' he says with a heavy sigh.

'Get Eva safely to a hospital for me,' I tell him, arching my eyebrows, 'and then I won't have any *reason* to shoot you, now will I?'

His chest shakes with a low, provocative laugh. 'I'm starting to see why Hathaway was willing to risk life and limb to save you,' he murmurs in his deliciously accented voice, suddenly lifting a nearly unconscious Eva into his strong arms as if she weighs no more than a feather. 'But do me a favor?'

'What's that?'

'When you find Hathaway,' he drawls, the corner of his mouth twitching with a brief, wry smile, 'please don't tell him that I allowed his woman to go off on her own without trying to stop her. I don't relish having him as an enemy.'

'Don't worry,' I reply. 'This will be our little secret.'

'Thank you, *solnyshko*.'

I give him a nod, wondering what he's just called me. 'Well, thank *you* for taking care of Eva.'

'I give you my word that she'll receive the medical attention she needs,' he says, before turning and quickly making his way back down the stairs with Eva cradled against his chest, which tells me just how worried he is about her condition.

I set off down the stairs as well, but at a slower pace, the gun held in my trembling right hand down by my side while I try to decide which floor I should start looking for Callan on. Since Pravik had said that Callan was searching from the first floor to the fifth one, I settle on five, terrified that it's going to take me forever to find him. And then I literally almost run straight into him not a minute later as I'm making my way down the fifth-floor hallway and he comes out of one of the rooms, looking every bit the gorgeous badass that he is.

'Callan!' I gasp, so excited and relieved that I nearly drop the freaking gun as I throw my arms around him. 'Ohmygod, I can't believe it's really you!'

Chapter Twenty-Two

LOTTIE

'Lottie!' Callan cries, my name rolling off his tongue like a fervent prayer. 'Jesus Christ, Lot, are you okay?' he asks in a graveled rush, touching my face and hair with the hand that doesn't have his own gun in it, frantically searching me with his worried gaze. 'Did he hurt you?'

'No. I think he was waiting for something,' I explain, though I still have no idea what it was as I stare up into Callan's handsome face with a wobbly smile. 'So I'm fine. I promise, I'm okay.'

'Thank God,' he groans, crushing me in a trembling hug that makes it clear just how terrified he's been for my safety. He kisses the side of my head, then my temple, before giving a heavy sigh and pulling back until he can look me in the eye again. 'I know it sounds crazy, baby, but your aunt and uncle are here.'

'What?' I frown up at him in confusion. 'That . . . It doesn't make any sense.'

'Tell me about it. But right now, I need to know if you've

NEW YORK SCANDAL 289

seen Eva.' He glances down at the gun in my hand, shaking his head as he asks, 'And how in the hell did you get a Glock?'

'Long story short, Eva saved me from a locked room, and there's a body in it. I think it's a homeless man who was probably living here, and Andrew killed him.'

'Fuck,' he curses, before waiting for me to go on.

'So Eva and I had to climb out onto a ledge to reach the stairwell, then ran into your new friend, Pravik. The gun is one of his, and he's hopefully gotten Eva out of here and to a hospital, because she was in bad shape. I think she's having some kind of reaction to the chloroform that Andrew used on her.'

'That son of a bitch.' He pushes my wet hair back from my face with his free hand, and I can't help but notice how it's shaking. 'Are you sure you're okay?'

'Yeah. Andrew hit me in the back of my head with his gun when he took me, and once with his fist, but I don't even think I have a concussion. He came into the locked room he was keeping me in maybe ten or fifteen minutes ago, but before he could try anything, there was a loud noise and he went to investigate.'

'I heard that too, but don't know what it was. Pravik and I were already searching for you and Eva when it came from downstairs.'

'Callan!' I say with urgency, the horrific events of the afternoon suddenly coming back to me as I grip a handful of his T-shirt. 'Andrew stabbed Thompson in my apartment!'

'I know, honey, but he's going to be okay. Clara and her detail got him to the ER.'

'Oh, thank God,' I gasp, nearly sagging with relief as I close my eyes. But then I pull in a deep breath and look back up at him, a frown tugging between my brows as I ask, 'How on earth did you end up here with Jack Pravik?'

'He called me and said that he thought he had a good idea where you were being kept.'

I take a second to process what he's told me, but still can't figure out how this happened. 'But how did he even know I'd been taken?'

'You're not going to believe it,' he says with a grim smile, 'but that was Clara's doing. She held a press conference just a few hours ago and pleaded with the city for information about where Andrew might have taken you.'

'Ohmygod, that's—' I have to stop and swallow against the knot of disbelief that's lodged in my throat, before I can say, 'It's as wonderfully sweet as it is crazy!'

'I know. But we can talk about my sweet, crazy family later,' he mutters, and there's a fierce look of determination in his dark eyes as he takes hold of my hand. 'Right now, I'm getting you out of here.'

'Wait!' I cry, refusing to budge when he tries to walk away. 'I have to help my aunt and uncle.'

'I'll come back for them,' he says in a hard, don't-argue-with-me tone that perfectly matches his expression. 'But I'm getting you someplace safe first.'

'I'm sorry, but I can't do that. I'd never be able to live with myself if something happened to them before we could get help.'

'Shit,' he curses, exhaling a rough breath, and I can tell by the strained look on his face that whatever he's about to say is going to be bad. 'I didn't want to have to do this here, but something's not right about this entire situation, Lot. They shouldn't be here. Leo, who works for me, found out that they flew into JFK last night, and when I saw them downstairs, they weren't even restrained.'

I gape up at him, unable to believe what I'm hearing. 'You . . . You think they're here to *help* him?'

His mouth presses into a hard, flat line. 'I don't know. But my gut is telling me this is off.'

'It . . .' I wet my lips with a nervous swipe of my tongue, my heart beating so hard it's a physical pain in my chest, and then force myself to tell him what I'm thinking. 'It might have something to do with my aunt. She's always been weirdly standoffish, and she's . . . I've just always had the feeling that she doesn't like me. But could she really be capable of . . . *supporting* him in a situation as twisted as this?'

Something flickers behind his dark, concerned gaze, and there's a new grittiness to his deep voice when he says, 'You know as well as I do, Lot, that women can do some messed-up shit, same as men. Hell, I still need to tell you about Jase's stepmom.'

'Caroline?' I murmur, not really surprised that she'd done something awful, seeing as how the woman had always given me the creeps. 'What about her?'

'We don't have time to get into it right now, but trust me when I say that the story is a bad one,' he explains. 'But if we're not running for it, then I need to get you hidden somewhere so that I can go and deal with this asshole once and for all.'

'You want me to freaking *hide*, while you go and face my psycho family all on your own?' I ask with a bitter laugh. 'Please tell me that's some kind of joke. Because if it's not, then you clearly don't know me *at all*.'

'Lottie,' he bites out, his nostrils flaring as he sucks in a sharp, frustrated breath.

'For the last time, Callan, I'm not Jessica!' I hiss, my chest heaving, wishing I could scream the words at him as guilt spreads through my system like liquid fire, burning me from the inside out. 'My biggest regret, for the rest of my life, will *always* be that I didn't go back to help Olly.'

'Lot—'

'No! Just listen!' I tell him, my voice shaking, though I'm determined to get the words out. To finally share this last secret with him, because I know that if I don't, it will just keep festering inside me, until the guilt turns into something ugly and vicious that completely destroys who I am. 'I've never told you . . . I've never told *anyone*. But Olly and I . . . we'd started arguing once we got to our stateroom that night. I'll never forget how he looked – a little terrified, and actually serious for once – when he told me that he wanted us to give our relationship a real go. And I . . . I just refused. Outright.'

His beautiful brown eyes are soft with understanding. 'There's nothing wrong with that, sweetheart. You didn't owe him anything.'

'But at the time, all I could think about was *you*,' I admit, my throat burning with unshed tears. 'About the fact that you were out there somewhere. And I knew that even if Olly somehow changed, and tried to make amends for all the horrible ways he'd treated people, that I would never be able to feel for him even a fraction of the way I feel about you.'

He says my name again, with so much emotion it makes my chest warm, even as I'm still drowning in my guilt.

'But even . . . Even knowing that I didn't want him that way –' I swipe my tongue over my lower lip again and sniff – 'he still put himself through hell to save me. And I . . . I just ran away.'

'Baby,' he rasps, pushing his hand into my hair as his dark gaze burns into mine, 'there was *nothing* you could have done.'

'Maybe,' I agree with another sniff. 'But we'll never know for sure.'

'Damn it, I don't want you carrying that around,' he grates. 'And Olly wouldn't have wanted it, either.'

'And I don't want *you* thinking that you always have to protect me. We protect *each other*.'

'Lot—'

'I mean it, Callan. We deal with this together, or there *is* no us afterward.'

For a moment, he looks so angry that I have no doubt he's going to keep arguing. But then the corner of his mouth twitches with a wry, fleeting smile, and he shakes his head as he rumbles, 'God, you're annoying.'

'Yeah,' I agree with an unsteady grin. 'But you already told me that you love me, and you can't take it back.'

'I don't want to take it back,' he husks, his molten gaze glinting as much with hunger as with protectiveness. 'I just want to put you over my damn knee.'

'Promises, promises,' I drawl, giving him a cheeky smirk, feeling lighter than I can ever remember feeling now that I've finally told him everything.

But his dark brows draw together in a sexy scowl. '*Now* you decide to tease me?'

'Just keeping you on your toes,' I say with a little shrug. And then, given the severity of the situation, I ask, 'So where are my aunt and uncle?'

He searches my determined expression for another heavy moment, but since he knows damn well that I'm not backing down, he finally answers my question. 'I only caught a glimpse of them, because *you* were the one I was desperate to find. But it was in a room down on the first floor that looks like an abandoned workshop.'

'Can we get to them without Andrew seeing us?'

'I'm not sure. But I think there's access to some kind of office that overlooks the workshop, kind of like a loft, on the second floor. If we can get in there, we should be able to get a good look down onto the workshop floor and figure out what the hell is going on.'

'Okay. Let's go.'

'Whoa! Before we go charging off to anyone's rescue, do you even know how to use that?' he asks, gesturing at the gun that's still in my hand . . . and sounding somewhat concerned that I might accidentally shoot him with it, same as Pravik had.

'Not really, no,' I admit with another shrug. 'But how hard can it be?'

'God help us,' he mutters with a shaky laugh. 'But it'll be okay, because I'm going to shoot the asshole between the eyes the second I get the chance.'

He quickly shows me how to take the safety off the gun, and I follow behind him as we make our way down the stairs to the second floor. Then he stops at the door to the loft and turns to face me. 'We need to be quiet, so no matter what you see, don't make a sound.'

I swallow against the knot of fear in my throat, my pulse rushing so hard that it hurts, terrified not only by what we're about to face, but by what I know I have to say to him, right now, before we go through that bloody door.

'Before we go in there,' I whisper in a breathless rush, staring up into his beautiful, thick-lashed eyes, 'I . . . I need to tell you that I love you too. Because I do. I am completely and totally in love with you, Callan Hathaway.'

'Jesus Christ, Lot,' he growls softly, suddenly looking as if he wants to eat me alive. 'You tell me this *now*, when I can't fuck you?'

I give him another wobbly smile. 'I'm sorry that my timing sucks so bad. I should have said it before, because it's true.' Then I reach up, pressing my dirty hand to the side of his ruggedly handsome face as I whisper, 'And you can fuck me as soon as we get the hell out of here.'

'Promises, promises,' he drawls, giving my earlier words right back to me, and I would laugh at how freaking much I love being with him if not for the fact that I'm completely panicked about what's going to happen.

Callan quietly opens the door to the office, and we creep along the edge of the loft as we make our way to the glass-topped wall that looks out onto the dimly lit workshop floor below. I spot Andrew's tall body almost immediately as he comes into the mostly empty room from a side door, carrying what looks strangely like a pile of white cotton sheets.

'Look at the side of his head, just above his ear, where his hair's matted with blood. Someone's hit him,' Callan murmurs, his voice so low I can barely hear it.

'That was me,' I whisper. 'He called me pathetic when we were in my apartment, and I've wasted enough energy thinking of myself that way because of this jerk. So I swung the candlestick that sits on my cherry-blossom table right at the side of his head.'

He reaches back to squeeze my free hand with his, his deep voice rough with pride as he says, 'Damn straight you're not pathetic, you beautiful badass.'

As we watch, Andrew sets the sheets on a rickety, dust-covered table that's propped against one of the walls, another table in the far-left corner of the room laden with expensive-looking computer equipment that seems jarringly out of place within this rundown, derelict building.

'What the hell is he doing?' I whisper, when Andrew walks over to what looks like a stack of transport pallets that have been carefully arranged into a rectangular shape, picks up a mound of chains that are piled on the floor beside a gasoline can, and starts working the chains through the pallets in an X-shaped pattern. 'Seriously,' I hiss, 'what in God's name *is* that?'

'You don't want to know,' Callan tells me, his low voice thick with disgust and rage, and that's when I see it. When the horror finally makes sense.

The psycho came in with a pile of sheets because he's making some kind of macabre cross between a pyre and a bed. And as I realize *who* he's making it for, and *what* he intends to happen on it, my blood runs so cold I'm amazed I don't shatter as I draw in my next shuddering breath.

'Lot,' Callan whispers, and there's an edge to his voice that has me bracing. 'Look in the corner on the far right. The one that's almost completely in shadow.'

'Ohmygod,' I gasp, blinking to make sure I'm seeing this right. But no matter how many times I shake my head and blink, the image of my aunt just sitting there quietly in a chair, dressed in a prim pink skirt and cream-colored sweater, watching her son make this deranged altar that he plans to rape and kill me on, remains. It's eerie and creepy as hell, the way she's just silently observing him, her face expressionless, while Andrew hums under his breath.

'Are you sure the building's secure?' she suddenly asks him, her tone so casual, you'd think they were talking about nothing more innocuous than the weather.

'I told you, I checked it. Whatever made the noise that spooked you, it was probably just another stray scrounging around for food.'

'Very well then,' she sighs, going back to sitting as still as a statue, her once beautiful face now sallow and heavily lined, while inside, she's clearly gone as stark raving mad as her son.

God, and here I'd thought Olly's family was screwed up. They didn't have anything on mine!

'This is going to give me nightmares for years,' I admit in a soft, unsteady voice, gripping the gun that's still in my hand so tightly my knuckles are turning white.

'You and me both,' Callan mutters.

'What are you doing?' I ask, when he pulls his phone from his pocket, wondering if he's getting ready to call the police.

Instead of answering my question, he taps his finger against the screen a few times, then turns it to show me that he's set his camera on record mode.

'Wow,' I murmur, as he slips the phone back into his pocket. 'You've got brains *and* a gorgeous bod, Hathaway.'

'I feel the same way about you, baby.'

'Where do you think my uncle's at?' I ask, worried that they've done something horrible to him.

But before Callan can even answer me, I hear a familiar, jovial voice come from behind us. 'I'm right here, sweetheart.'

Callan curses savagely under his breath as we both turn and find my short, balding uncle standing in the doorway to the office, dressed in a neatly pressed pair of trousers and plaid shirt, holding a bloody gun on us!

'Now be a good chap and lass,' he says, 'and toss those guns of yours right over here, onto the floor.' When neither of us moves, he frowns and points the gun directly at my chest, his voice sharper as he snaps, 'Now! Or I shoot.'

Callan curses again as we both do as he's said, while I'm still shaking my head in disbelief. 'What the hell?' I croak, feeling as if I've slipped into yet another outlandish level of this bizarre, twisted nightmare. 'I trusted you, you son of a bitch!'

'I really am sorry about this,' he replies with a heavy sigh, his tone shifting yet again, this time from sharp to contrite. 'I never wanted you to get hurt, sweetheart, but—'

'I'm not your sweetheart!' I shout, wanting to spit in his face.

'But he's my *boy*,' he goes on, sounding as if he's pleading with me to understand. 'My flesh and blood, Lottie. When I realized what was happening, after you turned sixteen and started maturing, I *tried* to help him. But there was no help for the things he wanted. So the best I could do was make sure that he never got caught.'

'You could have turned him in,' Callan snarls with so much fury his huge body is vibrating with it. 'That sick shit was terrorizing an innocent girl!'

'Yes, well, that was unfortunate,' my uncle murmurs, still holding his gun on me as he shifts his weary gaze to Callan. 'But Lottie is so much stronger than he is. I knew she would be okay. It's Andrew who needs me.'

'He murdered Oliver,' I choke out, shuddering from the memory. 'And he laughed while he was doing it!'

'Yes, well,' he sighs, returning his attention to me, 'once your fiancé hired those bodyguards to watch over you, I knew it was only a matter of time before Andrew would be caught. So that's when I helped him plan his trip to Italy.' His shoulders lift with another somber sigh, and he shakes his head as he says, 'I told him things had to come to an end, once and for all.'

'Holy shit,' I breathe, staggered by the wave of realization that's just swept through me. 'You sent him there to kill me, didn't you?'

'I *had* to! Don't you see?' he cries, looking frustrated that we're not simply nodding our heads in understanding, congratulating him on such a brilliant plan. 'There was no other option! But he failed – and he hasn't been the same since. He's deteriorated more and more over this past year, until I knew that something had to be done. So I took an overdose of a friend's medication to induce that heart attack, hoping that you might hear about it and finally reach out to us again. And we were ready when you did.' A scowl pulls at his brows and mouth as he mutters, 'But he was meant to kill you straightaway, Lottie. Not waste all this time just watching you.'

'Do you even care that he killed an innocent woman yesterday?' I ask in a shrill tone that's bordering on hysteria, unable to understand how I'd never seen what this man was hiding behind his shy demeanor and kind smiles.

'Unfortunate, that. But a necessary evil, I'm sure,' he says with another heavy sigh, before pulling his shoulders back and using the gun to motion us toward the top of the narrow staircase that leads down to the workshop floor. 'Now, down the stairs with the two of you.'

It's obvious that we both believe he's willing to shoot me, because Callan follows right behind me as I make my way down.

'Well, look at what you found, old man,' Andrew hoots with a wide smile from where he stands beside his sadistic pyre, clearly having overheard our shouting. 'Nicely done!'

My uncle's tone, however, is sour with disapproval. 'There's no need to gloat, son. It's unseemly.'

But Andrew is unfazed by the criticism as he stares at me. 'Oh, if only you could see the look on your face, Lottie,' he laughs as the three of us descend onto the workshop floor, and I notice that Callan is staying deliberately close to my side. 'Are you surprised? Are you? Because he loves me more than you!'

Glaring at my uncle over my shoulder, I ask, 'Did you know that the woman he kidnapped today is a mum? That she has a little boy?'

'And he's *my* boy,' he says, his expression imploring me to understand. 'Don't you see? I have to do whatever it takes to keep him alive.'

'Even if that means watching him rape and kill me?'

My uncle blinks at me in horror. 'Well, we weren't actually going to stay and watch, dear.'

'My God, you're as crazy as he is!' I shout, suddenly repeating a few of the moves that Callan had taught me during our self-defense lesson as I quickly step backward and stomp down on my uncle's foot as hard as I can. Then I use my entire body weight to lift up and ram the back of my head into his face. I hear a crunch and a howl, which I'm hoping was his nose breaking, and his gun skitters across the floor as I quickly do it again, ignoring the throbbing pain in my already injured head, and this time he slumps to the floor in an unconscious heap.

Then everything happens in slow motion as I watch Andrew pull his gun from behind his back, where he'd had it tucked into his waistband, while Callan is diving for the gun my uncle has dropped that's still skidding across the floor. Reacting purely on instinct, since I can see that Andrew is going to fire at him before Callan can reach the gun, I throw myself to the side, determined to take the bullet that's meant for the man I love . . . only Andrew never takes the shot.

Instead, he stumbles forward, howling in pain, and I lift my gaze to see my aunt standing behind him, holding the chair she'd been sitting on in her hands, her chest heaving from the exertion of hitting him across the back with it.

'You bitch!' Andrew cries, pointing the gun toward her as she drops the chair and starts running for our side of the workshop. But she's still running after there's an ear-shattering bang, and I blink as I watch the blood that spills from the small hole that's suddenly appeared in Andrew's upper chest, his expression one of shocked disbelief before he falls back against the floor. Looking over my shoulder, I see Callan standing there with my uncle's gleaming black gun still gripped tight in his hand, and he exhales a harsh breath as he lowers his arm and brings his narrowed gaze straight to mine. Then he clicks the safety on the gun, tucks it into the back of his jeans and starts moving toward me as I start running to him, and we crash together, desperate to make sure the other's okay.

'What the hell were you thinking,' he growls, gripping me with his shaking hands, 'throwing yourself in front of me like that?'

'I was thinking that I love—' I'm saying, when another gunshot thunders through the room, and we both gasp as we look over and see a brilliant splotch of red soaking through the front of my uncle's plaid shirt.

'I had to make it stop,' my aunt murmurs, dropping Andrew's gun back onto the floor, and I realize she must have picked it up while Callan and I were embracing. Then she looks over at me, and says, 'I'm so sorry, Lottie.'

'For what?' I whisper, clutching at Callan like a lifeline, since my legs are like noodles.

Her thin shoulders droop as if she has the weight of the entire world on them. 'For never protecting you.'

'All these years, I . . . I thought that you hated me.'

'No. No. Not at all,' she tells me, shaking her head. 'But I didn't know what I could do for you, except to . . .'

'To run me off,' I finish softly. 'Make me feel unwelcome, so that I would leave and not come back.'

'I should have helped you,' she says with more force, looking as if she's aging right before our eyes, 'but I let my fear of him control me. My fear of them *both*. And for that, I truly am sorry.'

'You knew Andrew was stalking her?' Callan asks in a hard voice, his muscles rigid with anger as he holds me close. 'You *knew*, and you never did anything about it?'

She gives a jerky nod as she looks at him. 'I was too weak,

Mr Hathaway. I couldn't save Lottie or my boy. Or even myself.' Then she pulls back the sleeve of her sweater, revealing a gruesome burn scar on her right arm. 'Whenever I tried, Liam would punish me. I earned this one after you came to talk to us last year about Lottie's disappearance, and I told you about her withdrawal when she turned sixteen, hoping that it might lead you down the right path.'

'Jesus Christ,' Callan and I both mutter at the same time.

'He would burn Andrew too, in places that couldn't be seen during his physicals, if he thought he was being too reckless. And I was too much of a coward to ever put a stop to it.' She lowers her sleeve, then brings her tormented gaze back to mine, and there's the briefest ghost of a smile on her trembling lips as she says, 'But you're just like your parents, Lottie. You would have made them both so proud today.'

I open my mouth, but have no idea what to say to her. And then the opportunity is gone, because the disgusting pyre that Andrew had been constructing suddenly goes up in flames with a mighty whoosh that seems to suck all the oxygen out of the room.

'What the fuck?' Callan snarls, grabbing mine and my aunt's arms and quickly jerking us back from the fire that's already roaring, the tips of the flames nearly reaching the high ceiling.

'It was Andrew! He's still alive!' I shout, coughing from the smoke that's billowing around us as I point toward the place where I'd just caught a glimpse of my cousin as he crawled around to the far side of the pyre. 'He must have had a lighter on him and set the can of gasoline on fire!'

Without another word, Callan quickly tosses my aunt over one of his broad shoulders, grabs my hand, and starts running like hell for the nearest exit. It feels like it takes forever to find our way out, though in reality I know not even a full minute has gone by before we're running out of a wide set of dirty double doors and into the deserted street. Callan sets my aunt back on her feet, and we're all coughing and trying to suck in deep breaths of the clean, crisp outside air as we stare in shock at the old building. The windows on this side are already glowing orange all the way up to the third floor, the fire spreading so rapidly it clearly won't be long before the entire structure is engulfed in flames. And as luck would have it, the storm has already passed, not a single raindrop falling from the sky.

'Get your aunt and move back to a safe distance,' Callan tells me, just as sirens start blaring in the distance. 'I'll be right back.'

But before he can even take a single step, I grab on to his arm, shouting, 'Where on earth are you going?'

At first, I think he must be making a horrible joke as he looks down at me and calmly says, 'I've got to go back and get Andrew and your uncle out.' Then a fresh wave of horror spreads through me as I realize he's actually being serious.

'Callan, no!' I cry, panicking even more as he breaks out of my hold. 'It's too dangerous!'

'I'll be careful,' he calls out over his shoulder. 'I promise.'

Then the too-brave-for-his-own-good man starts running back toward the building, and I nearly sob with relief when a fireman suddenly stops him right before he reaches the double doors. They're too far away for me to hear what they're saying to each other over all the racket the other firefighters are making as they ready the hoses and begin spraying at the windows, many of them already broken and billowing with smoke. I can't believe the emergency services have responded so quickly, given that the fire only started a few minutes ago and this area is completely abandoned, but I'm thankful as hell to see them.

Callan eventually steps away from the fireman who'd stopped him and starts making his way back over to us, while a group of firefighters with respirators attached to their faces go rushing inside the burning building to search for survivors.

And while I know it's probably wrong, I can't deny that I'm hoping my evil cousin and uncle are already dead, the world no doubt a far safer place without them in it.

Callan reaches us just as two ambulances show up, and it's chaos as the three of us are moved into an area that's being cordoned off by police officers. While an EMT looks my aunt over, the police captain comes over and pulls Callan aside for questioning. I can hear enough to know he's filling her in on what's happened, and then he plays the recording for her that he'd made with his phone, while one of the other EMTs starts checking the wound on the back of my head. As I'm pulling off my wet socks and gratefully slipping on the pair of flip-flops that one of the female cops has grabbed for me, I ask the EMT if it's possible for him to check with the local ER to see if an Eva Diaz has been admitted, and nearly keel over with relief when he calls and is able to tell me that she's in a stable condition and is expected to make a full recovery.

When the police captain finally shakes Callan's hand and walks away, my gorgeous guy heads straight for me. 'Who called them about the fire?' I ask, before he can get a single word out.

'No one. I had Deanna release your aunt's and uncle's photos to the press, and the taxi driver who picked them up from the airport and drove them here recognized them. According to the police captain,' he explains, his mouth kicking up on one side with a slight smile, 'the driver called Clara's hotline, and she apparently decided to bring the entire friggin' cavalry with her, including the fire department.'

'Wow,' I whisper, still amazed that his sister would do

everything that she'd done for us that day, basically putting her entire career on the line in order to help us. 'We're going to have to get her a *really* nice Christmas present, aren't we? But what do you buy for the woman who's been so completely selfless?'

'Whatever the hell she wants,' he replies with a gritty laugh. Then his beautiful brown eyes darken with concern as he stares down at me, and he asks, 'Are you okay, sweetheart?'

'No. Not really. I'm just . . . God, I'm still so furious,' I whisper, and we both flinch when we see a firefighter walk out of the building carrying my uncle's burned, clearly lifeless body over his shoulder. 'I always looked up to him, thinking he was this sweet, caring old man, when in reality he was every bit as much of a monster as his son.'

'Well, he's paid for his sins now,' Callan says, wrapping his strong, loving arms around me.

'Yeah,' I mutter, pressing the side of my face against his chest. 'But he should have paid *more*.'

The next firefighter to come out of the building is carrying a badly burned body as well, and while my view is obscured by the two police officers who pass in front of us, I know that it's Andrew. I'm filled with this strange combination of relief, shock and exhaustion as the long body is placed on a stretcher, then immediately covered by a sheet from head to toe, and as Callan's arms tighten around me, I think it's because he can sense how close I am to collapsing. But then I realize that he's not even looking at Andrew's sheet-covered body, but staring off to the side, and as I turn my head to follow his gaze, I gasp when I see a young police officer putting a set of handcuffs on my aunt, who's staring silently at the ground. 'What do you think will happen to her?' I quietly ask.

'I'm not sure,' he murmurs. 'But I imagine she'll get a psych eval, and they'll have to decide from there.'

I shudder so hard it makes my teeth crack together. 'God, that's grim.'

'What it is for you, sweetheart, is over,' he rumbles, pressing a soft kiss to the top of my head. 'You don't owe her a damn thing, and none of this evil is ever touching you again.' Then he moves to my side as he wraps his arm around my waist, giving it a gentle squeeze. 'Now come on. I'm getting you the hell out of here.'

CALLAN

Lottie and I make our way through the police cordon clutching at each other like Bonnie Bedelia and Bruce Willis at the end of *Die Hard*. And while it's no longer raining for the moment, the scene beyond the cordon is nearly as chaotic as it is in the movie, with media vans crowded around the police-tape barriers that are still going up, everyone shouting to each other in order to be heard over all the other voices, and our eyes are blinded by the flashes going off in rapid succession as photographers hurry to take photo after photo of us.

'What's going on?' Lottie gasps, looking completely stunned as she blinks up at me. 'Who on earth are all these people?'

'From the looks of it,' I mutter, pulling her along beside me as I start carving a path for us through the police officers who are standing around in clusters, 'I'd say we have about half of the city's press corps here, along with most of the local law enforcement. And if you look right in front of us, you'll see what appears to be my entire goddamn family. With the exception of Connor and Coco.'

'No, we've got them on FaceTime!' Chloe yells, holding up her phone, while Cade does the same beside her. And sure enough, I see Con's and Coco's worried faces staring back at us from the phone screens.

'Speaking of family,' Clara says, coming over and giving my girl a big hug, 'welcome to our crazy bunch, Lottie. We're so happy to have you!'

After we assure everyone that we're fine and that the danger is finally over, Clara introduces Lottie to Chloe and the twins, who are the only ones she hasn't met yet. When she's done, Lottie looks at Clara, and in a voice that's rough with emotion, she says, 'Thank you so much, Clara. For *everything*. I have no idea how I'll ever be able to repay you, but I promise I'll try.'

'Just take care of this big idiot for me, and we'll call it even,' my sister says, giving me a warm smile as she slips Lottie's backpack off her shoulder and hands it to me. 'He's always been my favorite.'

'What the hell, Clara?' Cade mutters with mock outrage, arching one of his dark eyebrows as he crosses his tattooed arms over his chest. 'You told me *I* was your favorite.'

She looks over at Cade with a laughing smirk. 'That was only so you would take Jasmine to that fundraiser.'

'I knew it! You're such a brat!'

My mom finally approaches, her brown eyes watery with tears as she asks, 'You're really both okay?'

'Yeah, we're good, Mom,' I murmur, hating that she'd been so worried.

'Thank goodness!' she cries, giving us both crushing hugs, before stepping back and swiping at her tears.

We've only just finished giving them all a brief rundown of what happened, when someone from the press calls Clara's name, and she sucks in a deep breath before turning and walking over to the cluster of reporters that are gathered on the other side of the police tape. 'I will not be giving a statement at this time, and please, no questions,' she says, and we've all gone silent, straining to hear her. 'I just want to say thank you to the incredible people of this city who helped us tonight. Without your heroic efforts, Lottie Fleming and Eva Diaz most likely wouldn't be alive right now. So my family and I owe you all an enormous debt of gratitude.'

'That's it?' I grunt, when she's made her way back over to us, ignoring the questions the reporters are still shouting, even though she'd told them she wouldn't be taking any. 'What the hell, Clara? You're a damn hero! You should be milking this moment for everything it's worth.'

She gives me a scowl that reminds me of when she was a child and my mom wouldn't let her have any dessert until she'd finished her broccoli. 'Tonight isn't about politics, Cal. My family is more important than all that crap.'

'All that crap?' I repeat with a rough bark of laughter, seeing as how she's devoted her entire life to it.

'You know what I mean. If I win, I'm going to love working to make this city a better place. But not at the expense of you crazy doofuses.'

'Aw,' Colin drawls, throwing one of his muscular arms around her shoulders, 'we love you too, ClaraBell.'

She growls in response to the hated nickname, elbowing him in the side, and Lottie and I catch my mom's gaze, letting her know we're taking off, then slip away while everyone's distracted by the squabbling siblings.

'You know, I seem to recall that you owe me a celebration,' Lottie says, pressing closer to my side as I pull my phone from my pocket so that I can call my car service.

'As soon as you're up for it,' I murmur, leaning over and pressing a kiss to her smiling lips as she tilts her head back, 'we can celebrate until we're too exhausted to even move.'

'Sounds perfect. But I actually think *you're* the one who needs to be *up* for it,' she playfully murmurs right back at me, and while it seems crazy that I can laugh after a day like the one we've just had, that's exactly what I do. But with this woman by my side, sharing my life, I have no doubt that laughter will always be a part of my days.

And I plan on enjoying each and every one of them . . .

And loving the absolute hell out of her.

Chapter Twenty-Three

Three and a half weeks later . . .

CALLAN

Unfortunately, the night that Andrew Fleming's hold on Lottie's life had finally ended, our celebration had had to wait until the following day. Instead, Seb and Jase had shown up just as I was about to call my car service, and after I'd made a heartfelt apology for ditching them at the office, explaining that I hadn't had any other choice because I couldn't risk pissing Pravik off, they forgave me – though they were both still irritated that they'd missed all the action.

I'd asked Jase to stay and help Clara deal with the press, since I knew the vultures were going to keep hounding her for an official statement, and Seb had offered to drive me and Lottie to the police station in the car Deanna had loaned him, since his Mercedes was still at the airfield. I'd promised the police captain that we would head straight there to give our statements, which had both been completely truthful, except for the omission of Jack Pravik's assistance. Keeping to our agreement, I'd made sure that Pravik had no connection to what had happened, telling the detectives that I'd simply received an anonymous tip about the building where Lottie and Eva had been taken. And with no other way to explain how Eva had gotten to the hospital, we'd suggested that perhaps Lottie's uncle had driven her there, after she'd left to find help, before returning to the derelict building and confronting us at gunpoint.

That night had also been when we'd taken the first steps in clearing all of the bullshit charges against Lottie. Seb had been instrumental in getting what could have been a long, grueling process fast-tracked, as did the recording I'd made which I'd happily transferred over to the police. But there'd still been a lot of paperwork to get through that first night, and by the time we'd finally been allowed to leave the station, the sun had already started rising over the city.

After grabbing a quick bite to eat at a drive-through, since it'd been hours since any of us had had a meal, Seb had driven us over to the hospital where Eva had been taken next, so that Lottie could see for herself that her friend was okay. Then we'd checked in on Thompson, who'd already been chomping at the bit to go home. Even now, the guy is still kicking himself over the mistake he'd made in escorting Lottie up to her apartment that day, but I'm not holding it against him. Hell, I wouldn't have any personal *or* professional ground to stand on if I tried, given how *my* plan had turned out. So that morning, I'd just told him to get back in fighting shape as soon as he could, because we needed him at Hathaway.

And while I'd known that Thompson's injury would be yet another piece of guilt that Lottie piled onto her already laden shoulders, she's proven over and over again how incredibly strong she is, regardless of how she sees herself at times. So I have no doubt that with the love that she gets from me, my family and her friends, she'll eventually work through everything that's happened and that she's been through, coming out of all of this stronger than ever.

When we'd finished visiting with Thompson at the hospital, the three of us had gone to say goodbye to Eva, and by then it'd already been well into Tuesday morning. I'd kept expecting Seb to bail, but he stayed the entire time, the concern on my friend's face as he'd stood in the corner of Eva Diaz's room and watched her while she talked with Lottie something I'd never seen before. I'd thought, at the time, that there might even be something there, until he'd simply told her that he wished her well as we'd headed out, and as far as I know, hasn't seen her since.

Before we'd left the hospital that morning, I'd insisted that someone take another look at the knot on Lottie's head, and after they'd assured me that she was fine, Seb had offered to drive us home.

'You're good people, Cassel,' Lottie had murmured with a grateful, but exhausted smile, when Seb had opened the back passenger-side door of his borrowed car for her. 'Even if you are as arrogant as Callan.'

'Aw,' he'd replied with a low laugh, 'I love you too, *ma chérie*.'

'And you can cut that shit out right now,' I'd grumbled. 'I already have one woman in my life who's in love with you, pal. I'm not letting it happen again.'

'Ah yes,' Seb had sighed, giving me a cheeky smile. 'The lovely Margot is quite special, isn't she?'

'Don't even think about it,' I'd warned, and he'd just laughed as he shut Lottie's door for her, but thankfully hadn't messed with me any more during the drive home, since I'd been too tired to deal with his teasing.

By the time I'd opened my front door and we were finally home, Lottie and I had both been in desperate need of a shower, so we'd climbed in together. We took our time under the warm spray of water, simply enjoying the fact that we'd made it through the nightmare in one piece. I'd washed her hair for her, and she'd massaged her tropical-scented body wash into my back, working out the kinks in my neck and shoulders. Then we spent long, steam-filled minutes just kissing each other's scrapes and bruises, until I'd finally lifted her up, pressed her against the shower wall and pushed myself inside her perfect body.

'I'm being too rough,' I'd grunted, immediately locked into a hard, driving rhythm.

'You're not,' she'd gasped, clutching at my shoulders. 'But even if you were, it wouldn't matter. I want you *exactly* like this, because it feels amazing, and it reminds me that we made it. That we're alive and together and there's nothing that can rip us apart.'

Then she'd pressed her open mouth against the side of my throat and nipped at me with her teeth, and I'd completely lost it.

'Love you so goddamn much,' I'd growled, my control in tatters as I'd grasped her wrists, lifted her arms above her head and started hammering my entire length inside her, hard and fast, fucking the ever-loving hell out of her until she came all over me with a breathless cry. Then my head had shot back, a guttural roar ripping up from my chest as I'd joined her to the mind-blowing sound of her telling me that she loved me, again and again, while I gave her everything I had.

'Wow. That was quite the celebration,' she'd murmured with a heavy dose of satisfaction, pressing her smiling lips to my cheek when we were finally able to breathe again.

'Baby,' I'd groaned, turning my head so that I could touch my own smile to hers, 'that was only the beginning.'

Somehow, after coming so hard I'd nearly blacked out, I'd carried her to my bed and held her in my arms, and my voice had been ragged with emotion as I'd said, 'I promise I won't ever plan things behind your back or try to cart you off again for your own safety, Lot. And I'm so damn sorry for screwing up so badly today.'

'What is it that you're always telling me?' she'd whispered, pressing her soft hand to the side of my face. 'You are not to blame, Callan. *He* was. So let it go. Don't let him have any kind of power over our lives anymore.'

And since my woman is the smartest person I know, I've tried to do like she said, and while the days since that terrifying night have been hectic, they've also been the absolute best days of my entire life.

We're still sorting out the last of Lottie's legal issues, but given that it's just formalities at this point, she's finally free to do whatever she wants, without any fear of retribution from Fleming. And if she'd said that that was to go back to England and start her doctoral program there, as she'd planned, I'd made it clear that I was ready and willing to go with her. But she'd just kissed me when we'd had the discussion a few weeks ago, told me that she loved me, and then insisted that she wants to stay here in New York and do her PhD at Columbia. It seems that despite the stress she'd been under during the past year, she'd fallen in love with the city, and now with my family too, and doesn't want to move away from either one of them.

But she's insisting on working her way through school, and though it took some serious convincing, she quit her job at the café and has been doing part-time work at Hathaway instead, updating all our promotional copy, as well as our protocol manuals. Deanna loves her, and the two often have lunch together, along with Eva and Clara, whenever my sister has been able to step away from the campaign long enough to enjoy herself.

Lottie has also been volunteering at Clara's campaign head-quarters, and the two are becoming close. The shadow that Andrew had cast over Lottie's life for so long had kept her constantly apart and alone, but she's flourishing now, and I love watching it happen. Love that I'm the lucky son of a bitch who gets to stand by her side and share her life with her, our connection growing so powerful, being together is simply the most natural thing in the world, like breathing and eating.

But then, it's also the most exciting, amazing thing that could have ever happened to us, and we're determined that no matter how busy life gets, we'll always take care of our relationship first.

'I can't believe that we're actually here,' she says with a small smile as she looks up at me, her cheeks flushed as we move within the cramped space on a makeshift, outdoor dance floor. We're at a charming, family-filled event for one of Clara's favorite charities, the South Brooklyn Women's Shelter, and we've spent the afternoon playing games with the kids, their ages ranging from toddlers to teens. Despite working night and day on her campaign, my sister had somehow found the time to raise enough funds for an incredible new garden and playground to be built on the lot behind the shelter, and this event has been for the official unveiling of the additions. We've got the entire family here, with the exception of Connor and Coco, since they're both still away at university. But if Clara wins in November, then the twins have already promised to fly home to celebrate with the rest of our crazy bunch, and I can't wait for them to meet Lottie in person.

'Why can't you believe it, sweetheart?' I ask, loving the way the late-afternoon sunshine is setting her golden hair alight, making her glow.

'It's just . . . we came so close to losing each other. Sometimes, things just don't seem . . . real.'

'I get that. I think it'll just take a bit of time,' I tell her, hating that there are moments, like now, when I can still see the shadows creeping through her beautiful blue eyes, though they're thankfully growing fainter each time they appear.

Andrew Fleming's body had been recovered from the burning building that terror-filled night when he'd kidnapped both Eva and Lottie, along with his father's. There'd been too much damage from the fire for a visual identification on either corpse, but dental records had confirmed that both Flemings were deceased, and there's no denying that I was relieved by the news. And I know Lottie was, as well.

'Thank you,' she murmurs, lifting up and pressing a soft, sweet kiss to my lips that makes me want to toss her over my shoulder and steal her away, taking her someplace private, where I can taste every tender, delicious inch of her.

'For what?' I husk, holding her tighter as she gives me another one of those gorgeous smiles, this one a little brighter, those shadows already receding, fading into the background.

'For everything.' She shakes her head slowly, and there's a softness to her expression that makes my pulse kick up and my chest go warm. 'I never thought I could feel this way about another person, or that someone could feel the way you do about me, but I'm beyond grateful for it. And I promise that I'll never take it for granted.'

'Love you more every goddamn day,' I growl, having to steal a quick kiss off her smiling lips, and she laughs that beautiful laugh of hers as I suddenly spin us around, her golden hair lifting off her shoulders.

'I love you too,' she tells me breathlessly, flushed with happiness as we move effortlessly to the live music, looking as if we've danced together for years, when this is actually our first time. But instead of being dressed for a romantic night out, we're wearing the event T-shirts that Clara had passed out to the family, along with jeans and sneakers, the weather still on the warm side as the afternoon blends into twilight, and I can't resist leaning over and pressing another kiss to the tip of Lottie's sunburned nose.

'Get a room already, you two adorable lovebirds!' a feminine voice calls out, and we look over to the group of tables on our right, at the edge of the dance floor, to find Julia McKellen grinning at us. We both smile back at the woman who is Clara's new campaign manager, and who's also become a good friend of the family.

To everyone's endless delight, Carl is no longer a part of the picture, seeing as how Clara fired him the night that everything had gone down with Fleming. According to Cade and Colin, the jackass had shown up before they all took off and started reading Clara the riot act for the things she'd said to the press. When she'd told him that she'd done it for her family and he'd responded, 'To hell with your family,' my sister had immediately clocked him in the eye, same as Lottie had done to Jase earlier that day. Only Clara had followed it up by firing the prick on the spot, and my brothers claim it was the most awesome thing they'd ever seen. As well as one of the most hilarious.

'Julia's right, bro. But if you guys bail out now, Clara will kill you,' I hear Cade say at my back, just before he claps me on the shoulder. He's been a huge hit today with the women and kids, his easy-going manner and hilarious sense of humor putting even the most guarded of them at ease. 'So stop hogging the prettiest girl here, you douche, and let me have a dance.'

'You're such an ass,' I mutter as I reluctantly let her go and step aside, loving how strongly my crazy family has embraced her. She's already laughing at whatever outrageous thing Cade has just said to her, and as I head off the dance floor, I can't help but grin like the lucky bastard I am, thinking that life just can't get any sweeter than this.

LOTTIE

'So, when do you think Cal is going to pop the question?' Cade murmurs, waggling his eyebrows at me like the goofball he is as we dance beside Colin and his wife, Zoe, who's not only gorgeous, but an absolute riot, constantly keeping the sexy soldier on his toes.

'And exactly what question would *that* be?' I drawl up at Cade, rolling my eyes at the mischievous troublemaker who looks every bit as handsome as his brothers in his casual clothes, his colorful, muscular arms showcased by the short sleeves of his T-shirt. I have no doubt that Cade is going to break a ton of hearts before he eventually settles down, but he's one of those guys who will likely stay good friends with all of his exes, not a mean or selfish bone in his entire body.

'Don't act like you don't know,' he laughs. 'The guy's so crazy about you, I'm surprised he didn't get down on one knee the night that shithead cousin of yours finally bit the big one.'

I shake my head this time at Cade's outrageousness, doing my best to ignore the knot that forms in my stomach whenever someone mentions Andrew. Even though he's been gone for nearly a month now, there are times when I swear I can still feel his malevolent presence like a sickly touch against my skin. I know it's probably a natural reaction after living through something so harrowing, but I'm thinking that Callan might have been on to something when he suggested a few days ago that I find a therapist to talk things over with.

As much as I enjoy being around Cade, I'm thankfully saved from his awkward line of questioning when the song draws to an end. 'If you see Callan, will you tell him that I'm just making a quick trip to the ladies' room?' I ask, after giving him a sisterly hug.

'Sure thing,' he replies, and I quietly laugh under my breath as I walk away, thinking it will be a miracle if he even makes it off the dance floor, since at least three women seem to be heading in his direction, no doubt determined to ask him to dance to the band's next song.

The restrooms are in the shelter, and I smile at several of the women I've met that day on my way across the garden, their stories ones that I know will stay with me for a long time. In fact, once Clara has clinched the mayoral race – Wainwright launched a brutal attack on her after all the craziness last month, but we're all confident that the creep's days of being able to lie his way to victory are behind him – I'm thinking that I'll start volunteering here in my spare time. Clara and I are meant to have breakfast together tomorrow morning, and I plan to talk the idea over with her then.

There thankfully isn't a line for the ladies' room, but I run into a fascinating woman named Estelle who works at the shelter as I'm coming out, and we have a lovely chat about the event and Clara's campaign, before she gets called away to deal with an issue in the kitchen. Realizing I've been gone long enough that Callan might be looking for me, I start making my way back through the shelter, toward the exit that leads to the garden. And now that I'm no longer in the hotseat, I can't help but smile as I think about how Cade was teasing me during our dance, knowing that if the day ever comes when Callan *does* ask me that all-important question, there's not a snowball's chance in hell that I'll say anything but yes.

'I'd be an absolute fool not to,' I murmur to myself as I near the wide double doors that lead outside. But just as I'm reaching for the handle, I nearly gag as a noxious odor hits me, the stench so strong I immediately cover my nose and mouth, worried that someone's been seriously ill nearby.

And then I hear a low, familiar voice come from just behind me, and know that I should have listened to my instincts these past weeks, whenever I hadn't been able to shake off the feeling that something wasn't quite right.

Because it wasn't.

'Well, hello there, little bunny,' my cousin laughs, quickly covering the hand I still have over my nose and mouth with his own, pressing so hard I can't even pull in a breath. 'Did you miss me?'

Chapter Twenty-Four

CALLAN

'Hey, where's Lottie?' I ask Cade as he strolls up to the table I'm sitting at with Chloe and her husband, Paul, without my beautiful girl on his arm.

He tilts his head in the direction of the shelter as he sprawls his long body in the chair beside Chloe's. 'She went off to the ladies' room after our dance.'

I frown as I move to my feet, my height allowing me a clear view of the bustling garden. Their dance must have ended nearly fifteen minutes ago, and I'm telling myself not to panic as I look over the different groups that are engaged in lively conversation, knowing I'll spot her soon. But there's no denying that my pulse is picking up when I can't find that golden head of hair, and I mutter a quick 'Excuse me' to the group as I swiftly walk away. I'm only vaguely aware of Cade getting up to follow me, the panic that I'm telling myself is nothing but a leftover reaction to what happened before impossible to shake.

'Whoa!' Clara says when I nearly run her down a minute

later on my way toward the shelter, mine and Cade's search of the garden turning up no sign of Lottie. 'Where's the fire, Cal?'

'Have you seen Lottie?' I grunt, my tone making her frown.

'Um, not for a while now. Why?'

Ignoring the worried look my mom is giving us as she talks to a group of her friends off to our left, I say, 'She went to the ladies' room around twenty minutes ago, but still hasn't come back.'

'I'll go in and check to see if she's still in there,' Clara says, and despite her shorter stature, she easily keeps up with me and Cade as we all head inside the four-story building. The restrooms are on the first floor, and it takes us only seconds to reach them. Clara gives me a worried look just before she hurries through the door that has 'LADIES' stenciled on it.

I pace back and forth while Clara searches the restroom, praying she's going to come back out any moment now and tell me that Lottie is just standing in there chatting away with one of the numerous women we'd met that day. Hell, I'd even be relieved if Clara found her puking her guts up. I'd hate it that she was unwell, but I'd still be relieved that she was *safe*, and I wonder if this horrible panic will stay with me always, or if I'll eventually find a way to put the terror of the day Fleming had kidnapped the love of my life behind me.

The second Clara comes back through the door, I know she didn't find anything before she can even give a quick, worried shake of her head. 'It's empty, Cal.'

I take a deep breath, still telling myself not to panic. Surely she's just wandered off somewhere, and we'll have a laugh about how fiercely I've overreacted once I've found her. But then I look at my brother and sister, taking in their grim expressions, and I know they're feeling it too. That strange, sharp heaviness in the air that says something isn't right.

'Okay, we need to think,' I mutter, shoving a hand back through my hair as I wrack my brain for what we should do next. I've bought her a new phone, but her purse is back at the table where Chloe and Paul are sitting, so I know it isn't on her. The only good news is that the shelter is on a busy street, so if someone's tried to take her, they wouldn't have been able to go through the front without drawing attention to themselves, and the rear exit leads onto the garden, which is teeming with people.

'Does this place have a basement?' I ask Clara.

She shakes her head again as she tells me it doesn't.

I take a second to listen to my gut, and even though it sounds preposterous, I'd be willing to bet my life on the fact that this has something to do with goddamn Fleming. 'We need to go up to the roof then.'

'This way,' Clara says, heading toward the front lobby. 'We can take the elevator up to the fourth floor and access the stairway that leads up to the roof from there.'

'What the hell would she be doing on the roof?' Cade mutters, just as the elevator doors ping open and we step into the empty car.

'I don't think she's alone.'

Something in my tone must alert him to what I'm thinking, because he shares a worried glance with Clara, before looking at me and carefully saying, 'Callan, man, the dude is dead.'

'Yeah, that's what we all thought,' I force through my clenched teeth, shoving the terror that's threatening to choke me down as far as I can, since it isn't going to help save her if she's in trouble.

'This doesn't make any sense,' Clara murmurs with confusion. 'Are you saying that you think he somehow faked his own death?'

'Who the fuck knows? But I know it bothered Lottie that the only identification the coroner could make was with dental records, and it's bothered me too. Because if anyone could pull off a crazy stunt like that, it would be Fleming.'

'Are you packing?' Cade asks me, eyeing me up for a gun.

'What the hell do you think?' I growl with frustration. 'We're at a bloody charity event!'

'I know,' he mutters, looking sheepish. 'I guess it was just hopeful thinking.'

Before I can respond, the elevator doors pull open, and as we step out into the fourth-floor hallway, there's a loud noise up on the roof that has Clara quickly saying, 'The stairs are this way!'

She reaches the door first, pulling it open, and Cade and I tear up the narrow staircase as quietly as we can. But any chance we had at sneaking up on whoever might be up here is blown when I open the heavy door that leads onto the roof and it gives an ear-piercing wail of sound. We come out on the west side of the roof, our view of the east side obscured by an oblong metal container that houses the shelter's air-conditioning unit.

With Cade and Clara following behind me, I move along the near side of the container, and all my worst fears are confirmed when the east side of the roof comes into view. Lottie is standing in the middle of the space between the metal container and a second, smaller brick structure, with Andrew Fleming at her back, the gun in his hand pointed at the side of her head. Even if I wasn't able to smell the putrid scent of infection coming from him, his puffy face and deathly pale, sweat-covered skin would have been enough for me to surmise that the jackass is seriously unwell. And I'd be willing to bet every penny of my hard-earned money on the fact that it's because of the bullet I'd put in his chest last month.

'I was hoping you would be clever enough to find us,' the psychopath says with a wide, gloating smile. 'It wouldn't be nearly as much fun to finally kill this annoying bitch without you here to watch, Hathaway.'

Clara gasps and Cade growls at my side, but I reach over and press my hand against his chest, silently warning him to keep his cool. I understand how he feels, because I'm seething with rage and fear, but I'm digging deep for my training, knowing that I'm only going to put her in greater danger if I lose my shit.

Looking at Lottie, I take in her fisted hands and defiant expression, and am thankful that while she's beyond furious, she doesn't appear to be hurt. 'You all right, baby?' I ask.

'Yeah,' she whispers, and I try to assure her with a look that this is going to be okay, even while I'm wracking my brain for a way to get her away from this jackass. And while she'd been able to use what I'd taught her when her uncle had her in a similar position, Andrew's height means she unfortunately won't be able to throw her head back and bash him in the face.

'That must have been some plan you had in place last month,' I say to him, figuring I can buy us some time if I keep him talking, hoping that maybe Chloe or Colin will realize something's wrong and call the police. 'What did you do? Kill some poor bastard who was roughly your height and build, then stash his body in the building on the off chance that you needed to use him?'

'There was no "off chance" about it,' he sneers with a low laugh, his bloodshot eyes burning with a maniacal gleam. 'I had the whole thing planned out to perfection.'

'Sure you did,' I drawl with a taunting dose of skepticism.

'I did!' he snaps, glaring daggers at me. 'You didn't actually think I would have planned to rape and kill her that night, and not have a way out already in place for myself, did you?'

Just hearing those vile words coming out of his mouth makes me want to rip his fucking throat out, but I beat back the fury and let him keep bragging.

'I'd already made my body double dress in the same things I'd been wearing, but I hadn't killed him yet, because I didn't want there to be any doubt that it was the fire that had taken "my" life. My mum didn't even know I had him locked in a secret room on the ground floor.'

'He was what made that loud noise, wasn't he?' Lottie asks, and I know she's referring to the sound that had pulled Andrew away from her that night, enabling her and Eva to get free.

A rusty laugh rumbles up from his chest before he answers her question. 'Bastard actually thought he could ruin my plans by trying to escape, so I had to cut him up a bit to shut that shit down.'

'And the corpse identification?' I murmur, piecing his plan together. 'You hacked into both of your medical files and switched your dental records, didn't you?'

'Of course I did,' he boasts, and I catch the way the hand that's holding the gun on Lottie is beginning to shake, his complexion starting to look a bit green. 'It was the perfect plan. I could kill the little bunny here,' he sneers, stroking the barrel of the gun against her cheek, 'and then be free to live my life wherever the hell I wanted.'

'Only you weren't counting on your mom bashing you with that chair,' I point out, arching one of my eyebrows. 'Bet that betrayal had to sting.'

His upper lip curls with disdain. 'I'm glad she'll be doing time soon, because she's always been a bitch.'

'And you've always been an asshole,' I shoot back. 'One who's not smelling too good, I have to say. Is your bullet wound infected, Andy? Because it sure as hell smells like it is.'

'Fuck you!' he snarls, just as sirens begin to sound in the distance, and I've never been so happy to hear that ear-piercing noise in my entire life.

'What exactly do you think is gonna happen here?' I demand, daring to take a step forward. 'You're outnumbered, and those police sirens are headed this way, meaning someone obviously spotted your ugly ass downstairs and has already called the cops. So there won't be any miraculous escape for you this time.'

'I don't care!' he roars, curling his free arm around Lottie's waist as he jerks her back a step. 'Nothing else matters now! All that matters is—'

One second he's standing there bellowing, holding a gun on the woman I love, and in the next I see someone behind him lift what looks like a heavy metal frying pan and bash him over the head with it! He instantly slumps to the ground, and as Lottie spins around to see what's happened, I'm gaping at the sight of my mother standing there with the pan in her hands, the rage on her face as she glares down at Fleming's unconscious body making me think she might actually kick him next.

'Mom!' Cade and Clara both shout in unison, while I'm rushing forward as Lottie turns and starts running toward me, my arms wrapping around her the instant she crashes against my chest.

'That's what you get for fucking with my family!' my mom shouts down at Fleming, before tossing the pan to the ground and stepping over his body as she pats her signature French twist, even though not a single hair is out of place. They never are, even when she's just saved the day and brained a deranged killer.

For a moment, my siblings and I don't seem capable of doing anything but gaping at her – not only because she's just done

one of the most heroic things we've ever seen, but she's also dropped the first F-bomb that we've ever heard from her! Then we snap out of it, and while Cade goes over and picks up Fleming's gun, keeping a careful eye on his still unconscious body, I ask her, 'Where in the hell did you come from?' at the same time that Clara cries, 'Mom, you're a total badass!'

'Thank you, dear,' she says to Clara, before shifting her still troubled gaze to me. 'And to answer your question, Callan, it was obvious downstairs that something was wrong, so when you didn't come back, I went inside to look for you just as the three of you were getting onto the elevator.'

'But you came up behind him,' Cade murmurs, shaking his head. 'How did you pull *that* off?'

'Estelle showed up while I was impatiently waiting for the elevator to come back down, and she said that a cleaner on the fourth floor had just called to say that she'd seen an armed man force a woman up to the roof with him. So she let me borrow the pan, insisting that I couldn't come up here empty-handed, and then showed me the second entrance to the roof.'

'Second entrance?' Clara asks.

'It's one that's no longer used, according to Estelle, and comes out right on the other side of that,' she says, gesturing toward the smaller rooftop structure.

'Thank you so much for saving the day,' Lottie cries, suddenly pulling out of my arms so that she can hug my mom. 'Thank you for saving *me*.'

'I'm just happy I could help, sweetheart,' my mom says with meaning, returning Lottie's fierce embrace. When Lottie eventually steps back, they both swipe at the tears on their cheeks, and I give my mom a fierce hug as well, before pulling my girl back into my arms. I'm so damn grateful that she's okay, I just want to keep holding her forever. But the sirens are almost here, and I know that we'll soon be having to deal with the police, while Fleming is undoubtedly rushed to a hospital. He smells so horrible, I can't believe that he's even still breathing, but it's obvious that his chest is rising and falling in an unsteady pattern.

'Did Estelle call the police?' Cade asks.

'No, that was me. I phoned them while I was waiting for her to come back with the pan from the kitchen,' my mom explains. 'Estelle's waiting out front so that she can point them up here.'

'Like I said,' Clara murmurs with a soft, proud laugh, 'total badass.'

We all agree, and then it becomes chaotic as the cops and EMTs make their way onto the roof. Cade hands Fleming's gun over to a policewoman, and then we all move down to one of the shelter's meeting rooms. While Estelle and Clara go to reassure the guests in the garden that everything is fine, Cade heads off to bring Chloe and Colin up to date, since we know they must be worried sick after hearing the sirens, and Lottie and I give our statements to the same detectives who had handled Andrew's *last* case of kidnapping and attempted murder. They're as angry as we are that the psychopath had been able to fool everyone so easily with his 'fake' death, and after assuring us that he'll be under constant guard at the hospital, we're given the all-clear to head home.

The detectives follow us out to the lobby, where my family is waiting for us over by the elevator, and just as we're telling them both goodbye, the taller of the two gets a call and immediately motions for us to stay put. As soon as he lowers the phone from his ear, he tells us that the call was from the uniformed officer who had accompanied Fleming in the ambulance. According to the policeman, not long after Fleming had been admitted, he'd apparently succumbed to the infection that had no doubt been raging through his body for weeks now. As Lottie and I absorb the news, we exhale rough, exhausted breaths, our hands locked together in an unbreakable hold.

'It's finally over,' she sighs, gazing up at me with a tear-drenched look of relief after the detective wishes us luck and takes off with his partner. '*Completely* over. He isn't coming back from this.'

'No, baby, he isn't,' I agree, pulling her into my arms again. 'He can't *ever* hurt us.'

'Amen to that,' I murmur as I study her expression. 'But are you sure you're okay?'

'I could definitely use a shower, but you don't need to worry that I'm going to fall apart on you,' she tells me, squeezing my shoulders. 'I know it probably sounds crazy, but I'm . . . Honestly, Callan, I feel better than I ever thought was possible. I feel like we're finally . . .'

'Free,' I finish for her.

She gives me a breathtaking smile. 'Yeah. And I know, without any doubt now, that he won't ever be able to take you away from me,' she says as a single tear slips from the corner of her eye.

'Christ, honey, have you actually been worrying about that?'

'I think it's been at the back of my mind all this time, like a splinter that you can't get rid of. And now that it's gone – now that *he's* really gone and there's no way he's coming back – I just . . . God, I just want to be with you, and be good for you. Forever.'

'Then marry me.' My deep voice is rough with emotion, but firm with conviction. 'Make me the happiest bastard alive, Lottie, and say that you'll marry me.'

Her beautiful blue eyes are wide with shock. '*What?*'

'You heard me.'

'You're serious?' she whispers.

The corner of my mouth twitches with a wry smile, my voice low as I say, 'It's not the romantic setting I'd planned on, but I can't think of any better time to do this than now. It just feels . . . right. And before you ask, I've known I wanted to marry you from that first weekend when we met.'

'Ohmygod!' she gasps, her eyes instantly filling with tears.

My chest shakes with a gritty laugh. 'That's not an answer, sweetheart.'

'I know, I'm sorry. I'm just . . . stunned. I had no idea you were even thinking of asking me. After watching me marry Olly, I figured you would just . . . I don't know. Maybe wait a while and—'

'I don't need to wait, Lot,' I murmur, taking her gorgeous face in my hands. 'I just need to know if you want the same thing. If you want *me*.'

'Then yes,' she breathes, smiling at me through her tears. 'A million times over, Callan Hathaway. I will marry the hell out of—'

I'm kissing her before she's even reached the end of her sentence, and we both break into ridiculously happy laughter when we hear Cade shout, 'Holy shit, Lottie just agreed to marry him!' Then my crazy family all start clapping and whooping, cheering us on, while I just keep on smiling and kissing my girl, beyond grateful to have her safe and healthy in my arms.

And determined to keep her that way for always.

Epilogue

Election Night

CALLAN

It took a hell of a lot to get here, but it's finally election night, and I'm feeling like the luckiest man in the world. Not only do I have my smiling fiancée in my arms, but the city has proven once again why it's one of the best in the world, backing my sister with a record turnout today. Though we'd all been worried after the shit that went down with Fleming – not once, but *twice* – it turns out that our fellow New Yorkers loved that a politician was finally being completely honest with them, drawing the curtain back on their real life, and they'd embraced the hell out of Clara in a landslide victory.

We're celebrating in the ballroom at the Fairfax, dressed to the nines, with me in a new Armani tux and Lottie in a beautiful black strapless dress that I'd bought for her at the Chanel boutique in Manhattan. She's cut her hair again, wearing it in the same style from when we'd first met, and I love it. As I spin her around on the dance floor that must be twice the size of the one we'd danced on the day Andrew Fleming had come back from the dead, there's the most beautiful smile on her flushed face, her blue eyes so bright I feel like I can see her every emotion burning there in those luminous depths. This girl . . . She's so damn gorgeous, it kills me. So utterly perfect for me, it's unreal.

And she's by far the most resilient person I've ever known.

By some miracle, no one was hurt the night that Andrew had reappeared in our lives for that brief, terrifying time, and while I'd worried about how Lottie and I would react in the aftermath, we've come through stronger than ever, both as a couple and as individuals. And the therapist we've been seeing has helped us to deal with the guilt that could so easily have crushed us down if we hadn't found a healthy way to process it. Even those moments of unease that would come over Lottie in the weeks after the fire are gone, and I truly believe that it had been her keen intuition trying to warn her that the danger wasn't quite as finished as we'd all assumed.

But now the nightmare is *finally* behind us, once and for all, and we've been having a blast celebrating all night with our family and friends. It's getting late now, though, and Eva just had to leave to pick up Nico from her mom's, while Jase and Emmy are off in a shadowed corner somewhere, making out like the newlyweds they'll soon be, their wedding set for May in San Diego, with mine and Lottie's happening just a month later in Mauritius. I wish Seb was here, since he deserves to be a part of the celebrations, but work has taken him back to Paris for the next few months. Lottie and I plan to visit him over the holidays, since she's never been, and I'm excited about showing one of my favorite cities to her, knowing she's going to love it.

I'll even enjoy visiting the museums I know she's going to drag me to, not only because I'm thankful for every moment we have together, but because Lottie somehow makes *everything* fun, and I'm impatient as hell to see a platinum wedding band nestled up against the beautiful engagement ring that glitters on her finger.

'So, I have to tell you something,' she murmurs with a smile, drawing me from my thoughts, 'but you have to promise not to freak out.'

I laugh, thinking of Jase's response when I'd said similar words to him the day I'd found Lottie – but unlike my friend, I'm smart enough to keep them to myself. 'The answer's yes,' I drawl instead. 'I will definitely fuck your beautiful brains out the second we get home tonight. In fact, we might not even make it past the entryway.'

She rolls those stunning eyes at me as she says, 'I said *tell* you something, not *ask* you something.'

'Oh, sorry,' I murmur, grinning like a jackass. 'But it's hard to concentrate when all the blood in my body is rushing below my belt.'

A soft, breathless rush of laughter falls from her lips, and I pull her closer as I tip my face over hers and rumble, 'Seriously, what's up, buttercup?'

She gives a feminine snort, same as she always does when I use my new nickname for her, which I came up with after Colin's little girl had said that the yellow sundress Lottie was wearing the last time we visited them reminded her of the flower. Then Lottie pulls in a deep breath, her blue eyes shimmering with emotion and her cheeks flushed the loveliest shade of pink as she softly says, 'I'm . . . pregnant.'

'Holy shit!' I gasp, my heart jolting so hard it's nearly lodged in my throat. 'Seriously?'

'Um, yeah,' she says with a nervous laugh. 'I wouldn't really joke about something like that.'

I pick her up and twirl her around so fast she yelps, but I'm too blissfully happy to control myself.

God only knows we haven't exactly been careful, so we'd been fully aware that this could happen. And while some people might think it's batshit crazy or far too soon to be taking this step, I think we're just so eager to start living in the *now*, rather than the past, that we're ready to embrace whatever life wants to throw at us . . . including a tiny, precious miracle that we can call our own.

When I finally stop spinning her around and just crush her against my chest, grinning so big that it hurts, she blinks up at me, asking, 'You're really happy?'

'I'm over the moon, baby. I'm losing my mind, I'm so happy.'

'Shh,' she whispers, looking around to make sure we haven't been overheard. 'I don't want anyone to know yet.'

'Why not?'

Looking back up at me, she smiles as she says, 'It's Clara's night, so now's not the time. And it's too early anyway.'

'When then?' I ask, wanting to shout it from the rooftops, I'm so excited.

'I read that most people wait until they've reached twelve weeks.'

'And you're at, what? About six?'

Her eyes widen with surprise. 'You figured that out quickly.'

I give her a cocky smirk. 'If it has to do with your body, woman, I pay attention. Closely.'

'Yeah, well, you're right.'

'Christ, Lot. I love you so fucking much,' I growl, just before I start kissing the hell out of her right there in the middle of the crowded dance floor. Someone claps me on the shoulder, no doubt Colin or Cade, while hoots and whistles fill the air around us, but neither of us gives a damn. We're too happy to do anything but stay locked together in our own private celebration, until we finally have to come up for air.

I take a moment to simply soak in the beautiful way she's staring up at me, then lean over again, resting my forehead against hers, and she lifts her hand, pressing it to my pounding heart. As I close my eyes, I'm more thankful than I've ever been as I hold the woman who makes that heart beat in my arms, determined – no matter what life throws at us, the good *and* the bad – to cherish her until my dying breath.

She'd kept telling me that she wasn't like Jessica, and, God, is that the truth. I never really understood what it would mean to have a true partner in my life, the way my parents had been to each other. The way that Jase and Emmy are, too. But now that I've got it, I honestly don't know how I ever survived without it.

After everything we've been through, I know there are times when life can be some seriously dark, messed-up shit.

But it can also be bold and bright and beautiful.

And if you get really lucky, then it just might shock the hell out of you... and end up giving you *everything* you ever wanted.

CLARA

I'm smiling so wide that my cheeks hurt, shaking hands with another group of supporters, when I look up and see an unexpected face in the crowd. He's as tall as my brothers, but with sharp, chiseled features and ink-black hair that's brushed back from his jaw-droppingly handsome face. And the suit he's wearing probably cost more than my entire wardrobe.

What's even more stunning than the way he looks, though, is the way he's looking *at me*, his gray gaze molten and sharp as it moves from my wide eyes down to my suddenly trembling lips.

Not really expecting a response, I mouth a silent 'thank you' to him for his help in saving Lottie and Eva, since Callan had told me the truth about how he'd found them that day. But I have no idea why Jack Pravik is here tonight. Hell, we still don't even understand how he'd known where Fleming was keeping the two women who have become my closest friends. Then I notice the equally tall man beside him, who's setting an enormous arrangement of blood-red roses down on a nearby table. It's the biggest, most lavish arrangement of flowers I've ever seen, and I shoot Pravik a look of surprise, wanting to know what this means.

What he wants.

But he doesn't answer any of my unspoken questions. He simply gives me the barest hint of a crooked, provocative smile, then turns and disappears into the celebrating crowd.

Dark secrets surround the Beckett family . . .

Can a fledgling relationship survive the damaging and
dangerous revelations to come?

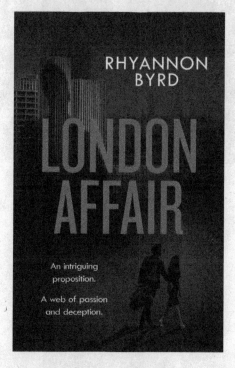

'*London Affair* is signature Rhyannon Byrd – exciting,
sexy, and romantic . . . I couldn't put it down!'
Virna DePaul, *New York Times* bestselling author

Available now from

HEADLINE
ETERNAL

Be drawn in by Rhyannon Byrd's
scorching hot Dangerous Tides series . . .

'No one writes lip-biting sexual tension and
sizzling romance like Rhyannon Byrd'
Shayla Black, *New York Times* bestselling author

Available now from

HEADLINE
ETERNAL

HEADLINE
ETERNAL

FIND YOUR HEART'S DESIRE...

VISIT OUR WEBSITE: www.headlineeternal.com
FIND US ON FACEBOOK: facebook.com/eternalromance
CONNECT WITH US ON TWITTER: @eternal_books
FOLLOW US ON INSTAGRAM: @headlineeternal
EMAIL US: eternalromance@headline.co.uk